For Sooz

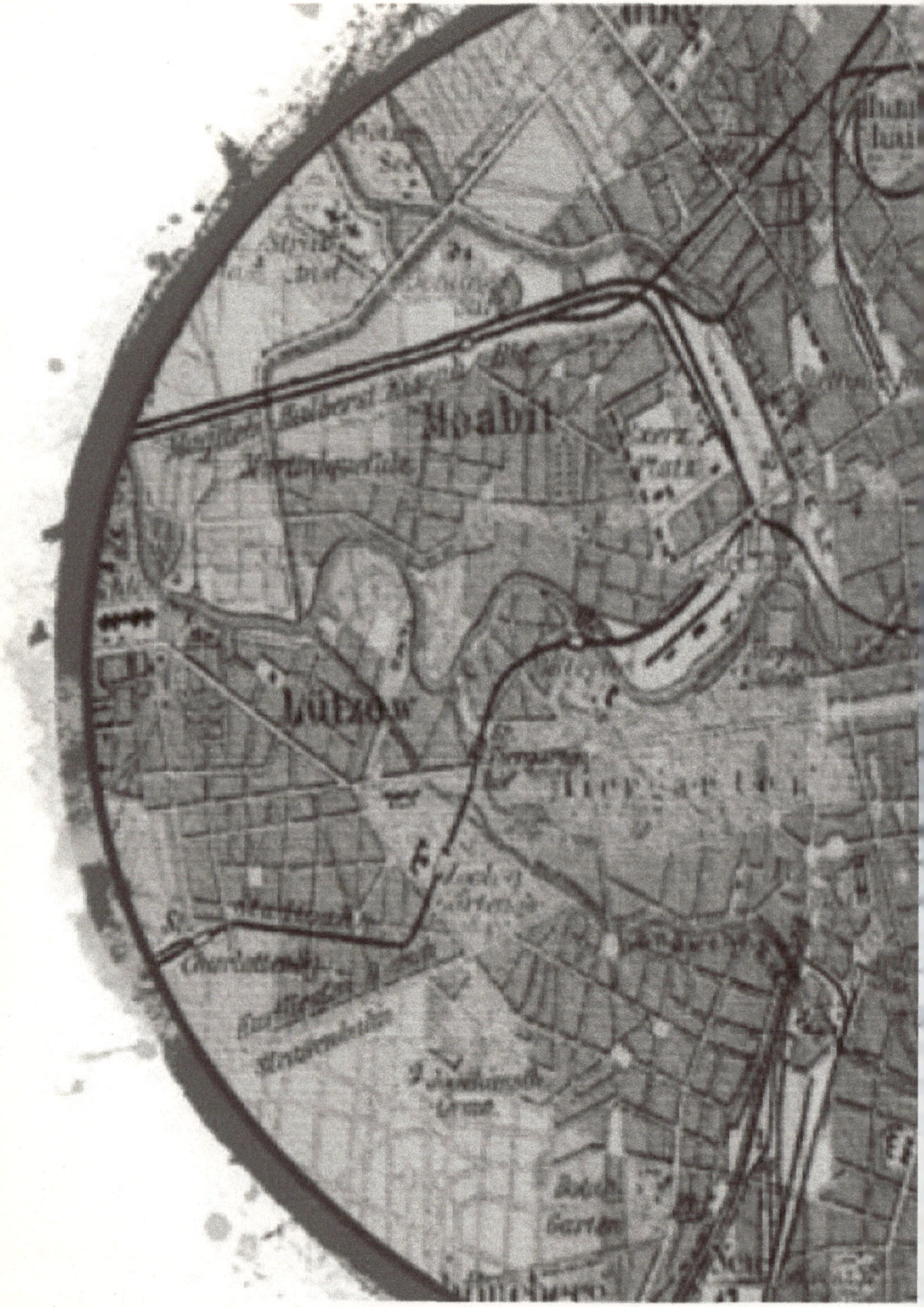
Moabit
Lützow

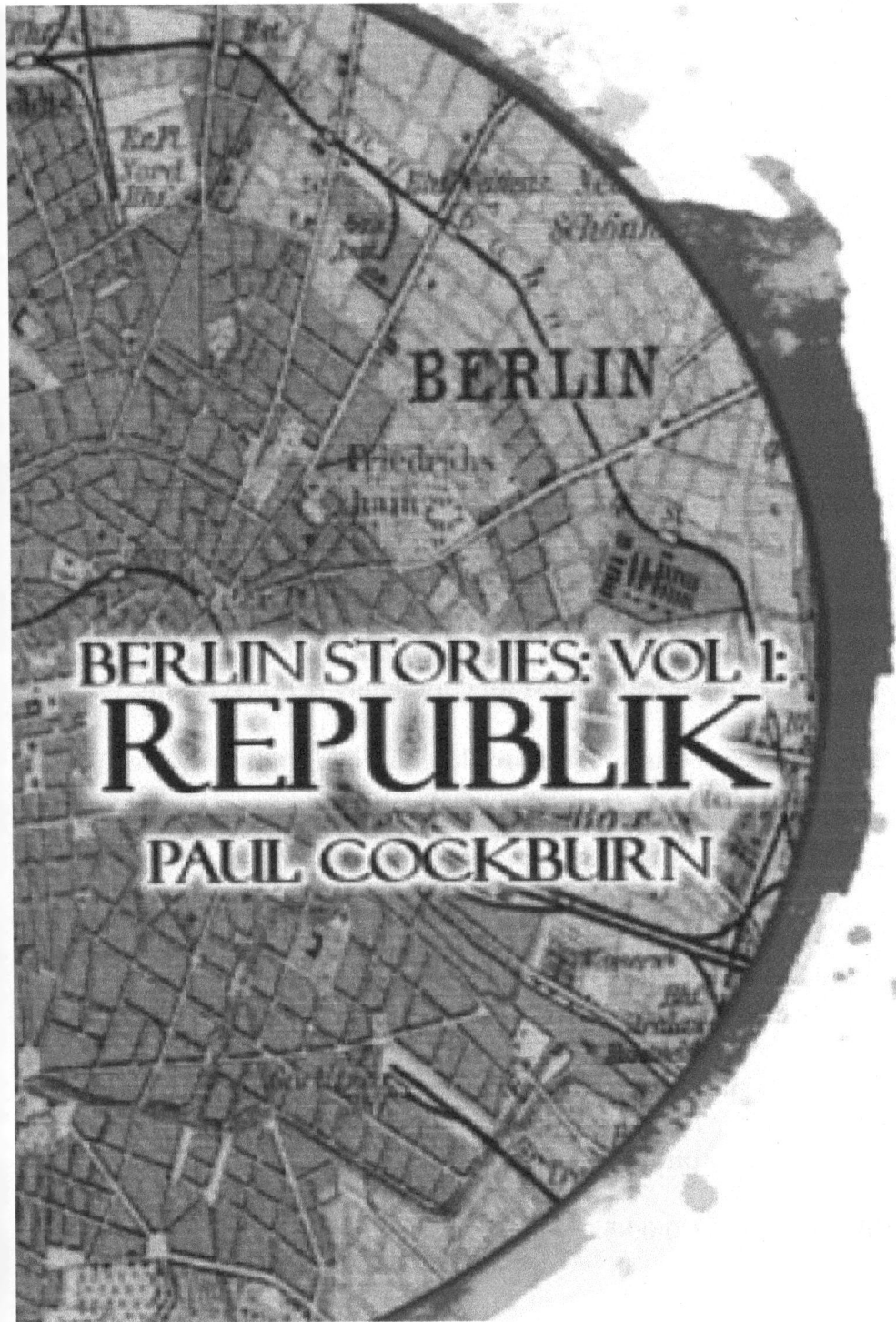

BERLIN

BERLIN STORIES: VOL. 1:
REPUBLIK

PAUL COCKBURN

This book is a work of fiction. The characters, incidents and dialogue are products of the author's imagination and are not intended to bear any resemblance to actual events, or to historical persons (living, dead or otherwise) *except* where they are. Any such resemblances are coincidental, and purely for the purposes of providing historical context for completely fictional events.

Ascendent Publishing
1640 Worcester Avenue, D613, Framingham MA 01702
www.ascendentpublishing.com

ISBN 978-1-963970-00-5

AN APOLOGY

This tale you're about to read began its gestation around the time of the hundredth anniversary of the events that transpire during its telling.

As the world-at-large found itself sitting comfortably at a point in time past their one hundred-sixth anniversary, I felt confident enough in the quantity of research books I'd amassed in that six-year interim to make it look like I know what I am talking about in the telling thereof.

I really don't.

Therefore, I apologise in advance to the people of Germany for the butchery of their language, and the people of Berlin for my ignorance of their city.

The main characters, Amt VIIIb of the Berlin police force and the central story are all fictional. Several historical figures make appearances, but I think I have treated them equitably, except for the fascists, and I don't care to apologise to them.
No apologies either for the number of German terms in this volume. For those who struggle with such things, there's a glossary to be found at the end of this volume. I do apologise for the existence of said glossary.

PROLOGUE

That dream again!

The room is filled with a billowing yellow cloud. Gas! Gas! I stumble forward, hands outstretched, but feel nothing ahead of me. There is no sound, save the roaring sound of my own breathing, each breath an inhalation of terror. I feel the pressure of the gas mask on my face, like a hand clasped over my mouth and nose. I feel the terror.

I want to tear the mask away. I know – I *know* – that this is suicide. It has been pointed out to us over and over again. We have even seen examples; we have all had that moment when we have realised a colleague is about to do just that. It's death. I know this.

But what if the cloud is *inside* the mask? What if ripping the gas mask from our head is the single action that will save me? I hear this voice, urgent and convincing, and it's telling me to liberate myself, to drag off the cursed mask, to gulp in lungfuls of liberating air. It even reasons with me. 'This is a dream. You know it isn't real. But you need to breathe. Go on, tear away the mask and breathe.'

And then I wake up. My eyes shoot open, but everything is distorted by the lenses of the gas mask. Off! Off! I'm in my own room. I'm safe, I'm safe, if I would only breathe...

And then I wake up, but this time it's for real. There is a cloud in front of my face, but it's just the vapour of my own cold breath. I'm lying on my bed, cocooned in my greatcoat and blanket, lying in the dark and silence of a Berlin winter night. My breath is rapid. I feel sweat on my face and wipe it away.

Goddammit... that dream.

TABLE OF CONTENTS

"The Case of the Missing Invalids"

TABLE OF CONTENTS

"The Case of the Body in the Tiergarten"

TABLE OF CONTENTS

"The Case of the Austrian Attaché"

Glossary

THE CASE OF THE MISSING INVALIDS

FRIDAY, 1ST NOVEMBER 1918

I pulled back the blanket and set my feet down on the floor. I let the nausea and the night-terrors ebb away, ran my hand across my face to wipe away the ghosts of night, then took a piss in the earthenware pot at the side of the bed. I checked the time, though I could see by the solid black square of the window that it was well before dawn. There was no point even trying to get back to sleep; it never works. Shuffling in the dark, I went to the washstand to inspect my face. A man who was almost a stranger looked back from the mirror, raw-eyed and disheveled. It had been a while since any woman had called me attractive, and even my blue eyes seemed jaded. I pulled a comb through my hair and noticed still more grey creeping into position among the black.

These morning routines never vary. I pulled on my boots, which was almost all I needed to do to be completely dressed. I found my suit jacket over the back of a chair, checked the contents of its pockets, and drew it on. I dragged on the greatcoat I had slept under, and that was it – the day could commence. If there was hot water at work, I would shave there. Clearing my throat, I spat into the chamber pot and pushed that under the bed with my foot. Then, with fumbling hands, I found my tobacco tin and matches, and lit up the first nail of the day. The nicotine sliced into me like a knife, and I reveled in it. I needed to roll up some more, but that too could wait until I was somewhere warm.

On with the routine. Most importantly, I flipped the mattress over. Johan gets in some time after six, and he'll be drunk, high, and incapable, so it's best to leave no obstacle to him getting a good day's sleep. Sharing an apartment is all about the little things.

The stove was cold, of course. Johan said yesterday that he thought he knew where he could get some fuel, but he'd said the same the day before, and the day before that. I didn't hold him to blame. There wasn't an ounce of firewood in Berlin, unless you knew some unguarded property that still had its furniture.

There was no food either. After a brief, forlorn look in the pantry (as we laughingly called it), my stomach rumbled. I would need to find sustenance elsewhere.

These were my living arrangements in November 1918, here in Berlin, the greatest city in Germany. One room, and that shared. No food and no fire; just a roof, a metal frame bed with a thin mattress, and the proverbial pot to piss in.

I am a *Kriminal-Kommissar* in the Robbery Büro of the Berlin Police, so you might think I would be paid well enough to afford better than this, but I'm paid as a Bezirkssekretär, a full rank below, because the Police are as broke as everyone else. I held the rank and responsibilities of Kommissar because that is what I had been in Hannover, back in 1914, before I had been stupid enough to volunteer for the Army. I'd been in Berlin since I was invalided out after Verdun, and this apartment had been 'home' ever since.

I was still on that first cigarette as I left, having completed my attire with a dark hat, which I wore as jauntily as I might, given how low I was feeling. Down the stairs, out through the front door and onto the street. I huddled in the doorway for a moment to look at my watch again in the limp light of a nearby streetlamp: a quarter past four. I wasn't due at work until eight. On the other hand, the Police Praesidium would be warm… warmer than this, anyway.

There was another option, one I took often enough, which was to walk in the direction of Friedrichstrasse and the railway station. This took me in the opposite direction from the direct route to Alexanderplatz, but Old Man Mauritz would be opening his café about now, to catch the early morning commuters. A coffee certainly; perhaps even a bread roll if he'd been able to find enough flour to bake that morning. I imagined the smell of that so vividly, my stomach rumbled again. Another drag of the cigarette, and I was off.

This was the first day of November, if I recalled right. Ah! There was a cold westerly blowing, so I thrust my hands even more deeply into the pockets of my greatcoat and cursed the stupidity that had made me forget my gloves yesterday, which were on my desk at the Praesidium if they hadn't been filched. The cigarette bobbed on my lip. I lowered my head and followed my nose.

I became dimly aware of the world around me as I approached the station. The tall buildings on either side of the street funneled my world forward and back, with the bulk of the elevated station across the junction just ahead. Someone, somewhere, was playing mournful music on their phonograph. At this hour! And there were shadowy figures on each pavement, moving as I was towards the station. I saw a youngish fellow on crutches, hurrying towards the main street the railway bridged at this point, the left leg of his filthy trousers hanging limply below the knee. He would be after one of the prime positions near the steps up to the platforms.

No-one else was walking briskly, but each, head-down, shuffled onward into the wind. Even those who progressed side-by-side held no conversation.

There is a reason why these are the hours military

planners like to choose for their attacks.

As I raised one hand to take a puff from my cigarette and flick off the ash, I saw Old Man Mauritz at the front of his café. He was putting out chairs on the pavement. I crossed the road and waved. Mauritz narrowed his eyes and tried to make out who I was. The matter of his missing eyeglasses was one robbery I had never solved.

"Ah, *Kommissar* Hoehner! You're up early. Do you want coffee? I'm afraid there isn't any bread…"

My stomach complained immediately. "Coffee is fine. Do you have any of the good stuff?

He laughed. Mauritz was in his eighties, and God alone knew how he kept his spirits high, given how things were, but that face was never short of a smile.

"Even the good stuff is ersatz these days, *Herr Kommissar*, but for good friends I keep the best of the worst. Come in, it won't take me a moment to –
At that same moment, someone else called my name. A man was crossing the street, just as I had moments before, almost as if he had been following me along the street.

"Kommissar Hoehner! I didn't expect to see you called out to this affair."

Even in the dark, I recognised the stooped, fidgety stature of Klaus Obermeier, and felt that slight fall in my soul that one does when meeting a representative of the fourth estate. Obermeier was a prematurely-matured fellow with a high forehead, a large nose and an unkempt face. His watery, dark eyes were big, under thick brows.

"Herr Obermeier. You're up early. What affair?"

"You're not heading to the station?" He gestured, as if I could possibly not have known where or what Bahnhof Friedrichstrasse was.

"What of it?"

I had a sinking feeling right away, and the growing,

knowing smile on Obermeier's face only made that worse. He wrote for a few of the Berlin newspapers, selling his stories wherever he could, though he took pains to use a *nom-de-plume* when he was published in *Vorwarts*.

As I looked past him, I realised that a few of the night-ghouls on the street right now were not the shambling figures on their way to or from the tomb I had witnessed (and been part of!) earlier, but energised men, and even a couple of women, more or less running towards Friedrichstrasse.

"Why would such a matter disturb the Robbery *Abteilung*?" queried Obermeier.

I didn't answer, but both of us obeyed the gravitational pull of whatever it was that lay ahead, and strode down the street. Obermeier, a much shorter man than I, almost broke into a run. No-one can smell out something dodgy like a journalist, and Obermeier was on the scent here.

At the foot of the steps leading up to the ticket hall and the Stadtbahn platforms, there were two *schupos* I didn't know, waving their hands and batons ineffectually as people brushed past them. Neither of them got in the way of either me or (to my slight regret) Obermeier.

There were a couple more uniformed police on the platform area, keeping themselves out of trouble over in one corner. I recognised Kempe, a *Wachtmeister* I'd worked with once or twice. I went over to him, gesturing to Obermeier to stay back, for all the good that did.

"What's going on?" I asked.

Kempe, a stout fellow with close-cut hair under his shako, and a jaw you might use to break down doors, pointed towards a growing group of people gathered around a railway official. There was a lot of indistinct yelling and gesturing. Beyond them, I could see a number of men in white coats, some of them bearing stretchers, who were moving to and from the far side of the station, where a train was parked in the gloom, its locomotive hissing and puffing quietly. Another train was just pulling out of the station, blocking my view of this first one, filling the space with noise, and the high, arched roof with smoke. I noticed one of the station clocks: it was still not even five in the morning. "There's some fuss going on, Herr Kommissar. Something to do with a train."

You could see why a mind like Kempe's was wasted in the uniform branch.

"Who is in charge here?" I asked.

Kempe started to say that Kommissar Brunner was on his way, but Obermeier pointed to the uniformed railway official at the centre of the loud press of people. "That's Gerhard Leider. He's the station master here."

"Everyone's starting early today," I muttered and moved towards the throng, passing between passengers who had recently stepped off the departing train, and who were now heading for the exits, looking back over their shoulders in some confusion at the disturbance. My journalist-dog followed at my heel.

As we got closer, I could see that many of the agitated people were themselves railway workers, and for a moment I wondered if I had stumbled onto an industrial dispute. That would have been a fate I didn't aspire to, but it transpired that most of the speaking was being done by three figures. One was the aforementioned station master, Herr Leider, a man with the stoic pomposity and upturned moustache normally seen in photographs of General Paul von Hindenburg. Actually, he was doing very little of the talking, but letting dignified silence do the work for him. This was not a successful policy.

More effusive was the woman immediately in front

of him. She was a typical Berliner *hausfrau*, it seemed on first acquaintance, in a plain blue dress and an apron. Her hair was grey and worn wildly. She gestured frequently as she spoke, and her demeanour was stern. I gathered immediately that Herr Leider was on the receiving end of a lecture a man of his station (if you'll excuse the pun) did not believe he deserved.

I knew the third person in the discussion, and my heart sank almost as much as when I had first spotted Obermeier. Franz Markwitz, formerly Franz-Josef von der Markwitz, was a local socialist city councillor, though local to where was anyone's guess. I'd crossed paths with him before. He was with the Independent Socialists, the breakaways, and was therefore anti-war, anti-business and anti-police. Today he was also anti-railway officials. It was his voice I could first make out clearly as I (we) approached.

"Frau Plommer received a telegram!" He pronounced with great emphasis, and my suspicion was that he had been making this same point over and over for several minutes. The lady in question waved a square of yellow paper under Hindenburg's moustaches.

"I cannot help you, or this good lady," Leider insisted, and that wasn't the first or last time he had said that either.

"Where is my son?" the woman cried, her voice genuinely grieving. She all but swooned.

Markwitz clocked me as I came up. His features became more animated as he recognised a new avenue to exploit.

"Ah! Kommissar Hoehner! Now we shall get to the bottom of this!" I suspected sarcasm.

"What is going on here?" I demanded, and for the next several minutes I was bombarded with accusations, denials, statements and demands. Let me try and summarise them for you. Frau Plommer was a widow, and it was important to this situation that her dead husband had been a railway worker, that being the reason all those other railway workers were present.

More germane, she had given birth to three sons just before the end of the last century, which had proven to be bad timing, since each had gone off to war in 1914. Two of them had been killed. Now she had a telegram informing her that her youngest son, Walter, had been wounded, and would be arriving in Berlin this very morning.

The expected train had duly arrived. That was it huffing on the far side of the station. But Walter Plommer was not on it.

Your first thought is probably the same as mine was, that this could hardly be termed 'unusual' in Germany in 1918. It was probably more unusual that somebody had been courteous enough to inform Frau Plommer of her son's transport, but that he had not arrived as expected… well, what did anyone expect?

Except…

"Privat Plommer *was* on the train," insisted Markwitz. It wasn't just the telegram. "There is a manifest," he added pointedly, glaring at Leider.

"I cannot help you," the station master intoned.

"You see those gentlemen over there?" shrilled Markwitz. He indicated the ambulance workers, who were still passing back and forth across the platforms, bearing souls away from the train and down to the lower levels where, presumably, ambulances awaited.

In summary, some wounded men had arrived at Friedrichstrasse Bahnhof, and I must assume Frau Plommer had checked that her son was not amongst them. All the same, I wanted to get a grip on proceedings before every aspect of the matter flew off in a different direction.

"Is there a manifest?"

"As I said to this good lady," the station master began, chin-up, rheumy eyes still and fixed on nothing. "Such things are not public documents."

"Yes, there is! He has it! I handed it to him myself!" This new participant was a small, dirty fellow with greasy hair and several missing teeth. I could tell from his accent he was no Berliner, which immediately made his evidence more credible. He said his name was Brandt, and that he had been the train driver who had brought the wounded soldiers to Berlin. Another even dirtier fellow nodded vigorously, as if to confirm this, or just because he liked the way this was going.

Almost without thinking, our little group was moving gradually in the direction of the parked train. Leider was a a stately battleship surrounded by fussing destroyers, though perhaps, given the trouble the German Imperial Navy were having up in Kiel (at least according to the hints in the somewhat censored newspapers), that wasn't the analogy I needed. Markwitz continued to bluster; the widow turned to weeping. At my side, the locomotive driver was still barking on about paperwork he had turned over to Leider, a man I suspected had never been handed paperwork he didn't read.

"Eight cars!" Brandt insisted. "Each one of them full of wounded. I saw 'em!"

By the time we reached the relevant area, my heart was sinking. I don't know what I had been expecting, but what I encountered brought back some of my darkest memories of being at the front, which were never about what had happened to me – that wasn't *all* that bad, I liked to say – but what I witnessed. No, I don't know what I had been expecting, but it wasn't eight freight wagons, doors thrown open, and disgorging a steady stream of broken men into the care of the ambulance crews. Of course, I might reason later, the railway company would never use passenger cars to transport these men; they would never get the bloodstains out of these wagons as it was. But surely these poor souls deserved better than this.

The ambulance men had been at this for a while, and still the wagons seemed full of casualties. The stench was unbearable. Had these wounded men just been piled onto the train, with no water, and not so much as a bucket to piss in? Had no-one travelled with them? A decent number were awake, and even lucid; others lay very still and pale. I counted three stretchers set to one side where the men had been covered over.

It made me irritable. "Who is in charge here?" I demanded.

No-one seemed to know. There were a few doctors on the platform, organising the transport of the wounded men, processing them according to the severity of their injuries in what was called the French method. This meant those who were least likely to benefit from treatment were set aside, much as were the three soldiers under their blankets. The medical personnel were also organising which casualties were to go where. It seemed that there were doctors and ambulance men from every hospital in the city, and that each was acting independently.

"Where is Kammerich?" barked one of the doctors, a tall, elegant man with eyeglasses who seemed quite unmoved by all the carnage he was wading through. No-one seemed to know the answer to his question.

"Who is Kammerich?" I enquired.

"I thought he was in charge," the doctor continued, peering this way and that briefly, but then returning to the soldier he was triaging. "This one to Charité," he told an orderly. He washed his hands in a basin of bloody water that sat on a bench as the fellow was carried away and another brought from the train for his attention. "We were told to meet the train," was all he had to add.

I turned to Leider. "He was here when I arrived," the station master insisted. "Doktor Kammerich told me that ambulances were on their way to meet the train. I told him that it was most irregular for casualties to be brought here, since they were normally delivered to the Hauptbahnhof. He said this train merited different arrangements. When it arrived, he started directing things. Here was still here when I was called away."

The doctor was becoming more and more disturbed. "I didn't see him slip away, but he has a lot to explain! These casualties shouldn't be here! They shouldn't have been transported in this state." He pointed to the man at his feet, who had some kind of abdominal wound, and lay on a stretcher swathed in bloody bandages, moaning and rolling his eyes. "These men should still be in clearing stations behind the front, not dumped in Berlin." He went back to work, cursing and vowing to wreak a terrible vengeance on the doctors in Aachen.

Brandt was skipping from foot to foot, agitated. He tugged at my arm. "See here, Herr Kommissar. You see here."

He led me to the eighth and final wagon. This was more or less identical to the others, with the same bloody interior. It was empty. He waved his hand at the interior. "I swear to you, Herr Kommissar, on my mother's grave, this one was full like all the others when we left Aachen; thirty, forty men. I saw them. And the manifest proves it." He shot an accusatory glare at Leider.

"Why was the train routed here? Is it right that other trains have gone to the Hauptbahnhof?"

"I only go where they send me, Herr Kommissar. But don't you see? The men on this wagon were removed."

"Perhaps this wagon was emptied first," I suggested, looking around at the chaotic operation on the platform.

"Herr Kommissar! That is not what we have been told by these doctors!" This was Markwitz. "They insist this wagon was empty. This Doktor Kammerich directed that the other wagons should be attended to. No-one seems to know what is going on."

"He has the manifest!" Brandt insisted again, jabbing a blackened finger towards Leider. I was going to get to that, but first I tried one more time to get an answer to a question I had posed earlier.

"Who is this Doktor Kammerich?"

There was some muttering among the medical professionals, but finally the Charité doctor suggested Kammerich was from Heilig-Geist-Spital, a small establishment not so far from the station. I was already picking up a sensation that the other doctors were regretting Kammerich's involvement in what was becoming a fiasco.

I was pondering all this for a moment, with Markwitz barking in my ear and the widow Plommer on the verge of fainting theatrically, when I noticed someone standing at the locomotive end of the train. He was a blank-faced fellow in the uniform of a basic infantryman, who I wondered if he was an orderly for a moment, until I noticed he was wearing a *stahlhelm*, with a curious crooked cross painted on the front of it. Bizarre. But then I was distracted by the clamour around me, and when I next searched for him, he was gone.

The throng had only grown larger by this time. Some of the more recent arrivals wore red armbands over their tunics, and I knew that that piece of symbology meant. Markwitz grew bolder with every arrival, insisting on answers and getting in the way of me finding them. Obermeier, who I spotted again for the first time in some minutes, was scribbling in a notebook, grinning broadly at the prospect of spending the fee he might get for this story. Things were getting out of hand for what was surely going to turn out to be a piece of administrative incompetence. Not very Prussian, but it happens.

The pushing and shoving was getting worse. Each new arrival, demanding to know what was going on, only increased the overall level of alarm. I wondered if Kempe was considering intervening in some way.

"I want that manifest," I told Leider.

"I fail to see how this is a police matter," the station master dead-panned. I gave him a moment to realise how feisty the crowd was becoming. Turning to Brandt, I commented: "Men don't just disappear from moving trains."

He was floored by this, but only for a moment. "We were held at a signal!" He waved an arm vaguely westward. "Just outside the station, on the Spree bridge."

"How long for?"

"Only three or four minutes!"

I couldn't see that being relevant. There was no way thirty or forty wounded men wandered off a train held at a signal, high up on a river bridge. Where would they go? Why?

The situation was getting beyond control. I looked across to where Kempe and the other *schutzpolizei* were standing. They had been reinforced a little, and was that Kommissar Brunner from Vice in conversation with them? No-one seemed minded to come over and lend a hand.

I climbed up into the doorway of the eighth wagon and demanded silence. I got it too, much to my surprise.

Even the doctors paused in their work, which had not been my intent.

"Listen to me. I intend to find out what happened here, but you are all getting in the way.

Clear the station. Go about your business. I will find out what happened here and will let Frau Plommer know the whereabouts of her son. In the meantime, disperse!"

Looking back, that was probably the last time anyone sporting a red armband obeyed the instructions of a Berlin bull. The idea would be laughable in a week's time.

"Very good," smiled Obermeier.

I probably needed to be grateful to Markwitz too, though I did not feel that way. He told the railwaymen that he would personally supervise the police in their investigation of the matter and would report to Frau Plommer directly. After a little more grand-standing from him, the railwaymen led the widow away. I should have liked to be away from this damn train myself.

The doctors continued their bloody work as all this was going on. A fourth covered figure was set to one side.

Seeing as I was up there already, I took a few minutes to look around the interior of the eighth wagon. It was like a charnel house in there. There was blood and bandages everywhere, and some other substances I stayed clear of. Glass crunched under my feet. I was struck again by the degrading way these men had been brought to Berlin… and now, if the story was correct, some of them were missing.

Among the detritus in the wagon, I stumbled across a couple of items. One was a very risqué photograph of a slender dancer, whose name was Charlotte, according to the autograph on the back. More pertinently, I found a paybook in the name of one Gefreiter Adolf Meinz. I pocketed both. Then, at the foot of one wall, I saw what seemed to be some scrawl, written in shit and blood. Someone had written 'Save Us.' At least, I think that's what it said.

"'Save us'? Save us from whom?"

My God, Obermeier was light on his feet. I hadn't heard him climb up at all.

"I don't want to read that detail in *Vorwarts*."

He shrugged. "I think *Freiheit* will pay better." Perfect.

"I thought I told everyone to leave."

"Oh, you cannot have meant to include the press, Herr Kommissar. This is surely a matter of great public interest. Was that a paybook I saw you –?"

"Never mind that. Let's not set the world on fire looking for a flame, Obermeier. I see one word of speculation in any socialist rag and I'll be coming to find you. This is all going to turn out to be a misunderstanding."

Obermeier shrugged and stepped down to the platform. I followed, and closed the door behind me. I was going to want to have the wagon properly searched at some point, just on the off-chance that there was anything else of interest.

I moved in front of Leider. "I want that manifest," I demanded, for what was going to be the last time.

"This is railway property!" he insisted. Markwitz took hold of the fellow's arm, and mentioned magistrates and the like. Suddenly, the railway was going to be cooperative after all. Leider reached into his inside jacket pocket and produced a sheaf of papers, which he handed to me without further protest.

The papers were standard forms of the KPuGHStE. The Königlich Preußische und Großherzoglich Hessischen Staatseisenbahnen liked their own name, heraldry and organised paperwork. The top sheet listed the train consist:

one locomotive and eight wagons (with associated numbers), with the driver and fireman also included everything in a neat written hand in the appropriate spaces. The route from Aachen was also detailed, with some scheduled times. The next eight pages listed the 'contents' of each wagon. What this came down to was a total cargo of two hundred and ninety-eight souls. Wagon Eight was listed as having contained thirty-four of these.

"See?" said Brandt, who had remained behind for just this moment. "They were on the train."

"Nothing else? No names?" I asked.

Brandt showed me the heavy leather wallet these documents were transported in, up in the cab of the locomotive. It was empty. He commented that there had also been a list of the transported patients, along with their injuries. We both looked pointedly at Leider.

"That was given to Herr Doktor Kammerich."

And, it came out, he had then handed this to the next doctor to have arrived, and that it had gone off with them as they took the first patients to hospital. That was inconvenient. The Charité doctor said he'd try to get it back.

I spoke with Brandt again. I asked him about the signal that had held him outside the station. Surely Friedrichstrasse wouldn't have been busy at that time in the morning? Brandt had no idea; he'd just done as he'd been told. And he hadn't seen anything back along the length of the train? No, it had been pitch black, of course, and you don't hear much of anything in the cab of a locomotive either.

I dismissed the two railwaymen for now. I made sure they knew I might need to speak with them again. They lingered for a while, but then went off to find breakfast.

Which left me, Obermeier and Markwitz on the platform. Oh, and the doctors, orderlies and their broken charges. We three moved off to the side. It was at this moment that a newcomer came over, a young woman in a smart red coat, dark skirt and a jaunty beret. She walked confidently past all the medical horror at the train, and came up to Markwitz.

"Ah," he said. "This is my assistant, Fraulein Irene Graber. Irene, this is Kriminal-Kommissar Hoehner of the Berlin Police Robbery Büro and…"

Obermeier lifted his hat. "Obermeier, Klaus Obermeier. A pleasure to meet you, *fraulein*."

"Likewise," the young woman replied.

"Fraulein, I am going to leave you in the company of these gentlemen. I will attend to the Widow Plommer, assuring her of our complete attention to this matter. Please accompany the Kommissar, and report back to me at the earliest opportunity."

"Yes, Herr Councillor."

"Wait a moment," I started, but Markwitz was already turning on his heel so my objection didn't go anywhere. Fraulein Graber stretched out her hand, and proffered an extensive smile with bright, small teeth. I felt compelled to be courteous.

"Fraulein, I have to warn you that this is an official police investigation. Anything you me hear or observe here or elsewhere today must be kept strictly confidential." We'd see how long that lasted.

The Heilig-Geist-Spital

I'll spare you the details of the conversation we had with the signalman. Ulrich Strauss is possibly the most tedious man I have ever encountered, a lifelong signalman

with the KPuGHStE and insistent that he could testify to
nothing unless we had a full understanding of railway
operations. I asked him a few questions that were designed
to elicit yes or no answers, and each reply lasted five
minutes. Strauss was about to go off duty, but even that
didn't encourage him to brevity. By the time he finished, I
could probably have operated the signal box myself,
though surely not to his satisfaction. He continued to throw
levers in what seemed an almost random fashion while we
spoke.

According to him, the next signal box down the line
had informed him of the approach of Brandt's train at
4:01am precisely. Everything was 'precisely' in the world of
Signalman First Class Strauss, of course, but he stressed this
point clearly. Anyway, at 4:03, a railwayman he didn't
know came into the box to tell him that there was an
obstruction on the track, between the bridge and the station
platforms. Despite his misgivings, he set the signal to halt
the train, and sent his assistant out to check the obstruction,
since nothing was visible from the signal box at that hour.
At 4:14 (and therefore a little later than Brandt had
imprecisely implied), the assistant returned to say there
was nothing there. Strauss released Brandt to bring his train
into the station.

The mystery railwayman had, meantime, vanished
as easily as he came.

I wasn't sure where that left us, but with my two
assistant investigators close at heel, I left Strauss to his
work, and went out to look at the area for myself. By now,
the station was starting to get busier as trains brought
workers in from the outer suburbs. Obermeier remarked
that the incident with 'our' train would not stay secret long.

From the western end of the station, the tracks cross
a small road called Reichstagufer and then go straight out

onto the bridge across the Spree. We looked at this from the end of the platform, with the train that was the focus of our thoughts at our backs. From there, we went down to the street and approached the bridge at that level. It was getting on for half-past-six at this point, and it was still dark. There was no light under the bridge at all. The road was quiet, though not empty, but I imagined that before half past four it might have been as silent as a tomb. I didn't expect to find witnesses.

There was a set of steps at the side of the bridge, leading up to the bridge deck. It was closed off at the bottom by a padlocked gate. If one was to imagine that the train was halted above at 4:03, and the eighth wagon was then emptied of its human cargo, thirty-four injured men must have come down this way in just eleven minutes. That just seemed like a flight of fancy. The orderlies at the station had been man-handling stretchers down broad, well-lit stairways, and that had taken time and effort enough. Carrying thirty-four badly injured men down what was little more than a ladder, in pitch darkness, this surely seemed impossible. And to what end? Where could they go?

Obermeier found a bloody rag caught on a railing. The blood was dried, and the rag could have been there any amount of time. There was nothing to be learned here.

I needed time to think. Cigarettes had got me only so far through the morning, and now I needed the coffee Old Man Mauritz had promised me earlier. I took my two new charges along, though they had to pay for their own beverages. These days, a bull's money doesn't go all that far (thought today was payday, I remembered). I watched Obermeier counting through pre-war coins that probably wouldn't pay for a single bean. Fraulein Graber took pity on the old fraud and paid for his coffee as well as her own.

And then, to my absolute delight, Old Man Mauritz announced he had three eggs. I reluctantly offered to share this feast with my new colleagues. Fraulein Graber announced that she had had breakfast, so Obermeier ate her portion too, as if his last meal had been back before Ludendorff was sacked. I made sure to give Mauritz my flour ration coupon, since if I was ever going to see bread again, it would be here.

Fraulein Graber took off her beret, and more curly chestnut hair tumbled out than seemed legitimately possible. I noticed she had a light dusting of freckles and eyes whose colour was open to debate. Green is far too prosaic.

Slightly more at ease, I leaned back in my chair and observed my companions. I informed them that I should probably go the Alex and report in. It had occurred to me that my chief would probably want me off whatever this was, but then I wasn't sure whose department this might come under. It was probably a matter for the War Office.

"They have quite a lot on their plate, don't you think?" asked Fraulein Graber, which was a valid observation. "The Councillor will hope to hear something soon."

"So, what do you think happened?" I asked this question directly of Obermeier, since Fraulein Graber had not been present for most of the incident, even if we had discussed it at length while we poked through the litter under the railway bridge.

"Well, it's a mystery," Obermeier observed. Less than helpful.

"It would be useful to have that list of patients," Fraulein Graber observed. "At least we could be sure that Frau Plommer's son was on the train."

"I'll make you a little wager," I suggested, with an

air of resignation. "He will have been on the last wagon." She raised an eyebrow at this. Most people get used to my pessimism eventually. "However, it should be obvious to all that this is a greater matter than the fate of any one son. Your employer is fixated on Plommer, but..."

"It makes for a strong human interest story," Obermeier interjected.

"If I can borrow a telephone at the Alex," suggested Fraulein Graber, after a delicate sip at her coffee (I was on my second), "I'll call some people I know. I'll find the list."

That was a useful division of labour. What use might Obermeier be? He found more work for Fraulein Graber. "The Ministry of Health may have information on this Kammerich."

And thus, at around half past eight, I reported for my shift at the Alex. The Police Praesidium was humming by the time we arrived. I took my new colleagues up to Robbery and left them (Graber) making calls while I went to see Radel, who was in charge of the Büro. The Oberkommissar was in a rush, as always, barely listening to my report, twisting his hand around in the air as if demanding greater and greater brevity. Like me, he was employed in a role that deserved higher rank, and rather more like me, he resented the extra work he had been tasked with, without the greater reward.

"Councillor Markwitz? I don't have time to deal with him. Try to get him off our back. Find this woman's son, and let's see an end to this."

I rejoined the other two. To my amazement, Graber had scored a success already, tracking down a doctor called Mueller who had the patient list! That was impressive! She arranged to meet him, hung up the phone and took up her coat and hat.

"Shall I meet you at Heilig-Geist? That's our next

port of call, right? I shalln't be long."

We had taken the Stadtbahn from Friedrichstrasse the two stops to Alexanderplatz, and now we were going one stop back in the other direction, to Hackescher Markt. The stations were all busy now that the day was advancing, with that cold wind still biting and a little threat of rain. People shuffled about their business, gaunt and silent, as if they were ghouls haunting a graveyard.

Obermeier picked up a copy of *Vossiche Zeitung* from the floor of the train and scanned the headlines with a look of distaste on his face, as if reading such centrist news would pollute his more radical mind. "It's a bad business this, with Austria," he insisted, jabbing a nicotine-stained finger at the front page. If they are out of the war, it leaves the Empire open to the south. What can they be thinking in Vienna?"

Mostly, I said to myself, they were thinking that their army was falling to pieces, they were in full retreat and there was revolution in the air in Vienna, Budapest and Prague. It didn't take a military genius to know that Germany had been propping up the Hapsburg Empire through most of the war, and that they didn't have anything much left to give.

"One might have expected as much from the Bulgarians and the Turks," Obermeier continued. "But this is Austria's war! It might not have come to this if she had been able to keep her neighbours in order." I wondered if history would record things that way.

"What now? Do we wait for the Americans to send us another of their infantile proposals? Can they not see that we are sincere about peace? Prince Max has been accommodating of their every demand, it seems to me, but still there is no ceasefire. Surely you agree, Herr Kommissar, that there must be a ceasefire?" He was becoming more agitated by the minute.

I didn't want to get into it. "I've been out of the army for about a year and a half, Herr Obermeier. I don't think about such things any more."

"Well, there are plenty of others who think of nothing else! We can't leave this in the hands of the Kaiser or there will be revolution!"

"I thought that would suit you, Herr Obermeier!"

"Bah! I'm a socialist, right enough, but after all this do you think I want to see Germans shooting other Germans? Look at this mutiny in Kiel! If they do finally send the army in, we'll have another front on our hands, fighting our own brothers! No, we need peace first. Then clear out all the dead wood, and finally we can make a German revolution."

A businessman just down the carriage tutted and shook his newspaper. Thank God we were only travelling the one stop, or the revolution might have started on the Stadtbahn.

After a short walk south down Spandauer Strasse, we reached Heilig-Geist-Kapelle. The old church was a treasured building in this locality, with its small, red brick church attached to a hospital.

We entered the chapel. It is an old, old building, with that special smell and sound that comes with antiquity. Nothing could be further removed from the privations of the city, or the brutal war beyond.

A young man who probably faced being called up into the army next year went off to find the sexton. Obermeier and I took a look around, like tourists. I didn't get the impression Herr Obermeier was a religious man.

When he finally appeared through a door at the far end, the sexton still took almost a full minute to reach us, and that was with us meeting him half way. He was a shrunken man, in a brown suit several sizes too large for his small frame. He had a crutch under one arm, the boy under the other. He was blind in one eye, largely deaf, and could barely remember breakfast, which altogether made him a less than ideal person to ask about Kammerich.

I'm being unfair. The sexton, Herr Seeckt, was a little bemused for a while, but with a little prompting he finally recalled Herr Doktor Karl-Heinz Kammerich perfectly well. The Holy Ghost hospital, which was at the back of the church, was a small institution, and it neither paid well nor kept a large body of doctors on staff. Kammerich had been a physician there.

"That is what had me confused, Herr Kommissar. Herr Doktor Kammerich was sacked in 1917. May, I think."

That was interesting, to say the least. I smelled scandal, but even though Seeckt hadn't needed to say even that much, he wasn't going to go any further.

"You'll need to take matters up with the church authorities," he insisted. I could imagine how much progress that would make. Instead, I asked about the hospital, and specifically if they had taken in any new patients that morning.

"War wounded? Kommissar – what did you say your name was again? We do have wounded soldiers here, but only those who are much further along in their recovery."

I tried to explain the source of my confusion, but it didn't interest Herr Seeckt at all. "We have a few patients who were wounded in the war, and are learning to walk again, that sort of thing. Also, a few who are beyond saving, and who live here in charity, awaiting their call to God. But mostly our beds are filled with those cursed with this damn influenza epidemic. We have more than enough trouble on that score, I can tell you!"

Obermeier enquired if we might be shown around the hospital. Seeckt was quick to deny that request. "Did you not hear me? We have dozens of influenza patients. They are in isolation. I will not have flat-footed policemen disturbing the peace of the hospital. We do not employ Doktor Kammerich any longer, and thus I insist that your interest here is at an end!"

Moments later, we were back on the street. I've had more cooperation in a brothel.

"Truly, a man of God," said Obermeier sardonically.

A taxi pulled up beside us, and out spilled Fraulein Graber. Beaming, she waved a folder at us, bound in pink ribbon. The morning was advanced enough that I felt I could stand a beer and a sit down, so we found a bar a couple of blocks away. At least beer wasn't in such short supply here in the city, even if much of it was watered down.

The three of us looked through the papers. Two hundred and sixty-three names, neatly ordered, with a brief note on the most serious of their ailments. A great many had suffered shrapnel wounds, and some had had emergency surgery in the clearing stations. I found it hard to believe that the Army Medical Corps had sent these men back to civilian hospitals in Berlin without additional and detailed records, but perhaps things were more disordered and chaotic at the front that we knew.

No Plommer. And no Gefreiter Adolf Meinz either.

"We were told there were two hundred and ninety-seven casualties," mused Obermeier. "Two hundred and sixty-three on this list. That leaves…"

"The thirty-four from Wagon Eight."

Obermeier nodded. Fraulein Graber looked from one of us to the other.

"Does this not mean the last wagon was empty all

along?"

"I don't think so. The engine driver was insistent on what he saw. We'll check the hospitals again, sure, to see if Gefreiter Meinz arrived on an earlier train, losing his paybook then. But I don't think that's what we'll find."

"But why? Why did the patients in the last car get off the train? How?"

Those were the questions. Why and, for curiosity's sake if nothing more, how.

"If they were taken off the train," Obermeier theorised, "that's a lot of help. Two men to a stretcher, that's seventy men organised specifically to meet the train and take these men off. And then what? Did they have ambulances on Spandauer Strasse? Even in the middle of the night, surely someone saw something."

"I agree, though that may not get us much closer to finding where these boys are now. Kammerich is the key. We need to make that call to the Health Ministry and see if we can track him down that way. Also, there was that doctor from Charité." Annoyingly, I hadn't got his name, but it transpired that the diligent journalist had.

I finished my beer. Obermeier had emptied his mug already, and he necked Fraulein Graber's once she stood up from the table to magically restore her hair to its plum-coloured hiding place.

"If this is more than just a misunderstanding," I said as we paid and left, "then it's something planned, something well organised. Someone at Aachen arranged for Wagon Eight to be added to this train, with those thirty-four boys aboard. Why them? Why would anyone want to hide the transport of thirty-four wounded men back to Germany." After all, there was no shortage of wounded to choose from here in the capital. "Why were they transported before they were ready? Also, someone let

Kammerich know the train was coming, so he could remove those boys, and muddy the waters with all the other doctors. They expected everyone to assume the last wagon had been added empty. Kammerich stole those patient records that spoke about the thirty-four. They wanted this to be a secret."

"Who are 'they'?" Fraulein Graber mused out loud.

"We won't know that until we find Kammerich. Let's use the rest of the day well, and track him down."

Regarding that, I went back to the bar and asked to use their telephone. One flash of my beer token so they knew it was police business and all argument ceased. After the usual tedious nonsense navigating the girls on the switchboard, I briskly summed the situation up for Oberkommissar Radel. I asked him to send a telegram to Aachen, to the army medical unit there, to get their copy of the full manifest sent over. I also asked for some additional manpower, but I had less success there. Robbery had their hands full, according to the Chief, which was amusing since we hadn't brought in a case for weeks.

A little later, and we were in the labyrinth that is Charité, the Universitätsmedizin complex. As we worked our way through layers of hospital bureaucracy, Fraulein Graber went off to work her contacts among the handsome doctors, which had already been a fruitful source. Obermeier looked pale, and skittish, constantly fidgeting with his shirt collar, and moving to light up a cigarette that he never smoked.

"I don't like hospitals," he confessed, fretfully. "I had tuberculosis as a child. I was terrified. My poor old mother came in with me, fainted, and six weeks later she was dead of cancer!"

All the same, he didn't leave. We were finally introduced to a Doktor Mueller, a distinguished physician of about fifty years, with that touch of grey at the temples that grants just the right level of authority. Mueller worked in the neurology department. I confessed I didn't know what that meant.

"We treat disorders of the brain," he said, in what felt like a particularly glib form of summary.

"You know Doktor Kammerich?"

"Not personally, no. I have only been here for a year, and he left Charité in... what would that have been... 1916?"

"What department was he in?"

"Neurology, same as me."

"And why did he leave?"

The doctor cleared his throat, straightened his white coat and looked around, as if worried he was about to transgress his Hippocratic oath. "I can't really say, but if you speak with the Ministry, they might be able to tell you. I hear - ah! - that he was suspended. I think there was talk of revoking his license?"

"You don't know why?" He did, but he wasn't saying.

"Do you know where he might be working now?"

 No, and I gained the impression that was true.

"Is that all, Herr Kommissar?"

"I think so. Oh, one thing. How do you know Fraulein Graber?"

Doktor Mueller looked utterly bemused, then amused. "She and I are old friends."

"It was fortunate that it was you who had the list we required."

He didn't understand what I was getting at, and in truth I had no rational idea. We shook hands, I thanked him for his assistance, and Obermeier and I went outside. The rain had passed and it was actually quite a fresh and bright afternoon. Cold as Moscow at Christmas, mind. We smoked cigarettes (mine, of course) and stamped our feet on the pavement.

'This Kammerich fellow gets more and more interesting," said Obermeier, more relaxed now what we were out of the hospital building, and that he had a story that might merit several columns. "A neurologist, eh? That gets you thinking." He didn't say what about, and I concluded it was some kind of joke.

The hour was getting late. I was impatient to move on. Just then, the doctor I had encountered at the railway station exited the main doors right by us. He had the look of a man who has been wrist-deep in guts all day.

"Herr Doktor!"

He glared at me as if I had insulted him. "Must this be now, Herr Kommissar. I have just spent twelve hours sewing those boys back together. I need a drink, a bath and eight hours solid sleep." Probably a long weekend with his mistress too, or perhaps that was only my preferred way of coping, at least in my imagination.

"Two minutes, Herr Doktor. I'll even walk with you to the station if that's where you're headed." He didn't take me up on the offer. "Well. When we spoke before, you said that when you arrived, Kammerich was directing matters, arranging matters for those boys at the station."

"I don't think that *I* told you that, but carry on."

"Did you know Kammerich?"

"Not well. I mean, I know he used to work here. But he was clearly in charge, handing out casualty lists, organising the orderlies. We went along with what he was saying; it was all perfectly correct."

"Did you know he had been suspended?"

The physician screwed up his face and shook his head, just once. "I had – have – no reason to believe he was

{ 40 }

not authorised to do what he was doing."

"Of course. Do you know what hospital he is working at now?"

"Is it not Heilig-Geist?"

"No."

"Then, no, I can't help you there either. Now, I'm leaving. If you have further questions, leave them until Monday morning, for God's sake." He went off, raincoat over his arm. Perhaps doctors don't feel the cold after a day like he'd had.

We finished our cigarettes. Moments later, Fraulein Graber came out, looking cheerful enough though she hadn't learned much more than we had, and that wasn't very much at all. I removed my hat and rubbed at my scalp. It felt like it had been a very long day with nothing much to show for it other than a list of soldiers who weren't the ones we were meant to be looking for.

"Herr Kommissar, the Councillor will expect us to attend Frau Plommer at her home, so that we might bring her up to date with our progress."

I groaned, but she was right. Still, if that was all we needed to do, it wouldn't take too long!

The Widow Plommer

Frau Plommer lived in a modest middle-class apartment on Eisenacher Strasse, on the northern edge of the Schöneberg district; quite a nice address for the widow of a railway worker. Perhaps he was a ticket inspector; they always seemed to have it easy.

There were several rough-looking men in the street outside, looking very out of place, and definitely not her neighbours. Though the evening was getting dark, I felt I recognised some of them from the dispute at the station (maybe it was just the red armbands), and I was certain they knew who I was. The loudest mouths demanded to know what was going on. As we tried to get by, there was some pushing and shoving. I had observed some *schupos* down the street as we arrived, but it was clear that they were going to keep their distance unless things got really ugly, and I was willing to bet that our definitions of 'really ugly' varied by a mile.

But then Fraulein Graber asked to be let through, and it was like the parting of the Red Sea (if you'll pardon the joke). With a little hissing at our backs, we entered the building found our way up to Frau Plommer's apartment.

The widow's sitting room was furnished comfortably, although not so well that it could accommodate all those currently within it. After stepping through the door, I made my way along a short corridor, partly blocked by two more of the armband-wearing railwaymen. They stood across my path as if this was something the fellows outside had neglected to do. But then a voice from behind them asked who was there. I recognised it as Frau Plommer's.

"*Gnädige Frau*, it is Kommissar Hoehner."

Instead of the good lady, it was the voice of Councillor Markwitz I heard next, telling the human barricade to let us through. Reluctantly, the two men did as they were told, but they made sure to jostle me a little, so that I properly understood I was here on sufferance.

There were more men around the margins of the room, standing with arms folded and stern looks on their faces. Not all of them were railwaymen, I guessed. At least two managed the trick of wearing the Emperor's military uniform *and* a red armband. Almost in the middle of the room, Frau Plommer was sat on a delicate dining chair, her hands folded in her lap, clutched around a handkerchief. She was flanked by two other women, stern-faced and ominous. The air in the room was stale with sweat and engine oil, but no-one was smoking.

I went into the middle of the room, to stand in front of Frau Plommer, holding my hat in my hands. I felt like I was appearing before the bench, with a hostile jury on all sides, and the judge in the centre, watched by all.

Markwitz had found himself a chair, of course, a comfortable armchair in one corner of the room, facing towards me. "Herr Kommissar, it is good to see you. I assume you come bearing news? We are all expecting, waiting to hear what it is you have to say."

Fraulein Graber stepped lightly over a patterned carpet to stand by her employer. She bent down to whisper something in his ear. He smiled.

"Well, Herr Kommissar?"

I cleared my throat. I would have killed for a cigarette right then, or better yet a drink. I noticed Markwitz balanced a cup and saucer on his knee. No-one was going to offer me coffee, that was for sure.

"*Gnädige Frau*, as I promised, I am here to let you

know what we have found out." Which was a shovelful of nothing. The widow, whose eyes had been set upon the floor, now looked up.

"Have you found my son?"

She was dressed all in black, as if in mourning. Out of the corner of my eye, I could see two photographs of young men in uniform, framed in black drape, set upon a dressing table. There was ample room for a third.

"No, Frau Plommer," I admitted. "At this moment, I cannot be certain that he was aboard that train. We have sent to Aachen for further information."

"I received a telegram..." the widow responded in a quiet voice. She waved a hand, and one of her lady companions stepped to a table by the window, and returned with that square of yellow paper. Frau Plommer indicated that she should hand it to me, which the woman did without getting too close, in case police was catching. I scanned the telegram quickly, noting who had sent it – a Major Steiner – and when.

"The train left Aachen several hours after this was sent, Frau Plommer. In such an interval, we cannot discount the possibility of error."

"If there is error, Herr Kommissar, it is at the hands of the authorities who have lost this poor woman's last son!" This was Markwitz, as you can imagine. I could see he had wanted to rise from his seat, but failed to free himself of his cup and saucer in time.

"We should hear from the authorities in the morning, I believe," I continued, genuinely uncertain this might be true. "I will telephone this Major Steiner also. We cannot discount the possibility that Walter was supposed to be on that train, but was not placed on it."

"Why would this error then not have been spotted in Aachen?"

"Herr Councillor, Frau Plommer. The situation is very confused at the front. Your son will have already endured a long and difficult transit to Aachen in difficult circumstances. We cannot discount that there has been some administrative error. Walter himself may be unconscious, or mute, or otherwise unable to announce his presence, and correct the misapprehension that he was sent off on that train."

These were not the comforting words I wrongly assumed they would be. Frau Plommer exhaled a little cry. Markwitz finally managed to hand the cup to one of the women, and rose up with all the authority he could muster.

"He would still have his *Erkennungsmarke*! Someone would know who he was!"

"*Hundemarken* get lost all the time," I said softly, using the nickname soldiers preferred for identity tags. "It's not at all uncommon." I neglected to mention that this most often occurred when the pour soul the dog tag identified was obliterated by the burst of an artillery shell.

"Preposterous!" insisted Markwitz.

I continued to address the widow. "We will make these enquiries, in Aachen and elsewhere. If your son was on that train, and has been misidentified somehow, it is my goal to search every hospital that took patients from that train. Frau Plommer... if I might trouble you for this... do you have a photograph of your son?" Preferably not taken from some shrouded frame, where it sits in anticipation of the worst...?

Such a photograph was produced. Walter was a good-looking boy, with a lop-sided grin and a crop of blond hair. He was wearing a brand-new uniform in the photograph, and holding his K98 rifle across one knee. Millions of mothers had photographs like this, some in plain sight, others shrouded. Once, I had had a photograph similar to this taken, though that felt like a very long time ago. That soldier wasn't mourned anywhere.

"Thank you. I'll leave you now. I will be back tomorrow, with good news, I hope." News, anyway.

I left the room between the two statues in the hallway. The door closed behind me. Of Obermeier and Graber there was no sign. I paused for just a moment, then descended the stairs with the photograph in my jacket pocket. I touched the breast pocket of my suit and felt there my own dog tags from my time in the army, which I carried for good luck. You could never be too careful.

Reporting In

It was properly night by the time I got back to the Alex. I expected that Radel would have gone home for the weekend, and that proved to be the case. I planned to leave a report on his desk in the unlikely event that he came in over the weekend, and a note for the shift commander in case any additional information arrived for my attention, but as I pushed open the frosted glass-paned door into Robbery, I was confronted with two unexpected occurrences. Sitting at my desk was Fraulein Graber, and as soon as she saw me, she held up a piece of departmental notepaper.

"Who is Kriminal-Oberkommissar Teske?" she asked.

A valid question that I didn't completely know the answer to. Teske was a boss, but not any kind of head of department. I'd heard about him, but I had no idea what he did, nor for whom, which undoubtedly made him political. I took the paper from Fraulein Graber and read it quickly. It contained just Teske's rank and name, an internal telephone number, and the instruction to call immediately on my return.

I reached for the telephone on my desk, glancing at Fraulein Graber as I dialed "How did you get in here?" She motioned in the direction of two of my departmental colleagues and gave them a winning smile and a wave.

Oberkommissar August Teske answered the phone on the first ring. He had a gravelly voice, radiating pedigree Prussian authority. I recalled him as being a large figure of a man, with a skull like a block of concrete.

"Kommissar Hoehner, Herr Oberkommissar."

"Stay there. I'm coming to your office now."

I replaced the receiver, taking a moment to breathe deeply. "What are you doing here?" I asked Fraulein Graber, while fumbling in my pocket for my cigarettes.

"We're working together, aren't we?"

"No. That ended the moment you whispered in Herr Markwitz's ear. I can't have you involved if you're going to feed him information before I'm ready."

"I didn't…" she began, then she bit her lip. "I didn't tell him anything about our case."

"It's not *our* case. You should leave. If Markwitz wants to tail around behind me himself, he can take it up with my Chief." I lit my nail and took a long drag on it. "But you can tell him that I intend to get this wrapped up by Monday."

At that moment, the department door swung violently open, and in strode KriminalOberkommissar Teske, every bit as solid as I remembered him. It seemed he remembered me too, because he came straight over to my desk. He took in Fraulein Graber, sitting awkwardly on the front edge, and I had a moment of horror imagining that he might think she was my girlfriend or something.

"Who's this?"

"She works for Councillor Markwitz."

That seemed to satisfy the Oberkommissar's curiosity on that score. "Is that a report on this business at the Bahnhof Friedrichstrasse?"

I wasn't sure what he was looking at. "No, Herr Oberkommissar. I haven't written that yet, since –"

"I expect reports at the end of every working day, Hoehner. Without fail." He sat down in my seat, leaning back so hard the chair groaned loudly. I thought it might topple over or collapse, but we avoided that catastrophe. "Tell me everything," he commanded, and as I started to speak added: "Use your notes. I want every detail."

That wasn't the kind of order ambitious *kripo* officers could ever ignore, even if I had no idea what authority Teske commanded. I took out my somewhat sparsely annotated notebook and began to fill him in on the day's events, extemporising where required, while he rocked on my chair like a child at a playground.

He didn't react, comment or question at any point before the end. He glared at my cigarette so hard I stubbed it out midway through. When I was finally done, he leaned forward and placed his beefy forearms on my desktop.

"This is a very unsatisfactory situation. There are soldiers returning from the front who have fallen in with the Bolshevists, and they have many supporters in the labour movement. Of course, many more of our brave men support the Kaiser and the government, but any excuse at all, and these disloyal factions will disrupt the government, and bring disorder and revolution to our beloved city. This... *incident*... has the power to be most disruptive. There could be battles on the street at any minute, and here you are stumbling around after this Doktor Kammerich. I want him apprehended and questioned – *immediately*. By the end of tomorrow, I demand that these missing soldiers are found!" He beat the table once with his fist to emphasise the point.

I didn't disagree with any of this as a concept, though a more by-the-book police officer might have pointed out that I didn't work for the Oberkommissar. What he was describing sounded more like a task for the Political Department... is that what his role was?

As I pondered this, Teske was reaching into his inside suit pocket. He handed me a piece of paper, which I noted at once had two addresses on it. Before I could fully comprehend the rest, Teske rose to his feet. He took a fob watch from his waistcoat and consulted it; tutted, and then moved away from my desk.

I consulted his note again. He filled in the background while I did so. He had accessed certain police records to find that Kammerich had a small house in Potsdam – quite a nice address. The local *schupos* had visited, but it appeared the house had been put up for sale and was currently shuttered. The neighbours had not seen Kammerich in months.

The second address was that of an apartment on a small street on the edge of the Wedding district, a decidedly less attractive part of town.

"That address was supplied by the Ministry of Health. Perhaps Kammerich is living there, perhaps he just uses it to receive mail from the Ministry. I strongly suggest you find out."

I was quietly impressed. This was more than Oberkommissar Radel had been able to supply. Perhaps there was more assistance I might call on?

"You already have all the manpower you are going to get," he said, and there was almost something of a smile upon his face. He started to step away, paused, and inclined his head slightly. "Fraulein Graber. My respects to your father."

Oh?

While I was dealing with that, Teske moved away, offering one last parting sentence over his shoulder. "I expect complete reports, Herr Kommissar!"

And with that he departed.

I was left with the feeling that, for the time being at least, I wasn't working for Robbery any more. I glanced at the uncleared case folders on my desk and felt no regrets. All the same, the ground had shifted under my feet somewhat, and I wasn't making much sense of it. I needed food.

"Where's someplace nearby we can eat?" asked Fraulein Graber. "We should talk about our next moves."

I didn't gainsay this, though it struck me how quickly she had moved from stammering excuses to being a key part of my 'team'. I can admire that kind of *chuztpah*. Instead, I picked up my coat and hat, recovered my gloves from the drawer, and tucked the Oberkommissar's information in my pocket.

"We'll go to Ascher's. It's a Friday night, and they'll be busy…"

"Oh, but I know the *maitre d'*! I'm sure I can get us a table."

This proved to be precisely the case. Ascher's was heaving, but one whispered word from Fraulein Graber and a space was found for us. We ordered hot soup and cold beer. One of the curiosities of late war Berlin was that, in a time of shortages and poverty, inflation and deprivation, the cafés, restaurants and bars were all doing solid business. Partly, it was people just wanting to escape the desperation for a while, but it was also true that it was easier and cheaper to sit in a restaurant and nurse a meal and a drink, than it was to heat your own home and cook.

It wasn't all good news. The soup was promoted as being potato, but it was really turnip. We ate ravenously (well, I did, anyway). There was very little small talk. I did ask who her father was, and it turned out he was some bigwig in Wilhem Solf's *Auswärtiges Amt*. I knew you had to have a pretty secure private income to even enter the foreign office, so perhaps that explained why Fraulein Graber had no real problem with Obermeier freeloading off her. I suggested that, in the current circumstances, her father was possibly very busy.

"Oh, I am sure he is, but we don't speak often. He

doesn't approve of my politics."

"And what are those?"

She smiled and struck a pose, holding her cigarette up by her cheek. She smoked rarely, I had noted, and then often only to be seen holding a cigarette, rather than puffing on it. A waiter passed by and I instructed him to bring two coffees, then lit up a nail of my own.

"Papa is one of von Hertling's people." She was referring to the man who had been our largely ineffectual Chancellor up until the end of September, a scion of *Zentrum*, the Catholic Centre Party. Did that mean Graber's people were…?

"Catholic? Yes. Papa is quite devout, but he married for money and I inherited Mama's scepticism. Later, I drifted into socialism, and Papa more or less disowned me."

Politics and religion at the dinner table. My own parents would have been scandalised.

"What's next, Kommissar? Do we visit Wedding tonight?"

"Good lord, no." Red Wedding after dark? The *schupos* patrolled that district in pairs, if at all, and certainly not at night. I didn't intend to go knocking on doors and waking up the good working people of that neighbourhood until morning.

We arranged to meet at Bahnhof Friedrichstrasse, at the tram stop that could take us north. We could take the tram out to Leopoldplatz and walk the rest of the way. Ideally, it being a Saturday, all the Reds would sleep in.

"How do we let Herr Obermeier know our plans?" I genuinely didn't expect that to be a difficulty.

SATURDAY, 2ND NOVEMBER 1918

I don't have a newspaper delivered. It's part of that routine I spoke of that I pick one up at a newsstand on my way to work, or as part of a late-morning stroll at the weekend. I certainly never have had one delivered by someone whose byline was included on page three. The drawback was that this newspaper was the USDP's *Freiheit*.

The front pages were dominated by news from Kiel, where sailors and stokers were pulling out all the stops to prevent the High Seas Fleet putting to sea. Most of the details had been removed by the censors, I was sure, but a certain amount of reading between the lines – with Obermeier's help – taught me that the sailors were forming what they called Workers and Soldiers Councils, and making representations to whoever was trying to control the situation up there. They wanted to have released those comrades who had been arrested when the original mutiny broke out a few days ago.

The latest news was that around 250 of their number planned to meet at the Union House in Kiel last night. They had the support of their unions, and both the Socialist parties.

There was a breathless quality to the writing as if *Freiheit*'s journalists were expecting red revolution to break out at any moment. By contrast, the article on page three under the headline 'Where Are Our Wounded Comrades?' was quite restrained. Obermeier played the grieving widow and mother for all she was worth, but there was no mention of Kammerich by name, or anything that hinted at mysterious activity. Obermeier had caught just the right tone of indignant outrage for *Freiheit*, with accusations of incompetence aimed at hospital administration and the Health Ministry.

"It's good, isn't it?" Obermeier was leaning against the frame of my front door, waiting while I pulled on my boots, found my keys, coat, hat, gloves and my Mauser C96. I was wearing a shoulder holster over my shirt and slipped the pistol into that. The Mauser was an awkward weapon for that kind of carry, but never mind. Regulations be damned: I wasn't going to Wedding unarmed.

Obermeier was uncomfortable with the idea, but determined to come along, even more so once he found that Fraulein Graber would be coming with us. He wanted to tell me what he had found out about her. I beat him to it.

The sun was up, though the deep streets were still heavy with shadow. It had rained overnight, and the pavements gleamed dully. At least that damned wind had dropped. The wise sages in Robbery who had read the auguries had been suggesting for days that snow was just around the corner, and it was surely cold enough.

Obermeier read his own prose out loud as we walked to the tram stop. I scarcely heard him. From the main street, I could hear loud voices, distorted in that way that only a megaphone can achieve. A flatbed truck went through the junction ahead, with several military men on the back throwing leaflets over the sides and haranguing passers-by with calls to beware the perils of Bolshevism.

Obermeier picked up one of the leaflets as we turned the corner, pausing to scoff at its crude imagery. He didn't even approve of the type face.

"'The Army has not been defeated!' they say! Then why are we not at the gates of Paris, tell me that!" He raised his voice just enough to be defiant, but nowhere near enough to be heard by the soldiers as they drove on.

"All people want is peace and bread," he continued.

"No-one is going to swallow the lie that all is well. Will they keep trying to sing the same song when the Americans are at the Rhine? Idiots. Ah, look, here is Fraulein Graber."

He tilted his hat in greeting, and they shook hands. I had my hands in my pockets; even with my gloves on I had not yet found any warmth. Graber was all in blue today, her fresh clothes a strong contrast to Obermeier – still in the same clothes he had worn yesterday – and I, who had at least changed his shirt.

Years ago, it had been proposed that a U-Bahn line be constructed along a north-south axis that would have run from Leopoldplatz, at the southern edge of Wedding, down through Friedrichstrasse to Templehof. Work had started, causing a lot of disruption, but had been halted at the outbreak of war for the want of labour. Some sites had been filled in, but others obstructed traffic where Friedrichstrasse gave way to Chausseestrasse, and then became Müllerstrasse. In addition, the trams were becoming venerable, and they had lacked maintenance during the war years. It was an uncomfortable ride.

Obermeier believed he knew the street Oberkommissar Teske had indicated, and that it was not so far from the main road, which suited me. We alighted the tram but soon realised he was mistaken, and we had to go back to the main road and continue much further north. The further we progressed, the buildings became more tired and worn, the faces leaner and grimmer. Off the main road, we passed a residential building that had been gutted by fire and not rebuilt. To my eyes, there were still people living there. An old man passed us by who appeared to be having a conversation with the Kaiser – and not the current one.

Red banners hung from balconies on all sides. Every inch of wall space was plastered with political posters.

Most demanded peace. The most recent were calling for the Emperor's abdication. A slogan painted in red on a bakery wall announced 'There Is No Bread!', though whether this was a simple pronouncement on the lack of flour or a more political one was hard to say.

"Feeling at home, Herr Kommissar?" smirked Obermeier. I winced, and he held a hand up in apology. I adjusted the set of my shoulders and felt the Mauser against my ribs.

Quakerstrasse was lined with large apartment buildings. They might once have been decent enough, but they were all a bit shabby now, and there were cracked windows and broken-down doors on all sides. Not a single building appeared to be numbered. There were people on the street, walking this way and that, but no-one seemed to be going anywhere. One younger fellow with a missing leg was slumped in a doorway, an empty bottle in his hand falling away to roll across the pavement and into the filth-strewn gutter. On the steps of another building, two women watched us pass, wary and hostile.

We were at the point of determining which was the correct building when a woman approached us. I would estimate she was about fifty years of age, with a mouth filled with rotten teeth and a poisonous accent. She was wearing what amounted to little more than a shift, which barely covered her full bosom, and was splattered with nicotine-coloured stains. She gave Fraulein Graber a hard stare and was still looking at her even as she addressed – I presumed – me.

"Looking for something saucy, handsome? I can always tell. Your girlfriend can watch, if that's your thing. If she's happy to do that naked in front of an audience –"

We didn't need to hear the whole pitch. "That's not what we're here for."

"Ah, I knew you'd be *kripo*," the woman snarled. "The girl threw me off, but I can always smell pork even when it comes with a bit of relish."

"We're not police," Obermeier interjected. He held up an identification card. "We're press, see?"

"You're not *kripo*," the woman announced, "but the pretty one is. She narrowed her eyes to take a closer squint at the card. "Do *you* want a fuck? Five marks. Ten for the back door. Or you can wank over these tits for 10 cigarettes."

We tried to move on before we heard the rest of her rate card. Obermeier thought he'd found the right building, but even as we got closer two men appeared from the basement of a neighbouring building, clad in just their vests and trousers, even though it was almost zero degrees out here. One threw a cigarette butt to the ground and a small child scurried up and bore away this treasure.

"*Kripo*," the woman announced again, louder than before. One of the men put his hand into a trouser pocket, and I figured he wasn't fumbling in there for loose change. We glared at each other.

"We're not police!" Obermeier insisted once more. "We're with the USDP." He obviously believed this appeal to socialist solidarity would curry favour, but it was a mistake. Nowhere in Wedding held to such bland political colours.

"We just want to speak to whoever lives in Apartment 9."

The woman seemed to find this amusing. "You're looking for Trude? At this hour? That little whore won't be awake until this afternoon. Why not spend a little time with me?"

The two men stared at me with dead eyes. They weren't drunk, but they weren't exactly sober. Even in the open air they stank of sweat, stale beer and a lack of reticence.

At this point the woman changed tack. She was willing to tell us anything we wanted to know for the price of a bottle of schnapps. Fraulein Graber reached for her pocketbook; I moved a hand to stay hers.

"Five marks," Obermeier offered. "Just let us talk to this Trudi."

"Ten," countered the woman, no stranger to haggling. I had a ten mark note in my pocket and produced it.

"Yours, as soon as we have spoken to Trudi."

The two men remained like a wall across the pavement. One of them scratched his arse, but they were otherwise immobile. The woman – and at some point she introduced herself as Helga, though I doubt she gave the same name twice to anyone – told us that Apartment 9 (and yes, we did have the right building) was rented by Trude Holstadt. Trude was, according to Helga (who would surely know and not judge), a prostitute, and a dancer at a nightclub called the Astrakhan. I hadn't heard of it, but there were a lot of new establishments springing up now that the government had weightier matters on its mind.

We asked about Doktor Kammerich, but Helga insisted she had never heard the name. You'd never know if that was truth or lie from that mouth.

"Trude does entertain a doctor, mind. Sees him regular. Useful thing for a working girl to have, that, a doctor who'll trade for favours."

This conversation was carried on in the full view of various windows along the street, some of which had been opened so that people could hear better what was going on. From one on an upper floor, an older gentleman with an unkempt beard and furrowed brow called out to ask what all the ruckus was.

"None of your business, Jew!" snapped Helga. Anyone tells you the Reds and the Jews have much love for each other, and I am here to tell you otherwise.

"I have no business with you ever, Frau Meissenberg. If you must whore in the street, could you not be a little quieter on the Sabbath?"

There was a little more to and fro between them, but then Helga abruptly asked the old man to go and knock on Trude Holstadt's door, and – equally surprisingly – he said he would do so. After another fifteen unpleasant minutes of being down-wind of the two meatheads, a disheveled, sleepy and very unhappy Fraulein Holstadt appeared at the front door wearing nothing more than a pink silk dressing gown and yesterday's lipstick.

I was quite happy to get straight down to business, though it might have been more conducive to be indoors, and without two draft-dodgers/deserters to work the conversation around and between.

Holstadt wasn't a beautiful woman, but she had that dancer's shape, and an angular quality to her face. At a guess, I would have said she was about thirty, but you know how it can be with working girls – they develop that hard look early. Being dragged from her bed by her old Jewish neighbour banging on her door cannot have helped her look her best. She was shivering on the steps, arms folded tightly across her chest, her blond hair lying lank about her face.

"Don't be alarmed," I said, with all the reassurance I could muster. "You're not in any trouble. We just need to find Doktor Kammerich."

"I don't know anyone by that name!" she insisted, her voice weak. I heard Helga hoot derisively.

"Think carefully," I counselled. "You have a friend

who visits. He gave this address to his boss." A small lie.

"We need to speak with him."

"Are you from the review board?"

"Yes." A bigger lie, but I hadn't hesitated.

Trude swallowed hard. "I've got your letter. The one you sent... to Karl. He hasn't seen it. He hasn't been here in over a week."

"Found himself someone better!" suggested Meissenburg.

I felt as if we were getting somewhere, which was just as well because a larger crowd was gathering all the time, and the mood wasn't improving with the increase in quantity. "OK. That's good. Can you go fetch the letter? And any others that have been sent to him here? We just want to be completely sure there's no mistake. "

She bought that, nodding as she turned to go inside again. I started to follow, but the wall of man-vest remained firmly in the way. "Come on, move aside," I said. "You can see she's fine with..."

Nothing. At least not from them. Helga was tapping Obermeier on the shoulder, urging him to hand over her ten marks and suggesting she had more to say for another ten. Obermeier stammered as she pressed closer towards him, insisting that I was the one in charge of the budget.

"Pay up," said the muscle in front of me on the left.

"Ten Marks," said the one on the right.

Helga shrieked that this was her money, and that 'Bernhard' (left or right?) should stay out of it. She spewed out words quickly, saying that 'Doktor Karl' had looked after a number of girls in the street, and not just Trude. He slept with Trude, stayed over some nights. He had last been there three nights ago.

I handed the money to Obermeier, from whom Helga snatched it immediately. Right-hand Bernhard demanded another ten, and I didn't want him to itemise the reasons why I needed to pay that. I believed I had at least another ten in my wallet, but that would mean opening my jacket to reach it, which would surely reveal the shoulder harness and the Mauser. Maybe that would work in my favour, maybe not. I decided to wait.

To my blessed relief, Trude was back quickly. She came up behind the two sweat stains and passed the letters through between them. I immediately noticed that they had all been opened.

"When did you last see the doctor?" I asked.

"It's been over a week." That didn't square with Helga's account.

"Fraulein Holstadt, no-one can get into any trouble if you tell us the truth.

Left-hand Bernhard decided to be gallant, and stepped forward. "She said a week," he growled. Helga called Trude a liar. Right-hand Bernhard moved towards her with a big fist raised. I moved into the space he vacated.

Things moved both slowly and all at once after that. Left-hand Bernhard tried to grab my sleeve, but I slipped under his grasp. Trude was directly in front of me now, eyes like saucers, clutching at her filmy robe as she stepped back towards the front steps. I could hear Helga screaming, and a yelp of alarm that I thought was from Obermeier. I caught Trude by the wrist.

"It's all right, Fraulein. There's a little money in it for you if you can help, We just want to speak to Doktor Kammerich."

Left-hand Bernhard was turning like a battlecruiser (not one of the self-detonating English ones, obviously), but I'd put myself in a bit of a spot. There were twenty or thirty people gathered in front of the building by this time, many of them restive. They closed in as I sought to pull myself closer to Trude. And through the hubbub, two voices. One was Helga, braying that we weren't from the fucking Health Ministry, that we were *kripo* bulls. And another young man's voice, screaming dementedly. "Don't let him near me!"

Planet left-hand Bernhard had completed his rotation about the sun, and was reaching to grab my lapel with one hand and slam the other into my face. I dropped Trude's wrist and pushed him back (he barely moved). Then, for good measure, I kicked him in the knee. Slow-witted and drunk he might be, but he felt that.

Another fist was thrown by someone that glanced off my shoulder. Trude was gone, tripping back up the steps. I saw a young man at the front of the throng, his mouth so open I could see the back of his throat, his eyes impossibly wide. He was standing on one leg, arms up, hands clawing at the air.

Another shove almost sent me sprawling. We needed to get out of there.

I burst out of the throng like a popped pimple. To my relief, I saw Fraulein Graber just ahead of me. She threw up one hand and a fluttering of bank notes exploded into the scene like butterflies. Were those twenty mark notes? I also noted that her other hand appeared to have produced a small pocket pistol.

This was all getting out of hand. I took hold of her wrist and guided her away from the throng, most of whom now were trying to divide six or eight banknotes between thirty people. Obermeier, who had been engaged in a shouting match with the lovely Helga, also managed to retreat. Some filthy children three stones at our backs but didn't hit us. We left Quakerstrasse and its inhabitants behind.

"Give me that!" I demanded, taking the pistol from

Fraulein Graber. "You could be arrested for this."

"It's just as well there isn't a policeman around," sneered Obermeier. "Really, Herr Inspektor, the city is awash with armed soldiery who have turned their back on all authority, and you are harassing poor Fraulein Graber for possessing that pea-shooter."

"If you're not prepared to use it, waving a gun around just invites trouble!"

"Who said I wasn't prepared to use it?" Fraulein Graber countered.

We continued our retreat to the main road. We were fortunate to find a tram passing, and boarded it, heading back south. No-one had pursued us. I suppose that's the kind of benefit 100 Marks will buy you.

"This is intolerable," I said, to no-one in particular. I could feel my pulse racing. Obermeier looked like death. To distract myself, and provide a space in which I might calm down, I took the opportunity to look at the mail Fraulein Holstadt had handed over.

Most of it was uninteresting. There was a letter from a lawyer confirming he had been retained to act for Kammerich in the matter of the sale of the Potsdam property. That was a couple of weeks old, and there was no follow-up, but I knew I could always speak with the lawyer to see if he – a Herr Trautman – had been in touch with his client more recently.

There was a handwritten note, signed 'S', which stated that 'here's the fifty marks you asked for'. If Trude had opened this and pocketed the money, as I suspected, she really should have disposed of the letter rather than keeping it with the others. On the one hand, perhaps this pointed to Kammerich having visited; on the other, perhaps Trude wasn't that bright.

There was the letter we had touched on with Trude,

the one from the Health Ministry regarding the review board. This informed the Herr Doktor that he should attend a meeting where he might make his case for his suspension to be lifted at 11am on Monday morning. That was useful to know, although I understood that if we were still looking for Kammerich come Monday, Oberkommissar Teske was going to have me moved to some frontier town in East Prussia. At best.

There was a leaflet amidst the mail, not addressed specifically to Kammerich. This promoted a meeting of spiritualists at a private residence that had taken place the weekend before. The leaflet suggested that a man named Father Olsen would address the meeting, and assist people in speaking with their lost, loved ones. I could imagine how sour my expression became.

"What's the postcard?" asked Obermeier.

I brought that to the top of the pile. It featured a picture of the Richard Wagner monument in the Tiergarten. The note on the reverse mentioned a time: 4 o'clock in the afternoon, and nothing else. The postmark suggested the card had been posted on Thursday morning in Lichterfelde.

"A rendezvous?" asked Obermeier.

"Probably." 4pm. Did that mean today, or some other day? The card would not have been delivered before Friday, but did that mean that the meeting had already taken place?

"It doesn't say where," Fraulein Graber commented in a quiet voice. I turned the card back to the picture.

"Perhaps this is a regular meeting, and the place is already known to Kammerich. Or perhaps this is the clue. Either way, this is where we will go next."

But when I said 'we'… who did I mean? I looked hard at my companions. Just what were we achieving here?

The Richard Wagner Monument

If I might have asked for any additional police at all, I would have dismissed Fraulein Graber, and perhaps Obermeier too. But that had never been on the table. And for this rendezvous, I would need more than just my own pair of eyes. When we got off the tram, I did find a *schupo* who I asked to accompany me, but he insisted he was going off duty at two o'clock, so I instead sent him back to the Praesidum with a note for the Oberkommissar.

The Richard Wagner monument is a memorial to the famous composer, catching him reclining in an uncomfortable chair while swathed in what looks like a toga. Maidens and other allegorical figures are at his feet, lifting a hand in salutation, or perhaps to ask why he is so much larger than they.

It is situated on Tiergartenstraße, on the south side of the park. It's a popular place for people to visit, pass and gawk at, and on a Saturday afternoon there was no shortage of citizenry doing just that. During a brief, brisk shower, a few gathered under the glassed roof keeping Wagner dry, but it wasn't especially a place to loiter, which I hoped would come in handy.

I posted Obermeier on a corner across the street, while Fraulein Graber and I took a turn along Tiergartenstraße like any man with a rich mistress might do on a Saturday afternoon. We were still a few hours before the proposed meeting, but I wanted to see if anyone was hanging around. Compared to other parts of the city that November, it was quite peaceful here, although there was a older man with one empty sleeve pinned to the rest of his jacket, selling copies of the *Nordeutsche Allgemeine Zeitung* and calling out headlines critical of the sailors' mutiny up in Kiel. As we went past, he begged for change, which implied sales were not all that brisk. I bought a paper. Such a prop is an essential disguise for any surveillance detail.

Obermeier suggested no-one had been paying us any attention, so we repaired to a café to pay over the odds for adulterated coffee and pastries. This was my treat, since Fraulein Graber found herself unaccountably short of cash.

The paper didn't have much to say that hadn't been covered in more detail and with more passion in *Freiheit*. It was a little better for coverage of government pronouncements and optimistic reports from the front, where it was estimated that the British had suffered over half a million casualties prosecuting the advance which another part of the paper suggested wasn't actually happening. It mentioned the two Paris-Geschütz guns that had been menacing the French capital until as late as August, and how they had been brought back to stiffen the defences of the *Siegfriendstellung*, which might have been impressive were it not for the fact that most reporting had accepted that those mighty defences had been overrun weeks ago.

"Perhaps they can use the barrels as water pipes," scoffed Obermeier.

We were back in position no later than three o'clock. Again, Fraulein Graber and I strolled along Tiergartenstraße like tourists. She took my arm – saying it looked more convincing – though I couldn't imagine anyone really took us for a couple. Some genuine couples (married or otherwise) were out for a late afternoon stroll, perhaps considering a venue for dinner, or 'my place or yours'. There were a few soldiers on leave (officially or otherwise), and some older gentlemen discussing the events of the day, and the future of Germany, looking sternly at anyone they thought should be sacrificing themselves at the front.

Just as we were passing the monument again, I heard one man suggests the Kaiser must abdicate to save the Empire, and a short argument broke out between him and a hussar officer. A passing *schupo* had them move on, and things settled down once more. I decided not to waylay the *schupo*, not even behind the 'disguise' of pretending to ask for directions, in case it gave us away.

At about a quarter before four, as we passed Obermeier and prepared to turn about, the reporter hissed: "Grey suit, homburg, umbrella, book. He's keeping an eye on the street."

Such a watchful man might have noticed if the same couple passed him for a third or fourth time, so we swapped places. Fraulein Graber and I stood on the corner, and Obermeier went to commune with Richard Wagner. From our new vantage point, we could see the individual he had spotted. This was a man lurking by one of the walls of the composer's shelter, outwardly reading a book, but also looking up at intervals to peer along the street in both directions. He was a pencil-thin fellow, with blackened glass spectacles (possibly a better descriptor than the homburg), blond hair, a good suit and (it will transpire) a limp. He lit up a cigarette precisely at the hour of four.

One drawback to our surveillance was that we didn't know with any certainty what Kammerich looked like. One of the doctors at Charité had provided the basics – short, dark-haired, blue eyes, shifty – but that could have been applied to me. So, we kept a watch for anyone, really, and I became convinced homburg was doing much the same. He smoked that cigarette, finished it, lit another. It made me twitch, so I lit a nail myself. It was seven minutes past the hour.

"He's leaving," whispered Fraulein Graber

He was indeed, and coming our way. I took Fraulein Graber's arm again, and we strolled eastwards, pausing to stop and discuss a poster advertising a concert at the Berliner Philharmonie. Homburg went past (this was where I noticed the limp). He looked back but once, by which time we two were well behind, and Obermeier was trailing him on the far side of Tiergartenstraße.

"What if this is not our man?" hissed Fraulein Graber.

"What if this was not the right day or place for the rendezvous? We must play the cards we have been dealt."

One thing I was confident about was that our quarry had not realised he was being followed. Fraulein Graber and I closed the gap a little, but not too close, and Obermeier slid along on the other pavement, innocuous and unremarkable. Homburg continued, past where Tiergartenstraße became Lennéstraße, then jinked onto Franz Strasse, crossing Wilhelmstrasse and finally entering a café on Glinkastrasse called *Annabet's*.

This being a Saturday, and this being the government administrative district, I was partly surprised *Annabet's* was open, but it was and was doing good trade. Obermeier found himself another street corner to loiter on. Fraulein Graber and I made a point of standing outside, pointing at the menu in the window, and observed our quarry order coffee at the counter, before going to sit at a table already occupied by an officer of the General Staff, an *Oberst*, who had been staring out of the window as we walked up. I had to hope our charade was convincing. We went in.

Homburg and the Colonel settled at their table, holding a sparse, low conversation. The Colonel was of your typical Prussian military persuasion; his fair hair was shaved almost to the skull; he wore a monocle over one of his cold blue eyes; and his uniform was rigidly correct. Quite the chestful of medal ribbons too. There was a free table just behind him, and I motioned Fraulein Graber to grab it, much to the disquiet of a waiter who had assumed that was his job. While she took off her coat and settled into a chair facing our persons of interest, I made a show of ordering coffee and complaining about the prices.

Annabet's was one of those places that seemed to trap sound, amplifying the conversations from every table, until there was just a morass of spoken words. I joined Fraulein Graber, my back to the Colonel, but much closer to him. I lit up a cigarette and enquired after Fraulein Graber's brother. I don't know if she had one or not, but she played along like a film actress.

I tried to focus all my attention on the conversation behind me. The Colonel kept his voice perpetually low, not much above a whisper, but the good news was that our friend with the Homburg was agitated and speaking with a little more vigour.

"I don't know what you expect from me. I told you: Kammerich didn't show."

At least we were in the right place. I could enjoy my cigarette. I hoped the coffee would not be long.

"Have you allowed him enough time?" I could sense the Colonel consulting his watch.

"He has *always* been punctual."

"Well then. What do you propose we do now, Herr Doktor?"

"He must have gone to ground."

The Colonel dropped his voice even lower. I wondered if the Herr Doktor could even hear him properly. "Or he has been exposed. But you have not answered my question. Perhaps we must shut the operation down. There is too much at stake."

At this moment, a waiter arrived with coffee for both Homburg and then for us. Fraulein Graber made a point of asking how late they were open. It was useful scene-setting, but it did mean I missed the next few lines of dialogue from the table behind me. When I next heard Homburg speak, he was even more agitated.

"Is that not premature?"

"This was always a risky project, and our window of opportunity is closing fast." "But, surely –"

"The risks outweigh any possible reward. You must shut it down! See to it at once, Herr Doktor!"

Someone at that table was stirring his cup vigorously. "Madness! Where am I supposed to move everything to?"

"Quiet!" hissed the Colonel. There was a clear pause behind me. I chuckled as if Fraulein Graber had just made an amusing remark and offered my congratulations. God knows what anyone listening in to *our* conversation would make of it.

"You know the answer to your own question. Use your resources, then it can all be explained as an administrative mistake. You know where to move everything to. As long as you are discrete, it should not be so difficult."

"Impossible! I say they cannot all be moved."

"Then eliminate …" The rest of the officer's words were lost. I realised he had leaned forward to give additional emphasis to his hissed commands. Then I heard the Colonel's chair scrape and felt him rise to his feet. I twisted in my seat as if I was trying to catch the waiter's attention, and saw from the corner of my eyes the Colonel drawing on his gloves, and picking up his cap.

"Good day, Herr Doktor. We shall not need to speak

tomorrow."

I couldn't be sure what dilemma had just been left for Doktor Homburg, but we had one of our own now. I had to rely on Obermeier to respond to the Colonel's departure, because it would have been too obvious if we had departed having barely touched our over-priced coffees. I wasn't too concerned; at a guess, Doktor Homburg was where we needed to concentrate. I leaned forward, drank half my coffee in a single gulp, and gestured for Fraulein Graber to come closer.

"I think you should take my amorous suggestion badly." She caught on quickly.

"Herr Blucher! What would your wife say?!"

With that, she grabbed her things and headed for the door. I uttered a word of protest as any cad would, then fumbled for coins to pay the bill. I heard someone mutter that I was a no gentleman, and managed to blush in response.

Outside, I caught sight of Obermeier, who shrugged theatrically and mimed steering a car, gesturing back along the street behind him. I caught the back of a large staff car disappearing into the distance. I suppose that drew a line under the Colonel, for now.

Fraulein Graber had hesitated on leaving the café, but before I reached the pavement she set off across the street. I hesitated a little myself, but then the door opened behind me (there was a little jangly bell to announce this), and Doktor Homburg came out. He paused and lit a cigarette while looking up and down Glinkastrasse. He turned up his coat collar, settled his Homburg more securely, and set off north, his limp perhaps just a little more pronounced.

Herr Doktor Luster

I remained in place, watching as Obermeier latched onto the doctor once more. Once he was nearing Behrenstrasse, I could be confident he was heading for Unter den Linden. Fraulein Graber returned, joining me outside the café.

"What was that about?" she asked.

"How much could you hear?"

"Not much. He told that officer that Kammerich didn't show, and after that I didn't hear much of anything."

Good. "Come on," I said. We followed Homburg and Obermeier up the street. I saw the doctor turn left onto Unter Den Linden, and we broke into something of a trot, although I was quickly struggling with my knee. I tried to keep this infirmity from Fraulein Graber. All the same, once we turned the corner, we were much closer. For a moment, I couldn't see Obermeier, but he had done his usual trick and was on the other side of the street.

"We need to be careful," I suggested. "He might catch a tram and we'll lose him."

"He would have done better turning the other way and catching one on Friedrichstrasse. No, I think he's going to cross Marschallbrucke."

She was right. We crossed the Spree about fifty metres behind Homburg. The Reichstag was off to the west, catching the wan afternoon light. It was getting colder by the minute. Finally, the pfennig dropped for us both. Ahead lay Charité. Doktor Homberg must work there. Once we were in the midst of the vast Universitätsmedizin complex, we might easily lose him. I decided it was time to bring him to a stop. At my urging, Fraulein Graber skipped after him, calling 'Herr Doktor!" every few steps. Eventually he realised this was about him, stopped and turned. I don't think he recalled her from the café, but the moment he saw me his expression turned first sour, then resigned, but finally defiant.

"What is the meaning of this? Who are you, and why are you following me?"

There was no point beating about the bush. I produced my beer token. "Kommissar Hoehner, Robbery."

"Robbery?" He looked quite shaken by this, which was interesting. "What do you want with me?"

"Shall we step inside the hospital, Herr Doktor? We're all cold, and I think I feel rain in the air."

He was almost willing to fight even that simple idea, but we continued the last few metres and passed through the main entrance.

"I demand to know –" he began, but then it must have struck him that he was in full view of other medical staff, perhaps his colleagues. "Tell me how I can be of help," he said, adjusting his tone.

"Might I trouble you for your papers, Herr Doktor?" He hesitated, but then complied as he was obliged to. I scanned them briefly: Doktor Hans Luster, born in Hannover – my old home town! –in 1868, now resident of Berlin, employed here at Charité as an anaesthesiologist. I handed the papers back.

"*Danke.* I believe you can help me with a matter of some urgency. I am trying to trace a Doktor Kammerich."

That cannot have come unexpected. All the same, Luster paled, and swayed on his feet. I was almost concerned we were about to make him a patient at his own hospital.

"I do not know anyone by that name."

"I find that odd, seeing as you sent a postcard to his

address, arranging to meet him at the Richard Wagner statue." I produced the postcard. "This is going to be easily proved to be your handwriting, I feel."

A reasonable but lucky guess. Luster took a handkerchief from his trouser pocket and mopped his lip. "Ah. Ah! Kammerich, you say! Well, yes, I do know a Doktor Kammerich. Not well, you understand, not personally, but I do know the man."

"And you arranged to meet him."

"Uh... yes."

"For what purpose?"

"It is a private matter."

"I insist on knowing."

The doctor's nerve stiffened. "Insist all you wish. It was a private matter, and I do not intend to discuss it."

"I see. Then can you tell me the name of the officer you were just speaking to at *Annabet's* café on Glinkastrasse?"

He was trembling. "I cannot. I do not know his name. This too is a private matter."

"That concerns Kammerich?"

"I told you: I will not speak of this! Am I to be interrogated like a felon, here, in my place of work, in front of my colleagues?"

"These are simple questions, Herr Doktor. I do not see why they are so difficult to answer. But I can solve another of your problems. If it suits you better, we can discuss this at the Praesidium."

He swallowed hard. I had hoped the threat of that would make him more amenable, but I was mistaken. "You cannot detain me!"

"In fact I can, Herr Doktor. I can take you in for questioning, and I shall. Or you can just tell me what I know right here, and then be on your way."

That surely had to appeal to him, but no. He insisted that he would not answer. "These are confidential matters."

"Come with me, Herr Doktor. You'll answer my questions at the Alex, and while you are our guest I shall get a warrant to search your office here, and your home. I give you one last chance to answer these very simple questions I put to you."

He went mute. He didn't have anything to say on the journey to the Alex, nor when he was placed in an interrogation room. I could tell he was frightened, but not of me. Not yet, anyway.

Reporting In

A little later, back in Robbery, I found a message waiting for me that had been dropped off at the front desk. A Doktor Thorssen had been told by a colleague that the police were looking for Kammerich, and as a good citizen Thorssen immediately dropped everything to send his information along. I wondered what the grudge would turn out to be.

The gist of what was quite a long-winded missive was that he knew a medical orderly by the name of Therodore Katz, who, deep in his cups, said he had been paid money by Kammerich on what would have been last Thursday evening. Thorssen was also keen to point out that Katz wasn't working this weekend, but that he liked to drink in a bar called the Trippel-A on Hannoverschstrasse.

It being Saturday night, I wanted to get there right away, but first I quickly prepared a report for Oberkommissar Teske. Actually, even that wasn't first. *First*, I asked one of the *kripos* on shift who Teske was, and what department he headed.

"Don't mess with Teske, Hoehner. He's thick with the Ministry. Von Oppen and he are thick as thieves." This reference to the big boss of the whole Berlin police force gave me pause for thought. Von Oppen was old school, a landowner and parliamentarian. I wondered why Teske didn't hold a more prominent position if his mate was in charge.

"Where does he hide?"

"Down the hall, the other side of the stairway. Amt VIIIb."

Not the Political Department, then. In fact, what

department was that?

I took up my completed report, placed it in a folder, labelled that in the correct manner and bound it with red ribbon. I told Obermeier and Graber to wait at my desk. I also told Obermeier to get out of my chair, but I didn't expect that to work any better.

Department VIIIb lay behind a door that just had the number painted on the glass, and no name or function. I knocked and went in, expecting to find an antechamber with a secretary, but instead I was directly into the office of Oberkommissar Teske. The old man was behind his desk, which was large enough to be suitable for a game of tennis. He looked up as I came in. I made a point of holding up the report so that he would know I came in peace.

Teske was not alone. Seated on one of the chairs in front of the desk was Councillor Markwitz. I could not conceive of any situation where those two came together and it turned out to be a good thing for me.

"Is that your report?"

"Yes, Herr Oberkommissar." I handed it over.

"Summarise matters succinctly for Councillor Markwitz."

"*Jawohl*, Herr Oberkommissar. We have made progress in the search for Doktor Kammerich."

This may have been a little too succinct. "*Progress?*" Markwitz responded, scornfully. "You still haven't found him after all this time?"

"No. But I do have another doctor in custody who I am certain can lead us to Kammerich. I am letting him sweat for a while in an interview room. I should like permission –"

"You have a *different* doctor in custody?" Markwitz was rousing himself to a suitable level of outrage, as I had observed before. He probably couldn't wait to visit the widow Plommer and tell her the bad news, preferably while a journalist or four was present to garner quotes.

"As you will see at the end, Herr Oberkommissar, another lead has come in that might lead us to Kammerich."

Teske grunted, dissatisfied with this level of progress. I hesitated to point out that if he released me to go to the Trippel-A immediately, it might lead to something more satisfactory.

"None of this, to my mind, gets you any closer to finding Frau Plommer's son and the other missing men."

Feeling defensive, I almost raised the point that we still couldn't be one hundred percent sure Plommer had ever been aboard the train. Perhaps anticipating this, Teske handed me a folder of his own. This was the response to yesterday's telegram to Aachen, bearing the full manifest of patients who had been placed on the train. Wagon Eight, exactly as feared, had contained thirty-four men, and there was listed Privat Walter Plommer (along with Gefreiter Meinz).

"May I take this?" I asked. Teske waved his acceptance. I felt like I had jumped in before Markwitz, which was a marginal and petty victory. "One other thing, Herr Oberkommissar. I would request warrants to search Doktor Luster's office at Charité, and his home."

Teske's eyes were flat and cold, but he agreed to my request and told me to pick up the warrants in the morning. I took my leave and hurried back to Robbery, gathering up Obermeier and Graber before Markwitz could find us. I may have neglected to tell Markwitz's assistant that her boss was in the building, but the Councilor had been settling into his next round of complaints to Teske as I left Amt VIIIb.

"Look at this," I said to them both, showing them

the paperwork from Aachen.

They glanced through the report together as we rode down to the ground floor on the paternoster lift. Normally, I preferred the stairs to this deathtrap, but it was slightly quicker.

"Most interesting," mused Obermeier.

"What?" Fraulein Graber demanded.

"Look at the injuries."

The thirty-four men had varied battlefield injuries. An amputated arm here; a lost eye there. Several had been the victims of mustard gas, which, even if the user is masked, blisters exposed skin. But what joined them all together was that all the victims had, either singularly or in common with these other maladies, been diagnosed with some kind of mental trauma. In some cases, the word used was 'pyschosis'; in two the word was 'catatonia'. A common word was *krieghysterie*.

"What does this mean?"

"We'll have to work that out," I suggested. "But in the meantime, after the day we've had, I am going to buy you both a drink. I know a place…"

Saturday Night

By the time we reached the Trippel-A bar, the evening was well advanced. Trippel-A is situated where Hannoverschstrasse meets Invalidenstrasse, a rough and ready corner drinking spot, with one main room accessed through the front door, and a back room for hardened drinkers, where a pianist plays popular music every evening.

I don't know what time things got going on a Saturday, but by the time we arrived it was packed. The exterior of the building was plastered in posters, some of which were calling for an end to the war, and the rest equating socialism with some kind of bacillus. The Trippel-A was clearly a popular haunt with students and medical staff from Charité, but leavened with some more senior doctors and administrators. A few people were out on the pavement, which was technically an offence. A young woman with long, braided hair remarked as I passed that the bar was just too smoky, even as she took a long pull on a cigarette through a long black holder.

As we walked through the door, the noise of music and conversation hit us like a hammer. Trippel-A was one of those few places that still favoured American-style Tin Pan Alley music. It wasn't music to dance too, at least not on a Saturday night, but that was all right because there was no room anyway. I led the way to the bar, edging my shoulder between patrons in the approved manner. Some joker at the bar glowered in my direction as I eased my way in as if fearing competition for the bar nuts. I let my jacket fall open a little, and after he'd glanced down, he left.

I bought us beers, and asked if there was any food.

The older man behind the bar scowled, but his pretty barmaid suggested there was some bread that wasn't too stale and some cheese that wasn't too hard. It sounded like a feast, and so that was dinner.

We drank slowly, while listening to doctor talk. It's not all about medicine: sometimes they focus on seducing the nurses. Obviously, any one of the lesser males might be this Katz fellow, and I'd have no way of telling. I smoked a couple of cigarettes, which ended my prepared supply, so I bought some more tobacco, of a brand I wouldn't normally touch. We ate the bread and cheese, drank a second beer. By then I had worked out that two men at the end of the bar were orderlies at Charité, so I edged my way towards them and asked if either of them knew Katz.

"He's working," one said, before the other pulled at his sleeve.

"Do you know where?" The fellow shook his head, and they both pointedly turned away.

I could have made sure, but I was just as likely to provide Katz with a warning if I continued this route. We finished our second beers (Obermeier sped this along) and left. Outside, the rain that had been threatening off and on had finally arrived. We ran to the nearest U Bahn station.

"We're done for the night," I suggested.

"What happens next?" Fraulein Graber asked.

I explained about the warrants, and that I'd probably interrogate Luster once he realised he wasn't getting any breakfast. If that didn't work, we still had Katz as a route to finding Kammerich. I thought about asking Graber to delay telling her boss what our meagre plans were, but figured she would do whatever she was obliged to do. With that, we parted company, having arranged our rendezvous for Sunday. Obermeier and I were travelling in the same direction, so I had the pleasure of his company for a little while longer.

"I doubt today has given you much of a story to sell," I remarked.

"That's when a writer truly shows his craft," he replied. He chewed his lower lip for a moment, then switched to something that had clearly been on his mind. "I couldn't help but notice you've been limping a little today, Herr Kommissar."

I didn't care for this having been noted. "My knee is a little painful."

"Ah." We carried on for a few metres, then he returned to his cause. "Is that why you were invalided out of the army?"

I cared even less for having the conversation continue along this path. This was not a memory I wished to revisit at all, but the best way to close this down was to be as terse as possible.

"My unit was gassed at Verdun, in October '16. We were defending Douaumont, but my division was down to around 3,000 men, and when the Moroccans advanced, we had nothing left. We abandoned the fort, but then were gassed during the retreat. I managed to get my mask on, but I was standing around like a scarecrow while I did so, and was hit in the knee when a shell went off along the trench from me. It didn't look too bad at first, but the surgeons decided it would never heal properly, so I got my papers. Every now and then I feel the metal shift around in there."

"Ah! No other lingering effects?"

"Just a hatred of talking about it."

SUNDAY, 3RD NOVEMBER 1918

The dream, but with a subtle variation. Normally I am quite alone within the cloud. Sometimes I can hear voices, but not what they are saying. That night, not only could I hear them, but there were shadows moving around in the yellow mist. They coughed and spluttered, stooped and stumbled. I knew some of them: men from my unit, the one I had been with when I was gassed. Their faces appeared, then drifted away upwards like smoke, gradually dissolving, merging into the gas cloud, becoming one with the poison.

They called my name as they faded away.

Those beers from the night before came back to haunt me, and the moment I was awake I needed to use the pail. The apartment was icy cold, and there was rain rattling on the window. Johan wouldn't be back for hours yet – he was always so late back on a Sunday morning – so I might have lain in, but the prospect of letting the Berlin Police pay the bill for keeping me warm appealed just a little too much.

As I left, Obermeier was just coming up the stairs, wheezing a little. He looked even more sallow than usual, and I saw he was carrying a suitcase.

"I am starting to think you're living in this hallway," I told him.

He offered a week smile. "We are neighbours, Herr Kommissar, but not that close. I would appreciate it, though, if I might leave this case in your apartment. Just for a few nights." I would consider it a most generous favour, in fact.

"Finding it hard to pay the rent, Obermeier?"

"Isn't everyone? No, it's not that."

"So long as you don't have stolen goods in there, or anything else I might regret," I told him, and opened the door. The only truly personal space I had in the world was a large steamer trunk on the far side of the room. I took the case and locked it in there. A wiser man might have demanded to know what he was getting into, but that has never been a virtue of mine.

"You live a spartan life, Herr Kommissar."

"There hasn't been a lot of emphasis on keeping police pay ahead of inflation."

We headed out onto the street. "You don't need to tell me! Some editors think we journalists live on promises and cigarettes. By the way, do you have a – Ah, thank you, Herr Kommissar."

Only fools like us were out so early on a cold, rainy, November morning. Us and the fools who still believed in God. Heads were bent into coat collars as the faithful went to church.

Fanatics of a different stripe were up early too. Against the backdrop of church bells pealing in the distance, another of those flatbed trucks bearing a squad of soldiers roared past as we were crossing over the canal on the Eisernbruche and turning onto Museum Island. The soldiers were chanting in unison, something about hanging every red from a lamppost.

"I thought there was a shortage of petrol," Obermeier observed bitterly. Then, after a few moments' reflection, he added: "You know what else we have never been short of? Soldiers in Berlin. We're told how the Allies have such a huge advantage in numbers, but all I ever see here in the capital are troops who have never been within a hundred miles of the front. What great threat to Berlin is there, that so many remain behind?"

He answered his own question. "This was never a war for Germany. No, it suited the *junkers*, the Prussian generals and all the hangers-on around the Kaiser, but not the working man. And there's your proof. All the soldiers held back to garrison Berlin! They're just here in case the people rise up."

I wasn't in the mood for a political lecture, especially not one quite so overtly socialist, but Obermeier was in full flow. By the time we passed the Berliner Dom he was onto the church's role. I think he kept going all the time as we passed under the railway bridge and entered Alexanderplatz, but I heard none of it. My mind kept returning to that manifest, and the thirty-four names on it. They were all strangers to me, but I felt a kinship to them. Not just because we were soldiers – I felt no such sense of brotherhood to those fools on the truck – but because of what we had all endured these last four years.

And I wondered about the damage that had evidently been done to those men's minds. For weeks after my wounding, I had felt a sense of panic at even the prospect of leaving the hospital, but that had faded over time, or at least that is what I told myself. I had become myself again, except for the dreams. What dreams were they left with?

Herr Doktor Luster's Office

Having picked up the warrants, along with Fraulein Graber, at the Praesidium, we found ourselves once more heading to Charité in the rain. Doktor Luster owned a comfortable home in the fashionable suburb of Grunewald, but we three agreed the more promising prospect lay within the hospital.

I had checked in on the doctor before we left the Praesidium, but his willingness to cooperate had not been improved by a night at the Alex. He refused to speak with me. Curiously, he not yet demanded to see a lawyer, even though I was certain he was intimate terms with several. Perhaps something from his office or home would provide a lever to open him up.

. This being a Sunday, I was able to take out one of the pool cars, a rather over-grand 1913 Horch. Since only I was permitted to drive this beast, Fraulein Graber and Obermeier sat in the back while I acted as chauffeur. Obermeier commented liberally on my use of the clutch, and on the route we should take.

Once at Charité, we asked to see the Direktor of Medicine. Being a Sunday, this august personage was nowhere near work, and so we were passed down the chain of command to a surgeon by the name of Ülbrecht, who insisted that we wait for one of the hospital's lawyers to arrive. I, in turn, said we were obliged to do no such thing. Ülbrecht next tried to maintain that he didn't know where a key might be found, but we had relieved Doktor Luster of his own copy last night, and so were well prepared.

Ülbrecht decided to step out of the path of this train and had an orderly take us to Luster's office. This fellow watched us unlock the door, but then chose to 'observe' us from further along the corridor, equally determined that he didn't want any part of what was running over Luster.

There had been a moment of confusion. Luster's card had suggested he was an anaesthesiologist, but the orderly brought us to all the way to the furthest depths of the hospital, where a glass door insisted Luster worked in Psychiatric Medicine. His office was, in fact, adjacent to a ward where, we were informed, around thirty patients were being treated for various disorders of the mind.

This caught my interest closely.

"Oh, yes," the orderly said, his Silesian accent thick with last night's beer and this morning's cigarettes. "Two in every three of them has – what do they call it? – 'shell shock'. Malingering bastards."

Though I might have mentioned that he was cozy enough in a hospital far from the front, I chose not to, and that was when he left to take up station ten meters away. I opened the office door.

The room beyond was comfortably furnished, with a row of sturdy wooden cabinets along one wall, a desk at the far end, and seating and bookshelves along the third wall. It was more of a study that a doctor's office to my point of view.

I handed Obermeier the doctor's keys and bade him open the cabinets while I browsed the doctor's reading materials. The books were mostly academic and medical textbooks, many well-worn, though a few were dusty with neglect, each bearing an unnaturally long title, and written by fellows with a lot of letters after their names. Additionally, I found works by Freud, Jung, Graf and others, mostly of the Vienna School. Yes, I knew all these names. Coppers are more interested in the workings of the mind than doctors, if you ask me.

In addition, there were books on psychotropics and other medicines, as well as surgical textbooks focused on the brain. One contained photographs of surgical procedures that I would never un-see. Ah, and here were his books on anaesthesiology, heavily annotated.

Doktor Luster had changed specialities during the war. His psychiatry books had contained nothing like this level of personal notation.

On the least accessible shelves near his desk, Luster kept some books on spirituality, phrenology and eugenics, as well as philosophical and political tracts that focused on criminality, *völkisch* nationalism, and antisemitism. There were two copies of the *Protocols of the Elders of Zion*, one in German, one in Russian, and writings by Houston Stewart Chamberlain, Henry Ford and Arthur de Gobineau. Interesting. On the whole, I don't work on the political stuff, but these were the kinds of books that were popping up more and more whenever one bumped into the right sort of crank.

Quite a few of these works were published by a company called Hammer-Verlag. I'd been called to their Berlin office once. Their walls were strewn with all kinds of posters and 'art' depicting Jews as twisted sub-humans. Perhaps that kind of decoration was frowned on at a teaching hospital like Charité, but I had no doubt what kind of man Luster was. In my book, a man's politics were his own affair, but this kind of thing was a poison.

By now, Obermeier had unlocked all the cabinets, and he and Fraulein Graber had started to assess the contents, discussing what they found as they found it. There were hundreds of patient files, stored alphabetically. Each contained detailed psychiatric diagnosis, treatment records and other information, including an extensive family background, which emphasised any 'racial abnormality'. Many of these records were pre-war; some even referred to men and women now deceased. Several more were from the 1914-18 era, though the notes in these were much less extensive. Nobody had that much time for record-keeping any more.

There were too many records for us to comb through, although we did at least make sure there was no mention of Plommer or Meinz. I told Fraulein Graber to remove a few of the most recent records; we'd have someone look them over. I had to trust that no-one would remove the rest, at least while we had Luster in custody.

That left the desk. This carried a jotting pad, telephone, an ornate lamp, an inkstand, and both in- and out-trays. The jotter contained a few telephone numbers: one, I noted, was an Aachen number. I suspected this would connect to the Steiner fellow who had signed off on the transport of the casualties. We could follow that up later; whoever had crated up thirty-four poor souls in Wagon Eight, might be worth our time at some point.

Obermeier then pointed at one of the others, here in Berlin.

"That's the Military Governor's office."

"Are you sure?"

"I've called it myself before now. It's in my notebook. Trust me: that's the number for General von Linsingen."

My mind went back to the colonel from *Annabel*'s café. High-ranking military officers were no rarity in this matter, it seemed.

"Open up the desk drawers."

Obermeier did so. Inside, we found a diary, with several recent entries suggesting meetings with "vO" and "KK", along with patient appointments and work-related meetings. None were scheduled with "KK" in the days to come, but yesterday's rendezvous was there, as was the plan to meet "vO" at *Annabet's*.

There were also two more books. One was a medical treatise on madness, not one that had been published by any academic publisher, but was again from Hammer-Verlag. It too was heavily annotated, and in Doktor Luster's hand, unless I was mistaken.

The other was a tattered volume entitled *The Drama of the Yellow King*, which appears to be a German-language commentary on a play I had never heard of. Having glanced at a few pages, I decided I would never need to see it, and I tossed the book back in the drawer, while pocketing the madness volume, and setting aside the diary to take also. Then, at the last moment, I took the drama commentary as well.

Finally, the desk also contained a decent amount of money, around 5,000 marks, I estimated. Once upon a time, that was a worthwhile sum, and even now it wasn't to be sniffed at. Obermeier looked at me, and I looked at him.

"Lock it up," I ordered.

Obermeier did so, and we locked the office securely as we left. I wasn't entirely sure we had achieved too much, although the diary was useful. Nothing here had provided evidence that Luster was guilty of any crimes, but he was connected to our mystery, and I was determined to make him realise that.

Herr Doktor Luster's Home

We went directly from Charité to Luster's home. This was in Grunewald, which was a very attractive part of the city. The house wasn't overly large, but it sat behind a high wall and wrought iron gates. There was an expensive-looking Mercedes Benz on the drive. I also noted an Opel four-seater parked in the street just along from the house, with a driver at the wheel, and another man in the back, both in uniform. The German military loved the Opel. The top was up, so I couldn't make out the passenger, but the driver was more or less in full view and didn't look happy about it in this weather.

The gate wasn't locked, so we walked up the drive to the main entrance. I noted that someone was watching from an upstairs window as we approached. I wondered what they made of the trio coming to their door.

I rang the bell and we waited. We waited for quite a few minutes, if truth be told. There was a portico of sorts, but the rain was being driven in under it. Finally, the door was opened, although we were afforded no glimpse inside. A solid mountain of a man stood in the opening, keeping us and the weather at bay.

I held the warrant before me.

"This is a search warrant authorising me to search Herr Docktor Luster's home."

The mountain didn't move. "Herr Doktor isn't here."

Information I already had.

"That doesn't matter. Step aside, *bitte*."

Still the mountain remained immobile. I couldn't be entirely sure from his unchanging, blank expression that he was even understanding the words he was hearing. If he was the butler, I doubted how well the family was served, and frankly, I feared for the safety of the crockery with this hulk moving around.

"Frau Agnetha is not receiving visitors."

I took a moment to assess the situation. Reasoning with this elephant wasn't getting me anywhere, but pushing past him didn't appear to be any easier an option. I considered shouting past him to attract the lady of the house, for all that this would mark me out as one of the low sort.

Perhaps a more personal approach. "What is your name, *mein Herr*?"

The giant was puzzled by this question. His brow furrowed minutely, and I swear I saw a little light in his eyes. "My name is Bruno."

"Herr Bruno. I am Kriminal-Kommissar Hoehner of the Berlin Police. This warrant –" I waved it again – "gives me the power to search this house. Do you understand?"

He nodded, but then added: "Herr Doktor Luster is not here."

I sighed and took a step back, perhaps about to commit to dodging past the obstacle somehow when I heard the squeal of the metal gate opening. I looked over my shoulder and saw a cavalry captain walking towards us. He paused and clicked his heels in salute. "*Guten morgen*. I am speaking with Kommissar Hoehner, is that correct?"

I confirmed that this was so.

"Might we have a word?" He looked past me towards the doorway. "*Danke*, Bruno. Please inform Frau Luster that I will deal with this matter."

I remained fixed on the captain as I heard the door close behind me. This new arrival was presumably the man from the back of the Opel. His uniform was impossibly well-tailored; his boots shone; his gloves were of a kind of grey kid leather that cost more than I made in a month; he wore a *pour le mérit* at his throat, which was some distinction for a mere captain. He had the kind of face that expressed a kind of smug superiority even when resting; high cheekbones, blue eyes, thin lips.

"*Herr Hauptman*, you appear to be holding the better ground. Might I see your identification?"

I could see he found this idea quite quaint, but he played along, reaching into a breast pocket to retrieve his military papers. Hauptman Ludwig Weiss von Beckman und Alderstadt. You'd get most of the way to the award of a *pour le mérit* for that name alone, I suspected.

"Why are you interrupting police business, Hauptman von Beckman?"

"Please, call me Willi. We're all friends here. Do you smoke, Herr Kommissar? Here, try one of these. American Camels. Machine rolled – aren't they remarkable?"

We lit up together. He didn't offer the packet around. In fact, he hadn't acknowledged the existence of Frau Graber or Herr Obermeier in the slightest.

"Well, this is better, nah? I am sorry for interrupting, but I am aware of something you may not know, which is that Frau Luster has a nervous condition. It affects her heart, you see. I do not think it is best for her to have strangers tramping all over her house, nah?"

That little affectation was starting to annoy me and I had only heard it twice.

"Herr Hauptman, I have a warrant."

"Yes. May I see?"

He had no right to, but I showed him anyway. I was hoping my cooperative sunny nature would illicit more information from him than arresting him for wasting police time and interfering in an official investigation. He glanced at the document briefly, then handed it back, thanking me graciously as he did so.

"Is Herr Luster under arrest?"

"He is at the *Polizei Praesidium*, yes." Which was both answer and non-answer, seeing as we appeared to be playing that kind of game.

"Is he charged with any offence?"

"Not yet."

"I see, I see." He breathed out blue tobacco smoke, and watched it curl into the sky. "When he did not return from work yesterday, Frau Luster became concerned. I am an old family friend, nah?" I was supposed to connect the dots myself. I didn't respond at first, but watched the captain, who I noted held his cigarette between his middle fingers in an effete manner I found offensive. It's possible my impatience showed. "Did Doktor Luster not ask to see his lawyer?"

"He did not."

"Curious. Might *I* be permitted to see him?"

"Family only." I looked back at the house. "If you wish to accompany Frau Luster to the Alex, that's fine, but you'll need to wait outside the interview room. We could all go there together, if that would suit the lady, *after* I have searched the house."

Von Beckman wasn't prepared to make that deal so easily. "As I have intimated, Frau Luster would find it distressing to have detectives going through her personal belongings."

"You could take her for a drive, then." Her and her butler/bodyguard.

This too was stonewalled. I checked my watch, feeling the day slip away. There were still other matters I wished to attend to, and I didn't have time to waste dealing with von Beckman's beautiful manners.

He and I finished our Camels at the same time. I stubbed mine out on the drive, while Beckman pinched his out, then retrieved both butts for disposal elsewhere. He would have made a far better roommate than Johan. "I will forgo the search at this time, Herr Hauptman. But only for today. As a friend to the family, perhaps you can find some way to distract Frau Luster tomorrow morning."

"Perhaps. In the meantime, when might I tell her that her husband will be released?"

"I shall question him again this afternoon. If I am satisfied then, perhaps he can return home."

For now, that seemed to be the end of matters. The captain snapped his heels and left. Obermeier, Graben and I followed not too far behind. As we walked, I quickly briefed the others. "Memorise the number plate of his car as it passes. Don't write it down until he is out of sight. There will also be markings on the side of the car; memorise those too. Step lively now, he is almost back at his car."

Searching For Kammerich: Dead End

I wanted to question Luster again before Hauptman von Beckman found a way to get a lawyer involved, so we raced back to the Alex. While I drove, Obermeier and Fraulein Graben compared notes on the Hauptman's Opel. Along with the number plate, the car had displayed a few different military markings. On the bonnet, the letters GKS and a numeral - either 508 or 808, depending on which of the two was correct - had been stenciled. On the passenger door, there had been a different combination of letters and numbers they more or less agreed on.

"You do not wish to follow them?" asked Obermeier.

"That would be a little too obvious," I explained. Besides, the numbers were enough. GKS meant the Opel was assigned to the Garde-Kavallerie-Schützendivision. Several of their reserve formations were stationed in Berlin; I had seen their personnel around often enough.

The stencil on the door identified which depot the car was from. That I couldn't assign from memory, but it could certainly be traced.

We were back at the Praesidium before lunch. I couldn't take the others into the interview room, so once I had returned the Horch I sent them off to find coffee or something, telling them to be back at my desk in ninety minutes.

I briefly stopped off at VIIIb, but Teske wasn't in. That wasn't the worst news ever. I would write up a report after I had spoken to Doktor Luster.

Gathering up my notebook, pen, cigarettes and matches, I made my way to the interview room where

Luster had been stashed overnight. He should have been more properly held in the custody area, but I had reasoned that a night in the cells would make him more obdurate, and likely to call his lawyer. This way, he'd be in a slightly more comfortable space, and I had asked the duty officer in Robbery to check in on him. He had seemed fine when I had checked in on him first thing.

This plan had clearly broken down.

The door to the interview room was solid; not half-glassed like most of the departmental doors. It could be locked from either side. When I tried the door, it didn't budge, and I realised it was latched from within. From that second, I dreaded the worst.

And I wasn't disappointed. Doktor Luster had hung himself using his necktie, affixed to the bars on the window. By the time I broke in, which roused just about every detective on the floor (not all that many, given it was a Sunday), he had been dead for a couple of hours. Later, a doctor would estimate he had died around ninety minutes hours before he was found, which put the time of death not long after I spoke with him this morning.

I'd like to tell you that deaths in custody are a rarity, but we all know it happens far too often. It just usually doesn't happen in an interview room, and the victim isn't usually a middle-class professional. No, those types like to blow their brains out at home.

As the afternoon progressed, more and more senior officers turned up to question me as to what had happened. Radel was mostly concerned that this involved Robbery, in a matter that really wasn't any business of Robbery, and that he would be forced to produce paperwork to account for events. Bernard Weiss, who was effectively Deputy Chief of *Kripo*, pending a more permanent appointment, turned up at about one in the afternoon, after the body had been taken down to the morgue. More politician than police, Weiss wasn't interested in hearing excuses from a mere Kommissar. He took in the scene, gave me a cold, flat stare, and went off to do whatever it is that exalted types like him do. My fellow Robbery detectives began keeping a greater distance.

Teske arrived just as Weiss was leaving. They exchanged a few words in the corridor, after which Teske beckoned to me while unlocking the door to his office.

With the door closed behind me, I came to something like attention in front of his desk. I handed him a report on what had transpired, which included the information from the two warrant searches, one completed and the other not. Teske read quickly. I saw he already had a companion report which undoubtedly included testimony from everyone in *kripo* who felt the need to point out that this was all my fault.

"This is a mess, Hoehner, and you don't come out of it shining that brightly. Where are Fraulein Graber and that journalist who has been tailing you around? What is the fellow's name?"

"Obermeier. They were not involved in this incident, Herr Oberkommissar."

He looked up, face slightly reddened, eyes blazing. "Get out of the habit of answering questions you have not been asked, Kommissar Hoehner."

I swallowed hard. "They are in Robbery. Fraulein Graber's notes are appended to my report, as you will have seen." Clearly, Herr Teske's instruction regarding how I answered questions hadn't taken root just yet.

"Don't tell me what I've seen." He closed the folder I had presented to him. "The Deputy Chief is meeting with Luster's lawyer and will speak with the widow. You are to stay well clear, is that understood?"

It was.

"I think this also means your career in Robbery is over. Herr Oberkommissar Radel isn't the kind of police who takes kindly to having to explain the actions of his subordinates to the higher-ups, which is odd, really, since most of you are more corrupt than even the Vice boys. That immediately means you need to make a choice, Kommissar Hoehner. Either you come work for me, or you are finished with Berlin Police."

I swallowed again. I had never been more desperate for a cigarette.

"Take a moment to decide. Have a smoke, Hoehner." He turned a lamp in my direction and pressed a button to reveal a compartment of cigarettes in the base. Teske evidently preferred Roth-Hendle "Red Death" tobacco, but it was a little too strong for my taste. I lit one of my own.

I had taken on a couple of puffs before he asked: 'Well?"

"Herr Oberkommissar, I don't know how I am to make such a decision. I have no idea what it is you even do here." I gestured at the room we occupied. As far as I knew, the entirety of Amt VIIIb was sat right in front of me.

Teske smoked one of his own coffin nails. Even the smell of it made me head reel.

"During the war, the Berlin Police have faced unique challenges. There has been a growing weight of concern around public order. So much anti-patriotism! Then also there have been the problems around shortages. The black market has thrived, with all the criminal activity that comes along with it. Finally, there has been a… loosening of public morals. After so much loss of life, the living have turned to a kind of hedonism that would have been impossible before the war."

This was all true, but I didn't see at all what he was getting at.

"All this at a time when the police themselves are weaker than they have ever been. It's not just the numbers, Hoehner; you know that. It's that those police who remain are... no longer the cream of the crop. Old men; the lame and the sick. The less... adept. Crime has flourished. And much of that crime is... new." He jabbed at the air with the end of his cigarette. "There are dark forces abroad in the city. Strange and unnatural forces. There are those who would corrupt this great city, morally, physically, politically, even spiritually."

"That sounds like work for the *sicherheitspolizei.*"

"And so it is. But they are focussed on rooting out Bolshevists and other traitors. No, they have their beat, and Amt VIIIb has its own. We are concerned more with... other behaviour."

This was also sounding rather vague, and not something I was that interested in. Teske continued: "Take this case you are involved in. What is it? Kidnapping? To what end? It presents endless questions. And now we have a suicide on our hands, someone who was a key witness, at the very least. Somebody well-connected."

He leaned back. "Even before the war, there were only so many resources to deploy against mundane crime. You've worked in Robbery since you joined us, Hoehner, so you know this. It is the same in Vice. Even the Homicide Büro struggles to clear cases. If a matter is likely to take more than a day or two, the Heads of Department would sooner drop it. But some cases merit more time. Some cases lead to some very deep waters indeed." He leaned back. "That is what Amt VIIIb investigates. We peer into the dark corners. I am quite certain that, as the war ends, as it surely must do soon, we will find ourselves busier than ever."

That was the end of his sales pitch, it seemed. He stubbed out his evil-smelling cigarette, leaned forwards on his elbows, and stared at me, his jaw set firm. "Now, you must decide."

"Who else is in the department?"

"Regular police? Only you. And I, of course. What do you think of Irene Graber?"

I hesitated. Surely, he wasn't suggesting...

"She is intelligent, observant... she knows people. But she isn't –"

"I have spoken to Herr Councillor Markwitz. He will not be offended if we make her an offer. I think we can make her a more intriguing proposition than being at the beck and call of a blow-hard like Markwitz. I am of the opinion that, after the war, women will play a much greater role in society. Why not within the police?"

This was... interesting. "I see. And what about Herr Obermeier?"

Teske's moustaches twitched. "I am less favourably inclined to bring him into the department, but he is already involved in this current business, and it will be easier to control him if he is on the inside, don't you agree?"

That was undoubtedly true.

"That much is settled, then. I must insist, Herr Kommissar, that you decide. You have your teeth in this business already, I think. Will you see it through?"

"It doesn't feel like I have any choice." I straightened my back and came to attention. "Is the pay any better, Herr Oberkommissar?"

"Worse, probably, but those kinds of details can wait. I think I know what your answer is. You will need to create a more... carefully worded report on the death of Doktor Luster. I shall provide you with some instructions you should follow carefully. After that, well, since you have lost one of your prime routes to this Kammerich, what will be your next move?"

What indeed?

Searching For Kammerich: The Astrakhan

I lost the rest of the afternoon dealing with the repercussions of the Luster suicide. There was this second, abridged report Teske insisted I write. Mostly, it left out any mention of the meeting with the Colonel at *Annabel's*, or the intervention by Captain von Beckman. I spoke at length with a homicide detective, Gelb, who was preparing the Berlin Police's official account, which would then draw in Luster's lawyer, the Ministry of the Interior, the press (Obermeier excluded) and the coroner.

Teske said he would have to discuss this whole matter with the Deputy Chief of *Kripo*, Bernard Weiss. This would take place on Monday morning. Teske wondered if I owned a better suit.

By the time all this was done, it was early evening. The rain had ceased, but outside the Alex the streets were still damp and the gutters flowing. Fraulein Graber, Obermeier and I repaired to Ascher's for dinner. On a Sunday, there was no problem getting a table, but Fraulein Graber worked her charms on the *maitre d'* anyway so that we had a booth where we could talk more privately.

"So, we are all to be on the same payroll!" Obermeier said brightly as we perused the menu. It was evident he was about to spend his first stipend on one night. "A government retainer. What have I become?"

"You have also reached an agreement with Herr Oberkommissar Teske, Fraulein Graber?"

She leaned back in her seat and waved the cigarette she wasn't smoking. "I think, Herr Kommissar, that now we are colleagues you should call me Irene, at least when it is just among the three of us."

"Perhaps."

"And what should I call you?"

"Herr Kommissar is fine." She laughed.

Unpatriotically, Obermeier wanted to order champagne. "To Amt VIIIb!" he toasted exuberantly, without even waiting for a waiter to arrive.

"No drinking on duty," I insisted, a protocol the Berlin Police has never followed. "We still have work to do."

Thus, after a meal of gristly sausage and sauerkraut, and some desultory conversation about our plans, we set off back across the city, first to see if Katz would turn up at TrippelA, and then to follow our only other remaining lead. Compared to our previous visit, the bar was almost empty on a Sunday, largely stripped of its normal clientele of doctors, orderlies and nurses. Apparently, no-one needed a drink after a Sunday shift. I could understand that; I didn't like being at work either.

We gave up there around nine o'clock. But instead of rolling away in our different directions, we stopped off in the Nollendorfplatz district, just south of the Tiergarten. This wasn't a particularly cultured part of town, but it came to life at night as a destination for citizens from the more affluent parts of the city. All along the main thoroughfares, there were theatres and nightclubs, garishly decorated to entice passers-by. We parked the Horch near the corner of Motzstrasse and Eisernacher Strasse, sitting in the car for a few minutes to assess the lie of the land.

"The Astrakhan!" exclaimed Obermeier, twisting in his seat. "This is where that dancer, if we must call her that, works. Trude Holstadt. But surely she will not be working on a Sunday? Such Godless heathens we have become."

"Did you attend church this morning, Herr Obermeier?" Fraulein Graber asked.

"I am what you might call an infrequent worshipper," Obermeier replied. "It is not that I do not believe, but more that I find it hard to see God at work in Berlin."

"This is not the time for that," I instructed. "Let us go and see who is visiting this particular communion."

The Astrakhan's name stood out in blue light from the building frontage, illuminating our path to the door. It boasted a large, well-lit main entrance, flanked by hard-looking men and a grinning doorman in red livery. Ignoring the two spanners, we looked to head inside. The door was opened, and we entered a foyer, where we checked our coats and hats. A stream of people entered around us, some laughing gaily, others looking worn-down by their responsibilities. Finally, we entered the belly of the club proper. This featured a 'ballroom' with a long bar and a stage, and a small restaurant. There were more rooms upstairs. I noted a side door, that I believed would open out onto Eisernache Strasse. There was probably a stage entrance too.

We had arrived at the Astrakhan before things truly got going that evening. We bought drinks and lounged at the bar, taking in the scene. The club's orchestra, working in a shallow pit in front of the stage, favoured bright dance numbers, but it was too early for the majority of the club's patrons to feel like dancing. At about half past nine, an elegant woman in a long sheath of a dress came onto the stage and sang a boisterous song about all the things she would do when her lover returned from the Front. It was an extensive list.

It was then that a curtain was drawn from a raised area at the back of the stage, revealing a relay of topless dancing girls striking poses against a brightly lit background. At about the same time, more topless women (incongruously wearing shiny top hats) began to move through the crowd dispensing watered-down sparkling wine, taking orders for actual liquor and selling cigarettes at inflated prices.

"What's this?" spluttered Obermeier. "When did this kind of thing become allowed?"

"It isn't," I responded, though I knew that the authorities had been turning a blind eye to such establishments for the last several weeks and months.

"Then where are the vice police?"

I pointed across the room. "That's two of them there, Pozen and... I forget the other one. So long as the girls stay this clothed, these things are permitted until midnight. It's believed that it keeps the soldiers away from worse vices."

"What happens at midnight?"

"The vice boys disappear upstairs, and the dancing girls perform a costume change – on stage."

Pre-war, Berlin had been a lively capital, but broadly a law-abiding and discrete one, at least when it came to its night life. Then, for the first few years of the war, it had taken on a more sombre tone, especially once it became clear how many young men would not be coming home. But since the tide of war had turned finally against Germany, as the state became less preoccupied with policing people's morals, and more concerned with saving its own skin, things like censorship laws had started to slip. Those who remained in Berlin could feel the coming storm and were determined to live life to the full before it fell upon them.

Fraulein Graber spotted Holstadt working the stage platform from around ten o'clock. In her heavy stage make-up and in what little she had that amounted to a costume, she was a different figure from that we had encountered in Wedding. It hadn't been easy to pick her out, because the dancing girls all wore wigs of black hair, short as was the coming fashion. Even the female clientele all had a certain look to them, parading their finest cocktail dresses, some showing their age. They drank, they smoked, they flirted with the men they'd come with, and often with those they had just met.

At intervals, the dancers moved about the room during short breaks, laughing with customers and accepting gifts from regular patrons. Assignations were arranged for later.

It was hard to keep track of Holstadt, but we were reasonably certain Kammerich did not make an appearance that night. The hours passed.

At around a quarter past one, on what was now Monday morning, there was an incident just in front of us. A group of four U-boat officers, wearing fresh medals, were seated at a table near the stage, all roaring drunk and having a grand time. This had been a frequent occurrence in Berlin in years past, but just lately success had been hard to find. Nearby, I spotted a larger group of eight soldiers from a Berlin garrison regiment, and I could sense tension brewing. The two groups exchange a few barbs, but it was nothing too spiteful or worthy of attention – it was just a feeling I got.

A dancer stopped at the naval officers' table, laughing and drinking with them. She shared a passionate, slightly comical kiss with the youngest of the naval men. It took me a moment, and several moments longer than Fraulein Graber, to realise this was Holstadt. Immediately, four tough-looking men in military uniforms that bore no insignia, beyond a black, white and red armband, stepped forward from the side of the room. One of them took hold of Holstadt's arm, and insisted she leave with them. He called her by name.

I've been police long enough to judge a situation that can only go downhill. The young U-boat officer jumped to his feet, directly in the goon's face. One of *his* companions pushed the young lad back. Another of the navy men took up a bottle and threatened the pair of them with it.

A push and pull kind of dance followed, and I eased myself away from the bar, just a little, to ensure I had room for manoeuvre. One of the toughs called out, and four more of their brethren appeared from the shadows. A table went over; glass shattered; a woman screamed. The first punches were thrown.

I let a few bystanders from the immediate vicinity get out of the way, then stepped forward. I hadn't worked out how I was going to intervene: I've never seen it go well when a single officer pulls out his beer token and yells 'Police!' in these situations. Another bevy of hard-looking men was coming into the fray – the Astrakhan's bouncers. The spanners' first concern was to let the numbers thin down a little first, but then they moved to break up the affray before it did any more damage. I did notice that their methodology for this was to attack the sailors, and to stay clear of anyone wielding chair legs or any other improvised weapon.

One of the armband-wearers was slipping around the edge of the fight. I saw something glint in his hand. That was a step too far for my taste, and I took an ice bucket from the bar and dinged him over the back of the head with it. The sound was extremely satisfactory, and he went down to the floor, surrounded by ice shards.

The sailors were still badly outnumbered. Their *kapitän* was holding three of the assailants at bay, and still being harassed by one of the bouncers. I really wanted to get around to the far side of the fight, where Trude was at the centre of the tug-of-war. As I started my circumnavigation of the struggle, the garrison soldiers from the nearby table joined in, partly out of respect for the U-boat men, partly because they sided with the out-numbered under-dog, and mostly because the spanners had pushed them out of the way as if they had caused the trouble.

The tide turned abruptly. Notably, the Astrakhan's men changed their tune, and began dragging the toughs out of the pile, and pushing them towards the exits. As soon as one fled, they were all of a mind to do the same, except for the gentleman I had served with the ice. I decided I needed a more conscious volunteer to speak to, and so tripped one of the thugs who was already stumbling and sliding on all the liquid spilled on the floor. *Now* I was prepared to announce myself as a police officer.

Everything de-escalated in a hurry. I pinned my new captive to the ground with one knee, while keeping my head up to make sure nothing caught me unawares. The sailors were all breathing hard, looking a little battered and torn. The garrison troops were congratulating themselves on a timely intervention and looking for something to drink. I caught sight of Trude Holstadt, who seemed to be fine, if a little wide-eyed.

I got one of the bouncers to sit on my prisoner, informing him that "If he gets away, you take his place in the cells." I went over to Trude, nodding to the sailors, treading on ice, broken glass and someone's teeth. It took her a moment to lock onto my face, as if her ability to remember anything from a couple of days before was gravely inhibited. Her eyes were greatly dilated; I suspected that she had enjoyed more than just a glass of champagne or two.

"Are you all right, Trude?"

She nodded, a little too vigorously. I waved Fraulein Graber over.

"Trude? I want you to go with Fraulein Graber here. We're going to want to talk to you about what happened here. I have to sort out these fellows, but I will come and speak with you as soon as I can." More nodding. I turned to Fraulien Graber. "Get her things, and take her to the Alex. Take Obermeier with you." Better that than nothing.

The fracas took far longer to disentangle than it ever had to break out. I made sure the Uboat men were generally unharmed and told some management suit from the Astrakhan to provide the lads from the local garrison with free beer. Some *schupos* arrived eventually, which allowed me to arrange for the transport of my two prisoners. I recovered the knife, at which point I found that I had split a knuckle throwing a punch I didn't remember throwing. I put some ice on it. There was plenty lying around.

I have no idea what time I got back to the Alex. The sky was still dark, save for a bright moon that flickered on and off behind fast-running clouds. The prisoners were handed over to the custody sergeant, who was quite disgruntled when I told him I wanted them kept separately, so that they couldn't get their stories straight. Even on a Sunday night, the cells were full of drunks and brawlers. Still, most importantly from my point of view, these two were not my responsibility for now.

I prepared a report for Oberkommissar Teske. Trude was asleep on a bench in the office (I was still working out of the Robbery Büro for now), wrapped in her threadbare overcoat. Obermeier was nodding off too, but Fraulein Graber remained quite alert.

I took her aside. "I'd like you to question Fraulein Holstadt. Let her sleep for an hour or two, but then wake her gently, and question her quickly. Find out if she knows the men that tried to abduct her. Ask her why she thinks they did so – I mean, we know it's Kammerich, but I want her to realise that herself. Then, before she gets her defences up, ask about Kammerich."

Fraulein Graber nodded and took herself off to sit at the end of the bench with her feet up on the seat, a cigarette between her lips and her notebook in hand. I watched her for a moment, then shook myself and went back to work.

Sometime around dawn, I went down to the cells to retrieve my prisoners. I had them taken to the interview room where Luster had killed himself. This place held disturbing and distressing memories for me, but I hoped to be able to use it to my advantage with these two.

I had no such luck with the first, the one I had tripped. He clamped his jaw closed and said nothing, even when I was reading an evident fact garnered from his identity papers. These had informed me that both men were from the 214th Division, and that they had permits to be in Berlin signed by that unit's commanding officer, Generalmajor Georg Maercker. Both were carrying modest amounts of money, much of it in newly-pressed banknotes.

The knife-wielder was just a little more unguarded and boastful, which fit the persona of the kind of hero who tries to get behind someone with a knife. He twitched a little when I mentioned Doktor Luster, clearly making the connection in his own mind that this was where that citizen had died.

"So many people looking for Kammerich, but who won't say why. And then it's too late."

"Never heard of him."

"One of you said that's who you were looking for." This was a silly bluff, in retrospect.

"That's a lie."

"OK. Then why were you trying to abduct the dancer?"

"Who says we were? Maybe we just wanted a dance."

"With that particular girl?"

"Sure. She's a looker."

"If you say so; I can't tell one from the other. Your friend called her by name."

"Did he?"

I could see that this knife-wielding bully was gasping for a smoke. He'd had nails in a little case on him when he was searched. Here in the interview room, I had lain my tin on the table between us at the start of the interview. Now I took it up, extracted a nail, and lit up. I didn't offer him one, but I did puff a generous amount of smoke his way.

"I need a doctor," he said, gingerly feeling at the back of his head.

"For that? Don't be such a child. That's the kind of wound you'd shake off in an hour at the front."

"What do you know about what it's like at the front?"

I didn't justify myself. "Why do you want to find Kammerich?"

He scratched the tabletop with a fingernail. "Like I said, who said we are?"

"No, you said you never heard of him. But you were after his girl-friend last night. Who sent you?"

"You don't know anything," he snarled. "If you did, you'd look the other way."

"What does that mean?" He didn't answer. I smoked for a moment, then pointed at the red-white-black armband on his sleeve. "What does that signify?"

He looked down, as if he'd forgotten it was there. "The imperial colours. Nothing wrong there, surely, unless you're a Bolshevist yourself, *bulle*."

"There's a picture of the Kaiser in the Robbery Büro," I retorted. "Doesn't mean I carry one around in my wallet. Does Generalmajor Maercker approve of his men embellishing their uniforms this way?"

No answer.

"Who sent you to look for Kammerich?"

No answer. He should have been that way from the beginning.

When I returned to Robbery after these largely fruitless interviews, the sun was up, someone had magically procured hot, sweet coffee, and Holstadt was gone,

"She is going to stay with a friend," Fraulein Graber explained. "I... we had no grounds to hold her, did we?"

"No. Did she say anything about Kammerich?"

"No. But, she's frightened."

"That's why you shouldn't have let her go. Where's Obermeier?"

"He's following her." I laughed. Fraulein Graber was spot on sometimes. "I have this for you as well," she added, handing me a note. It was the 'translation', if you will, of the information on the Opel Hauptman von Beckman and Alderstadt had been driven away in after we met at the Luster residence.

"The designation on the bonnet was for the Garde-Kavallerie-Schützendivision, as you suspected, Herr Kommissar. The depot number, though, is for the Hauptkadettenanstalt, out in Lichterfelde."

"Really? The officer training school? I know the place. It's on Altdorferstrasse."

"Yes. Why is the military academy involved with Doktor Luster?"

"Don't get ahead of yourself. Just because the vehicle is assigned to the academy, doesn't mean that the *hauptmann* was acting on its behalf. I'd really like to know if that other officer works there, the one who Luster met at the café."

"Can we ask them if they have an interest in all this business?"

"Hardly. The ground may not look quite so solid beneath the army's feet right now, but they do not answer to the likes of us. This is useful, though."

The final act of the night – or the first of the news day – was being called to hand my report to Oberkommissar Teske. I stood in silence as he read it through, tutting at a couple of points where I was concerned my spelling or my typing would be at fault. At one point I yawned, and he looked up at me, his countenance severe, as if yawning in the presence of a superior officer was top of his list of offences against the criminal code. I tried to breathe deeply, but silently, and to stare straight ahead in the approved fashion. "This investigation is treading on some dangerous ground," he summarised when he was done.

"Yes, sir."

"Generalmajor Maercker is a decorated war hero, venerated by the High Command."

"Yes, sir."

"You had better be entirely sure of the facts before you get anywhere near him."

"*Jawohl*, Herr Oberkommissar. As far as I know, the General is with his command at the Front. I have no cause to think he has anything to do with these matters that concern us. These men had fresh money in their pockets. Anyone might have provided that."

"Exactly. Tread carefully, Herr Kommissar. Now, where next with Kammerich?"

I reminded him that we had just one lead to follow.

He scowled and made a point of looking me directly in the eyes.

"Go home. Get a bath and a change of clothing. You could do with a haircut and a shave too. Then come back here ready to find this Kammerich and put an end to this case, Kommissar Hoehner. There are plenty more ships just over the horizon. We cannot spend the rest of our lives chasing after this one."

MONDAY, 4TH NOVEMBER 1918

I stepped out into the light of Monday morning, a day so bright it hurt my eyes. The streets around the Praesidium were crowded with people starting another working week, shuffling along in their worn shoes, in their patched clothes, in their despair and hunger, trying to last one more day through this abhorrent war.

A bath and a change of clothes – perhaps those were beyond me. But the great thing about Alexanderplatz is that it is surrounded by all kinds of establishments offering personal services. Not all of these could offer a wet shave and a haircut, but I knew a couple of places that did.

I like Oliver's. It is a one seat operation run by Oliver himself, who was a profoundly deaf man, which ruled out the kind of inane conversation normally associated with barbers. He was busy when I arrived, but there was a café across the street where I could read the morning papers and keep watch for my opportunity. I could have gone back to the apartment, but it would be Johan's turn for the bed, so there was no rest to be had there.

According to *Voßische Zeitung*, the Kaiser had left Berlin almost a week ago, and was at the front – well, at Spa, at least – with the High Command. I didn't understand what he thought he was doing there when there were clearly important political and diplomatic matters to be dealt with here in Berlin. Perhaps that was *why* he had absented himself.

The *Zeitung* and others were also preoccupied with rumoured message flying backwards and forwards between Berlin and Washington, through whatever intermediaries there might be, and the search for an honourable peace based on President's Wilson's frequently quoted 'Fourteen Points'. Wiser minds than mine pronounced that this would lead to a peace in which Germany might have to relinquish some or even all of the ground captured in the West, but which would leave the Empire with the enormous gains achieved at the expense of the Russians last year. Germany could draw breath, rearm, and then take the fight to the Bolshevists whenever she was ready.

I scratched at my stubble and waited for Oliver to finish with the earlier customer. My coffee was tasteless and gritty. I smoked and day-dreamed, almost missing the moment when Oliver became free.

Moments later, swathed in hot towels and watching Oliver strop his razor while mouthing the query "The usual?", I let my mind wander around this frustrating case. Kammerich was the key, of course. But once that lock was opened, what were we going to find? Why were thirty-four soldiers lost in the city? What possible thread wove this all together?

A half hour later I was still thinking the same thoughts, but now over a late breakfast.

At some point just after consuming the meanest portion of scrambled eggs I have ever been served, my mind returned to the officer Doktor Luster had spoken with at *Annabet*'s. Though I had somewhere dismissed the idea when talking to Fraulein Graber, I wondered if the *Oberst* was acting separately or independently of Hauptman von Beckman. But where did the Academy, of all places, fit in?

I ordered another coffee, smoked another cigarette, and let my mind wander. The *Hauptkadettenanstalt* went back to the very beginnings of the Empire. The old Kaiser, the current Emperor's grandfather, had founded the academy, which had been birthing cadres of aristocratic officers ever since. It was not the only officer training school in the Empire, but it was the most prestigious; all the big names had passed through its doors. I could not imagine it being involved in some unfathomable scheme, but there was some connection, no matter how small.

I didn't know anyone I could ask about von Beckman or the mysterious Oberst 'vO'. I couldn't just roll up there and demand answers, could I?

On the other hand, what else was I going to do? Much though I needed to sleep, my bed wouldn't come free until Johan tumbled out of it sometime in the afternoon. I hardly felt like sitting around in Robbery looking useless.

Eventually, I yielded my seat and went back outside, turning up my collar against the wind. As I crossed Alexanderplatz, I kept returning to the fundamental problem at the root of the investigation – what had happened to those soldiers from the train? Why had someone apparently gone to such lengths to arrange their transfer to Berlin on that specific train, on Wagon Eight, and then removed them from the train in such a seemingly impossible manner, like a stage magician might disappear his assistant? What purpose lay behind it all.

Of course, there was one factor in all this that I hadn't looked into at all. And to do that I would need to go out to Charité one more time.

The Handsome Doktor Mueller

I knew my way to the Neurology Department by now. It was at the back of the hospital, a particularly austere and cold area. This was where Doktor Luster's office was, of course, though I was not interested in that right now. Instead, I asked the duty staff where I might find Herr Doktor Mueller.

I suppose I might have surmised that he would have an office of his own, not all that far from Luster's. And, to my good fortune, he was in residence, with an unfortunate (from his perspective) window between patient sessions. I knocked on his door and let myself in.

"Herr Kommissar. I'm sorry, I forget the name..."

"Hoehner, Herr Doktor."

"Do we have an appointment, Kommissar Hoehner?"

"No. I appreciate this may be an imposition, but I wondered if I could steal some of your time."

He checked his desk clock ostentatiously. "Perhaps five minutes," he said, gracelessly.

"*Danke*. I'll come straight to the point. Could you explain the nature of psychiatric trauma to me, as it relates to soldiers at the Front?"

His eyes opened unnaturally widely, and he barked out a kind of laugh. "In five minutes? Herr Kommissar, even with what little we know, it would take much more than that to scratch the surface." He leaned back, gestured for me to take a seat, then picked up a paper knife which he toyed with as we spoke. "You are interested in what we call *Kriegneurosen* or *Krieghysterie*, yes?"

"Correct."

"You served in the Army at some point, I take it."

"I was at Verdun."

"Ah, well. I am sure you saw many cases. It was a mistake to leave men in that theatre for so long at a time... but I speak only medically, of course. So, what can I tell you that you have not seen for yourself?"

"Are there degrees of this malady, Herr Doktor?"

"Indeed. Some men are afflicted by insomnia, others by dreams, others yet by a sense of constant anxiety, perhaps. For the worst cases, the patient, enters a state of what you might call physical catatonia. What is that phrase you soldiers use?"

"The thousand metre stare?"

"That, yes. Others are subject to physical convulsions." We had words for that too. We called them *schüttler*.

"What is the treatment?"

He sighed deeply. "In many cases there is no treatment, only time, and who knows if some patients will ever recover their wits. But there has been some success with psychiatry, or with some extreme treatments. Electrotherapy is favoured by many."

That thought made me swallow hard. "These men, they do not return to health quickly? There is no drug...?"

"Ah, no, Herr Kommissar. I see what you are getting at. There is no miracle cure, not one that I have heard of. The patients who are referred to us here, and to the other hospitals, they will need years of treatment. I am afraid we have many patients on file whose malady dates back as far as 1914."

I looked behind him to the bookshelves that graced his office. His presented a much smaller library than Doktor Luster and – publicly at least – stayed well away from any political or race theories. He caught me staring and smiled thinly.

"I could suggest some reading materials for you, if that would help…?"

That seemed unlikely. "You do use drugs though, am I correct? Sedatives?"

He checked the clock again. "Yes. In the beginning, it is possible to reduce the symptoms of *krieghysterie* with things like ether. It is vital to keep the patient in a state of calm. Some suggest that morphine can calm the brain, but there are risks attached with all such treatments. It is best not to expect too much from drugs."

He stood up before I could think to ask any more questions. "I am sorry, Herr Kommissar. I have a patient to see at half past ten. A strict routine is essential, you understand. If you wish to discuss this further, please, make an appointment and I will do all I can to help."

"*Danke*, Herr Doktor. One last question before I leave… can nothing be done about patients who have… dreams, or night terrors, associated with the war?"

"That is a very specific symptom." He was ushering me to the door, but I could sense he had seen through my question.

"But common enough?"

We stood in the doorway. "Make an appointment, Herr Kommissar. These things cannot be solved in a five-minute conversation."

No, indeed. I thanked him again, and we parted company. He headed towards one of the wards, and I wandered back along the corridor. I paused outside Doktor Luster's office, then tried the handle. It was locked, of course, but then I still had the key. But what did I hope to find?

I was reminded that we had removed three items from the desk in there that I had yet to do much with; they were all back at the Alex. I checked my wristwatch, and decided this was as good a time as any to peruse those. But before I stepped away, I remembered how Luster had been an anaesthesiologist before he had moved into psychiatric medicine, and all those books on psychotropics on his shelves. Had Luster's interest in these subjects combined somehow? I felt like I needed a doctor to explain all this to me, but first, I felt, I needed a batter understanding myself.

I took the key from my pocket and opened the door. The room was completely empty.

Reading Matter

Returning to the Alex, I retrieved the three items we had taken from Luster's office from a drawer in my desk, but chose not to read them in Robbery. Instead, I went back out onto Alexanderplatz and found myself in the same spot in the same café I had been seated in earlier. The coffee was just the same too, alas. Sometimes, it feels like it would be easier and quicker to just chew hazelnuts instead.

Very well. What did we have?

First, of course, there was the diary. I spent an hour going through this carefully, trying to trace the steps of a man who now lay cold in the morgue. Much of it was self-evident (appointments with patients; meetings with fellow staff); a lot more was opaque (who was 'L', that he should have been meeting them every Thursday evening for around six months, before ending the assignations in September?). I observed how 'KK' had been a feature of his routine for around ten weeks, and 'vO' about the same.

Regular meetings in public spaces.

When I was done with that, and having realised that it didn't directly point in any direction we were not following, I laid the diary down and took up the Hammer-Verlag medical treatise. It was called *The Pathology of Madness*, and the title page informed me that it was a translation of a Greek work, which itself drew on even older knowledge. The translator was a Doktor Pfalz, supposedly of Salzburg, and the volume had first been published in 1887.

I could follow up on all that if need be, but I pictured some bewhiskered Austrian who had been in his dotage even then, and who was probably in his grave by now. One thing I could surmise about Pfalz from the very start was that German might not have been his first language – the translation was woeful. Or maybe it was just the subject material.

The text, as I have mentioned before, had been heavily annotated in Doktor Luster's rather cramped hand. Page after page would be free of any scribbled note in the margin, and then the next five or ten would be covered in scrawl. Not all of it was legible, and of that, only a proportion made much sense, but I scowled down at page after page trying to see what had fascinated the ancients, some Greek with time on his hands, then Pfalz and finally Luster. The answer was that they were all interested in the effect of certain chemicals on the brain. There was a lengthy chapter on hallucinogens. This wasn't entirely beyond my field of knowledge; there were plenty of people in Berlin consuming opium and morphine, and it was commonplace among soldiers to discuss the effects of battlefield morphine. Being old, the book mostly described the effects of using certain plants or fungi.

Luster's notes became more congested around chapters dealing with drugs which might be combined with, say, hypnotism to control behaviour. In some places, where the notes were a little faded, and by implication older, his interest was in using hallucinogens to take a patient out of the trauma in which they lived, so that healing of the mind might take place. In others, he showed what amounted to an obsession with drugs that made the patient more suggestible, so that through psychiatry or hypnosis or other treatment, they might be separated from the trauma that led to their mental condition.

I didn't read too much into any of this; the chemistry was beyond me, and I am a sceptic when it comes to things like hypnosis. If that art was genuine, we police would have been all over it by now. I day-dreamed for a moment about how efficacious it would be, if only it were real.

It was evident, though, that for Luster this was all scientifically proven, and had great potential. And not just as a cure for *krieghysterie* or other trauma. At one point, Luster's notes seemed to be extolling the routine use of certain drugs to bolster the morale of soldiers on the front line. It was a step up from giving the men a shot of schnapps.

I set the book down and smoked for a while. As I watched the smoke climb to the ceiling, drifting and curling, I considered my own condition, and how I almost seemed to rely on cigarettes to keep calm during the working day. And there was the liquor, of course. Were we all adherents to Luster's ideas already, self-medicating?

Finally, I took up the battered copy of *The Drama of the Yellow King*. I don't know what impulse had made me remove this from Luster's office, but it came from the same source as the diary and *The Pathology of Madness*, hidden away in the desk drawer. Would this provide another insight into his thinking?

The volume was physically curious. The cover was a deep red, cut from some kind of hide, but not leather, if I am any judge. The pages were flimsy, as if they might tear at any moment, and several were loose, having come away from the binding. The pages were not numbered, so I couldn't tell if any were missing, but I felt sure some must be. I leafed through it quickly and noted that it contained none of Luster's spiky hand. As to the contents, as I had surmised on first view, it was a commentary, in German, on a play called *The King In Yellow*. There was no mention of an author, nor where or when this play had been written. The name of the commentary's author, too, was missing.

The text made little sense. The commentary

suggested that the original play was about identity, and that the mysterious King, ruler of a realm I had never heard of, was masked throughout, or at least until near the end. The more I read, the more I became convinced that playwright and critic both had probably ingested a few of the wrong sort of mushrooms before setting word to page. It was all very earnest, but meant nothing to me.

I placed all three titles back in the briefcase in which I had brought them, paid my bill and set out into the streets again. The hour had progressed, and there were deep shadows across Alexanderplatz. As I headed back to the Praesidium, I was immediately passed by another of those flat-bed trucks, crowded with men, only these were not the helmeted and part-uniformed bully-boys I had seen on other days, but working men in rough jackets, wearing red armbands and displaying vast red flags emblazoned with the hammer and sickle, symbols the Reds were borrowing with increasing enthusiasm from their kin in Russia. Banners called for 'Bread and Peace'.

A second truck contained a smaller number of comrades, employed in tossing small bundles of newspapers onto the pavement, imperiling citizens who stopped to gawk. These were late editions of socialist papers, with the headlines that Austro-Hungary was out of the war.

I picked one up and started to read. A fellow came to my shoulder and scanned the first paragraph. "Hardly a surprise," he commented.

It might not have been unexpected, but the news had shock value. Austria-Hungary, whose *casus belli* had dragged us all into this fight, had capitulated.

I skimmed through the details. The armistice had been agreed at somewhere called the Villa Giulisti. By the terms of the agreed treaty, Austria – because, let's be accurate, Hungary was a separate entity these days – was to disband most of its army, and allow the Allies to use its railways and roads to move their troops freely, which opened up Bavaria and the whole of the south to invasion. There were other provisions, but this was what mattered. A whole new southern front had opened up overnight.

This surely was the end.

I put the newspaper under my arm and walked back into the Praesidium. Both Fraulein Graber and Herr Obermeier were at my desk, looking pensive. The duty shift was all gathered at Pressberg's desk, reading another copy of the newspaper I carried. I put the briefcase and paper down, along with my hat and gloves.

"What is to be done?" asked Obermeier.

"For us, nothing changes. We still need to find these men." I did concede that we were perhaps under a greater deadline than ever.

"We'll go to the Trippel-A. I'm prepared to question everyone there – someone must know where Katz lives." I counted my proposed progress on my fingers. "Katz, Kammerich, and then the soldiers. We cannot let this slip through our fingers any longer."

I checked the time: it was half past five. "We'll get something to eat, and then get over there."

There was one obstacle to that: Fraulein Graber informed me that Markwitz was in with Oberkommissar Teske, and that I was to attend on them immediately.

I didn't have a written report to deliver, but decided to go directly to the nerve-centre of Amt VIIIb. I bore my copy of the newspaper with me, in case this news had not filtered through to the Oberkommissar in his den. I knocked once, and was called in. I could tell just from that that Oberkommissar Teske was in a poor mood.

He listened impatiently to my verbal report. He

wasn't impressed. Neither was Councillor Markwitz, who offered theatrical sighs and grumbles to everything I said.

"Is that all?"

"I am confident we will soon have Herr Doktor Kammerich in custody."

Markwitz then began a tedious oration as if he was in the chambers of the City Council. He had just come from giving the KPuGH – the Royal Prussian and Grand-ducal Hessian State Railway – an earful over losing a wagon load of wounded soldiers. He had also visited the offices of the military economy department's invalids division at the Prussian War Ministry. The officials at both locations endured (briefly) their unwarranted scolding, but had urged him to speak with the police, since they had no ready answers. And so here he was, getting more of the same.

"So, you still have not found Frau Plommer's son!" Markwitz exclaimed with a flourish. This could not be denied. "Unbelievable! I warn you, by tomorrow this incompetence will be in every newspaper across the city!"

This, in the circumstances, I doubted.

Oberkommissar Teske insisted that Markwitz sit down and calm down, though the Councillor only managed the former.

"Placing unsubstantiated stories in the press at this time would be dangerous, as well as counter-productive. It can only stir up an already anxious city, and perhaps alert this Kammerich to our interest in him."

Markwitz suggested someone surely had spoken to *Vorwarts* and that the story was bound to come out. "It is not I who am responsible for this state of affairs! Now, I shall not hesitate to speak with the Military Governor!"

"General von Linsingen will not wish to interfere with police matters!"

"We shall see about that!" With that, Markwitz took

up his hate and coat, and stormed from the room. This did not improve my situation.

"We have received a letter, delivered by courier, from Frau Luster." Oberkommissar Teske was on the edge of fury. He indicated an envelope on his desk, so white it dazzled in the light from his lamp. "It was sent to the Deputy Chief, and he has passed it to me. She demands to know why her husband was arrested, and to receive a full account of his death. I take it we are in a poor position to deliver either."

I chose not to comment. It's often the best way of dealing with us police types.

Teske grumbled under his breath, then took up a separate piece of paper, a rather more mundane sheet of Berlin Police notepaper. "I have also had a telephone conversation with an aide to General von Linsingen. The General wished to enquire why certain members of the Berlin Police are interrogating senior German officers."

"Herr Oberkommissar, no such interrogation has taken place." I briskly detailed the conversation I had had with Hauptman Ludwig Weiss von Beckman and Alderstadt outside the Luster residence.

"Has there been any further contact with the military?"

I chose not to mention the link we had established to the Garde-KavallerieSchützendivision and the Hauptkadettenanstalt.

"Herr Oberkommissar, who was this aide to General von Linsingen?"

Teske's eyes narrowed. He glanced down at his notes. "A Colonel von Osterbruck. Is that relevant to anything?"

vO.

"I'm not in a position to say, Herr Oberkommissar. I

was just curious."

He grumbled again. He took up a pen, uncapped it, and wrote a note in a smooth hand on the bottom of the memorandum about his call with von Osterbruck. His desk clock ticked loudly. Only when his notation was complete did he next look up.

"Why is this investigation taking so long?"

I started to reply, but I had no excuse, none would be acceptable in any case. Instead, I reiterated that I was confident we would soon have our hands on Kammerich.

"You do not have any more time, Herr Kommissar." He gestured at my newspaper. "You have kept abreast with the news? If the unrest in Kiel spreads here to Berlin, we'll have our hands full. As it stands, I have two other matters I need you to attend to." He tapped matching folders in his In Tray, both fastened with pink ribbon. "Grave matters."

"More serious than thirty-four missing men?"

Teske's face went red. His big fists balled up, and he struck the desk hard.

"Do not lecture me about these men, Kommissar Hoehner. You are the one who has failed to find them. You say Kammerich is the key. Where is he? How is he able to masquerade as a working doctor so that others follow his instructions? He has a 'mouse' in Wedding, you say? Where there is one whore, there will be others. They'll all turn to him when they catch a dose. Have you even looked in such directions?"

I could not say that I had. Not successfully in any case. I doubted that the brawl in the Astrakhan would satisfy Teske's demands for progress.

"One more night, Herr Kommissar. When you come to work tomorrow, this had best be over." He tapped the uppermost of the two files in his In Tray. "You are to report to Homicide in the morning. They have a case which concerns them, a dead woman found in Tiergarten. I am confident that it fits our brief. *That* will be your primary concern tomorrow."

Which didn't turn out to be the case, but we'll come to that another time.

The Trippel-A Bar (Again)

By eight o'clock we were once again ensconced in the Trippel-A. Monday night was clearly one of those nights where the Trippel-A did good business, but then we all have Mondays where the only salvation is a strong drink. I could vouch for that.

Obermeier and Fraulein Graber went off to quiz the clientele. I approached the owner, a fellow by the name of Henz, who had a crippled left hand, bad teeth and an impatient manner. The only way to get anything out of him at all was to overpay for bad beer.

"Katz hasn't been in yet."

"Do you know a doctor by the name of Kammerich? He and yKatz have done a little business together, I think."

"I don't know a tenth of the names. You want a doctor? Wave a stick; you'll hit ten all at once."

I had not yet announced that I was police; I doubted it would help. Having quaffed that first beer, I next spoke with the pretty barmaid, who I learned was called Gerta. She smiled winningly as she poured me a 'fresh' glass.

"Do you know Katz?"

She laughed and tossed her cloud of blond hair. "Everyone knows Katz!" she insisted.

Her advice was to hang around, since he often came in just after eight on a weekday.

As she said this, I was jostled by a dark-haired fellow with a squint, who gave me the evil eye, set down his glass and made for the door. Ordinarily, I wouldn't have thought this worth much attention, but I kept my eye on him, and saw him approach another fellow in the street. At the same moment, Gerta chimed: "There he is!" and pointed out of the window.

The newcomer took off. He rounded the corner onto Invalidenstrasse and vanished.

"Obermeier!" I called and raced for the door. As I started to cross the street, squint tried to get in my way, but I pushed him aside and pounded down the street after my quarry.

He had a good start, but two things were going my way. First, he must have slipped as he rounded the corner, because by the time I hit Invalidenstrasse he wasn't that far ahead. Also, this isn't a part of the city with lots of handy alleys or hiding places. Now that he was in sight, he was going to stay there.

From the brief glimpse I had had through the window, Katz was a short, rangy-looking fellow, with black hair under an ill-fitting cap, a rough jacket and grubby trousers. He wore a moustache that wouldn't have suited anyone. At a guess, I would have said he was twenty-five years old, and I did wonder for a second why such a man wouldn't be serving as a stretcher-bearer with the army. Hospital orderly was no kind of reserved occupation.

Barely fifty or sixty meters up Invalidenstrasse, I found out why. Katz came to halt, leaning with one hand against a building there, gasping for breath. This came out later, but it transpired he had tuberculosis as a child, and his lungs were scarred. Why he took off, I never did understand.

"Papers!" I snapped, as I gripped his collar.

"Give me a smoke first," he gasped.

We traded. He lit up as I inspected his papers. Theodore Katz, medical orderly at Charité, born 1893 here in Berlin. His home address was close by, which still left him too far from Charité if he had to run home in the rain.

Obermeier and Fraulein Graber came up as I handed

Katz back his papers. "What's this all about?" he whimpered.

I showed him my beer token so he knew this was official. "It's about Doktor Kammerich."

"Karl-Heinz? What's he done?" Karl-Heinz? That sounded quite familiar for an orderly speaking about a doctor. I hoped this meant they were the best of friends, so that Katz would lead me right to him.

"We'll get round to that. Where can we find him?"

"How should I know?" Katz had a high, wheedling voice that would have grated on the nerves of a much more patient man. I gave him a shake.

"Kammerich paid you money last week."

"It wasn't just me!" Ah, a problem shared is a problem dumped on everyone else.

"What was it for?"

"He hired a few of us!" he reiterated, again keen to share the blame around. He held his hands up in the air as if surrendering to the Tommies. "Just a little freelance money to drive some ambulances."

"Ambulances? Where to?"

"Friedrichstrasse Bahnhof. The bridge across the river there."

Yes. "What for? What did Kammerich want ambulances for?"

"He wasn't there."

"What's that?"

"We met someone called Reinhold. Don't ask me who he is, I never saw him before or since. He was there with some soldiers. Pretty banged-up, some of them. Reinhold told them to get into the ambulances, and once we had them, we took them to the hospital."

"Which hospital?"

"Heilig-Geist."

Oh, he had to be kidding me!

"How many men?"

"I don't know! Twenty, maybe more like thirty?"

I reached into my pocket and took out the photograph Frau Plommer had supplied of her son, Walter. "Was he with them?"

"Come on, Herr Kommissar, I didn't check them all! Let me look again. Oh, maybe I did see this one. He walked right by me, I think."

"What physical state was he in? Was he wounded?"

"Look, Herr Kommissar, those boys, they all looked banged up, you know? Arms in slings, crutches, bandaged heads... I don't know. This one didn't stand out, I don't think. They all just kind of shuffled along, dead quiet. This Reinhold, he called the shots. He told them to climb onto the ambulances, and they didn't say a word."

"And who was with these men? Who carried them onto the ambulances?"

"No-one! It was just Reinhold. He told them to get into the ambulances, and they did. A bit slow, mind, but I helped where I could. They were all... quite docile, really. You know how it is with the *kriegszitterer*, they all twitch a bit. But these lads were quiet, never said a word. We loaded them up and took them to Heilig-Geist."

"What happened there?"

"We took them round back. Reinhold knocked on a door, and it opened up. He told the soldiers to go inside, and they filed in, good as gold."

"And then what?"

"And then what? Nothing! We took the ambulances back to the depot and got paid. Most of us had day shifts."

"So, you never saw Kammerich? He hired you, but you didn't see him when you collected the soldiers?"

"That's right. Only, well, he sent word around

today. He wants to hire us again. Tonight."

The Nighttime Return to Heilig-Geist-Spital

We found a patrol *schupo* just along the way and handed Katz over to him. I didn't really fear lightning striking twice, but told the *bulle* that Katz was to be watched over, and kept safe. I also wrote the most comprehensive note I could to Oberkommissar Teske on three sheets torn from my notebook. We needed back-up, and probably a warrant. Not that I was going to wait for either.

Katz had said that he and the other orderlies were supposed to pick up ambulances from the Charité depot at around ten. It was about that by the time we handed him over to the *schupos*. Luckily, we found someone had just managed to hail a taxi further along Invalidenstrasse, so I commandeered that and had the driver take the three of us to a street just around the corner from Heilig-Geist. On the way, we tried to make sense of everything we had just learned.

"Does this mean that old sexton –

"Herr Seeckt."

"– knew about this all the time? That he lied?"

I decided not. "I doubt it, Obermeier. I don't think the old man knows what's been going on, even if it was right under his nose."

We were all three of us smoking intensely as the cab rattled along the street. Obermeier waved his cigarette around, drawing smoke circles. "But how has Kammerich got away with all this? Hiring hospital orderlies, commandeering ambulances, hijacking a hospital... how does he do all this?"

"I think money helps," Fraulein Graber commented. Katz *had* mentioned a tidy sum.

"So, what now?"

"Let's get there and take a look around first. Katz says they were hired to be at the hospital at midnight. We can see what the lay of the land is before the rest of them arrive. Then, hopefully, Oberkommissar Teske will turn up with the cavalry, and we can finally discover what this is all about."

The taxi was abominably slow, or perhaps I was just impatient. It finally dropped us at the Friedrichsbrücke. We walked along the riverbank, then turned onto St Wolfgang Strasse. It was all very quiet.

"Be quiet and keep your heads down. We're just three friends out for a stroll."

We passed down the street, with the hospital buildings on our left. I made note of an old, heavy door in the wall that matched the description Katz had offered. In no time at all, we were on Spandaustrasse. I directed my colleagues round to the right, and we paused over by a tram stop where a few other people were loitering.

"Now we wait?"

"Now we wait."

From this new vantage point, we did not have much of a view of the hospital, but rather of the old chapel where it fronted onto Spandaustrasse. We smoked, discussed a few aspects of the case in hushed tones, and watched a tram or two come and go. They wouldn't be running for much longer. At around half past eleven, I sent Obermeier to a new position where he could look directly down St Wolfgang Strasse.

Two drunks walked past. One made a lewd remark to Fraulein Graber. I stepped forward, and they staggered off.

"I don't need your protection," she insisted.

"Maybe I was watching out for them," I offered.

Just as I said this, I saw her eyes open wide. I slipped to the side and turned, fearing we were about to be assaulted. In a way, we were.

"Herr Kommissar! What are you doing here?"

"Councillor Markwitz. I might ask the same." I glanced at Fraulein Graber who shook her head. She then stepped forward and greeted the Councillor.

"Kommissar Hoehner, what are you thinking? These streets are no place for a woman at night."

"She is perfectly safe."

"Hmmm. Heilig Geist. What are you doing here? This place came up early on in your enquiries, did it not?"

"I cannot discuss –"

"*Lieber Gott*! Are they here? Have they been here all along?" The thought clearly made him deliriously happy.

"Keep your voice down!" I hissed. At my side, Fraulein Graber placed a hand on my arm, and directed me to look back across towards Obermeier, who was giving the signal we had agreed on.

"I must insist you leave, Herr Councillor."

"What's that? Is something about to happen? I demand that you tell me!"

Obermeier was waving in an almost demented fashion, trying hard to be unobtrusive and attract our attention all at once.

"Stay *here*!" I demanded one last time. I took Fraulein Graber by the arm, and we walked slowly back along Spandaustrasse.

"My apologies, Herr Kommissar. The Councillor lives just round the corner. I could have foreseen that –"

"Don't concern yourself with that now. It's just bad luck." Or was it? The thought struck me so hard I almost stumbled. Fraulein Graber must have seen it on my face.

"No! Surely that is impossible! He is far too transparent to be involved!"

"Not now! Keep your eyes open. The next few moments could be vital."

As we started to cross St Wolfgang Strasse, I heard engines coming closer. I was about to glance back along St Wolfgang Strasse, but at that moment Fraulein Graber turned towards me, took my face between her gloved hands, and kissed me. It was a lover's kiss; full and lingering. It was not objectionable.

"Vehicles. I cannot tell how many... perhaps four? Two military trucks at the front. They are stopping in the street. Ah, the first one has stopped right by that door. There are two men in the cab. The passenger is getting out... he's in military uniform, no insignia. It could be Reinhold. He is just as Katz said: tall, very stiff, a scar on his right cheek."

I was aching to take a look, but this was the less obvious way to observe what was happening. At least that was what I told myself.

"He has knocked on the door. Some men are getting out of the other trucks. They are letting down the tailgates on their vehicles."

"We should move to the corner."

She dropped her hands, took my arm and we moved on. As soon as we were out of view of St Wolfgang Strasse, we dropped the charade. Obermeier crossed the street to join us. Back down Spandaustrasse, I observed Markwitz walking towards us. Damn that man!

I peered around the corner. Could-be-Reinhold was by the door, mostly in shadow. He wore an open military greatcoat and an officer's cap. I heard bolts drawn on the door, and it swung open, spilling light into the street.

Reinhold barked something and the light went out. Moments later, figures began to emerge from the doorway. They moved slowly, in something between a march and a shuffle, single file, each man with one hand on the shoulder of the man in front, like I have seen men blinded by gas attacks. Each was dressed in white, like bakers coming off a shift. They were cruelly under-dressed to be out on such a night, dressed like that. Dear God, some of them were bare-footed.

"Is this them?" asked Obermeier, urgently. I assumed they had to be, but I had not yet seen Walter Plommer. The first of them was being led to the back of the first truck. The others trailed behind.

We still had no back-up, but I could not wait. For one thing, soon the men would be loaded on the trucks, and I would surely lose them again. But for another, Councillor Markwitz was stepping out into the centre of St Wolfgang Strasse, hand raised, full of righteous indignation and ready to be the saviour of the situation. And that was when Reinhold pulled his gun.

Confrontation On St Wolfgang Strasse

One thing I'll say in Reinhold's favour: he had good taste in firearms. In a smooth movement, he pushed back his greatcoat with a flourish, like an American cowboy, then pulled a 'broomhandle' from a side holster. He levelled the weapon at Markwitz.

The Councillor was still demanding that everybody stop doing whatever it was they were doing. He didn't even see the weapon. I cursed under my breath.

With less aplomb, I pulled my own Mauser C96 out from the shoulder harness under my jacket. I took a half step forward, keeping the building between me and Reinhold as much as possible, though with this on my right-hand side, I was partly obstructed from aiming the weapon. Reinhold had no such immediate problem with Markwitz, although he did need to push through the file of walking wounded.

Now Markwitz saw the danger he was in, and yelped in alarm, throwing his hands up in front of his face like *that* was going to save him. Reinhold continued to move towards him, his pistol levelled. Frankly, part of me was ready for him to shoot the councillor and save me the trouble, but my better angels took control.

"Drop the weapon, Reinhold," I ordered, crisply.

He froze, the weapon still aimed at Markwitz. He didn't even turn his head in my direction.

"It's over. Drop it."

He didn't strike me as the go-down-all-(one)-guns-blazing type, nor could he have known he was facing just one *kripo*, and not half the Berlin police. I was certain he'd back down.

You can't be right about everything.

He fired once. In retrospect, I can see that he missed deliberately. The shot went comfortably over Markwitz's head, not that the councillor realised that. He dropped in what might have been a dead faint, though he crawled to the side of the street soon after.

Reinhold, meanwhile, turned his head in my direction and smiled. He hadn't moved the pistol at all. I watched him loosen his grip, and the gun twisted in his hand, pointing to the floor. He slowly crouched and lowered it to the ground.

I stepped out, moved towards him and kicked the Mauser aside. The scar on his face was very vivid; you'd never forget a face like that once you had seen it.

"Stand there, by the wall," I told him.

Further along the street, I realised, things were not going my way. The driver of the first truck, and one of the others, had stepped forward, clutching a heavy wrench. He wasn't prepared to gamble on winning with that versus a pistol, but he wasn't ready to back down either. Worse, behind him, the invalids were suddenly extremely agitated. Some fell to the ground, clutching at their heads, or curling up in the foetal position; others ran off down the street, screaming. The night was rent by their panic.

Fraulein Graber raced past me, heedless of the danger posed by the truck drivers. She pulled at the arm of one of the invalids, who shrugged her off and collapsed to the ground. She chased off after those who had fled.

In the meantime, I went to the door. There was no handle on the outside; it was designed only to be opened from within. I pounded my fist on the thick wood, a little awkward in that I had to keep my body turned and one armed raised so I might cover Reinhold.

"Open up in there!" I yelled.

Reinhold chuckled.

Obermeier was looking frantically up and down the street. "I'll find another way in," he snapped, and ran off. I opened my mouth to stop him, since I'd be alone in the street with Reinhold and the various drivers. By now, the latter had scattered, however. They might have driven off, but there was no route past the first truck, and Reinhold had been blocking the street during the best moment to have sped away.

"You are far too late to do anything," Reinhold said. He was alarmingly calm.

"Where is Kammerich?" I demanded.

"Who?" His voice dripped with sarcasm.

By now, I could hear the first police whistles. They were a long way off, and their direction was uncertain, but someone was responding, presumably to the gunshot, or perhaps to shrieking men in lightweight clothing running through a Berlin winter's night. Reinhold didn't react.

"Where were you taking those men?" I demanded.

Reinhold looked around theatrically. "What men?"

He was too assured to be broken in the street. I kept my Mauser aimed at his head until the first *schupo* appeared. I didn't recognise the fellow, but he appeared confident and capable. I told him to handcuff Reinhold and watch him, advising him that there was a discarded pistol on the other side of the street.

From there, I could turn my attention and my frustrations back to the door. I beat on the surface for several seconds, calling out to whoever was inside to open up. I had even considered where I might find an axe before I heard the bolts drawn.

The door swung open, revealing Obermeier, breathless. Behind him stood a startled older man, his eyes wide and jaw agape.

As Katz had described, the door gave onto a

passageway that led into the interior of the hospital, with a stairway immediately off to the side. I looked down, but the well was dark.

"What is down there?"

"I – I don't know!" the older fellow stuttered. "Storage? I've never been down there. I'm just the night nurse."

"There are men outside," I said quickly, gesturing both ways along the street. "Invalids, patients. Round up anyone else who is on duty and bring them back inside."

The nurse seemed bemused by this. "There's only myself and one other –"

"Then get out there and search by yourself! Klaus, come with me."

Obermeier and I made our way slowly down the darkened stairwell, only making it darker by our presence. I saw no sign of any switches of electrical cabling. At the very foot of the stair I found a door, under which a little weak light seeped. I listened at the door, and heard nothing, so, pistol in hand, I opened it up and stepped through.

We entered a large, vaulted space. The Heilig Geist was hundreds of years old, and still it felt as if this space predated it. The light came from a couple of oil lamps suspended from the roof. Along the walls on either side stood racked metal shelving, burdened with a great many boxes, some of which were labelled as having come from Charité, others of which were from various suppliers. There were bandages, splints and other medical supplies. Each box was open and had been partially emptied.

The stone floor was little damp underfoot. Motioning to Obermeier to be as quiet as possible, I moved along the room. A few boxes on lower shelves were open, and I saw within medical supplies of various kinds. One box caught my attention: it had large red lozenge printed on the side, with a stenciled label that read *Wiedergeburt*. From what I could see, the box contained numerous glass ampoule, each about the size of my thumb. These contained a dark liquid. Was this 'Rebirth'? I paused, took one from the box and held it up to the light. The liquid was a deep, rich red, like fine old wine.

I slipped the ampoule into my pocket. We moved on.

Beyond this first vaulted chamber there was a short passage, which turned to the right, so that now it ran parallel to St Wolfgang Strasse. This opened into a second chamber, vaulted like the first, but a little larger. There was more light in here, from kerosene lamps hanging from the walls on either side.

There were three men at the far end of the chamber, ordinary-looking fellows in the garb of hospital orderlies, or the nurse we had encountered above. Come to think of it, it was the same clothing as the invalids had been dressed in, though these fellows had allowed themselves the luxury of shoes.

They had been playing cards at a small, square table. This was abandoned as they saw us come in. Well, first, I imagine, they saw the muzzle, then the body of the Mauser. They were suitably surprised.

"Keep still! Raise your hands!" I showed them my beer token in the half light, moving deeper into the chamber as I did so.

"Who are you?" I demanded. "Identify yourselves!"

Two of the men were sufficiently surprised and alarmed to comply, I thought, but the third was made of sterner stuff. This was a bulky fellow with a scarred face, deep-set eyes and a missing ear. He had fists like hocks of ham.

"Say nothing!" he said to the others. And then to me: "What are you doing here? What right do you have to break in? This is a hospital!"

This much I was seeing for myself. Along both of the long walls of this room, and in a central row down the middle of the chamber, packed in tight so that there was barely space to stand between them, were various beds with stained mattresses and threadbare blankets. There were even a few bunk beds, still painted in military green. Many of the beds were occupied by silent, still men in grubby hospital garb.

By almost every bed, as far as I could see, there was a stand. Again, while most of these were official equipment, liberated from hospitals, I imagined, others were improvised. From many such poles a glass vessel hung, with rubber tubes leading down to the invalids, affixed to their arms by a needle. A dark red liquid was dripping from each vessel. I assumed this was the same liquid as in the small ampoules in the storage room. There were more of these glass vessels on shelves around the room, linked together with wires or rubber tubes.

The big man twitched. I moved my attention back to covering all three of them with the Mauser as I moved along the chamber, working my way carefully around the apparatus.

"What is going on here?" I demanded. None of the patients stirred as I passed.

"You have no right to be here!" said the bulky fellow.

"I very much doubt you have," I replied softly. "Who is in charge here?"

None of these misfits, I was sure of that. The youngest of the three (by my judgement), a scrawny-looking youth with a pitiable moustache, almost broke his neck trying not to look behind him at another door.

"You better leave!" snarled the big man, taking up a pair of scissors from a table, which struck me as a bold move, in the circumstances.

"Stand aside!" I commanded. The two lesser types shuffled off beside the last bed on one side. Scar-face didn't move. Perhaps that missing ear was handicapping him.

Because of the beds down the centre, as I moved along one gangway, he could step in the direction of the other. I ordered him to move back with the others, but he was happy to defy me. Then he paused, looked around the room, and slowly raised his hands. There was something about his expression that disquieted me, but I didn't understand why.

"What *is* this?" asked Obermeier from behind me.

I had no answer. Instead, I motioned him forward, and showed him the Mauser. "Do you know how to use this?"

I glimpsed his face. He was surprised, but not disquieted by the question. He took the gun carefully from my grasp. I steered him so that he kept it centred on the big fellow.

"Even if one of the others makes a move, shoot him first."

I left it unsaid that I expected *schupos* to be stumbling down the stairs at any moment. I wasn't wrong in that expectation.

Right now, I needed to see what lay beyond the end of the chamber and its silent human misery. I kept my eyes on scar-face, still unsettled by his expression. His eyes flickered to Obermeier, then back to me. Now his move to put one of the beds between us was to his disadvantage, and he made no move to undo his decision.

At this end of the chamber, there were two doors. A

glance showed me that each led into a short passage with more doors off to the side. On the left, the passage accessed two rooms, the first of which was an office, with an old, plain desk, filing cabinets and piles of documents. I stepped in, and glanced at an open folder on the desk, which was a patient record for a Privat Glueck. Reading quickly, I saw Glueck had arrived six weeks before, suffering from *Krieghysterie*. There was a detailed history of his being administered 'R'.

His record was stamped with the current date and the word 'Discharged'.

I estimated that Glueck's record sat atop a pile of perhaps ten or a dozen. How many more were in the filing cabinets? What did 'discharged' mean?

A wire basket contained more papers, the topmost of which was list of names. At the top, it read Wagen 8. I read the names again. There was Walter Plommer, and there Gefreiter Adolf Meinz. It was the missing page from the train manifest.

I took in a slow breath, feeling a powerful need for a cigarette. That would have to wait, though. I pocketed the paper and left the office.

The second room off this passage was half-glassed. Along the two longer walls, I could see benches, with stools set in front of them, and the kind of equipment I had last seen at school: the basics of a chemical laboratory. There were beakers of all sizes, retorts, paraffin burners, test tubes and pipettes. It was all haphazard, but also so still. I gained the impression that this room had seen little recent use.

There were gowns and aprons hanging on a peg just inside the door. Also, three gas masks. I pondered those just as I was reaching for the door handle. Perhaps it might be safer to examine the laboratory later. Now that the thought was in my mind, I thought I could smell blood, and the stench of mustard. My heart beat faster and I withdrew my hand. I needed that cigarette more than ever.

There were also three M1917 *stielhandgranate*, which the Tommies like to call potato mashers, lying on a table, wired together. Where lay three, there might be others. This confirmed to me that someone else could be the first to open this door.

Onto the second passage, then. I looked into the main chamber as I passed, and nothing had changed. I nodded to Obermeier; scar-face scowled.

This second corridor was shorter. Immediately within were doors to a washroom and toilet. I looked inside just to be sure they were both unoccupied.

The last door was slightly ajar, and I pushed it open the rest of the way with the toe of one boot. Inside, I saw a couple of cots, a table, and two rickety old chairs. These and the table were strewn with personal possessions, such as clothes, more food and drink, some pornographic novels and the like. The air was stale, rank with sweat and alcohol.

On one of the cots, lying on his side, there was a sleeping man. He was tall, angular, almost handsome, though he needed a haircut and a shave. He was wearing his trousers with the suspenders lowered, and holed socks. As I stepped closer, I realised he reeked of drink, and possibly something more potent. An empty bottle and a thick notebook lay on the bed with him. As I reached forward, I found this latter was actually two books, one a black notebook, the other an older volume bound in aged brown leather, the two bound in red cord. I moved them aside and laid my hand on the shoulder of the sleeping man.

We hadn't met, but I had heard a few descriptions of this gentlemen over the previous few days. At last, I was face to sleeping face with Herr Doktor Karl-Heinz

Kammerich.

Doktor Hammerich

"Wake up!"

I shook Kammerich roughly by the shoulder. This had no effect, so I shook him some more, and slapped his face. "Wake up, damn you!"

His eyes twitched, then snapped open. He had pale eyes, though any charm they had about them was ruined by how bloodshot and red-rimmed they were. We've all been there. He sat up by degrees, swaying. His tongue rolled around his mouth in a pathetic search for moisture. Giving him this moment to attempt recovery, I took up the notebook. It was full of formulae and procedures, a sketchbook of chemistry I didn't understand. I did note that it was written in two hands, and I would have bet my last cigarettes that one of them was Doktor Luster's.

Speaking of cigarettes: I lit two, handing one to Kammerich.

"Herr Doktor Karl-Heinz Kammerich?" He blinked and nodded. "Let me see your papers."

He gestured towards the table. I stepped back, never letting him out of my sight. His papers were in the inside pocket of a jacket that had been tossed aside. Nice cloth once, I surmised, but years old.

Kammerich's papers confirmed his identity, which I scarcely needed, given the circumstances. He was around thirty-five years old. He was a Silesian, from Wrocław. The papers gave his Berlin address as being on Quakerstrasse, and his employment as being at Charité. Not entirely up-to-date, then.

"Are you sober, Herr Doktor?"

"Regrettably." There was no trace of his origin in his

accent, though present conditions were hardly favourable to his speaking voice.

"Do you understand that you are speaking to a police officer?" I cautioned him.

He blinked again, before looking up to stare somewhere past my right ear. He didn't even appear to recognise where he was.

"What is this all about?" he asked, after a long draw on the cigarette.

"Who are those men out there?" I demanded, jerking my head in the direction of the main chamber.

It seemed to take Kammerich quite a while to work out who I might mean. Eventually, he proffered the idea that they were his patients.

"You are not a doctor at this hospital," I commented. "Or any other, I think." That thought too landed in his consciousness with a stubborn, reluctant weight.

"All the same..." he offered.

"Get dressed," I commanded. He sat still, smoking and swaying. I repeated the order.

"Yes, very well."

As he stood, and fumbled his way into shirt, jacket and shoes, I pressed him a little more. His memory might be off in a different country, but so was any reticence to reply, or any real sense of self-preservation.

"What have you been doing here, Herr Doktor?"

"Those men... are my patients," he repeated.

"What are you treating them for?"

His eyes cleared a little, and he stared directly into mine. I could see clarity being restored to his mind, as all the pieces tumbled back into place. It was as if I was being diagnosed.

"You have served? Surely, you must have. You

know… the horror of it all."

I could still feel that chill that had gripped me when I had my hand on the door of the laboratory, when the odour of that place had worked its way into my head with its suggestions and memories. In the back of my mind, I heard a cry from the past.

"Does it still trouble you?"

The voice in my mind grew from a distant, indistinct echo into an urgent whisper. "Gaz! Gaz!!"

I must have taken a step back. My thighs contacted the edge of the table. I gripped his notebook tightly.

"I see that it does. Do you receive treatment? Does it do you any good?"

I was breathing hard. The cigarette hung from my lip. The curl of smoke from its tip turned yellow before my eyes.

"Of course it doesn't. You cannot shake the memories. You dream of your terror in the night. Your mind is poisoned by what happened to you. Tell me, *polizei*, do you never wish you could just… forget?"

I lifted a hand as if I still held the Mauser, as if I could take control once more. I realised how foolish that must seem and moved my hand to remove the cigarette from my mouth. "Go out," I said, gesturing. I needed fresh air. Even the night air of Berlin would do.

He shrugged, and walked off in front of me, pausing only to steady himself against the doorframe before passing through. Before I moved to follow him, I took up the two books from the bed, and putting them in my jacket pocket, where they sat uncomfortably. We went back out into the main chamber. All was still as it had been, although I noted two uniformed police had joined the party, one standing behind Obermeier, another alongside Fraulein Graber, whose eyes were wide open.

"Stand with your men," I told Kammerich. He took a step to do so.

"No. Keep very still, Herr Kommissar."

My mind cleared very quickly, as I appreciated how far the tables had turned. Obermeier no longer had my Mauser in his hand, instead it was being levelled at me by scar-face. One of the two policemen, the one by Obermeier, did the same with his police-issued Luger P08 sidearm. This fellow, a narrow-faced, dead-eyed individual I thought I knew, put his palm on Obermeier's back and pushed him forward.

"We need to move, Moehnke." I got the idea that Moehnke, our scar-faced friend, might have liked to string this out a little, but he nodded and motioned his two fellow orderlies forward.

"Herr Doktor, let's go."

Kammerich looked at me, offered a small smile, then moved away and down the length of the chamber. Obermeier joined me over by the twin doors. "I'm sorry," he whispered. That was going to have to wait.

Kammerich moved on unsteady feet. Moehnke gestured to the other two orderlies who followed him along that aisle. One of them offered the doctor support, but as they came level with the second *schupo* and Fraulein Graber, he shook this off, and turned back, more animated than at any point heretofore.

"The woman too?"

"There can be no witnesses," growled Moehnke. I didn't like the sound of that at all. He started to move away as well, still covering me with what was, frustratingly, my own gun. "Do you have everything you need, Herr Doktor?"

Kammerich stared hard in my direction. "Yes," he said, flatly. I felt the weight of his journal in my pocket.

The second *schupo* pushed Fraulein Graber in our direction. She showed her concern, but there was determination in her eyes. "They can't escape," she whispered. "There must be a dozen police in the street outside."

Moehnke showed he had excellent hearing. "They will see exactly what they would expect. Two of their number leading out three prisoners."

He turned the Mauser in his hand and offered it to the second *schupo*. "No," the officer snapped. "When they find the bodies, it makes no sense for him to be unarmed. Leave it here." Moehnke shrugged and tossed the pistol clumsily onto one of the beds, where it struck the leg of one of the invalids, who didn't so much as flinch. The Mauser fell to the floor with a large clatter.

"Let's go."

Dead-eyes motioned for his colleague to go first, who did as he was told, leaving the chamber, followed by the other two orderlies. He, Kammerich and Moehnke paused by the door. "Do it," urged the *schupo*.

Kammerich moved a hand as if to stop what was coming. I felt the weight of his books in my jacket pocket – perhaps that was all he was concerned about. It was too late.

Reaching up, Moehnke grasped one of the many wires that were looped around the flasks and jars containing the dark red formulation. He pulled hard. Jar after jar began to topple from the shelves, each pulling its neighbour. Some landed on the beds – some even struck unfeeling patients. Others crashed to the floor, smashed and soaked invalids, bed linen and the floor alike. I didn't like how this was going at all. A little splashed onto Obermeier's coat, but otherwise we were not immediately affected by Moehnke's action, although the noise was deafening, and there was a powerful stench of iron and oil. My heart was thrumming harder than ever.

Dead-eyes reached into a tunic pocket, and took out what looked like a cartridge case. I knew what this was; soldiers had been making these improvised cigarette lighters from the middle of the war. He coaxed a flame from it. Everyone was as still as the unknowing invalids for just a moment.

"Do No Harm"

And then he tossed it onto the nearest bed, one soaked in the red liquid. The blankets burst into flame.

I doubted that Doktor Kammerich had placed the flasks that way as an instrument of mass murder, but really... had he never wondered why it was done? It seemed evident to me. If there was ever the need to 'clean house' in a hurry, they were obviously going to have to incinerate the evidence. Moehnke understood that; Dead-eyes too.

Later, I was going to find out that Rebirth burned like kerosene, because of the oils in its ingedients. In the greater picture of the risks associated with the formulation, this was one of the smaller ones, but it made Rebirth flammable. In the chamber under Heilig-Geist, this was about to become gravely dangerous.

"Mein Gott!" shrilled Obermeier.

More practically, Fraulein Graber first cried: "The patients!" and then: "Is there another way out?"

I had seen no such thing. We were underground, hemmed in by thick stone and good Berlin earth. I looked up at the ceiling briefly, but I knew the only way out was back the way we came, and where Moehnke and the others were ahead of us.

Being a practical man, I did have a moment where I considered that, if I had been Moehnke or Dead-eyes, I would have shot us first. Yes, that might have raised questions at autopsy, but there would be many more answers required with the method they had chosen to cause our demise. No-one had ever escaped a fire, ready to detail how it was set, when they were already dead.

I hesitated for a moment, because didn't want to give Moehnke the chance to reconsider shooting us, but Fraulein Graber's instincts were instantaneous, determined and solicitous. She went directly to the occupied bed nearest to the blaze, and tried to rouse the patient therein. The man didn't stir. With a gasp of effort, she pulled him up into a sitting position even as fire started to roll across the floor towards her skirts. Black smoke roiled up towards the ceiling. The moment she lost her grip, he slipped back down.

We were never going to rescue these men, not like this. I'm afraid this was one of those moments where we first needed to rescue the rescuers. I shrugged off my overcoat and looked around the room, hoping to spot our salvation, something Moehnke hadn't considered.

There was next to no water in the chamber, and though I recalled seeing a fire bucket in the laboratory, I suspected a couple of handfuls of sand were not going to solve our predicament. There were a few blankets in a cabinet by where we were standing, but these were as thin as those covering the men. I saw these as being just more fuel.

"We have to smother the flames!" I yelled, beating at one patch of crimson flame with my coat.

"The mattresses!" Fraulein Graber responded. Of course! Many of the beds were unoccupied, and surely those mattresses, no matter how poorly fit they were for use in a hospital would serve to at least slow down the fire.

This was true, to a point, but only to a point. I pulled a mattress from one of the beds nearest the exit onto a puddle of fire, and the flames vanished. But moments later, soaked in the Rebirth that lay all around, the mattress itself went up in flames. I had had better luck with my overcoat, but that could only last so long. We were just about holding our own against the growing blaze, but eventually, my coat was edged in purple and orange flame and was fuel to the fire. My hat went the same way, though without ever having contributed much to our firefighting efforts.

I dipped my head to peer out through the exit. The storage room was clear. Moehnke and the others must be on the stairs, or perhaps already out into the street. I couldn't imagine them hanging around. The two *schupos* would act out their dumb-show of taking their prisoners away, and no-one would be any the wiser.

"Obermeier! Get help!" I grabbed his sleeve as he came up. "Watch yourself. We don't know who's out there."

He didn't argue.

I went back to Fraulein Graber, dragging another mattress to fend off the tongues of flame that were flicking towards her and the invalid she was trying to rouse. The fellow was a skinny shadow of a man, but still she could barely move him. The flimsy gown he wore was slipping off his shoulders, and tore a little more as she pulled at him. The tubes that attached him to the flask of Rebirth tautened. I pulled the vessel off the stand it hung from, but this didn't really help, since now another ampoule of inflammable liquid threatened to fall to the ground and add its fuel to the fire. We didn't have enough hands to deal with man and medicine.

Fraulein Graber screamed in frustration and looked to detach the apparatus from the man's arm. As the needles came free, blood spurted from his vein. To my horror, as this splattered onto the flames, it spluttered and glowed and flared. An instinct made me turn, and I saw one of the other invalids become abruptly consumed by fire that climbed and swarmed over his bed. In that instant, his veins glowed red, and burned. I've seen death arrive in many forms, including by fire and flame, but I've never seen a man be taken that way.

And he didn't so much as twitch.

We were facing this choice: rip out the needles and bear the patients away, bleeding from the wounds we left, or leave them to burn. Even that choice was only available to a few. I looked back along the chamber and watched the expressionless, damaged faces of these men, doubly victims now, knowing that each would ignite just as certainly.

None of them screamed. I sincerely wished they would.

Rebirth

We saved eight. Eight from how many? Thirty? Forty? Some other *schupos* had appeared just when they were least likely to be of any use, when the chamber was full of smoke. By then Fraulein Graber and I were done, soot-blackened, coughing and retching on the street outside. There was a lot of running around. More *schupos* donned gas masks and went down, being passed flame-proof blankets and buckets of sand and earth by a human chain on the stairs. The fire brigade turned up with an antiquated vehicle and took over. About half an hour after the horror began, it was all over, and police, firemen and onlookers began to fall out from their various roles, standing around looking bemused and helpless. At one point a sergeant sheepishly handed me back my own gun. It was in better condition than most of us.

I shivered, though it felt difficult to imagine being cold ever again. My jacket, singed and blackened, lay on the ground at my side. Someone handed me a cigarette. I spat filth and guilt onto the pavement and took up the offer. It was from Obermeier.

"They were gone before I got back to the street," he said. He sat down beside me, heavily. "Do we know who those *polizei* were?"

"Two men who won't turn up their next shifts," I replied sourly. I knew we were unlikely to see either of the pair again. That was probably best for them.

At some point, HauptOberkommissar Teske showed up. He went down into the cellars and was gone for some short while. He was pale when he came up, but he was doing better than the rest of us. He stood in the street, hands on his hips, directing other *kripo* officers to the cellar in search of evidence. Then he looked back to we three.

"Go home and get some rest, all of you. I shall want your report in the morning."

Report! I almost burst into laughter. What report could sum up what we had just seen and endured?

"There is a box down there, in the storage room, with a red lozenge on its side. The contents are evidence."

I told Teske my belief, something that had been gnawing at me while I was sitting in the street, that whoever was behind this, if they were this willing to cover their tracks so abominably… well, I didn't fancy Kammerich's chances all that much. Judging by the way he was living, the way he was clearly drinking himself into a stupor just to sleep, he was more liability than asset, and I suspect he knew it.

"Don't be so pessimistic," the Oberkommissar rumbled. "For all this…" He waved his hands in the direction of Heilig-Geist. "You have had a success tonight."

I knew what he was referring to. Many of the terrified, fleeing invalids we had first encountered had been rounded up and were now in more suitable accommodation. Among them were Walter Plommer. Sadly, Adolph Meinz had not yet been found.

"We saved the patient records, well, most of them. There is that laboratory too. That's all useful evidence. And you prevented the removal of those poor souls; God knows where they were being taken, and for what purpose. They will receive the best care now."

"Frau Plommer will be *greatly* relieved. "

I realised this last was spoken by Councillor Markwitz. Where had he been skulking since setting off this conflagration?

"We should inform her *immediately*!" Markwitz was

almost out of the starting blocks, but Teske held up a hand to give him pause.

"Herr Councillor. This is now a most serious police matter. I must insist that you allow my officers to speak first with Frau Plommer."

Markwitz's face showed he didn't want to agree with that, but his voice muttered that he accepted the Oberkommissar's instructions. "I shall accompany them, of course."

"No, Herr Councillor," said Fraulein Graber. "We must let the Oberkommissar and the police do their job."

Teske had a small smile on his face, and a little glitter in his eye. "I expect nothing less of my officers," he said in a low voice. "*All* my officers."

Markwitz wandered off. I didn't really have the energy to pursue him, just in case he decided there was some method and profit in disobeying the Oberkommissar's instructions. All the same, I rose to my feet, picking up my singed jacket. I could hardly visit the widow Plommer dressed in that, but then I didn't own another.

Fraulein Graber took it from me. "We'll stop by my house. My cousin is staying with us. I am sure a suitable jacket can be found."

"Are you sure?"

"I am. She has impeccable taste."

TUESDAY, 5TH NOVEMBER 1918

There was no sleeping that night. No sleep, and no dreams. The visit to Frau Plommer's house had been the slightest of codas to what had gone on before. Once we had managed to rouse her, she listened to our news and wept. Walter, we could inform her, was at Charité. Or, at least, the outward form of Walter Plommer was there. I couldn't be sure what else Frau Plommer would find when she visited him in the morning. I made no attempt to warn her.

Six of the soldiers from Wagon Eight who had not been recovered; and were now abandoned, terrified souls loose on the streets of the city. I'd given Oberkommissar Teske the page from the manifest. The boars from foot patrol could find these six.

After reporting to Frau Plommer, Fraulein Graber and I found a bar somewhere nearby. Obermeier went off. I suspected he wanted to file a story to *Vorwarts* while everything was fresh in his mind. Maybe that would help him get it *out* of his mind.

Fraulein Graber and I sat in a corner while lovers danced and fondled before us, moving through cigarette smoke that danced around them in turn. I don't think I really heard the music at all. I smelled of shame and soot, even if a fresh shirt and an exquisitely tailored jacket had replaced my own ruined poverty. Fraulein Graber looked tired, and her eyes were heavy. She still smelled like a peacetime summer.

We drank schnapps. We smoked incessantly. We ate...something. I couldn't taste any of it. On his second visit, I had the waiter leave the bottle.

Eventually, because it had to be done, I took the two

books from the pocket of my borrowed jacket and turned them over in my hands. The black notebook was outwardly quite ordinary; cloth-covered, poorly bound. I imagined it had been manufactured during the war; like everything else in the civilian world, it was flimsy and badly made. It was a convenient size for a jacket pocket; I believed Kammerich took it with him everywhere.

The other volume was slightly larger. The boards were covered with old leather, worn smooth, dark with age. There was no title or other script. Once I had untied the crimson cord and separated the two, there was an unexpected lightness to it. I set it aside for now.

Fraulein Graber stubbed out a cigarette she had actually smoked, and moved along the bench we occupied to be closer to my shoulder. I opened the notebook.

For the most part, we read silently by the flickering glow of an oil tablelamp. Around us, people moved in the shadows, talking, dancing, drinking. The news from Austria had flooded Berlin with a sense of it being almost over. Why not dance away Germany's waning moments?

For Fraulein Graber and I, the world and the war narrowed down to successive pages of Kammerich's notebook. The first part was in Luster's spiky hand; twenty-something pages of notes and results concerning the formulation of what he called *schlafwandeln* or *lunatismus*. I would need his neurological mumbo-jumbo translated for me by someone with a lot more scientific understanding, but he did manage to speak in layman's terms here and there, especially when referring to a patient whose night terrors were 'calmed', or whose tremors subsided somewhat after treatment. His formulation appeared to aim to use sleep as a curative, sedating the patient to just the right level where they were 'alive', but operating at a level below true consciousness. Some of what we were reading drew extensively on the pages Luster had annotated in *The Pathology of Madness.*

"This is how the patients at Heilig Geist appeared," commented Fraulein Graber.

Yes, but there had to be more to it than that. We reached the pages where Kammerich took over the notebook. I wondered idly: had he been gifted the notes, or had he obtained them by some other method?

It probably didn't matter now. What we had here didn't quite count as a written confession, but it filled in the blanks in a way that allowed us to construct a version of the events that had brought us to this point. His first entry was dated four months ago. He spoke in the first person, as if relating the creation of *Wiedergeburt* for posterity.

His career, it appeared, had been perfectly normal up until the outbreak of war. He had trained as an anaesthologist, and this meant he was in great demand as the first casualties trickled back to Berlin from the Marne and elsewhere. He suggested that he had never been satisfied with simply reducing the pain and suffering of the wounded; that he wanted to *restore* them. And so, by 1916, he was performing unlicensed treatments and procedures at Charité, using refined opiates and other drugs. He worked with Luster for a time, but then he was caught administering his concoctions, and was fired.

A year later, and he was working at Heilig Geist. He was obsessed with finding faster ways to restore men to health, especially those suffering from *krieghysterie* or other trauma-induced mental disorders. Without explaining how he came to such knowledge; his account detailed his belief that the ancients had possessed knowledge that had been lost to European science. He suggested the mind could be repaired as easily as a broken limb, if we just recovered such knowledge.

He managed to learn just enough of some ancient languages to know what he was looking for. He undertook research at the Prussian State Library, and found an old book, which he stole. I looked at the other volume on the table, and at least could imagine where it belonged.

Kammerich's narrative provided context and excuse for all that he had done. His confession was self-serving, but I did get a sense that there had been a time when he had been genuinely concerned for the broken men who had passed through his care. But as the pages turned, they appeared less and less frequently. It became all about Rebirth.

There was more science at this point. I turned page after page of chemical formulae, and how Rebirth was formulated in early, unsuccessful incarnations. Kammerich referred to the 'Sumerian' compound, and to something, or perhaps someone, called Nammu.

"Is this making any sense to you?" asked Fraulein Graber at this point. I had to admit that I was increasingly lost. Kammerich's writing was wandering further and further from the world of chemistry and pharmacy, and into something altogether more fantastical, a mixture of alchemy and mysticism.

We flicked through a few more pages. It didn't get any more comprehensible. Even Kammerich's handwriting was falling apart.

I set the book down. More durable than I, Fraulein Graber took it up and read a few more pages. I lit two fresh cigarettes, and then took up the leather-bound book.

I was struck again how light it was. It seemed as though the leather cover should provide something more substantial, but no. I opened it up, and saw that the pages within were gossamer thin. There was no title page, no introduction, and no sign of Kammerich's scribbled notations. Instead, page after page was filled with symbols, evenly-spaced squiggles and shapes. It reminded me a little of a code book, but one where I had no idea what was being encrypted to what.

"What *is* that?" Fraulein Graber enquired, done now with the notebook. We looked through a few more of the filmy pages. "Is it some ancient script?"

"Possibly. If Kammerich stole this from the State Library, perhaps they can tell us what it is."

She nodded, though I think we both understood that this was not the kind of volume that was regularly consulted by scholars or academics.

I drank a little more. I felt my head swim and my remaining energy disipate. It was about four o'clock. Most of the bar's patrons had gone home, and the staff would willingly have joined them, were it not for us. The schnapps bottle was almost empty. We finished it off, and stood up slowly, picking up our possessions and heading for the door.

"What happens now, Herr Kommissar?"

"I really don't know." I chuckled. "We have a report to write,"

"Breakfast first, surely."

We wandered back in the direction of the central city. The air was biting, and I bitterly resented the loss of my overcoat. Fraulein Graber didn't seem to feel the cold, though she tucked her hands under her arms.

"We rescued the invalids," she said at one point as we crossed a broad street. A heavily-laden cart went past. In the buildings around us, a few weak lights were beginning to show. "Does that mean an end to it?"

"The Oberkommissar wants us to look at another case. A murder." How mundane that word sounded, how coldly professional.

"We are not to pursue Kammerich?"

I thought about how hard he had been to find in the first place, how it had been almost an accident that we had stumbled into his lair. He was in the hands of Moehnke now, and probably Reinhold. Originally, I had formed the impression that these men worked for Kammerich, that he had hired them much as he had employed Katz and the other orderlies. But as the night had unfolded, my opinion had changed.

"We don't pursue those other men?"

"I doubt we would ever find them. I think they were military. I suspect they will disappear, leaves in the forest." If the war was almost over, then soon millions of grey shadows would return from the front, clad in the last uniform the army had provided. There would be millions of them.

"I don't mean those... I mean the other invalids."

"The other..."

"You said there were patient records, stamped 'discharged'. Kammerich wasn't saying those men were cured, surely. He was saying they had been handed over to someone else."

We paused on one of the bridges over the Spree, looking along the river. The city was stirring around us, oddly unfamiliar, like a lover who had been keeping secrets, but who was now starkly revealed. A barge was making its way along the river. Curiously, a single white horse stood on its deck. Mist curled around its hooves.

"For how long do you think Kammerich has been doing this? Months? A year?"

I didn't have those answers, but I knew where her mind was going. "*Our* soldiers weren't the first. Those boys in the cellar..." My voice caught. "They weren't the first either. It's going to take time to go through Kammerich's records, those that survived, and find out just how many young men have been through this… Rebirth process."

"It could be hundreds."

I shrugged, leaned back against the wall and took a long draw on the nail between my lips. How many cigarettes had we smoked? "And knowing their names doesn't give us any further indication as to where they are now, or what *purpose* this all serves." I checked the bottle. There was possibly another tiny measure in it for us both. Fraulein Graber quickly shook her head, so I emptied the bottle into my mouth. My throat burned.

"This is so much bigger than Walter Plommer, or Wagon Eight, or even the murder of those young men tonight."

Fraulein Graber nodded her head. "There are surely more people involved. This isn't just Kammerich's work. How did he get so much of his formulation manufactured? Is that not beyond his simple laboratory?"

"Possibly." I heard how tired my voice sounded. "Ach, I should have checked the boxes in the storeroom more carefully. They could have told us where those ampoules were manufactured. I wonder if any paperwork of that kind survived?"

"I could look into that in the morning," Fraulein Graber suggested. "I'll go back to Heilig Geist and see what remains." Rather her than me.

"Then there is whoever works this from the Aachen end, and beyond. Someone selects these men, arranges for their transport, and for their collection here in Berlin. Someone gives *orders* for all this."

That was the key to where we were now. If we were to progress any further with the investigation, we were going to need to question figures in the military. At the front of the queue was the mysterious vO, who had managed Luster, who in turn, it appeared, had managed Kammerich.

"We need a friendly ear at the War Ministry," I suggested.

"Don't ask me," Fraulein Graber said, looking at her glass now with some regret. "I only date doctors."

THE CASE OF THE BODY IN THE TIERGARDEN

Curious Designs

Fraulein Graber went home for a few hours. I went back to the Praesidium and tried to sleep on a bench down in the basement near the mortuary, where I had expected things to be quiet. Of course, they were still receiving the blackened corpses from Heilig Geist, so the outer doors opened every few minutes as another body was carried in. I went back up to Robbery and stole a couple of hours on the couch in Radel's office.

Did I sleep?

In the sense that my eyes closed the moment my head touched the seat, yes. But I don't think it can have been more than a few minutes before the dream began.

It was, for the first time in a long time, different on this occasion. At its core, it remained the same: the cries of "Gaz, Gaz!" from voices I could not identify; the rolling, swelling cloud that enveloped me. But on this occasion, the cloud was black, and not yellow, and there was movement within. Shadows stumbled around, silent and ghostly. I felt that same terror as always, the compulsion to rip off my gas mask; I even seemed to feel fingers on my face, pulling at it.

I woke, drenched in sweat. I was nauseous and dry-mouthed. Swaying on my feet, I went out through Robbery, to the consternation of the early bodies on the day shift, to find the toilets. There, I retched into a urinal, sliding slowly to the grubby tiles of the floor. I didn't move for some time. I was beyond exhaustion, almost beyond caring.

Eventually, I got up, wiped myself down a little, and returned to Robbery. It was about half past six. For the next thirty minutes, I typed out a report. Some unseen Samaritan brought me coffee.

At nine on the dot, I knocked on the door of Amt VIIIb. I had tried to smarten myself up, pulling a comb through my hair and straightening the jacket that already had become unreturnable.

"Come."

Oberkommissar Teske read my report without comment. I believed he dwelled on the concluding page, in which I had outlined the options for the investigation going forward. In particular, I had urged him to provide the means whereby we might gain access to the Hauptkadettenanstalt, or to the Garde-Kavallerie-Schützendivision. Short of that, I had suggested, we should at least confirm the identity of vO, nd question him.

"Very well," he said, dropping the report into one of his many wooden trays. He consulted his watch with a flourish, then snapped his cold gaze up in my direction. "Have you yet contacted Homicide? You should speak to Kommissar Zimmerman. I told him you would consult with him today, without fail."

The new case? I didn't have the energy to protest. "I will go there directly."

"Good. Leave this other matter with me for now."

That was it. He reached for another folder on his desk. "Dismissed, Herr Kommissar."

Homicide was on the first floor, directly under Robbery. Their desks were packed in rather more closely than those upstairs, but the department didn't appear that much busier. I knew Zimmerman, a short, curly-haired fellow some years older than I, who had a reputation for solving cases in the first few hours or not at all.

"Oh, here you are at last, Hoehner! A few missing trinkets keeping you busy, were they?" He obviously hadn't heard I was now working for Teske, which made me wonder why he had been expecting me at all.

Zimmerman had been on the Russian front for a year back in 1914-15 and had picked up the habit of smoking foul-smelling Russian tobacco, along with a penchant for the kind of vodka that could fuel aeroplanes.

He offered me a cigarette from his tin, but I declined. He reached for a folder at the back of his desk.

"So, here she is," he said, as if he was introducing me to his niece. He removed a slew of photographs from the folder and started to spread them across his desk. "'Jane Doe', as they say in the American movies, no?"

The photographs showed a woman lying under some foliage. She was on her side with her legs tucked up, her wavy blond hair spilled across the grass as if she was sleeping. I estimated she was thirty years old, perhaps a little younger.

She was quite naked.

If I had to guess, the photographs had been taken at night, or just around dawn, using magnesium powder flash to illuminate the scene. There was a two-man team here at *kripo* that handled all that kind of thing, and they were pretty good. The photographs made the woman look extremely pale, and the flash cast an unearthly glow around her. Moving through the pile, I saw several close-ups of her face, her neck, her hands – and some rather unnecessarily intimate pictures of her naked body. A few more pictures set the scene, showing how she lay beneath a small tree. I believed I could see the river in the background, and thought I recognised the Moltkebrucke. Zimmerman confirmed this was so.

She wore no jewelry, not even earrings, but her fingernails were well cared-for, and I would have suggested she was from a middle-class background. From what I could observe, she wore little or no make-up. I sincerely doubted she was a working girl.

"No belongings?"

"Nothing," grinned Zimmerman. Naturally, he was enjoying waiting for me to notice whatever it was that made this body worth a consultation.

"Cause of death?"

"Strangulation. See here on this… no, this one. You can see the ligature marks."

Barely. "Is she down in the morgue?"

Zimmerman shook his head. "No, she's at Charité. Just as well. There's no room here after your adventure last night, eh?"

I ignored this. "What are these markings? Are they bruises?"

He grinned again. "Ah, now this is why you're here, Kommissar."

I peered closer. There were patterns of dark marks around the woman's ankles and wrists, swirls and circles, lines and what might have been shapes. "What are those? Tattoos?"

"No. I am informed they are painted designs, using what the Hindus call henna." He reached deeper into the pile of images. "These are sketches of the designs."

The sketches made the patterns much clearer. Around the circumference of each wrist and ankle, there was a five-centimetre band of inked illustration, with what looked almost like a musical stave affixed with symbols created from swirling lines and shapes.

"Well, what do you think?" Zimmerman demanded impatiently after I had stared at the drawings for a while. He tapped the photographs. "Can you tell me anything useful or not?"

"I should see the body," I said. Zimmerman didn't see how this would help. I didn't either, but nothing was jumping out at me from the drawings. But then how could it? What I possibly know about these symbols?

"Is this some kind of… ritual killing? Who paints a woman's ankles and wrists, strangles her, then drops her off in the park like this?"

"Are you confident she wasn't killed in the park?"

"Of course!" he snapped. "She was found at dawn

on Monday morning. The police pathologist thinks she cannot have been dead for more than a few hours. At that time, as you must imagine, there would have been plenty of foot traffic crossing the bridge from Alt-Moabit. If she was murdered there, surely it would have been seen. No, she was dumped in the park, but killed somewhere else. I doubt you have any useful opinion about that either."

"Can I have copies of these sketches?"

"We are working on some. I will have them sent to Oberkommissar Teske."

I nodded, looked through the photographs one more time, then stepped back. "I shall look into these markings. Perhaps they will tell us something about her. Someone must know she is missing. Have you checked the missing persons reports?"

That was a mistake. "This isn't my first homicide, Kommissar Hoehner. You stick to those markings and leave the detective work to me." And with that, Amt VIIIb was dismissed.

Wrapped In Brown Paper And String

I pondered just what it was I was supposed to do now. Thus far, Oberkommissar Teske had not fully explained to me what Amt VIIIb's role was – perhaps he didn't entirely know himself. I recalled his speech about 'dark corners'. And now there I was, being asked to offer an opinion on designs inked onto a dead woman's limbs. What did I know?

I was considering this aspect of the case as I pushed open the door into Robbery, finding Obermeier and Fraulein Graber at my desk. She looked remarkably fresh for someone who had had barely more sleep than I, but then she had taken the chance to change her clothes. That wasn't a luxury I could look forward to.

Obermeier appeared even more wretched than usual. He had been up all night writing his story.

"Now they will not even publish it!" he complained sourly. "The political situation is all they care about. Peace!" He waved a copy of that morning's edition of *Vorwarts* over Fraulein Graber's head. "Have you heard that Gustav Noske has been sent by the government to Kiel to negotiate with the sailors? Those fellows hold all the cards now!" His mood had improved as he spoke, but as he dropped the newspaper on my desk, it subsided again. "No-one cares about missing soldiers any more."

I pulled over a chair from another desk and slumped into it heavily. Across the Bureau, I could see Oberkommissar Radel in his cubby hole, looking back at me with the impatient and frustrated expression of a *hausfrau* who wishes her drunken husband would just move out. I don't know what he was so upset about; his small squad was rattling around in the office as it was. Why would he require my desk so urgently? It was then that I noticed a parcel lay on it, wrapped in brown paper.

I moved to examine it, but was interrupted. "So, what now, Herr Kommissar?" Fraulein Graber asked.

I told them about the homicide. Obermeier's wild and wiry eyebrows lifted higher and higher, as in search of his hairline.

"What is this to do with us?"

I shrugged. "According to the Oberkommissar, this is what we do now." Obermeier appeared ready to resign from this unorthodox post.

"The Murder Büro are concerned that this killing is… ritualistic?"

"I don't know what they think, Fraulein Graber. It's possible they are just a day or two away from classifying the case as unsolvable. We should see if there is anything we can do. We should start by visiting the mortuary at Charité; perhaps there is something we can find about her person that allows us to identify her." I didn't really believe this; Zimmerman had surely investigated that far.

"When we get the sketches from the Murder Büro, we should take them to the Prussian State Library," suggested Fraulein Graber, with a knowing smile on her face. "Perhaps they will have something to explain what the designs mean."

I liked that idea too.

"But what about Rebirth, and the soldiers we have not yet traced?" Obermeier clearly did not relish the prospect of a long afternoon following behind librarians as they trailed through narrow passages beneath cliffs of unread books. He lowered his voice. "What of vO?"

"Herr Obermeier. Do you think, in light of the fact that this terrible conflict is coming to an end, that our crowded newspapers would print an article about the terrible losses suffered by our most noble families?"

"What's that? Are you trying to drive me mad, or

perhaps deprive me of the little credibility I have left with my colleagues?"

"You could conduct some research at the Hauptkadettenanstalt."

Now he caught on. "Oh! Yes, I see. Yes, I am sure there are many illustrative stories one might find there. Yes." He took up his hat, tipping it towards Fraulein Graber. "I will have to leave the Library to you both." Seizing up his coat, he made for the door, his step a lot more sprightly.

Once the door closed behind him, I turned back to my desk. Ah, yes... the parcel!

"Open it," suggested Fraulein Graber, with a smile.

The parcel contained a dark woolen overcoat, double-breasted and bearing a black leather belt. I held it up; someone had proved an excellent judge of my size.

"I..."

"Please accept it, Herr Kommissar. It was going to be gifted to charity in any case. You know how the government feels about people hoarding winter clothing."

"It looks brand new."

"You can't go out in winter without a coat." She was right, but that wasn't an option for a lot of people, and I felt guilty taking advantage of my new connection.

"Your cousin is quite a tall woman."

Fraulein Graber chuckled. "She stands out in a crowd, yes."

I tried the coat on. It was a more than decent fit, and not as heavy as I expected. This was a serious upgrade on my previous attire. Would it be impolite to wonder if this Amazonian cousin had a spare hat?

The Moltkebrücke

Wrapped in my new overcoat, I set out with Fraulein Graber for Charité, which had featured so prominently in our activities of the last few days.

First though, we detoured to the Tiergarten, and the spot in the north-east corner where our mysterious victim had been dumped. We took the Stadtbahn, passing through Friedrichstrasse Bahnhof, and then one more stop to the Berlin Hauptbahnhof. I was reminded again of our previous – and perhaps ongoing – investigation, but as we made our way down to street level, turning south to follow Friedrich List Ufer down to the Moltebrücke, I was caught by the number of people on foot through here. Nobody appeared to be short of warm clothing in this part of town.

We paused at the north end of the bridge. A broad street ran along the riverbank, and the wide expanse of Alt-Moabit stretched off to the north-west. These were major thoroughfares. Moabit was home to the Zellengefängnis on Lehterstrasse, and the more recently-built Central Criminal Court on Turmstrasse. Prison and court; I had plenty of history visiting both over the last year or so.

Then, across the bridge, lay a number of embassies and government buildings, and it was only a short walk from here to reach the Reichstag. In other words, plenty of well-heeled gentleman walked these streets day and night. I tried to imagine how it must have looked the night before last, in those hours before our poor victim was found. I watched a couple of automobiles turn onto the bridge, but mostly it was foot traffic.

Where had she come from?

"If she was brought here by car, she might have been brought any distance," Fraulein Graber commented, her mind in the same vein as my own.

Where had she come from?

"If she was brought here by car, she might have been carried any distance," Fraulein Graber commented, her mind in the same space as my own.

"And she must have been. Would you risk carrying a body through these streets, even one wrapped in a carpet or something similar?"

I glanced back the way we had come, towards the station. There were hotels up and down the streets around here, and so it would be worth eliminating them as places where the woman might have emanated from. That should be delegated to the uniformed boys.

As we crossed the bridge, another of those interminable, unavoidable trucks passed, laden with troops. These were clad in field grey, with red-white-black armbands, and imperial flags flying. Every one of them was armed to the teeth, with rifles in hand, and pistols and grenades thrust into their belts. They were singing some rousing nonsense – old tune, new words – but a few paused to call out some lewd remarks to Fraulein Graber. As they faced our way, I saw that some had that same crooked white cross painted on the front of their *stahlhelms*, the same design I had glimpsed on the helmet of the man who had been observing the unloading of the train at Friedrichstrasse Bahnhof.

"Hakenkreuzen."

"What's that?"

"That symbol. I've been seeing it a lot lately, especially on soldiers, or on their flags."

"What does it mean?"

"I'm not sure. Nothing good."

She developed that idea as we continued across the bridge in the truck's wake. "I used to see it used by some friends of the family, who bought into the whole New

Templars idea ten or so years ago."

"Never heard of that."

"*Völkisch* types. There was this fellow – what was his name? Ach, it will come to me. Anyway, he had all kinds of extreme idea about how different races shouldn't intermingle, and how some had polluted blood, that type of nonsense. There was always someone spouting off about it at hunting parties back then. Oh, that was his name: Jörg Lanz von Liebenfels. Though maybe that was a pseudonym, I can't remember now. They disappeared during the war, I think."

"Perhaps not," I said. The truck and its awful songs had disappeared off into the distance.

Though it connected through to the Grosser Tiergarten, technically, this area was more correctly called the Spreebogenpark. It was mostly open grass, with just a few scattered trees flanking paths that angled across the space. The nearest building appeared to have a clear view across the whole area. It was hard to imagine, even in the dead of night, anyone laying out a dead body here, or having the confidence that they would not be seen.

"Where was she found?"

I tried to work it out from my memory of the photographs. In the end, I settled on a spot not far from the roadway which was heavily trampled. Other than appreciating even more what an overlooked spot this was, there was nothing to be gained here.

"When you said she was found in the Tiergarten, I imagined something more private."

"Exactly. What was the purpose of leaving her here? Most often, if you're looking to dispose of a corpse, you dump it on some waste ground, or in an abandoned building. The Spree is very popular with some criminals. But this is quite... deliberate."

We were both looking at the nearby building. "What

is that?" I wondered out loud.

"It's a city building, isn't it? It doesn't appear to be in use."

Now that she mentioned it, it did give off an atmosphere of being empty. We walked over, but the ground floor windows were too high to see into, and the main entrance was closed. It struck me as odd that such a large structure would have been left unused in the capital during wartime, but both the city and national governments had huge stocks of buildings.

"Let's find out what this has been used for," I said. Fraulein Graber made a note.

For now, though, I wanted to get to Charité, and to view the dead woman.

Unbekannt

No matter what department you worked in, as a *bulle* you got to see plenty of dead bodies in Berlin. It had become worse in the last couple of years – last winter had been brutal, and the *schupos* had got used to finding emaciated corpses on their beats, and we were always being called out to houses that had developed a particular odour. Last January, I had pursued a suspected burglar into a building on Singerstrasse. I caught up with him on the stairs, frozen with shock in front of a family of four who appeared to have been living on the landing. They had frozen in the night.

A mortuary is no place to encounter the borderlands between life and death. In the police mortuary at the Praesidium, it was a regular occurrence to have civilians brought in to perform the formalities of identifying a body. They are already stressed at the thought of confronting the final, absolute proof of the loss of a loved one, and then they step into that place. They smell that smell.

The duty mortuary attendant at Charité was not interested in niceties. I showed him my beer token, told him what – who – I was looking for, and he led the way to the cold room, cigarette dangling from his lip, leaning on a cane. He opened a metal door and drew out a drawer covered in a white sheet. He peeled this back without announcement or ceremony.

The young woman lay on her back, perfectly ordered, peaceful. Her hair spilled about her head. Her eyes were closed, mouth too. Everything was pale. Oh, with the exception of a red line about her throat, right up under the chin, and some odd bruising here and there.

I examined her for a moment, but there was nothing that hadn't been evident in the crime scene photographs.

She was pretty, and if I am any judge, in her late twenties. Her hands were smooth; she had well-tended nails. I could see no telltale sign of hardened skin where a wedding ring might have sat. But surely she was missed by *someone*.

"I need to see her feet."

The attendant sighed at being made to open the drawer wider. I lifted that corner of the sheet myself to save him the burden.

There was a tag tied to her toe, of course. It had the date of her admittance and the single word: *unbekannt*. But she wasn't unknown, couldn't be. We would surely find where she belonged.

I bent to look at her ankles. Again, there was nothing to see here that I hadn't noticed in the photographs back at the Alex, though I did take a moment to confirm that the soles of her feet were smooth. And then there were the designs.

"Do you think these marks are fresh, Fraulein Graber?"

I turned to my colleague in that moment and realised my mistake. I wasn't here with an experienced colleague, but with someone who had been a councillor's assistant, who was the daughter of a man who had probably sought to shelter her from all kinds of things. And here I was, bringing her into a mortuary, and uncovering a dead woman who was probably about the same age as she was.

"I'm sorry. Let's step outside."

"I'm fine. No, really… fine. It's just… that smell."

I took her arm, and we went out into the corridor. She asked for a cigarette, and I lit up for both of us. For once, she took a long drag on the nail.

"This is ridiculous," she said at length.

"Everyone is the same. My first time, I –"

"This *isn't* my first time. I…" She paused, unwilling,

in the end, to relate whatever that story was. Instead, she snapped: "We saw men *burn*. I didn't feel faint then."

That would have been the adrenaline. I wondered how she had coped in those hours since. I knew that I still smelled smoke, and felt flames, as if we had never left Heilig Geist.

She dropped the cigarette to the floor, only partly smoked. I lit her another one, before I retrieved the one she had dropped. Waste not…

"She looked asleep."

"That's often the way," I said, with as soft a voice as I could manage. "Unless there is obvious sign of outward trauma, a dead body can look… peaceful. As if they might wake up, and smile, and ask you what the weather was outside."

She nodded. We smoked for a few minutes more while she stared at the ceiling. "What did you want me to look at?" she asked.

"Never mind. I think I know the answer for myself; those designs on her wrists and ankles are fresh. If they were painted on her much before the night she passed, I'm a Dutchman. And therefore, somehow, they relate to how, or why she died."

"Some poisons can be absorbed through the skin, isn't that right?"

I confirmed this, but at the same time I told her that isn't where my mind was going right now. "I want to talk to the pathologist here. I can do that alone, if you prefer, Irene."

She smiled weakly at my use of her given name. "It's all right. Shall we go?"

The hospital pathologist at Charité had an office just along the corridor. His name was Doktor Julius Bamberg, and he was about sixty years of age, with a few wispy strands of white hair, an extensive beard and the bushiest eyebrows I had ever seen. When he admitted us to his office, he had just concluded an autopsy report of a man who had dropped dead at work the day before.

Doktor Bamberg closed that folder, and once I had explained why we were there, reached for another.

"I have chosen to call her Anna," he said. "What would you like to know about her?"

"Anything you can tell me that might lead me to her people, or to those who did her harm."

Bamberg's hands trembled a little as he worked. He wore strong eyeglasses, and there was something about the way he turned his head and watched my mouth as I spoke that made me suspect he was a little deaf in one ear. I don't suppose the dead minded that he was not a more spritely man.

"I would surmise Anna to be between twenty-five and thirty-five years old. She has been in good health, although there is an abnormality in her left leg which makes me think she broke it, possibly as a child. Her heart, lungs and other organs were in excellent condition. She was 1.65 metres tall and weighed 54 kilograms. You might be interested to know she was... uh..." He glanced at Fraulein Graber, then whispered: "...*virgo intacta*." He lay down the file he had read this from.

"I suspect you would like to know cause of death?" There was a slight smile about the man's lips. He flicked his gaze between Fraulein Graber and I several times.

"Asphyxia, correct?"

"Yes. She was strangled with a ligature. I would surmise it was something like a silk scarf, perhaps the woman's own, eh? Pulled tight from behind. But, I would strongly indicate, it is likely that she was sedated before she was killed."

"Oh?"

Bamberg was enjoying the theatre of this. "Two

things. First, there are no tell-tale marks on her throat, or skin under her nails, to show she tried to fight back."

He smiled apologetically to Fraulein Graber. "When someone is strangled from behind, the first instinct is try to and pull at the ligature. One… claws at the rope, or scarf, and in so doing scratches at the neck."

"I see."

Bamberg turned back to me. "Also, I have examined the contents of her stomach. She ingested a small meal some hours before death – an evening meal, perhaps. Chicken and salad. Later, she drank a quantity of alcohol; several glasses of champagne. Finally, prior to death, she ingested a heavy sedative, in liquid form. She would have been rendered incapable of resistance within minutes. It was then that she was strangled."

I considered this for a moment. I could imagine a sequence of events, dinner, drinks, a private assignation, and then death. But at what point did the painting of her wrists and ankles factor into the sequence of events?

"Now, Herr Kommissar, we come to the more interesting aspects of the mystery behind Anna's death."

"The inking on her limbs?"

"That! Bah. Medically and pathologically insignificant. No, I am taking about what happened to her immediately post-mortem." He paused for effect. "She was suspended; hung upside down." What was that? "Did you see the discolouration of her face? It is what we call hypostatis, or livor mortis; the settling of heavy red blood cells into the lower extremities once the heart stops pumping. You can see this too in her hip, and along the side of her body where she lay on the ground after death."

I lifted a hand to give him pause. "Forgive me, Herr Doktor. I need you to speak to the consequences of what you have just told me in the plainest of terms. First, she is strangled."

"I think it is important to remember that first she was drugged, and that she drank alcohol. But yes, she was then strangled."

"But afterwards she is suspended by her ankles? How soon afterwards?"

"Oh, quite soon. Her arms must have been fastened at her sides." He drew a child's diagram on a sheet of paper he pulled from a drawer. "Like this. With her arms by her side, and not dangling below her head, because blood did not settle in her hands."

"For how long?"

He shrugged. "More than half an hour, but perhaps more like three or four hours. A lot depends on the temperature where this happened. Then she was taken down, and laid on her side, as I know she was found. She lay like that for just a few hours more."

My mind was racing. "So, you would estimate the time of death to be perhaps six, or even eight hours before she was found?" That would push the time of death back to as early as midnight.

"There are other indicators, particularly body temperature, which provide a more reliable estimate, but yes... She died at midnight, give or take a couple of hours before or after."

"And in the period after, she was suspended for a time by her ankles, and then lay on her side for a time up to when she was discovered."

"Yes, correct."

Fraulein Graber immediately caught onto what was rolling around in my brain. "She was not placed in any other position? Lain on her back?"

"Not for any length of time."

We sat in silence for several seconds. Bamberg watched our faces; he seemed to enjoy watching us catch up. Eventually, I asked him if there was anything else he could tell us, and he mentioned just one last thing before we rose and left his office.

Anna had been washed clean. Thoroughly. Her hair remained damp even by the time she arrived at Charité.

An Indecipherable Cypher

We ate a dissatisfying and hurried lunch in a dark and cheerless café near Charité, then raced back to the Praesidium to see if Zimmerman had delivered our copies of the sketches. He had, though these were as carelessly produced as had been our lunch. I had to hope they were accurate enough for our purposes.

I collected another item from my desk, which had been edged even further back towards one corner of the Robbery Büro. This was becoming intolerable, and I would need to speak with Teske about it, but right now we needed to get to the Prussian State Library.

The Library, on Unter Den Linden, was more properly known as the Royal Library, or the New Royal Library, to distinguish it from the old library on Bebelplatz, just across the street. It was a big building, and really needed to be, since it housed a copy of just about anything that had ever been published in the German language. And if there's one thing you can say about we Germans, we like to write a lot.

Fraulein Graber took charge of enquiring at the Information Desk inside the main hall. The attendant here was a stout, weary fellow in a uniform that not only did not fit him, but rendered him more like a hotel doorman than a state functionary. Eventually, he informed us that the fellow we wanted was up on the fifth floor, in part to put us as far away from him as possible, but perhaps also hoping to deter us from an arduous ascent. Fortunately for us, the elevator was in use.

On the fifth floor, we were guided to the office of the Direktor of Ancient Texts, a charming old rogue by the name of von Theriesenwald. He kissed Fraulein Graber's hand as if he was greeting some Bavarian Princess, and offered us coffee. A young fellow with one arm wa summonsed, and then dispatched in search of some.

Von Theriesenwald had a beautiful, cultured speaking voice, and would have been, one could imagine, quite handsome perhaps back in the days before Bismarck came to the fore. His blue eyes glistened whenever he turned them on Fraulein Graber.

"You say you have a book of ours?"

"I believe so." We had gained admittance on the back of the leather-bound volume we had found along with Kammerich's diary. I handed this now to Herr Professor von Theriesenwald, whose eyebrows shot upwards as he turned it over in hands. He opened the cover, then turned to the back.

"You are sure this belongs here? There are no stamps or identifying marks to suggest so."

I realised that I wasn't completely certain, and that we had simply associated the book with the confession in Kammerich's diary I explained this to the Direktor.

"The older parts of the royal collection do include some curious volumes, and ones which we have been historically reticent to mark in any way. These are kept in boxes, and the boxes contain their index classifications, and so forth. Your Herr Kammerich would have been quite privileged to have gained access to that part of our collection. Hmmm. It will be difficult to ascertain if this is such a book, since I cannot see a title, or author... or anything, really, which would identify it."

Until then, he had not looked at the body of the book, with its strange sigils and inscriptions. The moment he did so, he was even more bemused.

"What do we even have here? This is... well, it is not a language I recognise. What did you say this Kammerich believed it to be?"

"Some kind of ancient medical text." I realised I

should have brought the diary to consult.

"He called it 'Eastern'."

We were interrupted at that moment by the return of the young, one-armed man, bearing a silver tray with a tall coffee pot and three glasses. I could tell at once that this was actual coffee, not the ersatz nonsense we Berliners had become accustomed to. The aroma alone made my stomach grumble. The assistant poured three generous servings; von Theriesenwald heaped sugar into his, another luxury that I had grown out of.

"What were we saying? Ah, yes, the comment made by your Herr Kammerich. Well, Herr Kommissar, most everything appeared 'Eastern' to scholars back in the day. You say this Kammerich was able to read this book?"

"So he suggested," I said with waning confidence. "Assuming this is the right book."

Von Theriesenwald leafed through a few pages. "From this, I cannot so much as tell if it is meant to be read right to left or left to right. Or even top to bottom! These symbols… I do not think some of them are even complete. But if I had to guess, I would say that these are supposed to be pictograms, like hieroglyphics."

"Egyptian?"

"Ah, Herr Kommissar, Egyptian hieroglyphs are merely those we are most familiar with in the modern world. In truth, many ancient societies used them."

I nodded. Then I recalled something Kammerich had mentioned in his account. "Could it be Sumerian?" I took my first sip of scalding coffee. It was bliss.

Von Theriesenwald was intrigued by my question. He took up the book and peered at it more clearly. "What put that idea into your mind?"

"Something Doktor Kammerich wrote."

"Hmmm. It is possible… Sumerian writing was created by pressing a stylus into wet clay, we call this text cuneiform. I could… imagine… that some of these markings relate to Sumerian in this form, but I stress again that I do not believe the symbols are complete." He turned a page, then turned back. "Perhaps rather than being in Sumerian *per se*, that style of writing is being used as a code, a cypher."

"How might we discover what it says?" I asked.

Von Theriesenwald was still fixated on this one leaf. "Hmmm? Oh, you'd need an expert, and there are few of those around! Sumerian is a language we barely understand; it is quite isolated from almost anything else. I think you need to speak with someone at the Kaiser Friedrich Museum. They have the greatest collection of artefacts from Mesopotamia in the world! You should speak to Professor Schumann, I think. Although he might be in Istanbul right now…"

Less than useful. I was about to move onto the matter of Anna's henna tattoos when the Direktor repositioned the lamp on his desk and held the book so that a single leaf was exposed to the light. He squinted and moved closer.

"This is interesting…" he said, in a whisper. "The symbols on each side of the page line up precisely. Come and look, Herr Kommissar. Do you see? Now each symbol becomes more complex, more complete. A simple deception! These *might* be cuneiform symbols. Yes, I do think this is an avenue you should pursue with the Kaiser Friedrich Museum. It is outside of the purview of this library."

"Thank you, Herr Direktor. If I might take advantage of your time a little longer, at least for as long as it takes to finish this delicious coffee, could you look at these, and give me your opinion?" I passed him the sketches.

He chuckled as he took them. "I had no idea the

Berlin Police were faced with so many academic mysteries. What are these? Another cypher? These look like pictograms... on a musical stave? How intriguing! Where did you find these?" He made a point of holding these pages up to the light likewise, but there was no additional complexity to be found on Berlin Police notepaper.

"These two mysteries are not connected," he said, posing the remark midway between question and statement. I told him that they were quite separate.

"I fear your enquiries will follow similar paths. You will need to translate or decode these pictograms to understand the purpose of the designs. But what strikes me is that these could be chants. The pictograms represent the words to be sung, and their position on the lines shows the pitch at which they are to be sung. Modern musical notation has moved on from such methods, but a few hundred years ago, you might find designs such as these in manuscripts in monasteries and other places of worship. Well, perhaps not quite like these, but something similar."

Fraulein Graber and I shared a silent glance at each other. Von Theriesenwald observed this and smiled. "You two have quite the quest on your hands, I feel. I am sorry I can't be of any further assistance." He handed back the book and the sketches, with a finality that suggested his mind was already moving onto other things. I quickly finished my coffee. "One last question," Fraulein Graber said, as she rose to her feet.

"Of course, of course, my dear."

"You say the Library here exists to preserve and study texts in the German language. If we do have the correct book, as spoken of in the diary of Doktor Kammerich, why would it have been here for him to steal?"

Von Theriesenwald had risen and was moving around his desk to help her into her coat. "Ah, I see. Well, although that is our current purpose, it was not always so.

The Library was originally based on the private collection of Frederick William, Elector of Brandenburg, back in the Seventeenth Century. It was he who ordered that the collection be catalogued and made available for public reading. His successor, Frederick I, more than doubled the collection, and he introduced the first legal deposit law, which means that a copy of each book published in Germany should, by law, be here. In those early days, in particular, the collection was far more eclectic than it is today. We have a separate department which looks after volumes outside of the German language."

"I see. Would the Direktor there know more…?"

"I am afraid Herr Abst died three months ago. This dreadful flu epidemic."

"Ah. My condolences. Is there someone else…?"

"I regret that there is no-one who can help you in this regard, Herr Kommissar. I am so sorry."

We shook hands. Moments later, Fraulein Graber and I were out in the corridor. Nothing about von Theriesenwald's demeanour had changed at all, but we had been courteously shown the door.

"That was odd," Fraulein Graber suggested, as we headed for the stairs. "He never once asked for the return of the book, even if just to check that it was theirs."

I placed the items back in the briefcase I carried. We paused at a balcony overlooking the interior of the building. Fraulein Graber fussed with her green hat and matching gloves. "Did we learn anything useful?"

That was debatable. I let my eyes wander about the library, trying to imagine what secrets might be buried on its least accessible shelves. I suspected that I would be a long time finding out.

"What now?"

I wanted to get outside so I could enjoy a cigarette and a longer chance to think. "Back to the Alex. We should get a photograph of 'Anna' circulated around where she was found."

"Because she was murdered nearby…"

"Precisely."

vO

Obermeier was back in the Robbery Büro when we returned, battering the life out of my Adler 7 typewriter. He was most assuredly in a hurry with whatever he was doing, since he had not even removed his hat. A cigarette dangled from his lip, trembling with each impact of his paws on the typewriter keys.

"Are you also writing reports for Oberkommissar Teske now, Herr Obermeier?"

"Ah! Gerhard! Irene! No, I leave such official reports to you, Herr Inspektor. These are my notes to allow me to write a front-page article for the newspaper!"

I peered over his shoulder, which he found disturbing. "Have you solved our case?" I asked him.

He took the sheet from the machine and stacked it with three or four others, then turned the chair to lean closer to Fraulein Graber and myself. His voice was low, conspiratorial.

"I have, perhaps, deepened the mystery."

I was intrigued, but I didn't want to discuss this in Robbery. At my urging, we three stepped out into the hall.

"I have found 'vO'," Obermeier said with pride.

We moved further along the hall, closer to Vice. At this time of day, there would be next to no-one on this part of the floor.

"Well?"

"Colonel von Osterbruck. Here is a decorated war hero, no less, who served at the headquarters of Eighth Army during the Battle of Tannenburg, and who commanded a regiment on the Western Front until it was more or less wiped out during Operation Michael. He was then reassigned. And that is where things get interesting."

Obermeier was almost dancing with excitement. He

drew us close, into a cloud of dark tobacco smoke.

"His new assignment was with the 214th Division. That's right. Generalmajor Maercker's command. That's a very tidy connection, wouldn't you say?"

He wasn't wrong. "Those men from the 214th, the ones I arrested. We should talk to them."

"Yes, we should, and I already made enquiries. However, it turns out they were released that same morning we arrested them. Orders from on high."

That was my fault. I had taken my eyes off the ball with them. At the very least I should have made sure I knew where they were reporting to here in Berlin.

"So, where did you find von Osterbruck?"

"I haven't encountered the gentleman directly, not yet, but I did speak with a Feldwebel at the Hauptkadetten-anstalt, who said that von Osterbruck had been back in Berlin for about a month, on the direct orders of Generalmajor Maercker and with the agreement of the commandant of the Academy. The word is that Maercker, and he is not alone in this, considers the war against the Allies lost, and that it is the duty of the German Army to prevent a revolution by the Bolshevists. The suggestion was that this was why the Kaiser took himself to Army Headquarters in Spa, so that he could lead the troops back to the Fatherland in person. It is believed that there are loyal regiments in the garrisons here who could be relied on in such circumstances."

I listened to those words with a growing sense of foreboding. The right-leaning newspapers had been spewing out a diet of fear and hatred against the left ever since the Mutiny had started in Wilhelmshaven and Kiel. And those uniformed goons I had been seeing with greater and greater regularity; what else were they preaching other than the suppression of revolution before it could even begin.

"What is von Osterbruck doing in Berlin, if it is the Army in the West that is going to be used in this way?"

"Generalmajor Maercker has been mooting that the Berlin garrison, along with others throughout the country, should be ready to strike against the Reds, even without orders or authority from the government. They are suggesting, for example, that the troops who were moved from the front to shore up the Austrian front should be ordered to put down the Reds in Munich. Apparently, it is chaos down there."

"They have the Kaiser's authority for this?"

"No! What would that even mean? The Kaiser has been a figurehead for most of the last four years. That is all he would be to these counter-revolutionaries. No, these elements do not march to the orders of any organised government any more. They are starting to call themselves *freikorps*."

"What's that? Like they used to call the irregulars who fought against Napoleon?" It was a heady part of our national identity.

Obermeier sneered. "These modern army types like the romantic allusion. Poets and students standing shoulder to shoulder against the common enemy. Pah! They're freebooters who like the idea of murdering socialists without consequence. The government better quash these notions quickly!"

This was worrying news, sure enough, but it didn't yet draw a path through to a solution of our case.

"Where is von Osterbruck now?"

"That I cannot be certain of. My Feldwebel said these people are active all over the city." Judging by what we had seen, that was likely to be true.

"Where do the invalids fit in?" asked Fraulein Graber, proving more the most focused of the three of us.

"Find von Osterbruck, and we'll find the invalids," I

suggested with greater confidence than I truly felt.

"Where do we start?" Obermeier was brimming with enthusiasm.

"Slow down, Klaus. We have this other matter to work on. The Oberkommissar isn't going to accept us ignoring the woman's death, especially if it means butting heads with the Army. Fraulein Graber, would you mind going down to Homicide and using your charm to get me a photograph of the dead woman's face?"

"Of course."

"With what we learned today, I am certain she was killed somewhere near the Hauptbahnhof or Alt Moabit, and if the pathologist at Charité is correct, it happened around midnight. We need to find someone, anyone, who saw something curious in that area around that time. Whatever Anna went through, it took time to organise and execute, and it required privacy. We need to find where she died."

Interdepartmental Cooperation

It proved easier to get the Alex's tame photographers, Goldstein and Blau, to make prints from the negatives than to prise anything from the grasp of Zimmerman and his posse in the Murder Büro. It would, however, take a few hours for them to get me sufficient copies, and so I returned to Robbery to type up the day's report, and then to call on Oberkommissar Teske.

"Ah, Kommissar Hoehner. Is that your report?"

I handed it over. "We have made some progress, Herr Oberkommissar. I have confidence that the woman was killed in the vicinity of where the body was found."

Teske lifted his head enough to study my face for a moment. "That is not the opinion of Herr Inspektor Zimmerman." He tapped another report that was already set on his desk.

"I shared the Kommissar's… concerns… originally. It seemed most likely that the woman was killed in one place, and then brought to the Tiergarten by vehicle, a truck perhaps. She could then be swiftly dropped near the road. This theory meant that the murder scene could be anywhere, up to three hours drive from the centre of Berlin."

"Exactly."

"Now, with better information from the pathologist at Charité, I believe she remained at the murder scene for a few hours, and then was dropped in the Spreebogenpark a couple of hours before she was found. That reduces the window in which she might have been in the back of a lorry considerably."

Teske was reading, chewing on his lip as he did so. "We believe this because of the scientific evidence, as provided by this Doktor…"

"Bamberg."

"Yes. Julius Bamberg. Is he a Jewish gentleman, by any chance?"

"I didn't ask. Does it matter?"

"Not to me. Have you shown this information to Kommissar Zimmerman?"

"Was I supposed to, Herr Oberkommissar?"

"Not before you showed it to me, Hoehner. Now, how do you proceed?"

"I want to show the woman's picture to every night porter in Moabit, and every station worker on the night shift at the Hauptbahnhof."

"Good. Another sleepless night, Herr Kommissar."

"That doesn't worry me at all, sir."

"Good, good. Now I have some news for you. From tomorrow morning Amt VIIIb will have its own offices. Room B2. Desks are being moved in as we speak, and you should have a telephone connection by the morning. Give me a list of anything else you need. I will also need a report on how things are working out with Herr Obermeier and Fraulein Graber. There will need to be formalities."

"B2? Where is that?"

"In the basement. You are going to have to work your way up, Kommissar Hoehner"

He thought this was very droll.

Herr Obermeier's Thesis

We ate dinner at what was becoming our habitual table in Ascher's. Though the waiters still deferred to Fraulein Graber, they had at least learned which brand of schnapps I preferred. We were served promptly, and then they kept out of the way so we could talk.

Obermeier was greatly amused at being coopted into the establishment. He felt like he would need to keep it secret from his colleagues on *Vorwarts*, but he added his opinion that the socialist movement was riddled with police spies.

"The political police probably contribute more to socialist discourse than the socialists!" he exclaimed, a little too loudly for my tastes, waving his cigarette around. "Of course, we will all be standing against a wall, come the revolution." He was remarkably sanguine about this.

"Can we try to solve this new case before you have us all shot?"

"Of course, of course."

I pushed thin slivers of what might have been meat around my soup, my appetite not up to par. It's an old adage along soldiers that you never turn down a meal, because you can't be certain when you'll see another one. I had drifted a long way from that life, even in ration-stricken Berlin. "Who do we imagine 'Anna' to be?"

"No working girl!" Obermeier observed, still a little loud. "Thirty years old, and still a virgin. A nun perhaps?"

Fraulein Graber's expression was quite sour on hearing this. Obermeier noticed her irritation and apologised.

"A nun would not have such soft hands," she remarked.

"She was not used to manual labour of any kind," I

agreed. "A girl from a good family, perhaps? But why, then, have we not heard enquiries from them? No concerns have been raised that I know of."

"Perhaps she is not from Berlin?"

Obermeier's point was valid. "But why bring a girl all the way here for... that?"

"Perhaps precisely because of the confusion we now experience. She is *unbekannt*. If she had a name, an identity, perhaps we would then see the link to those who took her."

"Her anonymity may well be the whole point," Fraulein Graber agreed.

"A recent arrival," I said, letting my imagination wander. "She arrives in the city, looking for a place to live and a job. She meets a man; perhaps om the train. He suggests that if she presents herself at a particular hotel room, at a particular hour, she might find what she is looking for."

"You are convinced that there is some connection to a hotel, Herr Kommissar?"

"More in hope than expectation, Fraulein Graber. But, in my imagination, she had to have been murdered somewhere that is both quiet, but well-trafficked. A place where the comings and goings of a number of men, and one woman, would not be out of place."

Obermeier leant in, looking around in a way that surely only made us look more conspiratorial. "We should discuss the other concern with this affair. The method of her death. Am I alone in thinking that this is the work of some kind of sexual maniac?"

Fraulein Graber seemed to lean a little further away from Obermeier. She grimaced and tutted. "What makes your mind go in that direction?"

"Again, *gnadiges fraulein*, I mean no offence. But does it not strike you that there are certain... ritualistic... qualities to this crime?" He paused for a moment, then began to list the reasons for his assertion on the fingers of his left hand.

"For one, consider that she was found... nude. Then, there are the ink designs on her feet and wrists, and the possibility that these are connected to some kind of chant. And, also, she was suspended upside down. These are uncommon factors in a murder, as I am sure the Kommissar would agree."

"Before the weekend I was a humble Robbery detective," I remarked.

"Of course, but you have some experience of how these things go. Violence against women is altogether too common in our paternalistic society." I gestured for him to continue. "'Anna' showed no signs of violence, beyond her strangulation. She was not beaten. This is no crime of passion, or an assault by an angry lover. This was deliberate, calculated."

"Murder is murder," Fraulein Graber murmured. And then more forcefully she added: "She is no less dead for all these things you mention."

"That is correct. But we cannot ignore the method of her killing." He paused to stub out the last fraction of one cigarette, and light another. "May I explain?"

Fraulein Graber shrugged. I told him to proceed, but to keep his voice down. He took a moment to consider where to begin his exposition, then leaned in once more.

"This war has done terrible things to Germany. Think back, if you are able, to how things were in 1913. How ordered everything was, how... routine. The Kaiser may have been erratic, but he represented stability – a sclerotic, illiberal stability, but still."

"I do not think this is the time or place for one of your political lectures," I advised Obermeier.

"That is not my purpose. I merely wish to illustrate how our world has changed. Our Germany. Our Berlin. The old certainties were destroyed; the old order has been consigned to the dustbin." He anticipated my objections. "I know, Herr Kommissar. It seemed for a time that things had become *more* ordered, with the military in charge of almost every aspect of our lives. But, in reality, they were focused on one goal only – victory in the war, and in the meantime every other function of government was neglected and allowed to wither."

"Where are you going with this?"

"I admit: I am explaining this badly. What I mean to say is that society has been profoundly altered by the war. It is not just the privations that afflict us, but a breakdown in all the structures that bound us together. These protests we see on the streets every day are just the most recent manifestations, the last writhing paroxysms against the old ways. Soon, something new must come to take their place."

I was ready for more schnapps. Obermeier held up his hand to give me pause. "When I was at the Hauptkadettenanstalt, my friend the Feldwebel told me that 3,000 graduates of the academy are known to have died at the front. Not so many, when millions have died, no? But these were the sons of the highest families in the land. Such loss has been unbearable. For even the richest, most privileged among us, it has been unbearable. Perhaps even more for them, who had more to lose."

"Please, Obermeier. Stop dancing around and get to your point."

"Very well. Do you understand what I mean when I speak of spiritualism?"

"Hmmm? Are you speaking of those charlatans who profess to be able to speak with the dead?" I was reminded that Kammerich had been invited to a Spiritualist gathering. Was this another link between our two cases?

"There is more to it than that," Fraulein Graber said, before Obermeier could continue.

"Yes, yes," he said. "They have been around for decades, of course, both the charlatans you speak of, and those who believe, or yearn to believe. It is a false 'science', naturally. But, I can assure you, they are no longer utterly on the fringes of society. That is the consequence of so many dead, of so many more grieving. There are more people than ever who believe that, through some medium, they could reach out to the soul of their lost sons. And that may be just the beginning."

"What do you mean?"

"If you had lost a son to the war, what would be the one thing better than being able to talk to that son once more?"

I struggled to see what he meant, but Fraulein Graber understood immediately.

"You'd want to get him back."

The Hotel Graz

We continued this conversation fitfully as we made our way across the centre of the city. The sun had long since set, and there was a chill in the air that made our breath steam in front of our faces as we walked, huddled, through the darkened streets.

"Are you suggesting… *black magic*?"

"Let me be clear, Herr Kommissar, I do not believe in such nonsense myself. But I am aware that there are some who, quite frankly, have become desperate enough to stoop to witchcraft and superstition. There have been whispers in the last few months, years even, of societies dedicated to dark arts, to ancient knowledge. It may all be hocum, but there are those who follow such beliefs, and therefore others who will exploit them. As authority breaks down, this can only become worse."

"In God's name…" I sighed.

"It is the absence of God that allows this to spread. This is why I spoke of the collapse of order in Germany. When all the different pillars that propped up the Imperial German state have failed, then why should they stand any more? Why should people not cleave to new beliefs?"

"You know people like this?"

We were on the Stadtbahn, heading for the Hauptbahnhof once more. As we lurched about a curve, Obermeier dropped a cigarette he had been rolling. His language was profane. "My pardon, Fraulein Graber," he said, regaining his self-control. "I did not previously use such language. I feel as if the last few days have strained my last nerve. I have not slept for several nights now."

He picked up the spilled tobacco and set it back in his tin. "I shall need more tobacco before this night is over."

"There is a kiosk at the station," I reminded him.

"Finish what you were saying."

"What was it you asked? Do I know people who have taken up such beliefs? If you mean frightened, bereaved, unstable people, then yes, yes, I do. If you mean am I acquainted with wizards and warlocks, then no. But…" He pointed at me dramatically. "I could give you the addresses of at least five prominent men, where, as regular as clockwork, seances are held, or other gatherings. There is a Minister I could name… but I shall not. Meanwhile, the poor gather at meeting halls or in the cellars of theatres, to listen to charlatans. Didn't we find a leaflet for such a gathering among the post held for Doktor Kammerich? Even rational, scientific men are caught up in it. It's a disease; worse than the Spanish Influenza, if you want my opinion."

"But you're not suggesting that these are all…" What was I going to call them? "Demon worshippers? Satanists?"

"That is not what these people are," insisted Fraulein Graber. "That is not what he is saying."

"Then what?"

Obermeier chuckled. "Look, most of these gatherings are just opportunities for fraud and deceit. And all those I have ever heard of were just excuses to get drunk and fondle pretty girls." He tilted his hat. "I apologise, Fraulein Graber."

She replied irritably: "If we are to work together, you should both get past feeling you need to apologise each time you speak about such matters in front of me."

I was still taking in the import of what Obermeier was revealing. "These gatherings are excuses for debauchery?"

Obermeier shifted in his seat and looked out of the window. "We are almost there. Yes, yes, Herr Kommissar. Masked men and naked women; drunkenness and narcotics. It is just the same as we encountered at the Astrakhan, but with some gibberish incantations and a priest who will promise power and sex to those pay. You understand what I am saying now?"

I felt that he had changed his tune somewhat during this journey. He almost seemed to be downplaying the seriousness of the things he had revealed.

"You think there was some... ritual... behind this girl's murder?"

"Perhaps. Who knows? But this 'Anna', she wasn't murdered for sex, or in anger. She was... sacrificed."

We stepped out onto the platform at the Hauptbahnhof. Obermeier went off to buy tobacco.

"What do you make of that?" asked Fraulein Graber.

I couldn't answer that straight. "Have you never read his articles in *Vorwarts*? Obermeier has an over-active imagination." I wondered if I still had the leaflet we had recovered from Trude Holstadt. I had a feeling that we would need to visit one of these spiritualist gatherings if we were to obtain a better understanding of their form and purpose, untainted by a newspaperman's need for sensationalism.

Frauline Graber smiled weakly. I paused to look at one of the prints we had obtained from Goldstein and Blau, a slightly grainy image of the face of the dead woman, a modern death mask. There was a rigidity about her expression that did not suggest she was merely asleep. I wondered what the last thing had been her eyes had seen, before they closed for the last time. Disturbed by Obermeier's assertions, my own imagination was running just as wild.

Moments later, Obermeier returned, and we descended to street level. I handed my colleagues separate copies of the print.

"We'll split up. Herr Obermeier, if you would begin

on Alt-Moabit? Fraulein Graber; perhaps you might try north of the station. Any hotel, any rooming house, even the bars and cafés; show them this photograph and see if they recognise her. But also ask if they saw or heard anything unusual two nights ago. Anything unusual at all. But especially anyone carrying an awkward load towards the Moltkebrücke. I'll be down that way, so come and find me if you hear anything interesting. We'll meet back here at…" I checked my watch. "Half past ten. Please keep to the main streets, Fraulein. Anything we can't cover, we'll have the *schupos* look into."

I had selected for myself the short road that led directly from the Hauptbahnhof to the river and the Moltkebrüche, having observed several hotels on our previous visit.

The next hour was frustrating. Generally speaking, the hotels weren't seeing much trade at this time. It was winter, the economy was completely skewed because of the war, and they were struggling for staff. In this latter instance, what it meant was that the concierges and desk managers at different establishments were not of the finest quality.

Take the fellow I met at the Great Northern Hotel. I walked up to hotel reception and asked to speak to the desk manager. The fellow behind the counter informed me that he was Friedrich Bodenhof, the assistant manager, and that his chief had finished for the day. Bodenhof was a man of about fifty, with straggly white hair and a lazy eye. He was also an invalid, with his left arm amputated below the elbow. He made a point of barely looking when I produced my beer token and introduced myself.

"Were you working two evenings ago, Herr Bodenhof?"

He continued to focus on the paperwork he was engaged with. "I work most evenings, Herr Kommissar.

Except for Sundays, which is my night off."

"That is unfortunate. I am looking to find a young woman who may have been in this hotel on Sunday evening."

He lifted his head and fixed one good eye on me. "The misfortune is mine. Herr Föster, who would normally work Sunday evenings, was ill. I had to come in."

"So, you *were* on duty?" Why couldn't he have said that in the first place? "Take a look at this" I produced the print without warning Bodenhof what it showed. He glanced at it.

"I do not recognise her."

"Could you take a closer look? Obviously, it is not always easy to recognise a living person from such a photograph."

He grimaced, but then made a grudging effort. "She is not… *has not* been a guest at this hotel."

As Oberkommissar Teske might say: never answer a question you weren't asked. "But might you have seen her on Sunday evening?"

"I think not." He made a point of not glancing towards the photograph again. I struggled with his attitude, but this was not the first, nor will it be the last time, that a potential witness had kept solidly distant to something the police were interested in. Not everyone you meet is a crook, but an awful lot them are strictly agnostic when it comes to the law.

I took up the photograph and placed it back in my pocket. "One last question. Did this hotel host a private party of any kind on Sunday?"

"Not that I know of."

That was so vague and dismissive that I almost left there and then. 'Not that I know of'! How often would there be a party in this place, and they wouldn't know anything about it on the desk? But I decided to ask the last question on my mental list.

"You didn't see anything unusual?"

Bodenhof was still on the question before. "There was a party at the Hotel Graz, though. You might want to ask there."

Oh. His answer was purely a ploy to get rid of me, of course, but little did he know how valuable his information was to become. I thanked him and turned away from the desk.

As I left the Great Northern, I looked south along the street, and caught sight of the sign for the Hotel Graz. There were a couple of intervening establishments, I noticed, but I decided I would go to the Graz first. As I started to walk, I heard a voice call my name, and turned to find Fraulein Graber walking towards me at a brisk pace. There was something about her gait, and the way she twice looked back over her shoulder, that caused me a small tremor of anxiety.

"Fraulein Graber?"

She came up and took my arm. "Herr Kommissar…" Once more, she looked back the way she had come.

"Is something wrong?"

"It's nothing. I was just… unsettled for a moment there."

As she spoke, I saw someone in the shadow of a building on the other side of the street. They had been walking south from the station, but now paused, loitered for a few heartbeats, and then turned back, head bowed, shoulders hunched under their overcoat. In the hard darkness of that night, illuminated only now and then by light spilling from a window or doorway, I could only make out that the figure was quite tall, quite broad, and quite heavy.

"Did something happen, Fraulein Graber?"

Her gaze followed mine, back along the street. "I'm

sure it's nothing. I just felt as if someone was… following me for a moment there."

"That man?" I asked, deciding that if the figure was a creep, it had to be male.

"No, no. Someone much smaller. I think he was in uniform."

The big shadow was slipping out of sight as they approached the station. They pressed brusquely past an older couple and were gone.

"It was just a feeling, Herr Kommissar. I had no luck in the few hotels I visited, and then I felt a little uncomfortable. I walked back to the Hauptbahnhof, and that was where I became convinced a man was following me. I came through the station, to assure myself that he was not just simply making his way to catch a train, but then I saw him again as I came down the stairs to the street." She came up onto her toes and peered into the darkness. "I can't see him now. Perhaps I made a mistake. I feel foolish for my apprehension."

"Perhaps it was a mistake to separate."

"I was fine on my own at first, although it was difficult to get any information out of anyone. They refused to believe I was associated with the police in any way."

That was something we were going to have to deal with. I checked the time and took one more hard look along the street. The old couple passed us; he a bent old man leaning on a cane, she emaciated and under-dressed for such an evening.

"It's just after ten o'clock. We'll go back and meet Herr Obermeier shortly. But I want to stop off at just one of these last few hotels." I indicated the Graz. We set off together, crossing the road to fall in behind the elderly couple. Fraulein Graber still had her arm linked with mine. I wasn't minded to stop her.

The Graz was a more modest establishment than the

Great Northern, with a cramped vestibule just behind the entrance. The night manager was not behind his desk, and only appeared after I rang the bell, pulling up his suspenders over a grimy vest that featured a great number of small holes burned by cigarette ash. He was portly, balding, and sweated profusely. He coughed into his fist as he came to the desk.

"For the night, or just by the hour?" he asked, with a lascivious grin towards Fraulein Graber. I showed him my beer token. "My mistake! I didn't mean anything by it!"

"I'm Kommissar Hoehner of the Berlin Police, and this is my colleague. Are you the manager here?"

"No! He's never here. Could be dead for all I know."

"Did you work Sunday night?"

"I'm always here!" he announced, as if he was filing a complaint. He took up a cloth and gave the desk a wipe, though that surface was beyond saving. "Eight in the evening to eight in the morning, seven days a week."

"Tell me about Sunday. You had a party here?"

His eyes widened. "Why do you ask?"

"Just answer the question."

He dropped the cloth and leaned a little closer. His breath drank of alcohol. "I wouldn't call it a party, exactly. Some army types, they hired the room downstairs. Lots of booze. I told them we had a couple of rooms upstairs that might be more suitable, but they said they wanted the privacy."

I leaned my own head a little closer as well, trying not to breath in the fugue coming from his body. "Privacy for what?"

"Look, Kommissar…"

"Hoehner. Kommissar Hoehner."

"Right, right. Look, you know how it goes. They were planning to let off a bit of steam, OK? A lot of drinking and patriotic songs."

"Women?"

The night manager winced. "It was nothing illegal! You know how it is. A few girls... well, things have changed during the way, wouldn't you say? The rules are different these days."

I wasn't at all interested in his views on the changing social mores of late war Berlin.

"Show me this room."

The door that led to the basement was close at hand, just beside the stairway that led up to the main body of the hotel. The stair down to the basement was pitch dark, and we had to guide ourselves down by the scant illumination provided from the vestibule. In the basement itself, the night manager quickly lit a few oil lanterns. It was still quite gloomy down there, but we could just about see the noses in front of our faces.

"It's mostly used for storage," our host informed us.

That was apparent. There was an assortment of mismatched chairs along one wall, some stacked on top of each other, and several boxes of assorted junk, including candle holders, ashtrays, cushions and pillows. I kicked an empty brandy bottle that was lying on the floor, and it clattered against the stair post.

"What time were they here?"

"They got started at about ten, and it was all over by... perhaps two o'clock?"

"Did you clear up afterwards?"

He shrugged. "I came down to pick up the glasses."

I continued to look through the boxes. Fraulein Graber slipped past me and went to the far end of the room.

"You didn't come down here to see what was going on?"

The fellow scratched his head, then his belly. "Herr Kommissar, I don't need to know what goes on with these parties."

"Parties? These events have happened before?"

He looked stricken with regret. "They just pay me for the room, Herr Kommissar! I don't pry."

I noted the pronoun. I suspect it was easier to make a little money on the side renting out the basement for an evening than it might be to skim the takings from the by the hour trade. 'They' struck me as regular and valued customers.

"You said there were girls. How many?"

"I didn't count, Herr Kommissar! Six, maybe?" I reasoned that he probably knew some of them as well as the men who hired the room.

I showed him the photograph. "Was she one of them?"

His eyes grew wider than ever. "Is that...? Is she *dead*? Look, Herr Kommissar, this is all –"

"Do you *recognise* her?"

"No, no. I swear! The girls all looked the same... pretty, blonde, lots of make-up. She could have been one of them, but..."

"And how many men were there?"

He swallowed. "Eight, maybe? Ten? I don't know." Liar.

"But you spoke to one of them at least, correct? You must have. Someone hired the room, and you talked about a price, and you've already said that you discussed giving them a better room upstairs."

The night manager was looking quite pale. "It didn't take so long..."

"So, who was this fellow?"

"I didn't get a name."

"No? But you can describe him surely. He was a soldier? What rank?"

"I don't know..."

I took a moment, offered some cigarettes around, lit up for the three of us. Fraulein Graber was still poking around at the far end of the room. I heard her shifting boxes. I held her cigarette for her.

"Tell me your name, *Mein Herr*."

"Seydlitz. Joachim Seydlitz."

"So, Herr Seydlitz. Don't try to sell me any horse crap. You've served, right?"

He swallowed hard, then nodded. "Sure. Two years."

"We're brothers in arms, Herr Seydlitz. I was at Verdun; got gassed there."

The cigarette wobbled on his lip. "I was in at the start. I got wounded on the Marne, and then again on the Somme. That was a belly wound." He started to pull at his vest as if we were about to swap scars and war stories. I held up a hand.

"You were lucky, my friend. Those things are not so easy to survive." I didn't remark that he looked like a man who could take a hit to the gut. "So, let's be straight with each other, shall we? Who was this soldier who booked this room?"

Seydlitz took a long hard drag on his cigarette, fidgeted with his suspenders. "I didn't get a name. He was a captain. They were all officers, or senior NCOs, but he was definitely in charge. They were all in their ordinary uniforms – not dress uniforms like this was going to be some formal affair. I didn't think they wanted the room for a regimental dinner!"

"Good, good. What more can you tell me about him?"

"You know the type, Herr Kommissar. Tailored uniform, slicked back hair, too good-looking by half. Not the kind who would ever get shot in the gut and lie in the mud begging for help." As he said, this, and twisted his lips in a sour expression, Seydlitz tapped his throat. "Still got himself a Blue Max, though."

I felt my heart skip a beat.

"A *pour le mérite*? Are you sure?"

"You don't mistake one of those! I've only seen two of them ever, and he was the second. You wouldn't normally see a medal on an ordinary uniform, right? But a Blue Max, well."

"What else can you remember?"

"What else? I don't know. He was tall, I guess…"

"Did he smoke?"

"Oh, yes! He even offered me a couple of his smokes. American. Didn't like the taste myself, but…"

I looked away. My mind was reeling at what I was hearing. Of course, it wasn't definitive proof, but how many holders of the *Pour Le Mérite* were there? They didn't hand them out like Iron Crosses (even I had one of those somewhere).

As I tried to take in what I had learned, I heard Fraulein Graber call my name. There was an edge to her voice that suggested she felt she had found something, but I was sure I could trump just about anything!

I don't pretend to be right every time.

Signs

I went over to her, feeling broken glass crunch under my shoes. Before I got to where she was standing, she held up a hand to make me pause. I handed her the remains of the cigarette I had lit for her.

"Look on the floor, Herr Kommissar."

I did as she suggested; a glance, at first, then I took an oil lantern from a shelf and knelt to look more closely. The floor of the basement was made from large stone flags, most of which were cracked. This area had been buried under more of the boxes that lay strewn all over the basement; Fraulein Graber had moved several to one side.

"I'm sorry, Herr Kommissar, I disturbed them when I moved the boxes."

She was indicating some scuffed chalk marks. Two lines met at an acute angle. I could see part of the arc of a circle stretching off to one side. This latter mark consisted of a series of parallel lines, with curious symbols on them.

"*Liebe Gott,*" I muttered.

"It's the same, isn't it?"

"Say nothing here, Fraulein Graber."

She nodded briskly; her eyes gleaming. "Now, see here, Herr Kommissar." She was pointing over the top of the remaining boxes, towards the wall at that end of the room. Propped against the brickwork, stood on one end, was a heavy iron bedstead.

I was at the point of telling her to go and fetch Obermeier, when I remembered her scare from before. Instead, I barked at the night porter, asking if the establishment had a telephone. It did not. I told Seydlitz to run at once to the railway station and find a *schupo*; they should normally be one or two hanging around there at night. I added a description of Obermeier, just on the off-chance he might spot him too. Seydlitz opened his mouth to protest, reluctant to abandon his post, but I imagined he realised that trade was about to drop off for the night. It was only after he left that I wondered if he might just hoof it altogether, but that was a chance we were going to have to take.

I put out my cigarette; Fraulein Graber had hardly touched hers, but she handed over the pinched-out remnant, and I put both back in the tin.

"Give me a hand with these boxes. We'll leave the ones that are actually on the floor, so we don't wipe off any more of these marks. Here, take this one, it's not so heavy."

It only took a few minutes to complete this task. None of the boxes were heavy; in fact, a few were empty. I peeked into a few, but the contents were mundane, except for one which contained some leather belts. These seemed a little out of place.

Oh, and then there was the box containing a full set of clothes, including shoes. A woollen dress, a well-lined topcoat, underslip and stockings... I held the coat up and Fraulein Graber and I inspected it together.

"Can you recall how tall 'Anna' was?"

"One meter sixty-five."

"You're a little taller?"

"One seventy."

"This looks about the right size for you." Fraulein Graber agreed. "This is almost too good to be true. Check to see if there are any laundry labels, or anything that might identify whose property this is. Check that box over there. It would change everything if we could find a purse."

But we weren't that lucky. Fraulein Graber noted that the coat had been purchased from Hermann Tietz. There were a couple of these department stores here in Berlin, including a huge one on Alexanderplatz, but they would not record the names of customers who bought such a coat. In any case, there were branches all over eastern

Germany.

"Do you think she was a Berliner?"

I didn't. "A girl like 'Anna', surely someone would have missed her by now. I checked the reports; there is nothing."

"She must have lived somewhere."

I still couldn't shake the impression that she was a recent arrival. All the same, that should mean that there would be a hotel with a tenant who had failed to extend her stay and had left luggage in her room. Uniform would have to investigate this, but with their lack of resources, this wouldn't happen quickly.

With the boxes moved, we had a clearer view of that end of the room. There, against the wall, were not one, but three old, iron bedsteads. Two were on their sides, but the one that had caught Fraulein Graber's attention was propped on one end. We stood side-by-side examining this for a moment, wondering if the bed frames were just innocent storage items, or had some bearing on our case. I would need to speak to Seydlitz about that if I had the chance.

"Do you think… this is where she died?"

I did, but I also knew it never paid to leap to conclusions. I was also very puzzled as to the means and motive for her death.

"If she was hung on this contraption first, and then strangled… well, that just seems implausible. Her head would be almost to the ground; the killer would have had to lie down or something. On the other hand, if she was strangled first, what was the purpose of then hanging her upside down in this bizarre manner?" And what was the point of inking her limbs?

"Is it… some kind of bizarre… sexual ritual?"

I wasn't comfortable discussing that with Fraulein Graber. But it couldn't be denied that a private party with several soldiers, women, and copious amounts of booze didn't give off an air of a literary gathering. I cursed the situation that had compelled me to send Seydlitz off to find help; I had many questions I now wanted to ask him, especially around what he had seen when the party broke up. The killer or killers must have carried 'Anna' up the narrow stairway, and out of the hotel – right past Seydlitz's nighttime eyrie. He surely had to have seen something.

Of course, after around half an hour, I realised my mistake had been compounded. Seydlitz wasn't coming back at all.

Furious with myself, I climbed the stairs, checked his cubby-hold and knocked on the door to his apartment, then went to the hotel entrance to peer out into the street. I was as reluctant to leave Fraulein Graber on her own down in the basement as I had been to send her back out onto the dark streets in search of Obermeier.

Thank God, there was the latter, pacing the pavements outside the hotel impatiently. It was now past the hour we had arranged to meet, and he had become anxious when neither of us showed.

I sent him off again to find some *schupos*, then returned to the basement. Fraulein Graber was sitting on one of the boxes we had moved, smoking a cigarette with trembling hand. I joined her. We didn't have long to wait; a one-eyed officer stumbled down the steps just a few minutes later. I sent *him* off to rouse Kommissar Zimmerman. Obermeier and another *bulle* came down the stairs almost immediately afterwards.

The *schupo* went by the name of Rogel. I told him to wait at the top of the stairs, and to admit no-one to the hotel (nor to allow anyone to leave) save for police. Then the three of us carefully began moving the remaining boxes from the area in front of the bedsteads while we waited for Zimmerman to arrive and tell us how well we had done.

Inverted Logic

"What the hell do you think you have been doing?"

"Herr Kommissar, we have just –"

"You were supposed to advise us on the unusual aspects of this case, not take it over!"

"This is where those questions led us." I refrained from asking why he had never checked the hotels close to the site where the body was found. "And you can see what we have found."

He wasn't impressed with that either. "What? What is it you think you have found? A few scuffed chalk marks?" He kicked at one with a toe of his shoe. "What does this signify, tell me?"

We were standing side-by-side at that end of the basement, looking down at what was left of the markings on the floor. He was right to call them scuffed. Before the perpetrators had covered them with boxes, they had made some rudimentary effort to erase the markings. The rough shape remained, but the details were largely obscured.

"Come on, tell me, what do you suggest I am looking at? I see a circle, and what – is this a Jewish star?"

"You mean a Star of David," I suggested. Zimmerman pouted. "But that has six points, and this has only five. This is something called a pentagram, or, more specifically, a *drudenfuss*."

"What's that? Is this some Satanic sign?"

"Not exactly." In truth, I didn't know a great deal about the symbology, merely that it existed. "But from the look of this, these boys were indulging in a ritual of some kind."

"I don't see how you can tell that from this! Shouldn't there be candles everywhere, and all that other paraphenalia?" Clearly the Kommissar was a devotee of the kinds of films that had been all the rage in German cinemas during the war, once we were starved of French and American movies.

"There are signs of candle wax on the floor…"

"Oh, nonsense!" Zimmerman scoffed.

"… but look here. On the lines that make the circle, do you see?"

"See what?"

"These are the same designs that were on the dead woman's arms and legs. See here?" Sadly, I didn't have the sketches on me to prove my point, but I pointed out the clearest markings. Zimmerman huffed and puffed some more, completely skeptical as to my observation. We had already shown him the woman's clothing from the boxes; he hadn't been impressed with that either. He was downright condemnatory about me letting Seydlitz slip away, and on that I agreed with him.

"And then look here, Kommissar. At the bottom of this bed frame. Do you see them, caught on the metal?"

Zimmerman reached into a pocket for a pair of spectacles, which he perched over his broad nose. He squinted and twisted his head. "Hairs? How long might they have been there?"

"Blonde hairs, like our victim's. The right length too."

"Pah! Didn't the night manager tell you the girls all wore wigs?" Another valid point. "This is what you got me out of bed for?" At least he had had some sleep. "This is useless!"

"You should find out who these soldiers were," Fraulein Graber said in a low voice. That was the final straw for Zimmerman.

"Oh, so now I am to be told how to run a murder investigation by a girl?" That was as far as he was willing to acknowledge her. "Now, listen here, Hoehner. You were asked to find out what those markings were on the girl's wrists and legs. Have you done that?"

"I think so."

"Then send me a report. Beyond that, get out of my way. I don't have time to indulge your theories. There's another case I need to take care of, do you understand, and you can bet it won't be long before there is yet another. Now, you think you have found trace of our dead girl; I am here to tell you that I spoke to the other girls at this party already, and they assured me that they all left, together, a little the worse for wear, but perfectly safe. I know all about the soldiers too, and I have spoken to their commander."

"Hauptman von Beckman and Alderstadt?"

I could see from Zimmerman's face that he had never heard the name before. He scowled and leaned in close.

"Stay away from my case, Hoehner. This is no place for amateurs."

Short of causing a scene, there wasn't much I could do to argue. A few minutes later, we three were out on the street once more. A raw wind was blowing up from the south, and the first flurry of rain struck us hard while we watched a little of the coming and going. Turning up our collars, we hurried back to the Hauptbanhof. We stood in the ticket hall, hearing rain fall on the glass roof above. I noticed the many shapes huddled against the walls under thin coats or ragged blankets: homeless, crippled veterans; alcoholics and lunatics; the destitute and lost.

I was exhausted and completely frustrated. We smoked cigarettes. A man with shrunken eyes and a mouth devoid of teeth came up and begged for a smoke; I gave him the last one I had rolled. He stumbled away and went down the nearest stairs, quickly followed by another pitiful wretch whose feet were wrapped in rags. I could almost picture the struggle that might soon take place.

"Go home and get some sleep," I told the others.

"What about you, Herr Kommissar?" asked Obermeier.

Sleep was the last thing on my mind; the last thing I thought I could bear. "I'll see you in the morning,"

I had nothing more to say and left them there. I made my way down to street level and walked briskly through the dark canyons of the city, my head buried in my coat as I tried to stay out of the worst of the weather. I didn't have a plan, or a destination in mind, but followed my nose, and allowing myself to be buffeted by the wind like a sailboat. Freezing cold water dripped down my neck.

I was dragged from my restless, aimless thoughts by a bright blue light, and realised I had fetched up outside the Astrakhan. The better angel of my nature told me this was a mistake, but I went in anyway.

What was this now, early Wednesday morning? The club was almost empty, and those few patrons who had found their way in exhibited a sullen, lifeless quality. I took a long turn about the room. Here was the same band; the same women; probably many of the same customers, but none of the same energy. Perhaps they could all sense the end was coming. It was so cold in the main room that I kept my coat on even as I perched on a bar stool, rolling a series of thin cigarettes with my trembling fingers, pausing now and then to drink beer with schnapps chasers. Maybe the cold was real, maybe it was all in my head, but I couldn't break free from it. My mind was foggy with the lack of sleep, but there was no way I could go back to my cold apartment, not right now. If I closed my eyes, I would dream either of being gassed, or I would see the smug smile of Hauptman von Beckman. It was hard to be sure which would be worse.

WEDNESDAY, 6TH NOVEMBER 1918

"Lonely tonight, handsome?"

One of the dancers had come up, a silk wrap around her shoulders as a nod towards modesty. She looked as cold as I felt.

"No, thank you." I moved one hand towards my beer token, in case she was one of the persistent ones. I needn't have worried. She had already turned to the fellow seated two stools down from me, who was clean-shaven, better-dressed and further along in his solitary drinking. He turned her down too. Wednesday morning was not going to pan out so well for a working girl.

I had glanced at my neighbour when she spoke to him and took a longer look after he replied and she slipped away. I had caught something in his accent, something that placed him as being from somewhere far away from Berlin. In fact, I could place him by his uniform. Instead of Prussian *feldgrau*, this fellow wore the blue of Austria-Hungary. Judging by the edelweiss insignia, he was from one of their mountain regiments, the *kaiserlich und königlich gebergsinfantrie*. He was clearly an officer, and undoubtedly of aristocratic birth – I could tell that just by the monocle. He had slicked-back hair of a sort of hay colour, an obsessively-trimmed moustache, and piercing blue eyes, though these latter were getting more bloodshot by the minute.

He caught my eye and lifted his glass. "It's not a night for fucking, eh?" I toasted him in return, and had the barman fetch us more schnapps. The Austrian had been drinking champagne (or whatever the Astrakhan served in recycled champagne bottles), but he didn't turn down a free drink.

"Major Olivier Sattlberger," he announced. After I

introduced myself likewise, he said he was a military attaché. I've never heard a man announce his profession with such distaste.

"Not that this means anything any more, Herr Kommissar. Have you heard the news? Everything is over. Everything." He threw back his schnapps and ordered us both another. I could see where the night was headed.

"The army is *kaput*. The fucking Magyars, the Slavs, the Czechs, they have all deserted!

Cowards! Traitors! Curse them all. The Italians have swept what was left aside. Bastards. They offered us a ceasefire, but delayed it for twenty-four hours so they could take as much territory and as many prisoners as possible. There was nothing we could do to prevent it! Now the Hungarians have broken away, and God knows the Czechs will follow. The Empire is finished. Yes, I believe it. Emperor Karl is hanging on by his fingernails, but there are reports from Vienna and everywhere else that there are Reds marching in the streets, calling for him to abdicate or be overthrown."

This and more tumbled from his lips in fits and starts. There were tears in his eyes; it seemed as if his whole world was gone. He lifted his glass once more. "Here's to His Excellency, Gottfried, Prinz zu Hohenlohe-Waldenburg-Schillingfürst, Ratibor and Corvey, ambassador for an Empire that no longer exists! You Germans are on your own now. There can be no ambassadors when every country in the world is against you, eh? No, it is all done."

"Let me tell you the future, my friend. The fucking French and Serbians are in Belgrade. They could be in Vienna in a matter of days. What then lies between them and Germany? I hear Munich is in a state of revolution already. Is it true? Pah! No matter. It will all turn to shit soon enough. Let me tell you who are the masters now.

There is a man in my country, a dog by the name of Friedrich Adler. A socialist. Do you know, two years ago he assassinated the Minister-President of Austria? Shot him three times! The man demands peace, and yet kills a political opponent. What do you think of that?"

"Well, now everything is turning to shit, he has been released. I am not joking! These are the types of men who run things now, socialists and assassins, anarchists. Nothing will be left standing. And, you mark my words, it will not be any different here in Berlin. You have your own Adlers here too; traitors, turncoats who have stabbed their own country, their own Emperor in the back. Think what the Russians did. Will it be any different here?"

He was, by now, so drunk that he could barely maintain his seat. His champagne bottle was empty; we had also finished off a bottle of schnapps. He called for another magnum, then lurched to his feet, swaying like a tall-masted ship in a storm.

"I need a whore!" he bellowed. It didn't take long for him to stagger off with a girl under each arm, cursing socialists, Jews and Hungarians in graphic terms.

"What about you, *mein Herr*? Need a tumble?" My mind was so mixed up I couldn't even work out which direction the voice had come from, but finally met the bold glare of a broad-faced woman in a red wig. She winked at me and plumped up her bosom, which burdened a flimsy camisole.

Then there was a second voice: "This one is with me, Mimi." Mimi's red lips twisted in an ugly sneer, but she walked away.

Trude Holstadt perched herself on the stool next to mine and leaned on the bar. "Buy a girl a drink, *bulle*?"

With what little composure I had left, I did as she asked. The barman's attitude had soured a little more, but brought Trude black coffee and Polish vodka. I irritated him more by asking for coffee for myself, after which he pointedly absented himself. Trude and I toasted each other wearily.

"You look awful, Herr Kommissar. When did you last sleep?" I hadn't been keeping track. She slipped an arm through mine, and leaned in to whisper in my ear. "They keep rooms upstairs for us girls to… entertain. We could…"

I didn't have the heart or strength to tell her I felt I way beyond that. She didn't seem to care, but laid a hand on my cheek, steering my face so that she could look more or less directly into my rolling eyes. "Please stay with me tonight, Kommissar, I'd feel safer with you here. Please. You only have to pay for the room."

There was a corridor behind a curtain at one end of the bar, and a stairway that led to the upper floors. We struggled to ascend, as if we were Alpinists scaling the Matterhorn. A key was produced, and we fell into a dark room hung with velvet drapes, rank with body odour barely masked by stale perfume. I hit the mattress as if I had been dropped from a Zeppelin. I think I probably fell asleep on the way down.

.

THE CASE OF AUSTRIAN ATTACHÉ

'Anna'

The attaché and I had drunk enough between us to tame a wild bull, which certainly afforded me a few hours of unconsciousness on a soft mattress. Slight though she was, Trude managed to wrestle me out of my overcoat and shoes, but gave up there. She threw a thin coverlet over me, then crawled under the sheets on the other side of the bed. At least I assume that is what happened; there might have been a military band practising in the room with us and I wouldn't have noticed.

But there was still the dream. My subconscious had the decency to leave it until a few hours had passed, but then the familiar, distorted memories returned. The shelling, the screaming, the billowing clouds of yellow fog. My heart began to pound; I could feel cold air on the sweat that had broken out all over my body. My hands began to move, groping for my gas mask case, but I couldn't find it. I should scream for help, but dared not open my mouth as the poisonous mist drew closer. Besides, there was something already lying across my mouth, something light and wispy. I tried to pull it away, but it was almost intangible. The cloud rolled in.

Then I realised it was light. Wintery sunbeams were streaming through a partly-opened curtain, catching dust motes as they floated lazily in the air. There was also a sound…

I rolled over and opened my eyes. Trude was squatting over a bedpan, still clad in her dancer's garb – such as that was. Once she was relieved, she stood up and pulled up a tiny g-string, smoothing down her short, flared skirt. She turned around to find me looking, my brain not quite awake enough to consider her privacy. I doubt it bothered her.

"I'm sorry, Herr Kommissar, did I wake you?"

I sat up slowly, wiping at my mouth. There were a few loose long hairs there, which I brushed aside. My tongue felt furry.

"No, it's fine. What time is it?"

She laughed. "I didn't steal your watch, *bulle!*"

This was true. It was a little after half past nine. My stomach growled as I sat up, and my bladder added to my body's list of complaints. I tried rising, ended up tripping over my own shoes, then felt a wave of nausea. I stepped over to the window and looked out into the day, squinting against the bright light streaming down from above. Then I found my cigarettes and sought to straighten myself out. I caught a whiff of my own odour (or perhaps it was just the ambience of the room). I needed a bath and a change of clothes.

Trude sat on the bed, wrapped in my overcoat, smoking the cigarette I offered her. A little bell went off in my mind, and I looked at her closely. She looked as gaunt and tired as she had the first time I laid eyes on her, but there was also some warmth about her, that certainly wasn't coming from the room.

"What are you doing here, Fraulein Holstadt?"

She seemed puzzled. "Please, call me Trude. It sounds so official when you speak to me the other way."

"Very well. But answer my question: what on Earth are you doing, working at the Astrakhan? Those men were looking for you before; do you not think they'll come back?"

"I haven't seen them," she replied. "I'm sorry about what I said last night; I didn't mean to worry you. I just felt safe with you."

I considered this. For a while, finding Kammerich had seemed to be uppermost in everyone's minds, but I supposed that moment had passed after the Heilig-Geist incident. He was still a wanted man for everything that had happened in that basement, but I had no sense that this was a priority any longer. The fire itself had barely merited a column in the newspapers, and the details had been obscure, erroneous or just plain false. No-one was facing up to the horror that had happened.

"I don't suppose you have seen Kammerich," I asked. Trude shook her head.

She was probably safe enough, then. I was confident she had no idea what he had been involved with. Part of me wasn't sure he had been entirely clear about it either.

"I'm late for work," I announced, and I drew on my shoes and started lacing them.

"Are you still looking for Karl-Heinz?"

"I am on a different case now," I said, feeling a little sour even admitting it to myself.

"Oh, truly? Who are you looking for now? That's what you do, isn't it? You look for people?"

"Sometimes."

She put out the cigarette she had been smoking, shrugged her way out of my coat and handed it over. "The streets aren't safe," she commented. "Not these days. I hate going home in the dark. All the girls say the same thing, especially after that poor girl was found in Tiergarten."

I glanced up at her. "You've heard about that?"

"Of course. We all talked about it. Some of the girls wondered if they knew her."

"What's that?"

"Oh, you know. We all work the same kinds of places, and we all love to talk. Some of the girls who also work at Schone Grune thought they might know who she was."

I was very, very awake by now. "Who? What are they saying?"

Trude was struck by my abrupt question. "It's probably nothing, Herr Kommissar."

"Tell me anyway."

She shrugged and begged another cigarette. "There's this girl, Lotte, who works the cabaret hours at Schone Grune. She got hired for a private party, and she said there was this one other girl in the group who nobody knew, like she was fresh off the train or something. Anyway, they all got hired for this private party."

"Did she say where?"

"I forget. Some hotel, I think. Anyway, the girls all left, except for the new girl. And then, when the description of that murdered girl was in the newspaper, Lotte just wondered, is all. Said it could have been her."

My mind raced. I just needed one more small detail to convince me that the idea forcing its way to the front of my mind might be possible.

"Did Lotte say who the girls were there to party with?"

"No-one she knew, but she said they were all army types…"

I dragged my fingers through my hair and tried to think, difficult though that felt. I questioned Trude about Lotte a little more, and then sent her on her way. Well, not before she asked me for money.

"I didn't think we…"

"For the room, Herr Kommissar."

Ah, of course. I reached into my wallet and found the price required more or less cleared me out. Just as I was wondering how I was going to get through to Friday, there came a hammering on the door.

"Trude! Trude! Is that *bulle* with you?"

I opened the door to confirm to one of the house spanners that this was so.

"You better come quickly," the fellow said, glaring at me through pudgy eyes. "Some Austrian bloke just blew his brains out!"

'Forever, L'

The military attaché was sitting on a plain wooden chair in the corner of a room, not unlike the one I had just left. His head was lolling on his chest, and beneath one draped hand a Steyr M1912 service pistol lay on the floor. The walls behind him were soaked in blood and brain matter. His monocle, dotted with blood itself, lay on his chest.

I knelt down so I could see his face. Though this was hardly my field of expertise, I reasoned that he had put the muzzle of the pistol into his mouth and pulled the trigger. They say it's the most effective way.

Taking a deep breath, I felt his tunic pockets, and found his identification and a silver cigarette case. He wore an expensive wristwatch, and, of course, his clothing and boots were of the highest quality, though the former was stained with his blood.

I found a wallet in his trouser pocket, as well as 60 marks in a gold clip and a few coins. God knows how much he had spent last night, but it seemed he had more of a cushion than I had. I pocketed the valuables and the pistol. I also found a photograph, loosely inserted into his wallet; an attractive young woman with strong features and wavy hair. On the back was written: 'Forever, L'. Poor L would soon find out that nothing lasts forever.

"Do you have a telephone here?" I asked. The bouncer looked back at me, wide-eyed, as if frightened I might ask him to use it. I gave him the number for the Praesidium. "Ask for Kommissar Zimmerman. Tell him an Austrian military attaché has blown his brains out in a back room at the Astrakhan. That should motivate him."

I stood up. The two girls Major Sattlberger had spent his last night on earth with were sat on the bed, arms about each other. One was a blubbering mess, incapable of coherent speech. The other had been talking in clipped sentences while

I searched their client, saying how they had both been asleep up to the shock of the report from Sattlberger's gun. They had called the spanner, and he had come to me. The capable girl said neither of them had touched the body, which I could believe since he still had his valuables on him. I was certain someone in the establishment was going to enquire about their payment eventually.

"Go and get some clothes on," I suggested. "Don't run off, because Kommissar Zimmerman is going to want to hear from you. You're not in any trouble. Go on, now." They fled, quite naked, still linked arm-in-arm, out of the door.

I took one last look around, then left and closed the door behind me. I handed the key to another bouncer, who I told was to keep the door locked until Zimmerman arrived.

And with that, I left. I had no desire to cross swords with Zimmerman again, and it wasn't as if I was a witness or anything. Homicide would soon see this for what it was: a self-inflicted wound from Sattlberger's own pistol. I'd draft a statement on how he had seemed at the bar, and all that we had spoken about, and that would be about that. This was not my case, and I saw no reason why it would ever be so. Besides, I had Trude's information, and what that might mean for 'Anna', which would be a far more satisfying way to screw with Zimmerman.

Thus, from the Astrakhan I went home, picked up my last clean shirt and some underwear, ran a finger over my teeth and a comb through my hair. I might have been in and out so quick that Johan would barely have stirred in our shared bed, but I needed some money. My share of this week's rent was in a tin we kept hidden at the back of a wide shelf above the bed. I retrieved it, noting that Johan, snoring heavily under the quilt, had contributed his portion, which was a rarity. I took that too. Old man Blocher would be around tomorrow morning, but I figured I could replace the cash by then.

I headed to work, delaying only to use the public bath

on the edge of Alexanderplatz, in and out in ten minutes, and then dropping off my laundry at a place near the Praesidium. A shave wouldn't have gone amiss, but I felt I had wasted enough of the day. I was down in the basement at a little after a quarter past eleven, damp, but a little more fragrant. Even my hangover had diminished somewhat.

Fraulein Graber and Obermeier had been hanging around in B2 all morning, directionless, wondering when I might appear. Obermeier had been reading out a story he hoped to see published in *Vorwarts*, asking for her opinion. She was delighted to see me arrive. They were both so out of place in this new environment that they almost stood to attention.

I took one quick look at our new accommodation as I shrugged out of my coat. B2 was a large, windowless room, with green walls; desks for four people, two with typewriters, one with a telephone; two large metal cabinets; a couch; a hat stand; an over-sized wall clock; a small stove in one corner and scuffed, bare floorboards. It had the air of a storage room that had been pressed into our service. That couldn't matter now.

"Fraulein Graber. At midday, a young woman by the name of Lotte should present herself upstairs. She has information we need to hear. Would you mind loitering by the entrance to make sure she comes to the right place?"

"Of course."

"Thank you. Now, listen, we might have caught a lucky break." I explained the situation quickly. "It's possible this Lotte didn't see what happened; in fact, it's reasonable to assume that it's certain that she didn't. But she can tell us what was going on when she and the other girls left. More importantly, she can perhaps tell us who 'Anna' is."

Obermeier brewed coffee on the stove as we talked. I needed to complete my statement for Zimmerman, and to record the items I had taken from Major Sattlberger. It took Obermeier in particular a few minutes to realise I was talking about a wholly unconnected incident there. He handed me that morning's copy of *Vorwarts*, which confirmed most of what Sattlberger had complained of. The Hapsburg Empire was surely about to disappear.

"These days will make the French Revolution look like a mere vacation for the crowned heads of Europe," he said, with some pleasure. "Wilhelm is lucky he is tucked away with the army in Spa."

I put the newspaper to one side. "This chaos is not our friend, Obermeier. If all order breaks down, we'll never close the case on those invalided soldiers."

He raised his eyebrows. "That is still a priority?"

"Why wouldn't it be?"

Obermeier shrugged, then smiled, and went to the stove to pour coffee into three enameled mugs.

"*If* Hauptman Beckman is somehow connected to 'Anna', that gives us all the excuse we need to question him. If it so happens we can draw anything out of him on the other matter, so much the better."

I rushed my typing which appalled Fraulein Graber, who took the sheet from the typewriter, shooed me from seat and rolled in a clean statement form (the administration people had made sure we had every variety possible of Berlin Police paperwork, because even in the depth of defeat and despair Prussian bureaucracy does not bend). She retyped my report, without all the mistakes. I signed it, and was about to ask Obermeier to take it up to the Murder Büro when the door to B2 opened abruptly.

"Ah, good, you're here," said Hauptkommisar Teske, filling the doorway. He looked around the room with his cold eyes, and I was convinced that we would rarely ever see him down here again. "We shall need some method by which I shall know when you are in the building, and when out on the department's business."

"Of course, Herr Oberkommissar."

"Meanwhile, I need you to come with me. We have a

most important meeting to attend. Top floor."

That wasn't good news. Only the most severe grillings took place in the bosses' offices.

He and I took the paternoster. Oberkommissar Teske looked about as comfortable in the device as if he been strapped to an artillery shell and fired at the moon.

"What is this about, Herr Oberkommissar?"

He didn't answer. I trailed behind him along the carpeted halls of the top floor, where smart-suited young men scurried between offices, and the ambience was more like a cathedral than a police station. Teske marched directly to a set of double doors at the end of corridor, beyond which one of the smart suits conducted us through a second such doorway into the presence of Heinrich Karl Wilhelm Ehrenfried Hellmuth von Oppen, Chief of the whole Berlin police force. I swallowed hard.

Von Oppen was almost sixty, I believed, and had probably not aged well in the post he occupied. He was a narrow, aristocratic type, with a full moustache and thinning brown hair which he fussed at constantly. He had been in post for the last couple of years, in which the authority of the civilian police had played second fiddle to military commands. The government had kept up stringent demands on the force, even while it was denuded of competent manpower. The lines about his eyes suggested many sleepless nights.

"Ah, August, good, good. Come in and take a seat. This is…" He looked at me as if I might just be a member of the cleaning staff, completely out of place. I thanked God under my breath that I had changed my shirt.

"Kommissar Hoehner," Teske said tersely. He indicated the chair – off to the side – I was to occupy.

There were two other figures in the room (three, I suppose, if you counted the adjutant who had ushered us in); one of whom I knew, the other of whom I could guess. Bernard Weiss, Deputy Chief of *Kripo*, was standing behind

Von Oppen. He took off his round glasses, polished them with a handkerchief and placed them back on his nose. He had the kind of features it was hard to imagine ever wore a smile. He wore a charcoal grey suit and fiddled with a wedding ring. I don't recall him saying a word, or so much as registering a reaction, throughout the entire meeting.

Finally, seated on a high-backed chair in front of Von Oppen's desk was a man in a frock coat, his pale grey trousers so sharply creased they were a hazard. Ambassador Gottfried, Prinz zu Hohenlohe-Waldenburg-Schillingfürst, Ratibor and Corvey was about the same age as the Chief, tall and greying, with the kind of haughty demeanour I imagine is a job requirement for someone in the diplomatic service of the Austro-Hungarian Empire. A memory flashed into my mind of one part of the

conversation I had had with Sattlberger. I say conversation; it was part of his diatribe about the state of affairs. He'd said that Prinz von Hohenlohe-Schillingfürst was a decorated military officer, a major-general, and that he had first been suggested as the Ambassador to Berlin long before the war, only to be blocked by his predecessor refusing to return to Vienna. He had taken up his post in 1914, and thus had served throughout the worst times imaginable. Sattlberger had been convinced that the Prinz would be recalled any day now that Austria was out of the war. I wondered if he would depart with any more grace than the last fellow.

I wasn't introduced to the Ambassador, nor was he to me. I felt like a spectator.

"A sorry business, August," said Von Oppen, as if continuing a conversation Teske and I had not been present for. I remembered being told that Teske was a protégé of the Chief, but there was a stiff formality between them here.

"Indeed."

Von Oppen tapped a closed case file that lay in front of him. "I have the crime scene report from Kommissar Zimmerman. It all seems quite… straightforward."

"It would seem so." How had Teske learned anything so quickly?

"Such a tragedy. A man of honour. Again, I offer my condolences, Your Excellency. It seems cut and dried: Major Sattlberger clearly felt that... well, in the current circumstances... in keeping with his honour as an officer..." Von Oppen's voice trailed off.

"There is no reason to think otherwise, Herr *Polizeipräsident*."

Von Oppen offered a thin smile. "Good, good. And therefore, we need not delay the return of his remains to his grieving family. Nor should there be any need to... uh... burden the family with extraneous details. He took his own life at a gentlemen's club? The report will... confirm this?"

"It will, Herr Polizeipräsident."

"Good." Von Oppen gestured apologetically to the Ambassador. "Herr Weiss will make all the arrangements."

Von Hohenlohe-Schillingfürst's voice rumbled in his throat. "I shall telegram Vienna immediately. When may I expect the return of his personal effects?"

That was the only moment I was there to facilitate, it seemed. Teske looked at me. I nodded. Teske looked at the Chief and nodded in turn. Von Oppen folded his hands together. "Immediately, Your Excellency. A courier will bring them to the embassy this afternoon."

That was that. The Ambassador stood, and the rest of us rose up in unison. Teske gestured to me, and we headed for the door while the higher-ups performed more elaborate farewells. Once out in the broad corridor, we spoke of the matter for what would be the only time.

"Send your statement to me, Kommissar Hoehner. Within the hour."

"*Jawohl.*"

"Can this 'Astrakhan'" in any way be described as an officer's club?"

"Not at all."

That was entirely what he had expected. He stroked his moustache as he thought for a moment. "Leave the name out of your statement. I'll make sure Zimmerman does the same. Bring those effects to my office when you deliver the statement. Keep everything simple, but above board, you understand?"

I did. I suppose it suited me that I wouldn't have to explain why I was at the Astrakhan myself. A gentlemen's club made it sound as if I had been in some paneled smoking room, drinking brandy and discussing the bourse, instead of drooling drunkenly onto a pillow in what was no better than a cat-house.

A win all round.

Rules Of Engagement

Given that I now had an additional task on my hands, I went straight back down to the basement. I gave the others a highly redacted account of the meeting I had just encountered, then took up the statement I had written, and Fraulein Graber had retyped, and drew pencil lines through certain details. Fraulein Graber looked at me a little askance, as if I was criticising her work.

"I'm going to have to ask you to interview Lotte," I said, glancing up at the large wall clock, whose minute hand trembled in anticipation of another step towards midday. "The top floor has other plans for me. Do you think you can handle it, Irene?"

Fraulein Graber beamed. "Of course."

"This might be for the best anyway. This girl might speak more easily with you. Have Obermeier with you if you wish, but he might chase her off."

"This is calumny upon my character," Obermeier complained.

"Perhaps I should take her to a café," Fraulein Graber speculated. "This place is so oppressive."

"That's actually an excellent idea. Keep it informal, but don't allow her to give you the runaround. It's important we get what we need. We want every detail possible about this party, about the girl Lotte suggest was fresh off the boat, about the officers present, who left when. She'll ask for money; agree to nothing, but hint that there are things you might be able to do for her. A girl like that won't have avoided trouble and will find it again."

"I understand."

"Take her to Ruben's. It's quiet there. I'll come and find you when I'm done."

"Yes, Herr Kommissar. I should leave now, I suppose."

It was indeed that time. I wished her luck, and watched

her gather her purse, hat and coat. As the door closed, I took up her version of my statement, and laid it beside one of the typewriters.

"Shall I do that for you, Herr Kommissar? The way you type, we could be here until dinner time."

"I have to do this alone."

"I see. You think I will see something I shouldn't? A few facts that the Top Floor don't want to see in the newspapers tomorrow morning?"

I leaned back. "We have never discussed exactly how this role fits in with your journalistic affairs, Klaus. There will be times when you cannot report on what you see."

"You've read what I have published these last few days. There's nothing in there that wasn't out in the open, for anyone to see."

"All the same…"

He took his hat off the stand. "Very well, Gerhard. I see how it is. If I am not needed here for a few hours, I have a few things to chase down on my own."

I should have asked what he meant, but I felt rushed by the need to get the statement retyped. I was stumbling over the first words as he left VIIIb.

Lotte's Recollections

I did a better job of getting the statement completed than anyone expected and took it up to the second floor and Oberkommissar Teske's office. He took it from me, read it briskly (I had kept the account extremely concise) and grunted with satisfaction.

I handed him a list, and then the items. "One gold watch, one silver cigarette case, his identification papers, one photograph."

"Is that all he had on him?"

"There was a pistol. Will the Ambassador want that, in the circumstances? Anyway, that's all I took. He spent a lot of cash at the bar. He wore no ring."

Teske looked hard at me. "Good," he said at length. "The embassy are collecting his other possessions from his apartment. Everything will be sent on to Vienna by nightfall." He carefully dropped all of the items into a large manilla envelope, pausing only to study the photograph for a few seconds. "There. It's not much to mark a man's life, is it?"

"It's more than they will find on me, when my time comes," I replied.

"Well. If anything else turns up, get it to me before six o'clock, do you understand?"

"Of course, but surely this is no longer any affair of ours. Zimmerman will have spoken to the girls Sattlberger was with, but I expect he has been told to lose their statements."

Teske looked up at me. His eyes were quite cold, unblinking. "That is the last I expect to hear on this case, yes. Now, where are matters with this painted girl from Tiergarten?"

I brought him up-to-date, at least as far as things had progressed yesterday. I pointedly didn't reveal what Fraulein

Graber was up to at that very moment, nor what had led us to that.

"Have you provided Kommissar Zimmerman with everything he requires?"

That too needed careful consideration. I knew what Zimmerman would say. "There are some details around those markings on her limbs, Herr Oberkommissar. I can't rule out that they signify some occult behaviour. We have spoken to an academic, but I need to confirm what he told us, and see if we can make more sense of them."

Teske breathed deeply. "This is precisely what I told you was my concern, Kommissar Hoehner. The crisis in which Germany finds itself is leading people down all kinds of dangerous paths. I hope you are starting to see the importance of the work this department has been formed to do."

"I am."

"Good. Go and continue your enquiries. I shall want a report on my desk…"

"… by the end of the day. *Jawohl*, Herr Oberkommissar."

That done, I retrieved my hat, gloves, coat and smokes, and set off for Ruben's. As soon as I stepped outside, I regretted not bringing a scarf, because the wind had turned bitterly cold. The streets around the Alex were almost empty. I hunched my shoulders and headed for Rathausstrasse, passing under the railway bridge which provided a little shelter. I noticed two old men sat against the wall, passing a bottle between them. God help them get through the night.

Ruben's is in the basement of an office building, and it's a dingy, poky affair, which means it has never been popular. I rarely use the place myself, though it does sell some of the best pastries in this part of town. I felt like I could use the sugar.

Fraulein Graber was sitting alone by the time I arrived. I joined her and ordered soup and coffee. Fraulein Graber declined anything, other than to accept one of my cigarettes.

On top of everything else, I was going to need more tobacco.

"She didn't want to stay long. She was very nervous at being questioned. She kept asking if I was really police, and what it was we were hoping to find."

"But she did give you some information?"

Fraulein Graber nodded, and produced her notebook, page after page of which was filled with her neat, dense hand. "First, I asked her about the party. She said that another of the girls, Madeleine, had been asked to bring a group of girls to a party by an officer friend of hers. The money was good, so Madeleine agreed, and she persuaded Lotte and some others."

"Did you get the name of this officer?"

"No, she refused to name him. She did confirm that they were all from the same regiment, though she didn't name that either."

"What excuse was she given for this party?"

"A birthday or somesuch. She didn't believe it, not once she arrived at the Hotel Graz. She said she had attended parties with these officers before, and it was always at some club, or a private house. She thought the basement of the Graz was an ugly place."

"You have to wonder why they changed the venue."

Fraulein Graber didn't speculate, but turned a page in her notebook. "Lotte says the party was the normal kind of affair. There was lots of drink. The boys sang marching songs and groped the girls. She said for an hour or so, there was music on a phonograph, and dancing, but the machine broke down. After that, a couple of the girls went off with officers, singly or in pairs. Lotte and the remainder stayed until two o'clock. She wasn't completely sure of the time, Kommissar, but thinks it was around then. She left with an officer by the name of Horst. She doesn't know his rank, or his surname."

"What about *our* girl?"

"This is where it gets interesting. After they arrived, the girl went to one end of the room with two of the officers. They didn't join the dancing. Lotte says the girl looked uncomfortable and tried to fend off their advances. Her dress was torn. One of the other officers went over, and told them to behave, but it didn't do all that much good. She says the men stole the girl's shoes and laughed about it. She wanted to leave, but she didn't know where to go."

"Keep going."

"Lotte says she spoke to the girl and offered to take her back to her hotel – but, in all honesty, Kommissar, she may just have been trying to put herself in a better light with me."

"Did the name of this hotel our girl was staying in come up?"

"Yes. The Great Northern."

At last. If nothing else, Zimmerman could go back there and hopefully find the girl's other possessions, and perhaps her name. I remembered the assistant manager, Bodenhof, giving me the run-around. I looked forward to turning the tables on him.

"Keep going."

"There isn't much more. Lotte left with Horst. She doesn't remember seeing the girl again. She said the lights had burned low, and she was busy with Horst. Most of the men had gone by then, but she recalled one officer she knew, who was at the far end of the room in conversation with another officer. Lotte says they kept looking down at the floor and laughing."

Better still! "Did you get a name?"

"Waldemar Pabst. A captain, she thinks."

Perfect. Fraulein Graber looked up from her notes. "How did I do?"

"Excellent. That's really good work." I checked my watch, and compared it to the clock in the café, only that was about an hour behind. "If we hurry, we can deal with the hotel today." I picked up my coat from the back of the chair and helped Fraulein Graber into hers. "Genuinely, Irene, that's good work. Now, come on."

"What about Obermeier?"

"We'll fill him in later. I don't want to waste any time chasing this."

Soon we were back in familiar territory near the Hauptbahnhof. On the way, we had discussed the case, trying to recreate in our minds what had happened to 'Anna'. It seemed she was alive when the other girls left, even if subject to persistent and unwelcome attention from Pabst and his mate. As Lotte left, she had been hidden out of sight, perhaps behind those same boxes. What had happened to her there? How did things progress from a drunken party to murder and some bizarre ritualistic display?

The Girl From Posen

It was every bit as pleasurable to reacquaint myself with Herr Bodenhof at the Great Northern Hotel as I had hoped. He had not started work as we arrived, but was due shortly. We spoke with the day manager, a Herr Pfödel, who suggested that there was a room on the fourth floor which had been taken for one night by a young woman who had, he believed, just arrived in Berlin. He had not seen her since that first day.

"She said she was going to look for work. I expected to see her on Tuesday, either checking out or extending her stay. But nothing. I checked the room this morning, and her luggage is still there, such as it is."

Naturally, he had seen nothing unusual in this. Hotel clerks are some of the most cynical people alive; they'd make great police officers if they cared a damn about the people they meet.

"What name did she check in under?"

Pfödel consulted the book, peering at the pages through a *pince-nez*. "Fraulein Elisabet Nowak. It lists a home address in Posen."

Fraulein Graber noted the information down, while I took the room key. "When do you expect Herr Bodenhof?"

"Any minute, really. His shift doesn't start for a couple of hours, but he usually eats here before work."

Bodenhof didn't vary his routine that day. We waited in what passed for the lounge, in seats that gave us a good view of the entrance. I read some of that day's *Norddeutsche Allgemeine Zeitung*, which I wouldn't normally use for kindling. It was mostly vexed that Prince Max von Baden had sent Gustav Noske, a member of the leadership group of the SPD in the Reichstag, up to Kiel, and instead of calling in the army to deal with the mutineers, he had ended up being elected chairman of the soldiers' and sailors' council. The paper was convinced that the socialists were betraying the country; they were almost giddy with the hope that the Kaiser might soon march back from Spa at the head of a dozen loyal divisions of the western army, as if that front had manpower to spare.

At around five o'clock, Bodenhof came through the front doors, whistling a tune I didn't recognise. He clocked me at once. He wasn't thrilled we were meeting up again.

"I need you to come up to Room 411 with us. Fraulein Nowak's room." I watched his face carefully as I said the name. His eyes grew even wider, and he looked at Pfödel as if he had been betrayed.

"I have to work –" he stammered, but we caught him out in that lie at once. I took him by the arm and led him towards the elevator.

The Great Northern might have been quite a pleasant place to stay in its heyday, but it was a down-at-heel hotel now, without so much as a lick of paint anywhere during the war years. It felt as if even basic cleaning was beyond them; there was dust on tables in the hallways upstairs, and the carpets looked faded and worn.

Room 411 was about as far from the elevator as possible. I handed Bodenhof the key. He had been jabbering on about how the hotel wasn't fully occupied, and how they had left Fraulein Nowak's belongings there, expecting her to return. It sounded utterly insincere.

The room was a dark and shabby, lit by a single window that looked out onto the alley between this building and its neighbour. The curtains were drawn. There was a narrow bed with a lightweight mattress and a patterned coverlet; a wardrobe with squeaky hinges; a night-stand; a small desk and chair. There was little else. We had passed a shared toilet just along the hall; the nightstand bore a washbowl and a cracked chamberpot in matching dingy grey.

I told Bodenhof to wait by the door while we gave the

room a quick search. The bed was made, and everything else appeared undisturbed. If it wasn't for the boxy little suitcase we found in the wardrobe, one wouldn't know the room had supposedly been let. The case had an address label tied to the handle, which matched the Posen address in the register downstairs; it had no locks, so I popped the clasps and opened the lid. The immediate view was that the contents were just ordinary items, like underclothes, stockings and one very thin shawl.

I recalled the items Fraulein Graber and I had found in the boxes in the cellar of the Hotel Graz, just a short distance up the road. The green woolen dress; the quality topcoat; neat, sensible shoes; underslip and stockings. Here were the rest of her belongings.

We packed everything back into the case and told Bodenhof we were taking it with us. He accepted that without argument, not even asking for a receipt. Then I asked him about the last time he had seen Fraulein Nowak.

"I never met her. She checked in during the day."

"You didn't meet her during the evening?" He shook his head. "She didn't ask where she might find a cheap place to get an evening meal?"

"Nothing like that."

"Did your colleague tell you that she was looking for work?"

"Not that I recall." I nodded, as if taking it all in. Everything about Bodenhof screamed that he was withholding something.

"You didn't suggest that there was a party about to take place at the Graz, something a girl might earn some money from if she attended? You might not have let it seem sordid. Perhaps she could have worked there as a waitress?"

"No, no, nothing like that!" he insisted.

I went to the desk and opened the drawer. There was a pad of hotel notepaper in there, from which a few top sheets had been torn off. A couple of envelopes were tucked at the back. Who knew how many years they had dwelled in this drawer?

"Did she send a letter to anyone?"

"I told you; I didn't see her. Ask Wilhelm – Herr Pfödel.

I turned on the desk light and held the top sheet in such a way to let the light shine through, but the lamp was too dull to be of service. Instead, finding a stub of a pencil in the drawer too, I did the old *kripo* trick of lightly scribbling over the top sheet to reveal indentations left when the previous top sheet was written on. It wasn't clear, but I thought I could make out the words 'your loving daughter' at the bottom, and some other words further up the page.

We took the notepad with us as well.

"Do you know a Captain Pabst?"

"No."

I nodded again and took a final look around the room. "I'm struggling to believe you, Bodenhof. You'd do best to not mess me around. Your employer isn't going to be thrilled when he finds you've been pimping out girls for private parties." Bodenhof was shrill in his denial. "No need for that to come out," I continued, "unless you are lying to me about anything else."

He looked quite pale. I had little doubt that the version of events I was putting together was correct. All the same, he offered no comment. After this silence had stretched out for a while, I told him that I would require him to come to the Alex and give a statement. Primarily, I didn't want him running off as Joachim Seydlitz from the Hotel Graz had done.

"Listen, Herr Kommissar, I don't know what happened!"

"It will be a short statement, then."

Sixty Marks

We deposited Bodenhof in an interview room back at the Police Praesidium, having informed Pfödel that he would need to come in tomorrow morning to look at photographs of our victim, to confirm that she was Elisabet Nowak. The Day Manager wasn't thrilled; he was already going to have to work late to cover for Bodenhof's absence, and he would have to inform the hotel's owner of the scandal that was brewing. Pfödel mentioned that he had told Bodenhof about the new arrival, and that she was 'fresh off the boat' and looking for work. That would give me something to go out with the night manager.

We also carried back the few belongings Fraulein Nowak had left in Room 411 before she stepped out into the night. These, along with a duplicate of a report Fraulein Graber typed out efficiently while I dictated, I took up to the Homicide Büro. Zimmerman wasn't thrilled to see me. He read the report at lightning speed, his frown deepening with every word.

"Why are you still working my case?" he demanded.

"Someone has to."

I took the top copy of the report to Oberkommissar Teske. It was early evening, but he was still at his desk, and read through my account with a slow deliberation. At one point he paused to comment: "Leave Bodenhof's interrogation to Kommissar Zimmerman" and held up a hand to pause my protest before it started. He laid the report in his In Tray.

"This is excellent work, Kommissar Hoehner. Not at all what I was expecting, but excellent work all the same."

"Thank you."

"Unless you feel that you can uncover more of the meaning of the symbols painted onto the girl, or chalked upon the floor, this matter is at an end with regard to Amt VIIIb".

I didn't comment on this, but he must have been able to

see that I was unhappy at such an instruction.

"Go home and get some rest, Hoehner. You look like a man who hasn't slept properly in weeks."

"*Jawohl*, Herr Oberkommissar."

"You may be interested to hear that we have received a letter from the Austrian Ambassador, the Prinz zu Hohenlohe-Waldenburg-Schillingfürst, thanking us for our discretion in the matter of the unfortunate death of Major Sattlberger. That matter too can be considered concluded."

"*Jawohl*."

"Go and get some rest," he said again. "The situation isn't getting any better for Germany. I fear what may lie around the corner. We will need to be at our best."

"*Jawohl*."

I accepted his advice. I went back to the basement, and instructed Fraulein Graber, in turn, that she should take the night off. She looked beat.

"No word from Obermeier?" I asked.

"Nothing."

"He'll show up. Go home, Irene"

I found a lonely dinner in a dimly lit café along my route home, then stumbled through the dark streets, eyes cast down, feeling the cold seep into my bones. I passed an old man lying in a doorway under a few sheets of newspaper, and – I'm ashamed to admit it – I didn't check to see if the old fellow was alive. I stopped at a kiosk to buy more tobacco, which was when I realised I was still carrying Sattlberger's gold money clip. I stared at it for a moment as if it was some mystery as to how it came to be in my coat pocket.

I paid for the tobacco with some of the 60 marks the clip contained.

This was the earliest I had been back in the apartment for days. It was cold, and the wind howled beyond the window. I took a blanket from the bed and sat under it on a chair, smoking, thinking. Part of me wanted to go out and use more of Sattlberger's money to buy alcohol. Instead, I repaid the rent tin. I suppose that let me feel a little less like a heel.

THURSDAY, 7TH NOVEMBER 1918

I don't know how early the hammering on my door started. It was still dark outside, but November in Berlin felt like night all the time. I crawled out of bed and stumbled to the door. I was still fully dressed; all I had shucked off in the night had been my overcoat and boots. I swear ice cracked under the weight of my feet.

"Who's there?"

"It's me, Herr Kommissar! Obermeier. Let me in, for pity's sake, it's colder than a snowman's arse out here."

I unlocked the door and admitted my excitable colleague. He was immediately crestfallen to release it was no warmer in the apartment. "You don't light your stove?"

"I'm never here."

"I can't believe you live like this. Don't you earn a decent salary as a *kripo* kommissar? Ach! Look at this! Even I live better than you! That's one good thing about renting a room from the widow Moskowizt, she keeps the place warm."

"I don't know how she can afford the fuel," I commented, fumbling my way into my boots. My fingers were so cold it took a solid minute to tie my laces. When I looked up, Obermeier was making an obscene movement with his hands to suggest just how his landlady kept the place stocked with wood. I shook my head and looked away at such a calumny on the woman's character.

"Have you seen this?" He waved a copy of *Vorwarts* under my nose, still hot from the press or so I imagined. There was no need to reply, and no need to have read anything. Obermeier quickly digested the salient points from the front page. "We're saying that it is widely accepted that the Entente is prepared to negotiate a truce. The Americans are bossing the show. All that is required is for the Emperor to abdicate, and then we can have peace."

"The Americans are demanding that?"

"Pah! Not in so many words, but everyone knows which way the wind is blowing. They wouldn't deal with the military government, not even with Ludendorff kicked out. President Wilson wants a proper republican government established, so that it reflects the popular will. Did you know Ludendorff fled to Sweden? What a hero he turned out to be; now others have to clear up after his mess."

"Is the Kaiser still in Spa?"

"It seems so. We're reporting that the leader of the SPD wants to go there and persuade him that he must step down."

"I don't know if that's a good idea for Ebert to try. Wilhelm is surrounded by troops..."

"Ach! They won't support him. If the sailors have mutinied, the Army can't be far behind, especially the front-line troops. And look here, at the bottom of the page. It looks as if King Ludwig is preparing to flee from Bavaria! As one King falls, so shall they all, eh? Saxony, Baden... what is the point of any of them? There was a huge protest in Munich on Monday, on the Theresienwiese, demanding peace and a republic. For all I know, he's already fled as well. The Emperor Karl is tottering in Vienna; I tell you, the whole rotten edifice is falling. Hurry up, can you? I have more news for you. Can't we at least find a coffee shop that's open?"

I pulled on my coat and we headed out. I only realised when we reached the foot of the stairs that I hadn't made the bed. Johan would be livid.

The day was advanced enough that Old Man Mauritz was already open, and Obermeier and I found a small table deep in the interior, where the air had had the edge taken off. Obermeier slapped his newspaper down on the table, and glanced around at the rest of the clientele, looking quite pleased with himself.

"These royals think they can make a few cosmetic changes and everything will be fine. The Americans will be satisfied, the people... ah, but they are so wrong. No, believe me, it's over for them. Look at Bavaria; Ludwig III was facing demands for change a year ago. He waited until last week to announce constitutional reform. Too late! People don't want a constitutional monarchy; they want a republic!"

A few people at nearby tables tutted. Even Old Man Mauritz frowned. That delighted Obermeier all the more, and he was almost ready to jump up onto the table and proclaim the Revolution right there and then.

"Ha! A few weeks ago, speaking like this, I should have been arrested. But not any more! Those political prisoners that remain are being released – even the Bolshevists! You mark my words, in just a few days time, the Bastille will fall!"

I sighed and tapped the back of his hand where it lay on the table. "Is this the news you wanted me to hear?"

Obermeier settled down a little. Old Man Mauritz brought coffee, and two of the smallest bread rolls you have ever seen. There was no butter, but he had found some jam, by God!! We broke open our rolls and spread the delicious fruit on them, for all that it would only be a mouthful.

"Spare me a cigarette, Herr Kommissar? I got through all my tobacco last night. It was worth it, mind… you wait 'til you hear! Ah, thank you."

I lit both nails, and we puffed away for a moment, before Obermeier leaned forwards.

"I found Pabst!"

"What's that? Where?"

Naturally, I had to hear the 'how' before the 'where'.

"It turns out that a year ago a friend of mine tried to write an article about him for one of the Army newspapers – *Kriegs-Echo* or one of those. I met up with him last night, and he told me that Pabst returned from the front back in '16 and served here with the General Staff. No less a luminary than General Ludendorff himself than arranged for Pabst to join the Garde-Kavallerie-Schützendivision earlier this year. Most of the division are still at the front as part of the Crown Prince's army group, but various headquarters units are here in Berlin. That's where Pabst is, at their depot in Potsdam."

I thought about that for a moment. The Garde-Kavallerie-Schützendivision had come up before, with Captain von Beckman, who was attached to the Hauptkadettenanstalt. And, of course, Beckman had been instrumental in arranging the party at the Hotel Graz at which Fraulein Nowak had met her end, quite possibly at Pabst's hands.

Obermeier was still reeling off all that he knew. "They're not really a cavalry formation any more, of course, just dismounted infantry, and they number just a few hundred. However, they are still barracked in the old cavalry barracks by the Neues Palais. My friend said he had seen a few of them at different places around the city. He thinks they have been held back in case of disorder."

He leaned in even closer, so that he exhaled warm tobacco breath into my face. "Guess where I was last night."

I could have berated him for taking such a risk, but I was intrigued where this tale was leading.

"That's where I saw him. Pabst! My friend had shown me a photograph..."

"What was he doing? Pabst, I mean."

"Nothing exciting. I saw him in the courtyard of the barracks. He was giving orders to a platoon of men who then left the barracks on trucks. This would have been at around eight o'clock. The barracks were dark as Hell. I don't think there were many solders left there."

"You are sure this was him?"

"Completely. But listen, I haven't got to the interesting part. About midnight, Pabst left the barracks with another officer, another captain, a fellow I didn't recognise. They went to another building just along the street. It looked like an old armoury for the Prussian Guard Corps. There was a sentry outside, so I couldn't follow, but they were in there for about thirty-five minutes. Then Pabst came out alone and went back to the cavalry barracks."

"I see."

"Then, at around two o'clock, that other fellow comes out of the armoury with perhaps thirty other men. He forms them up in a column, marches them up the street, then back, and they disappear into the armoury once more. *Ein, zwei; ein, zwei*... like clockwork. A curious time for drill, no? I was hiding across the street, and I got a good look at them. They weren't part of the Garde-Kavallerie-Schützendivision; at least, they wore no insignia to suggest they were. None of them had a sergeant's stripes. It was just them and this one officer. That's not normal, is it?"

It didn't feel like it. I didn't entirely know what to make of this account, other than that there were altogether too many men in uniform up to no good in the capital. I drank my coffee and smoked a second nail while I considered what I had been told.

"Do we arrest this Pabst?" Obermeier demanded in a lone tone.

"Let's get out of here," I suggested. Second only to the hostility shown to Obermeier's politicking, our hushed and conspiratorial whispering was drawing a lot of attention. I paid Old Man Mauritz. He asked what ration coupons I could spare. He had never asked before. It seemed times were getting harder for everyone.

We stepped out onto the street, back into the biting cold of pre-dawn. I was so busy drawing up the collar of my coat that I didn't notice there was a small car parked there, its driver wrapped in rugs, nor that there was a truck across the street bearing several pale-faced, keen-eyed young men. A door opened on the car, and out stepped Hauptman Weiss von Beckman und Alderstadt.

"*Guten morgen*, Herr Kommissar. Do you have a moment you can spare me?"

"I am due at the Alex," I said, trying to sound nonchalant.

"I will give you a lift!" Von Beckman replied brightly.

"Come. Just you, Herr Kommissar. Perhaps my men can drive Herr Obermeier where he needs to go."

A Deadly Trade

Compared to the four-seater Hauptmann Beckman had had access to when he last intercepted me at the Luster house, his ride this time was an Opel, a 4/8 PS two-seater. It bore no military designations. The driver got out, bundled up the rugs and carried them over to the truck, onto which Obermeier was being encouraged to climb. Beckman gestured for me to get into the passenger seat; then slid in on the driver's side. He was smiling broadly as he coaxed the car away from the kerb, his hands wrapped in kid leather gloves. He was wearing a long woolen greatcoat, and didn't seem at all discomfited by the open nature of the car, whereas I was freezing. I wished the driver had left the rugs.

"Isn't this a little bourgeoise for the holder of a *pour le merité*?"

I wasn't proud of such a petty remark; it isn't as if I owned a car at all. Still, von Beckman didn't appear at all phased. "Oh, don't you like it? These are reliable, well-built little cars, I find. Inexpensive, too; less than 4,000 marks before the war. Also, there are times when one doesn't want to be sat behind a driver, if you take my meaning."

"Every doctor in Prussia seems to drive one. Those fellows love a bargain."

He thought this amusing. We passed under the railway east of Friedrichstrasse Bahnhof and crossed the Spree via the Weidendammer Bridge. Von Beckman was quiet and thoughtful as he navigated to Ziegelstrasse, but got to his point quickly thereafter, as the little Opel puttered eastwards.

"Your friend, the socialist journalist... he has been poking his nose into some things best left alone."

I decided to make the point early, just so that there were no misunderstandings, that Obermeier worked for the Berlin Police now.

"Oh, hardly!" A pedestrian stepped out in front of the

car and Beckman swerved around them. "Idiot! Get out of the way! No, if you are referring to the... arrangement supporting Oberkommissar Teske's appointment, I'm afraid I cannot consider that true police work."

He glanced across at me, with a supercilious sneer on his face.

"A waste of your talents also, if I may say so."

"Where are your men taking Herr Obermeier?"

"They are technically not my men, Herr Kommissar, so I am afraid their actions – whatever those may be – will come as much as a surprise to me as to anyone."

We were sat close side-by-side in the little Opel. Von Beckman was in the driver's seat on the right. I was very aware of the Mauser under my left arm, and equally aware that it was buried under my jacket and overcoat in this cramped space. Nor did I wish to wrestle von Beckman for control of the car. What good would it have done anyway – the truck had gone off in a completely different direction.

"I would not expect to get off scot-free, were something to happen to him, if I were you."

Von Beckman did not respond at first, and when he did so he was quite indirect. "While we are offering advice, Herr Kommissar, mine would be that you merely listen to what I have to say. It is important, at this juncture, that there be no misunderstanding."

I wrapped my arms across my chest, feeling the chill all the more each time the car speeded up. "You're driving the car, Herr Hauptmann. Why don't you see where it takes us?"

At that moment, von Beckman was turning right onto Oranienburger Strasse. As we passed the Centrum Judaicum, he made a sucking noise with his lips, rolling his eyes. "This is a dangerous time, Herr Inspektor. Disorder is everywhere. Surely you must see that, as a police officer?"

"I'm aware of quite a few crimes that have been committed in the last few days, yes."

He didn't rise to the bait, but continued with a speech I

could tell he had rehearsed. "Social unrest, strikes, protests. The very fabric of the state challenged. And all this while there is a war to be won."

I almost laughed out loud. But von Beckman had intended for me to misinterpret his words, all the more so he could make his next point with greater emphasis. "You scoff. You think the war is lost because of what has happened in Sofia, or in Vienna? Our army holds still on the Western Front! But even that is not what I am speaking of. I do not refer to the war against the Entente, but the war to come."

His words were tinted with enthusiasm. He looked across at me with a gleam in his blue eyes.

"Yes. As soon as we achieve an honourable peace in the west, the true conflict begins."

"What are you talking about?"

"Socialism! Bolshevism! Think of all the gains we have made in the east! Must all that be risked because the Americans have been tricked into siding against us? Because the English are jealous of our success in the world?"

Was he trying to sell me on this concept? His voice was bright, animated, determined. His gloved hands gripped the steering wheel tightly.

"You are a police officer. You are responsible for the maintenance of order."

"In accordance with the law."

I could see that didn't land with him. "When the Bolshevists are rioting in the streets, stabbing the fatherland in the back, committing treason, what will you do?"

"I'll enforce the law. What will you do, Herr Hauptmann?"

"My duty."

We had to slow down near the Hackeschen Markt tram stop, where the road narrows. An ancient truck was parked at the side of the road, holding up a tram. Von Beckman beat the steering wheel with a fist and leaned out of the car to berate the truck driver, then pulled his head back sharply. I realised in that same moment that the vehicle carried a party of Reds, sorting through piles of leaflets in the bed of the truck. Two others loitered at the back carrying rifles. They turned around slowly to see who had shouted at them.

Von Beckman cursed, and looked over his shoulder, but a second tram was pulling to a halt behind us (in fairness, its driver was every bit as aggrieved as von Beckman about the hold-up), and nor could we squeeze past the first tram. One of the Reds, a tall fellow with the kind of moustache that seemed to wander far and wide, gestured towards us.

I was tempted to step out of the car, but I didn't move. In part, I wanted to see how this might play out. But mostly I was determined that von Beckman find his own way off the bed he had made for himself.

The Red was continuing to make obscene gestures with one hand while trying to keep his rifle shouldered. The tram at our side lumbered past, and von Beckman revved the Opel's engine, though this didn't create a particularly intimidating sound. He snarled and prepared to pull out once the tram had passed, only to see that another one was coming from the tram stop. Von Beckman braked and reached to his hip. However, he had much the same problem I did; his sidearm was under his greatcoat. The Red had no such problem; whether by accident or design, he had unslung his rifle, and was no carrying it at his side, as he walked towards us.

I realised matters were about to get out of hand. Once the tram was finally passed, I slipped from the passenger seat and walked a few steps along the street, reaching into my pocket for my beer token.

"Hey, what's this?" the Red cried out. "You can't stop us delivering leaflets."

"You're blocking the street," I said, searching for a calmness I didn't feel.

He didn't look bothered. "Your friend can drive his pram through there!" He started to peer at von Beckman with narrowed eyes.

"Just move the truck," I insisted.

The Red shifted the rifle, just a little. "You're not in charge here," he insisted. His colleague, the other one with a rifle, had caught wind that something was happening and was coming up to join in. He was an ugly fellow with little rat eyes, and there was something in his expression which suggested he was spoiling for an argument.

"Is that an officer?" he demanded, nodding towards the car. "Some staff shit still thinks he can give orders to real soldiers?"

"Move the truck," I said again, with greater emphasis. "I don't give a shit about your leaflets, but you can't block the street."

"Fuck off!" said Rat-eyes.

I took another couple of steps forward. Neither of them had their rifle levelled at me just yet, but there was a sense of threat in the air. The tram behind von Beckman's car rang its bell. Passing pedestrians hurried their steps or ducked into doorways.

"And put those rifles back in the truck," I continued.

Rat-eyes lifted his rifle to his hip. It still wasn't being aimed at me, but it was only a twitch away. I could feel my breathing accelerating. Just then, the truck's driver leaned out of his cab. He was an older man, with an unshaven chin and a faded blue cap on his head.

"Fritz! Max! Leave it! Come on, we've work to do!"

The two Reds looked at each other. Moustache nodded to Rat-eyes. They both took a step back. Moustache even shouldered his rifle once more as they retreated alongside the truck. I exhaled slowly as the tension eased down a fraction, and then I became aware that von Beckman was at my shoulder.

"Red scum! Get out of here!"

Brilliant.

Moustache hesitated, but at least he was most of the

way back towards the passenger door. Rat-eyes was at the tailgate, about to hand his rifle up to one of the men in the back. He turned and snarled at von Beckman.

"What did you call me, you prick?"

"Fucking traitor. Get out of here before I shoot you here in the street."

That was a bold statement of intent for a man whose service pistol was still holstered under his greatcoat. I hissed at von Beckman to calm himself, but he marched on, head erect, boot heels snapping crisply on the roadway.

"You can't give me orders!" Rat-eyes snarled. His fellow Red, leaning down at the back of the truck, had taken hold of the barrel of his rifle. Rat-eyes tugged at the weapon.

"I'll bet everything I have on me that you're a deserter," von Beckman continued, still moving forwards. "Shall we see if I am right? You can pay me before they hang you."

"If anyone is going to hang, it'll be you, you reactionary pig. The people have no need for officers! Give it a few days, and I'll see you swinging from a lamp-post."

Von Beckman bristled, and there was a moment when Rat-eyes was about to get the rifle back, but I had taken the last few moments to unfasten my greatcoat and reach into my jacket. The Mauser is a clumsy weapon to draw from a shoulder rig at the best of times, and this was hardly those. It was as well that von Beckman had stepped ahead of me, so that Rat-eyes and his colleagues were occupied by that flashing *pour le merité* and the clipped accent, because the pistol's front sight snagged on my jacket at the first attempt. With a second pull, however, I drew the C69 clear.

"Everybody, stop what you are doing!" Rat-eyes looked at me as if I had appeared from nowhere, and the other Reds glared at me from the back of the truck, some open mouthed, others ready to put up a fight. I wasn't aiming the Mauser at anyone, but it was in clear view. Those pedestrians on either side of the row who had been persuaded to watch the show now took off in varied directions.

"Move that truck!" I instructed. Old man driver snarled, but then called to the others to get in. It took a few moments for everyone to settle, but then the old truck coughed into life, and rattled off down the street. There was a moment of peace, and then the tram behind von Beckman's car rang its bell impatiently once more, as if we had been the problem all along. We climbed back into the Opel and went back about our business.

"That was a demonstration of everything I mean," von Beckman commented. I agreed that it definitely indicated something.

We didn't exchange much more conversation for the journey to Alexanderplatz. Von Beckman pulled up to the kerb a short distance from the Praesidium, turning in his seat.

"When the socialists begin their revolution, Germany will depend on upon men like us, Herr Kommissar. You need to decide where your duty lies."

"I have never doubted it."

Von Beckman narrowed his eyes, correctly certain that I had evaded the thrust of his implied demand.

"You know I work at the Hauptkadettenanstalt. During this war, three thousand of our cadets have given their lives for the Fatherland."

"So I have been told. So many more have, from all walks of life."

"Indeed. We cannot let their sacrifice be in vain. If peace must come, let it be an honourable one, delivered quickly, so that we can turn our attention to the Reds. There is much work to be done in the east."

Peace so that there could be new war? I must have let my incredulity show. Von Beckman's voice became terse, snappy. "Only a fool thinks matters are finally settled."

I decided to let a little of my own impatience and irritability show. "Where have you taken Obermeier?"

"I have already explained..."

Now I was the one changing my body position, bringing my face directly in front of his.

"Don't try this with me, Herr Hauptmann. Return him immediately, unharmed, or our next conversation cannot be so civil. He is police now..."

Von Beckman snorted derisively. "Police? Come now. He's a paid informant at best; little better than a snitch. He has been sniffing around matters that do not concern him."

This made me angrier than ever. "This is not a discussion, Hauptmann von Beckman. Either he is back here within the hour, or I'll come and find him. And when I do, I'll bring the whole Berlin police force down on whatever you have going on on Altdorferstrasse, you and Colonel von Osterbruck and Herr Doktor Kammerich. You remind them both that we still have much to discuss about what happened at Heilig-Geist-Spital. Your protectors are running out of road, Herr Hauptmann. And when they are gone, nothing we stop me coming to find you all."

Misdirection

I didn't entirely follow through with this bravado. It was at least ninety minutes before Obermeier turned up at the Alex. The moment the door opened, I knew he had taken a beating; he was stiff, unsteady on his face, and he talked with the quiet of a man who could barely cope with the sound of his own voice.

Fraulein Graber sat him down and brought him water. He asked for brandy; they compromised on coffee.

"What happened?"

"I suspect you had the more rewarding conversation, Herr Kommissar."

"It remains to be seen how rewarding it was. Now, I insist, tell me what happened."

"I promise, I've suffered worse, Herr Kommissar. Those boys from the academy, they just wanted to show me who's in charge."

I ground my teeth. Colonel von Osterbruck or whoever was finally in charge of this sorry band must be getting bold or desperate to act with such impunity against the Berlin Police. No matter what disrespect they had for Obermeier personally, or his unorthodox position as part of Amt VIIIb, they had only drawn even more attention to themselves.

We drank ersatz coffee and smoked ersatz tobacco, grumbling about both, and discussing what was to happen next. I told them that I had deliberately avoided mentioning Pabst or the Potsdam barracks, allowing von Beckman to draw the inference that we were only interested in what was going on at the Hauptkadettenanstalt.

"We need to go out to Potsdam. I think they know everything is coming to a head, and they have proved they are desperate, ruthless men. We cannot afford to let them clean house like they did at Heilig-Geist-Spital."

"Herr Obermeier needs to see a doctor!"

"No, no, *gnadige* Fraulein. The Kommissar is right."

Fraulein Graber rounded on me, eyes flashing. She showed no anxiety or fear, just a calm and rational understanding of the situation, and the risks involved. "Can we not ask for help?"

"With your help, I intend to fully acquaint Oberkommissar Teske with our plans. Hopefully, he will provide support for our actions from one source or another."

"And just what *are* our plans?"

"I'll know when we get there."

As I had just suggested, we quickly put our heads together to create a report for the Oberkommissar which outlined what we knew, what we believed, and what we hoped we might uncover. I didn't deliver it personally, but had a passing *schupo* take it up to the second floor.

Immediately after, we went to the armoury in the basement. My two colleagues were a little anxious at this, as I took out an American Winchester 1897 pump-action shotgun, a weapon the armoury had 'inherited' after it had been deployed in a robbery at a jewelers shop back in 1915. Fraulein Graber expressed some surprise that the Berlin police would think of keeping such a weapon.

"Didn't our government protest about the Americans using these things?"

"They did, *gnadige fraulein*," Obermeier responded. "But it is an unfortunate curiosity that the Hague Convention on Land Warfare from 1907 does not apply to the civilian world. In any case, the Americans rejected our protests."

I asked if Obermeier would be comfortable with a rifle, but he declined. "I'll take a pistol if I may, Herr Kommissar, for personal protection, but should matters get so bad that I am required to do more, well… I doubt my poor skills would tip the balance."

I considered the shotgun in this light, but took it anyway. Its weight was reassuring.

Fraulein Graber had her pocket pistol, a Schwarzlose

1908. I reminded her that if we faced any danger at all (and I tried to sound confident we would not), it would be from trained soldiers with rifles. Her six-shot toy wouldn't make a lot of difference. She took offence. Obermeier suggested she stay behind, which shifted the point of her anger.

"I am as determined to see this through as either of you!" Obermeier backed down.

'Just don't start anything," I insisted. She scoffed, casting her eye at the heavy shotgun, which was likely to set off a war all by itself.

From the armoury, we three went down to the garage where I took out a pre-war Mercedes Tourer, after a brief argument with a quartermaster who appeared worried we were going out for a joy-ride. Obermeier climbed in the back; Fraulein Graber sat by my side in the front passenger seat, with the shotgun propped between us. The Tourer was a comfortable ride, but Fraulein Graber kept as far away from the weapon as possible, pressed against the door.

It was no great distance to the Guard Cavalry Barracks in Potsdam, following the main highway away from the city to the south-west, passing Potsdamerplatz, and then the southern end of Wannsee, before crossing the Glienicke Bridge to enter Potsdam itself.

Navigating the city, we passed the Garnisonkirche, with its tall and elegant spire. Obermeier, who had been pensive throughout the journey, remarked how the church was full of captured French regimental flags from the time of the Franco-Prussian War. "My father served then," he commented. "He was at Sedan when the French Emperor surrendered. Such triumphs are hollow now."

Up front, neither of us chose to add anything to that. Instead, I circled around to the north, heading towards the various barracks of the Imperial Guard on Jägerallee.

Following Obermeier's advice, we pulled up just along from the city courthouse. It was a dark day under heavy cloud, but we had a perfect view of all that Obermeier wanted us to see. On the opposite side of the road, a boxy-looking building housed the barracks, with an entrance at one end into a courtyard where, presumably, horses were stabled. The building was smart, functional, but with little moments of whimsy such as the purely decorative towers at the corners, with their useless crenellations.

"Then, down there, that's the other building I spoke of," said Obermeier. "The one where the other soldiers marched out from." This was an altogether less desirable or fanciful construction, with high, narrow windows and a single door facing the street. Nothing stirred there; even the pedestrians along Jägerallee seemed to avoid the pavement outside.

We sat for a while observing the street, and particularly the barracks. There was very little movement here either. I could imagine more triumphant times, and a military band emerging from the courtyard playing martial music, followed by ranks of horsemen in their plumed best. How ridiculous the past seemed now.

From where we sat, I could see a café in the distance, more or less opposite the mysterious building with its forbidding aspect. Hiding the shotgun behind the front seats, we stepped out of the car, and almost at once there was a *schupo* to tell us that we could not leave the car there. Where had he come from? I showed him my beer token.

He wasn't impressed. Out here, we were in the domain of the Brandenburg police. I had had dealings with these public servants often enough in the past to know that they hated the Berlin force with a passion.

"You're out of your jurisdiction," he explained, casting his eye over Obermeier and admiring Fraulein Graber's ankles as they descended from the Mercedes.

"We're on the hunt for a dangerous Red," I said in a low voice, bringing him into this fictitious manhunt. The *schupo*, a tall fellow with close-cropped blond hair under his *shako*, looked at Obermeier as if he might be this imagined suspect.

"Here?"

"Don't make a fuss," I advised. "For all we know this Bolshevist is watching us as we speak."

The *schupo*'s eyes widened with excitement. "Should I call for back-up?"

I leaned in even closer.

"My boss is probably calling your boss even as we speak. How far is it to your Praesidium? I suggest you continue along your beat as normal, but stay close. You never know when this fellow might appear."

The buffoon let out a crisp "*Jawohl!*" and saluted. I made a mental note to never rely on the Brandenburg police for undercover work.

As he marched off, stiff and incapable of doing anything other than looking around at every step, I left it for a few minutes before I spoke to my colleagues again. I was very conscious of the rows of windows in the barracks building, imagining a face behind every pane of glass, watching us and the awkward *schupo*. My imagination had Kammerich telling Pabst who we were, and von Beckman and von Osterbruck dispatching men to watch our movements and plot our demise.

We let the *schupo* move off, and then made our own way to the café opposite the dark building Obermeier insisted on calling an armoury. As we drank coffee and smoked cigarettes, I gave the place a long look over. It was certainly sturdy enough to be an armoury, set behind a wall and a closed gate, with a small number of narrow, barred windows. The wall acted as a continuation of that surrounding the courtyard, which seemed to confirm that the two were connected. However, there were no signs on the 'armoury', nor any indication that it was army property, nor yet any guards at the door.

"I'd like to get a look inside," I said quietly, more for my own benefit than to inform the others.

"Can't we just knock?" asked Obermeier. I didn't answer.

There was very little foot traffic along Jägerallee, for all that there were a number of Brandenburger government offices in this part of the city. A maidservant passed with a shopping basket on her arm; two children with in the company of an older woman were called back as they skipped ahead of her, to be diverted to our side of the street. I should have liked to ask that woman what made her so cautious.

Minutes passed. The café proprietor grew impatient as we occupied the window table without buying anything. Fraulein Graber tried to charm him with her smile and the purchase of thin sandwiches. We even purchased more coffee.

This had only just been delivered when Obermeier nudged my arm. A Daimler Marienfeld truck was pulling up on the other side of the road. It was painted in army drab, but the canvas cover was a dirty white, and featured a large red lozenge. Obermeier nodded as he observed that I too had recognised it.

The driver stepped gingerly down from the cab and limped slowly towards the armoury gate.

"We need to get a look at his cargo," I said urgently, rising to my feet. Obermeier was first to react, leaving his coat behind as he rushed through the café door. I scattered some change on the table, picked up Obermeier's coat (feeling the weight of the Luger he had stashed in a pocket), and guided Fraulein Graber out onto the pavement.

"Go back to the car; if there's trouble, go to the Potsdam Praesidium and get help."

The driver had finally managed to unlatch the gate, which squealed loudly as it opened. Obermeier had reached the back of the truck, but the canvas was tied down tightly. He reached into a pocket and drew out something metallic. Anticipating his next move, I waved at him to leave well alone.

I made for the cab, keeping the bulk of the Daimler

between myself and the armoury door. Looking through the cab, I saw the driver rap on the door with his fist. Several moments passed before the door was opened. I didn't see who had answered the summons, but these two had a brief, staccato conversation. The door then closed, and the limping driver came back to the truck.

He spotted me immediately, screwing his face up in an ugly scowl as he hobbled back through the gate, waving and shouting. As he came closer, I saw his face was pockmarked with scar tissue on one side.

"Hey, you! Get away from there!"

"Take it easy," I replied, producing my beer token. "I was just taking a look."

Various emotions crossed his face, defiance and fear uppermost in the fight. "Nothing to concern you, *bulle*."

"Medical supplies?" I gestured to the manifest he had left on the passenger seat of the truck. He didn't answer. "Where have they come from?"

"I'm just the driver! You want to know what this stuff is, ask those inside, *polente*." He dragged himself into the cab, looking a little sheepish at having used that old insult.

"Why so hostile?"

Again, he didn't answer, but kept his expression fixed in that same defiant scowl as he put the truck into gear and pulled away from the kerb, the motor stuttering a little in the cold. I stepped away and watched him go. As the Daimler trundled awkwardly along the street, I saw the back flaps of its canvas were snapping open and shut until a hand appeared momentarily to draw them closed.

"Christ!"

Fraulein Graber came up to my shoulder. Her voice was filled with concern. "Where is Herr Obermeier?"

There could only be one place. I felt like a fool, stood there in the middle of Jägerallee with his coat over my arm, and his pistol in its pocket. I also felt a chill caress my skin that was more profound than just the cold wind.

"Back to the car!"

I took her arm, and we scampered back towards the Mercedes. The truck moved ahead of us along the street, progressing slowly, until it reached the entrance to the barracks' courtyard. It turned in, pausing at the gatehouse. I saw the driver hand his manifest to a uniformed guard, who went back into his gatehouse. He pointed back to where we had all been just a few moments before, but he didn't seem to catch sight of Fraulein Graber and I as we raced back to the car.

I couldn't blame him for that. Equally, until the last moment, I didn't realise there was someone in the Mercedes sitting in the driver's seat with the Winchester shotgun across his lap.

"So, Herr Kommissar. I am ready to hear your report."

Supplies

"Herr Oberkommissar! What are you doing here?"

"You asked for back-up," he said, which left my racing mind wondering if Herr Oberkommissar Teske considered himself sufficient reinforcement. He then continued: "Events elsewhere are moving briskly. All police are on stand-by to defend against a possible uprising. I came to warn you that we are on our own."

That 'we' wasn't all that reassuring. I opened the passenger door and folded the seat down so that Fraulein Graber could step inside. With one foot on the running board, I leaned in under the canopy.

"That truck, Herr Oberkommissar, contains, I believe, a delivery of *Wiedergeburt*. I further believe that the building back there may be the location to which the missing invalids – those removed from Heilig Geist before we discovered what was going on – were taken.

Oberkommissar Teske grunted and observed the Daimler for a moment. The guard had not yet returned.

"You were instructed to abandon that case," he said, though there was little about his voice to suggest I was being reprimanded.

"Herr Oberkommissar, if I may – there is an immediate situation to be resolved." I swallowed before I delivered the bad news: "Herr Obermeier is in the back of that truck." I handed Obermeier's coat through to Fraulein Graber. "He will surely be discovered when the truck is unloaded."

Now I was reprimanded. "What were you thinking, Hoehner?" Herr Teske was almost grinding his teeth now as he stared across the road. The guard reappeared from his station, handing the manifest back to the driver. There was some pointing, and then the guard lifted the barrier, and the Daimler crept steadily in.

"*Verdammt*. Get in," the Oberkommissar directed in a

low growl, shifting his weight awkwardly across to the passenger seat. I was about to climb in beside him, but he made me pause and insisted Fraulein Graber leave the vehicle. "Do you see the green Daimler back along the street? That is my car; my driver will take you to the Potsdam Praesidium. Ask there for Polizei-Major Trapp; use my name. Explain the situation and ask for any men he can spare. Hurry."

Fraulein Graber gave no hint of how she was feeling as she followed the Oberkommissar's instructions. Once she had departed, I swung into the driver's seat, noting that the Oberkommissar had held onto the shotgun. "I expected better judgment from you, Hoehner. A leader does not put his team at risk. Come now, drive to the gate!"

I did as he instructed. The youth at the guard post looked surprised; perhaps he had never seen so much traffic at the gate before. He looked about sixteen or seventeen, with big eyes, an angular chin and barely a whiff of facial hair. His greatcoat was too large, and even at a first glance I could see it was shoddily made, with the seams looking fit to burst even though the coat hung so loosely on his shoulders.

'Halt!" he said, his immature voice scarcely radiating authority. Teske decided to show him how it was done.

"Is this how you perform your duties, private? Fasten your collar; straighten that cap!"

The young man jumped as if he had stabbed in the arse. He all but saluted. He was stammering out an apology even as Oberkommissar Teske produced his identity papers. "Let us through. That truck contains a wanted fugitive, and black-market contraband."

The guard's mouth opened and closed like he was a dying fish. He stared at the document for several minutes, but it might just as well have been in Swahili. Something told me he was not a vital cog in the machine.

"Move the barrier!" Teske commanded after he was handed back his papers. The Daimler was out of sight, having passed through an open gate in the perimeter of the barracks compound that appeared to lead to a yard behind the armoury.

The young guard clearly hadn't been instructed in what to do when faced by the kind of policeman who once had harassed him and his mates for loitering on street corners. With an expression of 'don't tell my father', he hesitated, then lifted the gate. Oberkommissar Teske nudged my leg with the back of his hand, which still grasped the shotgun, and I released the handbrake and took us off behind the truck. As we left, Teske commanded the boy to fetch the officer of the watch.

"Do we *want* the officer of the watch?" I wondered out loud.

"It's best if someone is present who has the sense and authority to understand the situation they're in." The situation in which we were inside a military compound containing evidence and perpetrators of an horrendous crime? That situation? "Fraulein Graber will be here soon enough. Polizei-Major Trapp is a good man."

The Oberkommissar seemed far more comfortable with our position than did I. In the Mercedes' rearview mirror, I saw the young guard lower the gate and then scurry off to a door in the main barracks block. Good on him. This was beyond my pay grade too, and we only needed the one fool in these circumstances.

It had been a tight fit for a big beast like that Daimler Marienfeld through the interior gateway, and the big Mercedes Tourer wasn't so slender that there was a *lot* of room, but it wasn't my paintwork to worry about. I trod down hard on the brakes and we slithered to a halt across the gravel, almost running into the side of the truck, which had been reversed up to a loading bay at the back of the armoury.

The driver was up by a narrow door at the side of a larger entrance at the top of a ramp. To my mind, it looked as if he had just come out of the door, probably having announced his arrival to whoever was stationed within. His face had coloured with anger as he watched the Mercedes almost pile into his truck; it screwed up even more as I exited the driver's seat.

"Hey! You can't be back here!" he began, taking a couple of halting steps towards the edge of the loading bay. He froze as he saw me pull the Winchester out from the Tourer. Perhaps it wasn't a hard and fast rule that we weren't allowed back here after all.

Oberkommissar Teske now hove into view, like a battlecruiser steaming out from behind an island. He marched stiffly to the back of the truck. I followed meekly, noticing that the back of the canvas was unlaced. I tried to peer inside the truck, but I didn't want to appear too interested.

"What do you have in here?"

"M-medical supplies," the driver insisted, lifting a hand to scratch at one of the many scars on his face.

"Show me your paperwork!" the Oberkommissar demanded. He remained by the side of the Mercedes, arms folded, jaw set hard. The delivery driver froze in place, then looked around for assistance. There was none, of course.

"You – you can't do this!" the driver responded, his stammer getting worse by the minute. His eyes were wide disks.

"I am Oberkommissar Teske of the Berlin Police." That sounded like enough authority to me. "Show me your transport papers."

"You have no right!" The driver was obstinate, I'll give him that. I hefted the shotgun. He quickly indicated that he had left the paperwork in the delivery office behind him. Quite right; the Winchester obviously made this someone else's problem.

Oberkommissar Teske marched up the ramp, gesturing for me to follow. I took a look around, very much aware that we were in the lions' den, and that Obermeier's precipitous behaviour was becoming a whole division of rash choices. The Oberkommissar motioned for the deliveryman to go through the door ahead of him.

Now I took a slightly longer look into the back of the truck, pushing the canvas back with the barrel of the shotgun. There was quite the load of boxes and wooden crates, all marked with the red lozenge. I could see no sign of Obermeier, who, I was starting to believe, must have jumped off the truck as it pulled up to the loading bay, or possibly when the driver reported his arrival inside. Where was he now?

I scurried up the ramp to follow the Oberkommissar into the armoury. The door opened into a unloading area with a small office attached, and doors which led further into the interior of the building. The space had a funereal air, cold and quiet. The walls were whitewashed and festooned with military instructions. Smoking was *verboten*.

Through some glass panes, I could see the Oberkommissar talking to some fellow seated behind a desk. I moved up behind the chief and took a quick look into the office to gauge the situation for myself. The fellow behind the desk was a scruffy, pasty-faced individual with reddish hair and dark rings around his eyes. He was dwarfed by the Oberkommissar, and not just in purely physical terms.

"Who is in charge here, Unteroffizier? Stand up when I am talking to you!"

The NCO rose slowly to his feet, letting a hand linger near the drawer of the desk in front of him. I looked at him, and he at me. Or, more accurately, he let his eyes dwell for a moment on Herr Winchester.

Oberkommissar Teske was on a roll. "Call yourself a soldier in the Guard?"

"He isn't," I ventured. It had taken me a moment, but I had recognised him. The last time I had seen this individual, it had been at Heilig Geist and he had been wearing the garb of a hospital orderly. My mind went back to the moment Moehnke pulled on the cable by the door, and this fool, Moehnke and the other orderly, along with the two *schupos*, had left the ward. I recalled the first flask as it tumbled off the shelf; the last moments before the inferno.

"What's your name, friend?" I snarled, not feeling at all amicable. I don't hold grudges often, but I felt justified with this one.

"You've made a big mistake," he replied, surely nowhere near as brave as he sounded. Once again, it seemed, the first line of defence with these fellows, was to insist we had no right to be on military property.

I decided to get straight to the point. "Where is Moehnke? Where is Kammerich?" "Go to hell."

His hand was trembling as it edged nearer the edge of the desk. I flicked the muzzle of the shotgun up and down to ensure it had his attention. He took perhaps a half step back.

"You are going to lead the way into the rest of the building," Oberkommissar Teske announced in a flat tone that brooked no refusal.

"L-look, I'm just the delivery d-driver," scar-face began. He was backed-up as far into the corner of the room as possible.

The Oberkommissar took one of several pieces of thin paper from the desk. I glanced at it quickly. It appeared to be a delivery note, listing medical equipment, chemicals and three cases of what was listed as 'WG'. The only printing on the manifest was a red lozenge; there was no consignee address or anything.

"Where did all this come from?" Teske pressed, waving the paper.

"Say nothing," snapped the NCO.

"Do not take this man's advice. You're right – you are just a delivery driver. But this man is going to be tried for murder. Don't become part of that."

The driver didn't take this new possibility well. His face paled, and his stammer grew so bad it wasn't possible to understand what he was saying, though it was evident he didn't want any part of being accused of murder. The Oberkommissar took hold of his lapel and drew him away from the desk. "Where do these supplies come from?"

The driver looked across at the NCO with panicked eyes. I took that to mean it was time they were separated and gestured with the shotgun.

"Let's go see what's going on through there."

Reluctant though he was to take any orders from me, the Winchester tipped the balance. Scuffing his boots on the floor, the NCO came out from behind the desk and stepped up to the door. I had him pause there for a moment while I opened the drawer. As expected, I found a pistol there – a rather worn Luger P08. The NCO scowled as I pocketed it. Herr Winchester directed him out of the door.

The armoury was constructed of large stone blocks, which made for very thick walls, and a feeling of cold weight about us on all sides. The office had been set behind a rough wooden partition, but the wall at the back of the loading area was a metre thick at least. Two trolleys were leaning there, under more notices and instructions. A large metal door stood ajar.

I had to keep nudging my guide forward with the shotgun. He was obviously stalling. I could understand why, given the situation, but that didn't make it any less irritating. He also decided to start talking, and not in any kind of informative way, either.

"How long do you think your luck can hold?"

"Longer than yours, Unteroffizier."

He mocked that assertion with a hollow laugh. "What do you think is going to happen when my commander learns what you are doing here?"

"You better hope he makes himself scarce. Don't worry about me, brother, you worry about what happens if I decide these walls are thick enough that no-one will hear me scatter you all over them. I haven't forgotten what you did." Nor would I ever.

This next area of the armoury was divided up into

pens, akin to a cattle shed. Some of the pens had open faces, others had bulky metal doors of which about half were closed. A couple were empty, but the rest of those I could see into were piled with munitions. One contained crates of Gewehr 98 rifles, still in their delivery crates from Mauser, along with box after box of 7.62x57mm ammunition; in a second, there were four DWM Maschinengewehr 08 on their tripod mounts, again with crates of ammunition; in a third there was an assortment of other hardware – bayonets, M17 Stielhandgrenate, even two Flammenwerfer M16s. One crate contained a couple of dozen modern lederschutzmaske. These alone made my blood run cold.

"Not bad for a few dozen men," I observed.

The NCO sneered. "You underestimate us, *bulle*. Soon, there will be thousands of us on the streets."

"Haven't you heard? The war is over, mate."

"We *are* the war!" he snapped back, in a confident manner which suggested he had heard and used that line before.

"Who are 'we'? Come on: let's not pretend. You're not with the Garde-Kavallerie-Schützendivision. Are you even in the Army?"

He laughed raucously. "You don't understand anything!"

I tried to goad him into adding more, but he didn't rise to the bait. I poked the Winchester into his back, and we moved on.

Beyond another heavy door, the next area contained more gear: rations, medical supplies, uniforms. I saw the red lozenge on several of the boxes.

"You moved the operation here from Heilig Geist." He didn't comment beyond yet another variant of his scornful sneer. I took a quick look around while keeping him covered. Here was the door out onto the street I had observed from Jägerstrasse. There was also a staircase going up to the next level. I also noted something that really chilled me. Racked on wooden shelves sat at least twenty large metal cylinders, some marked with a yellow cross, others with crosses of green.

"My God… are you people mad?"

The NCO stared at me dumbly. I jerked my thumb towards the cylinders.

"Phosgene? Mustard gas? You're keeping mustard gas here?" I heard the tremor in my voice. "What possible *reason* can there be for this?"

"You'd fumigate a house to get rid of rats, wouldn't you?" the NCO replied, glibly.

My heart started pounding. I found myself almost sinking to the ground as sweat broke out from every pore, and my voice became thick with phlegm. Drawing on all my strength, I pointed towards the stairs. "What's up there?"

"Fuck off."

"What's *up* there?!"

I was close to belting him with the shotgun by this point, and he knew it. Maybe he hoped he could provoke me; perhaps he sensed I was weak and distracted at that moment. I pushed him towards the stairs.

"Go up!"

He hesitated, but then took a couple of faltering steps upwards. He paused and looked back at me. I thought I could see fear in his eyes. He was on the brink of saying something when we both heard a door open at the top of the stairs, and then heavy boots moving along the landing up there. I kept the shotgun trained at the NCO's back. The steps creaked a little as we started to climb.

Breaking The Chain

We were barely started when a voice called out to us to halt.

It was darker on the upper floor, but as we paused the electric lights on the stairwell revealed three figures moving into view. I had no idea who the first was, but he radiated authority and Prussian self-confidence, bolstered by the general's oak leaves on his lapels and the blue *pour le merité* at his throat. I started to wonder if they were giving those things away wholesale.

I would have placed him as being in his late fifties. He had quite a weak chin, narrow eyes, and a bird's nest of brown hair. He was so far above us, both literally and figuratively, but didn't register much of a reaction to seeing both an unteroffizier and a civilian on his stairs. Instead, he turned his head slightly to speak to the man behind him.

I didn't recognise this one, not for a moment. He was a Colonel, tall, blond-haired, with a nose that sought to define the word aquiline and a uniform so well-tailored it put even the general's to shame. He wore a monocle in his left eye, and had a small duelling scar on his left cheek, to compel the idea that he was a proper Prussian officer. No *pour le merité*, though, the lightweight.

"What is this?" the general asked.

The Colonel reached into the holster at his waist and produced a Luger of his own, which was a bold move. I guess he couldn't clearly see the Winchester.

"This must be the Berlin policeman we were warned about, Herr Generalmajor." The Colonel stepped past his superior while I wondered what those words revealed. In that moment, a third figure appeared at the head of the stairs, one I did recognise. It was the *schupo* we had encountered in the street.

"That's him, Herr Generalmajor! There's a girl and

some old man as well."

"Step out of the way," the Colonel said crisply. Just from that phrase, I knew who he was; that accent and manner were impossible to miss. The constable stepped back while the Colonel raised the pistol. In front of me, the NCO quivered. In a competition between the Luger and the Winchester, he knew he would be the loser.

"Herr Generalmajor. Before the Colonel here makes a rash move, I should inform you that one of my subordinates is bringing reinforcements; they should already be on their way."

"The Potsdam police?" the Colonel sneered. The *schupo* laughed scornfully.

"Also: I am not alone. Others from the Berlin *kripo* are wth me, as is our chief, Oberkommissar Teske."

The Colonel didn't find that so amusing. "He's bluffing."

"I only suggest that no-one does anything hasty," I concluded. The Generalmajor took a moment, then laid his hand on top of the Colonel's, lowering the pistol.

"Very well. Let us hear what you have to say, Herr…?"

"Kriminal-Kommissar Hoehner, Herr Generalmajor."

"Do you know who I am?" I wasn't against taking a guess, but it turned out his question was rhetorical. "I am Generalmajor Maercker, commanding officer of His Imperial Majesty's 214th Infantry Division. This is Colonel von Osterbruck, my chief of staff. You are trespassing on Army property, Herr Kriminal-Kommissar."

Von Osterbruck, we meet again. That brief acquaintance we had forged in *Annabet*'s felt like a lifetime ago. And now here he was with almost the whole of the rest of the gang.

"Is this man also under your command, Herr Generalmajor?" I asked, giving the NCO a nudge with the Winchester, just so he remembered the American was still in charge here.

Maercker was wise enough to avoid answering that. "I am going to insist that you leave immediately, Herr Kriminal-Kommissar. However well-intentioned your actions, you are interfering with Top Secret operations."

That was an even more solid argument than the trespassing one.

"Herr Generalmajor. This man in front of me is wanted for the murder of approximately thirty army personnel at Heilig-Geist-Spital, as well as being part of a criminal conspiracy."

Maercker's thin mouth twisted. "You have proof of these accusations, Herr Kommissar?"

"I witnessed them."

Maercker considered this for a moment, nodding his head slightly. "I see."

"I further believe that others guilty of the same offence are on these premises. I am going to insist on being allowed to... complete my search."

The nodding continued. "Do you have a warrant to that effect?"

"No. But I do have the Oberkommissar of Berlin's *kriminalpolizei*, who can issue such a warrant. It amounts to the same thing."

The Generalmajor stiffened. He whispered something to the Colonel, who disappeared from view. The staircase standoff continued.

"I insist on a proper warrant, Herr Kriminal-Kommissar. Until then, you must leave."

"I cannot agree to that, Herr Generalmajor. These conspirators have already committed murder to cover their tracks. I cannot allow them to take flight."

We watched each other for a long moment. I doubted that someone like Maercker was accustomed to negotiating, but he was proving a quick learner.

"Who are these other suspects you think might be here?"

"There is a man named Moehnke; a third individual I cannot name, but who is connected to Moehnke and this NCO; and finally, there is a Herr Doktor Kammerich. All of these are wanted for the murder of German soldiers at Heilig-Geist." I let that sink in for a beat. "I would welcome also the opportunity to speak at length with your Colonel von Osterbruck." The Generalmajor narrowed his eyes and folded his hands behind his back. We took a moment, we two, to give the chessboard a long appraisal.

I understood clearly what the Generalmajor was trying to achieve; he wanted to know what we knew, what we could prove, what we proposed to do about it. I imagined the calculations going on in his mind. My suspicions were that he was wondering what he might be able to keep obscured if he sacrificed these few names. Judging by his body language, the NCO was starting to appreciate where he figured in that calculation.

During the pause that followed that laundry list, it occurred to me that I might as well kill as many birds as possible with the one stone. "I also want Hauptman Waldemar Pabst for questioning in relation to a different murder."

Generalmajor Maercker's expression went from thoughtful to dismissive. "Impossible. You exceed both your authority and my patience, Herr Kommissar."

As he finished berating me, I heard a noise off to the side down at my level and in walked Oberkommissar Teske. If he was at all perturbed to find his subordinate at the bottom of a flight of stairs, aiming a shotgun in the general direction of a divisional commander of the Imperial German Army, he didn't show it.

"Kommissar Hoehner; what is going on here?"

I made introductions and outlined the state of negotiations for the benefit of my Chief. He and Generalmajor Maercker sized each other up.

"Herr General. It hardly behooves men of rank to

conduct themselves like widows at the back of a tenement building. Can we speak privately?"

Maercker puffed himself up, perhaps having enjoyed the higher ground thus far. "This needs to be brief."

"So. Shall I come to you, or shall you come to me?"

Maercker stepped back. As he did so, Colonel von Osterbruck reappeared and whispered something in his ear. Maercker nodded and Osterbruck went out of sight again. Oberkommissar Teske hauled himself up the stairs. Once the ascent was complete, he and the Generalmajor saluted each other, shook hands and then walked off out of view. Colonel von Osterbruck reappeared, and this time he had company: Moehnke, in the greatcoat of an army *feldwebel,* along with the third 'orderly' from Helig-Geist.

Through all this, the NCO had been standing uncomfortably on the lower portion of the stairs. I could smell his sweat. He had been pressed to the wall as Oberkommissar Teske went by, but now he was piggy-in-the-middle once more. "Moehnke, you need to get me out of this!" he called.

"Shut up, you idiot!" Moehnke snapped back.

At his rear, the Colonel made some kind of deliberate movement, and when I next saw his hand, it was occupied once more with the Luger pistol. "Go down," he instructed.

Moehnke's face twisted in surprise. He looked back to find von Osterbruck and the Luger impassively squared up behind him.

"What is this?"

"Go down."

Moehnke looked down at me, then back at von Osterbruck. "Oh, no. You're not sacrificing me to –"

"Shut up. Go down." Each word was enunciated separately, like four pistol shots. Von Osterbruck's posture was designed to make the point just as forcefully. He lifted the muzzle of the Luger to Moehnke's forehead.

Moehnke ground his teeth, but he made the first step. His colleague was pale and open-mouthed. Moehnke made sure he went down first.

Even with a shotgun, I wasn't entirely comfortable with how this was going. Once I had all three 'interns' from Heilig-Geist down with me, I would have my hands full, and certainly I wouldn't be well-placed to assist the Ober-kommissar with whatever was going on upstairs. I cursed under my breath, and wondered how long it would be before Fraulein Graber arrived with reinforcements. Of course, we had to reckon with the possibility that the Potsdam *polizei* would not necessarily consider themselves on *our* side.

Speaking of which: "You as well," von Osterbruck said in a low voice, and he indicated that the *schupo* should follow the other two. The fellow looked dumbstruck. Von Osterbruck leaned in and removed his police-issue pistol from its holster.

"All of you, go down the stairs."

The trio moved with a glacial slowness. That suited me, since I needed time to decide what to do now that von Osterbruck was successfully encumbering me with these 'prisoners'. They had barely moved halfway down the stairs; the third intern in the lead, then Moehnke, then the bewildered Potsdam *schupo*. The shotgun felt heavy in my hands, and my nostrils were filled with the stench of the *unteroffizier*'s sweat.

"I'll not swing for your botched scheme!" snarled Moehnke.

The next seconds passed in a blur. Moehnke made a move with his right arm, using the others to hide his actions. He must have a pistol in his right coat pocket, I realised. Von Osterbruck knew it too and delayed just enough to allow Moehnke to begin to pull it clear. The Luger barked.

The *schupo* yelped as if he had been struck, but von Osterbruck hadn't been aiming at him. A jet of blood and grey matter splashed along the wall, and Moehnke went down like a felled tree. He bounced off the third 'intern', crashed onto the steps, bounced again, and slid down a few more steps to wind up just above where the Unteroffizier was standing.

Someone yelled out 'No! Don't shoot!' In a high, hysterical voice. It could have been any one of the three surviving occupants of the stairway. Come to that, it might even have been me. I certainly joined in.

"Stop shooting, von Osterbruck! Don't you know what's down here? You'll kill us all."

The Colonel lowered the Luger slightly. His expression suggested he didn't think he believed there was any danger at all. He'd hit what he was aiming at. Moehnke had been the go-between, the one Kammerich had placed in charge of the day-to-day care of the invalids at Heilig-Geist. That had been the chain of command: von Osterbruck (with whoever was pulling the strings above him), Doktor Luster, Kammerich, Moehnke. Two links in the chain were broken.

"Unterwachtmeister Dorn. What did you just witness here?"

Out on the street, the *schupo* hadn't struck me as the sharpest tack in the tin, but he caught on *very* quickly here. The bullet must have passed close enough for him to have felt it, and he quickly worked out why it had been fired.

"Sir, ummm... The uh... *feldwebel* was being placed under arrest. He – uh – reached for his weapon... and you shot him, *Herr Colonel.*"

"*Sehr gut.*" Von Osterbruck was almost smiling as he holstered the Luger.

The third intern was trembling. The back of his head was covered with the blood and gore of his fellow suspect, and his uniform was soiled. Not all of that was down to Moehnke.

Tidying Up

Abruptly, breaking into this curious, fatal interlude, there came a thunderous hammering at the street door and a strong, if muffled, baritone voice.

"Polizei! Open up!"

This was good news (I hoped), though it added one more complication to my situation. I took a step up and grabbed hold of the Unteroffizier by the back of his collar, dragging him off the staircase with the shotgun pushed hard into his back. He didn't resist too much, partly because Moehnke had been bleeding all over his boots.

"Open the door."

I had to step well away from the stairs to keep both him and the trio descending the stairs covered. It was not an ideal situation. My back bumped into a metal rack against one wall, and I looked around to see that it was one of those containing the large metal cylinders. My heart jumped a beat or two. The thought jumped into my mind again that one stray bullet and one of the canisters could be spewing mustard gas into an enclosed room. When I could speak, I bellowed at the *Unteroffizier* to hurry up.

At last, the bolts were drawn, and the doors opened. Daylight flooded into the chamber, backlighting a whole squad of bodies in police green. To my relief, I could see Fraulein Graber immediately behind a *schupo Polizei-leutnant*. He looked more than a little taken aback at the vista in front of him.

"Stay *exactly* where you are, Herr Leutnant." I used my free hand to draw out my beer token. "I am Kriminal-Kommissar Hoehner of the Berlin Police. Upstairs, Oberkommissar Teske of Amt VIIIb is speaking with a senior officer of the German army. These men –" I encompassed a wide range of people with a movement of the shotgun – "are involved in a criminal conspiracy, which includes the murder of several soldiers of the German army. Put this one in handcuffs." I gave the *Unteroffizier* a little shove.

The Leutnant had spotted Dorn on the stairs. "Unterwachtmeister, is this correct?"

Dorn, naturally, glanced briefly at von Osterbruck. Nothing was exchanged between them, but Dorn had quickly learned on which side his bread was buttered.

"*Jawohl, Herr Leutnant.*"

The Potsdam *Leutnant* looked sceptical, but gestured for one of his squad to take hold of the *Unteroffizier*, and they did at least slap iron on the man. I had no way to be sure if he would stay that way, but what else was I supposed to do?

"Don't come in," I told him. "There are munitions stored in here, including *giftgas!*"

The *Leutnant* technically outranked me, but the threat of poison gas trumped everything else. His men took several steps back.

I had the third intern come down to the ground floor and handed him over to the Potsdam lads. Dorn came down under his own steam and left the building without a word. For a moment, we all stood there like fools, watching Moehnke's blood dripping down the stairs and pooling out onto the stone floor.

"What would you have us do?" the *leutnant* asked.

"Secure the building. If I was you, I'd clear the street just in case."

That sounded good to all the gathered *schupos*. Some of them took the prisoners to a waiting van; others marched off to form a cordon around the armoury. Everyone was prepared to stay *well* back.

Soon, that just left me, the *leutnant*, Colonel von Osterbruck and Fraulein Graber. Before I could even think to say otherwise, she had pressed her way into the armoury, coming to my elbow. I told her to retrieve Moehnke's weapon. As she did so, I stared up at von Osterbruck. The Colonel was completely calm.

"I'm coming up," I told him.

"That is an ill-advised move," he replied.

"All the same." I made my way up the stair, taking great care to keep the sleeve of my coat away from the bloodied wall. I carried the Winchester as casually as any man could. I was almost at the top when I realised Fraulein Graber had followed me, which really was ill-advised. Von Osterbruck looked past me, one eyebrow crooked in disbelief, though he chose not to comment on her presence specifically.

"Your presence here can only complicate matters," he said in that same measured voice. "What are you looking for?"

"You've stolen Moehnke from me, as you did Herr Doktor Luster. I want Kammerich."

He chuckled softly. "To what end?" When I didn't answer, he stepped back and gestured for me to to go on. "You'll be disappointed," he remarked as I passed. "In any case, from here on, matters are being decided at a much higher level."

"I've come this far. I'd like to see things to the end."

"Would you? Well, I suppose you have seen most everything already."

At the head of the stairs there was a long, wide passageway, with narrow, barred windows on one side and doorways on the other. Hearing no further obstruction from von Osterbruck, I tried the first door. This led into a room not unlike those pens downstairs. It had functioned as a office, I imagined, when this place had been used as an actual army magazine, and still retained some drab, functional military furniture, specifically a desk and chair, and some cabinets. In the far corner, a cot had been laid out, and on it a figure lay prone, quite still, hardly breathing. I hesitated, then moved a little closer, and drew the man back by his shoulder, to that he faced upwards.

Kammerich's eyes were open, but he didn't see me. Instead, he stared blankly up at the ceiling. His mouth was slack, and his lips wet. I shook the same shoulder I had used to roll him over; he didn't respond.

"What has happened to him?"

Von Osterbruck chose to shrug, which irritated me. Fraulein Graber was in the doorway, open-mouthed. I shook Kammerich more vigorously. Still nothing.

"What happened to him?"

"Who can say? An overdose of his own preparation, perhaps?"

"Rebirth?"

"I genuinely don't know. Doktor Kammerich was… indisciplined. Perhaps that worked for him as an experimental scientist, up to a point. He rolled the dice once too often."

Fraulein Graber spoke up with a soft voice. "Has he seen a doctor?"

"Interesting turn of phrase. No, he has not been visited by a doctor. What diagnosis could they offer without knowing the cause? And we cannot speak of the cause, can we? No. On the other hand, perhaps if we had his notes, we might…"

"His notes are gone."

"Ah. Are they? That's a pity. Well, that being the case, as you can see the whole affair ends here. A pity."

"A *pity*?" I was completely incredulous at his blasé assessment of all that had happened.

Von Osterbruck, who had been over by the door beside Fraulein Graber, came completely into the room and took up the chair, placing it by Kammerich's bedside. Unexpectedly, he stroked the doctor's lank hair, akin to the touch of one man for his brother.

"Are you even aware what he had achieved? The potential!"

"I'm keenly aware of what has been done, Herr Colonel. You seem more… comfortable with his discoveries than I."

He ignored the moral judgment I had left implicit in what I had said. Instead, he continued assertively: "Imagine if

Rebirth had been available at scale two years ago, or even one. Imagine. Thousands of men who had reduced to nothing by mental trauma, restored to active service."

"I fail to see..."

"Herr Kommissar, you have been misled, only seeing those men undergoing treatment. But when the full course is complete, these men are as good as new! You would be *amazed!*"

He sounded delighted, almost enraptured. "And it's not just the mental scars that are healed. *Wiedergeburt* can do so much more. Imagine a man who has suffered a debilitating wound. Well, you don't have to imagine that, do you, Herr Kommissar? Yes, I am aware of how you came to be discharged. So let us speak of a soldier subjected to shrapnel wounds, or scarring of the lungs through a gas attack. The wounds heal, yes, but underneath the scars, the pain endures. So, what if that pain was... eradicated?"

He sat back, crossing his legs and straightening his seams, looking up at me with something approaching a light in his eyes.

"The German Empire has suffered over two million military deaths in this war. The Reich has made an extraordinary sacrifice. How might that be justified?"

"Perhaps by ending it."

He ignored such talk. "Additionally, an estimated four million have been wounded. Now, many of those men, brave men, dedicated to the cause, returned to their units after treatment. As it should be. But how many more have been lost to the fight through being invalided – or, perhaps more accurately – discarded because of their infirmities?"

Fraulien Graber made an odd little noise. I found my own voice reaching a high note of its own. "What are you suggesting, Herr Colonel? That amputees be returned to the trenches?" I thought I was joking.

"Oh, you have seen these fellows all over Berlin, Herr Kommissar! They do just fine. Those men who have suffered facial disfigurement, for example…" He made a vague gesture around his own features. "A porcelain mask here, a tin mask there. They may not excite the ladies any more, but they can still fight!"

Dear God.

"It's all in the mind, Herr Kommissar. That is where the problem lies. And Rebirth cleanses the mind, heals the mind. All trauma is forgotten, all pain. The soldier is made whole."

We remained in silence for a few seconds. I was struggling to process what I was hearing. Fraulein Graber looked over at me, and I could see she too was appalled.

"These men… have been completely broken by the war we made. And you want to send them back into it?"

He made a noncommittal gesture, completely at odds with how forthright he had just been.

I looked down at Kammerich. Was he 'made whole'? Von Osterbruck misinterpreted my thoughts: "Take him if you wish, Herr Kommissar. He has no value to the Reich any more."

I wasn't ready to make that decision. I stepped away from the bed, pausing by Fraulein Graber to guide her from the room ahead of me.

"Herr Kommissar!" came von Osterbruck's urgent voice from behind me. "You have been provided with everything you demanded. Now, I must insist that you leave!"

I ignored him. Fraulein Graber and I went into the next room, where we found Oberkommissar Teske and Generalmajor Maercker standing at the foot of a pair of hospital beds. The room had been converted into a basic infirmary, bleak though it was. As well as the two beds, there was a small cabinet for supplies, and two chairs. By each bed, there was a stand, with a glass ampule hanging from it, slowly drip-feeding *Wiedergeburt* into the arm of the figure lying on the bed. I felt nauseous.

"Herr Kommissar, you should not be here." This was from Teske. His voice was quiet, almost subdued. As he looked at me, I saw his eyes were gleaming.

"You know what this is?" I asked, gesturing loosely about the room.

"I read your reports," he replied.

Von Osterbruck pushed into the room past Fraulein Graber. He had that feverish look about his face still.

Generalmajor Maercker picked up on my Chief's last remark. "Those reports need to be secured, Herr Oberkommissar. Along with the other evidence you have accumulated." "Yes, I will attend to that."

Now, more than ever, I couldn't believe what I was hearing. "What's this? You're handing over everything we found to these people?"

"Be still, Kommissar!"

Maercker stared back at me, chin lifted, eyes hardening. "Herr Kommissar. Your Chief and I have discussed this. There is nothing to be gained by pursuing matters further. This… experiment was unauthorised. No matter what the perpetrators –"

"We can't just brush this under the carpet!" I cried in vain appeal.

Unused to being interrupted, Maercker took a moment. "As I said, we have agreed that it is best that this whole matter be forgotten. The perpetrators, where their misdeeds can be proven, are gone now. Do as you will with the prisoners you have taken, but I personally recommend that they be charged with lesser crimes, and handed lighter sentences on the basis that they keep their mouths shut."

My mind was racing. I would have killed for a cigarette right then; in fact, I would happily have blown up the whole armoury for a nail. "Herr Oberkommissar! Tell me you aren't agreeing to this!"

Teske took his time formulating his reply. Of course he could have just commanded my obedience, but I think he was preparing to justify his decision to himself, and not just to me and Fraulein Graber.

"Kriminal-Kommissar Hoehner. You have done great work in this matter, but it is over. This... abhorrent project has been brought to an end. It has been agreed that the pharmaceutical manufacturer of *Wiedergeburt* will be closed down, and all stocks seized. I am told that the manufacture of the treatment was, at best, problematic, and that without Kammerich, is considered impossible."

"That's why they want his records!" I insisted. "They're not going to just give up."

"The most... sensitive records... will be sealed away."

That was news to von Osterbruck, and clearly wasn't what he and Maercker had been cooking up here. Unlike me, though, he had the self-discipline to keep his trap shut in front of a superior officer.

"Even as we speak, the old order is collapsing," Maercker added. "I was just telling the Oberkommissar – Ebert is on the brink of traveling to Spa to see the Kaiser – a socialist going to make demands of the Emperor. I think everyone is now agreed that abdication is inevitable; if it does not come, a revolution is the only other possible outcome. The situation is becoming worse by the hour. Bolshevists and revolutionaries are everywhere, pressing all the territorial rulers to step aside. I hear that King Ludwig fled Munich in the last few hours. Anarchy is knocking at the door, Herr Kommissar."

"What does that have to do with the crimes we know to have been committed?"

"When the abdication occurs, authority must endure. Whatever new government takes the Emperor's place must maintain order. The army and the police owe this duty to Germany."

So, that was the play? We were going to let everything slide because of *duty*?

During much of the latter part of this conversation, I had been staring at the figures on the two beds. Both were sat up, looking back at me with dead eyes, as if listening but unable to follow. My eyes wandered to the medical charts hanging from the bedframes. I noticed their names. Privat Werner Winter, and Gefreiter Adolf Meinz.

Adolf Meinz. They must have found him on the street after that fracas outside Heilig-Geist. He looked little more than a boy, sitting there in his hospital gown, poison dripping into his veins, melting his mind. *Guten Tag,* Adolf. I have your paybook in a drawer.

My lack of further objections must have suggested to Generalmajor Marecke that this conversation was over. He turned to the Oberkommissar. "We should speak to your superiors at once. They should be provided with an explanation that fits the known facts, without all the extraneous details."

"Of course."

"Wait!" I cried. "What about Hauptmann Pabst?"

Maercker sighed theatrically. "Pabst is nothing to do with this business, nor with me. If you think you can bring a charge of murder against him, then do so."

They started to move towards the door without so much at a backwards glance at the two men lying on hospital beds. Oberkommissar Teske did pause as he went by me, laying a hand on my shoulder.

"Go home, Kommissar. Get some rest. You've been going at this non-stop for days. It's over now."

That was it. He followed the Generalmajor out of the room. I swear I heard them start to discuss politics before they reached the head of the stairs. If I heard Maercker expound on what would be required to deal with Bolshevists one more time, I was convinced I'd join the revolution myself.

Breathe Deeply

So, there we were, the five of us, not saying a word as we listened to the brass making their way out of the building, bonding over a proposed future of order and law. Two of us were silent because our brains had been chemically neutered; two more of us were trying to process all that we had just heard with brains that were scarcely more intact. Only one of us was silent because he thought it was all over.

Von Osterbruck took a silver cigarette case out of his pocket, along with a trench lighter, the type we liked to call Tommy lighters, because the British .303 cartridge case made for such a good lighter. Von Osterbruck's was highly-polished, and looked as if it was engraved. I watched him stroke his manicured fingers over the brass, but he thought better of the moment, and placed both back in his tunic pocket.

"Well, then," he said.

I walked over to Gefreiter Meinz's bed, leant the shotgun against the frame and took up the chart. Someone had been taking his temperature every few hours, checking his blood pressure, monitoring his liquid intake; presumably they had spooned food into the man a couple of times of day – what else was there to record? Ah, yes… the regular intake of Rebirth. Meinz' record only went back a day or two. When I looked at Winter's chart, he had been receiving Rebirth for weeks. I could not ignore that this 'experiment' had been going on for weeks now. Somewhere, there were others like Winter, others who had been victims long before I had stumbled across that train.

Von Osterbruck didn't like my ongoing curiosity. "You should go now."

"What happens to these men?"

"That is not your concern."

I decided it might be. "I want Gefreiter Meinz

transferred to a hospital here in Berlin."

Von Osterbruck had no idea who that was, of course. I had to point the man out. Von Osterbruck stared at the Gefreiter as if seeing him for the first time.

"Why this one?"

"Meinz has only been fed this poison for a couple of days. When would he first have been injected with it – in Aachen? Before? Well, I want to give him the best chance of coming back to his family, wherever they are. These others…"

Von Osterbruck seemed both surprised and amused by my compassion. "If you have read Kammerich's notes, you know there is no way back."

"Perhaps he was wrong. Indulge me."

He chuckled. "Very well. I'm surprised to see such a sentimental side in a policeman."

I still wasn't quite done. "How many more have there been, von Osterbruck? How many train wagons, how many men passed through Heilig-Geist before we found you?"

He smirked, and I knew I'd never get that answer. Nor would I have known where Privat Winter and however many others lay in beds here in the Armoury were to be taken, were it not for von Osterbruck's ego and one last twist in the tale.

"I could follow you," I said, though that was the last thing on my mind. He knew that too.

"What use are these men to you now, von Osterbruck? The war is over. I hear talk of you fighting Reds, but where? You can't have these men on the streets of Berlin. What possible use are they to you anyway?"

"You just don't listen, do you? This is over for you."

"Perhaps. But if I find out you are still in Berlin, I'll make sure it ends badly for you."

He sneered at this. "I have bigger matters to attend to. You, Kommissar, are an irrelevance."

"You'll find out how wrong you are one day," I countered. And that was when he felt he had to prove how superior he was.

"Would you like the answer to your question? What use are these men to me?" His lip curled even more, and he brought himself into an upright position, as if on parade, and drew in a long, deep breath.

"Company! Awake!"

That was loud. I saw movement out of the corner of my eye. Meinz twitched on the bed, but what had really caught my eye was Winter. He had jack-knifed into a completely upright position. His eyes were fixed straight forward. The ampoule and the rubber tube leading down to his arm jingled against the metal stand.

"Mother of God!" shrilled Fraulein Graber. I was rather more speechless.

"Company! Stand up!!"

Winter kicked himself clear of the sheets under which he lay. His movements were stiff, but he came to attention beside his bed, barefoot and with his arse hanging out of his hospital gown, but as rigidly Prussian as ever a man was.

I was taken aback enough that, as I stepped away, I tripped over the shotgun, which clattered to the ground. Winter didn't even twitch.

"Now, I think you start to understand." Von Osterbruck almost split his cheeks open he was grinning so widely. "Not so useless after all, eh? Company! Assemble in the hallway!" I saw Meinz twitch again, but he didn't rise. Winter, though, set off at a brisk march, arms swinging as if he was on a parade ground. The stand trembled and then fell to the ground, skidding the ampoule across the floor. The needle fell from his arm. He passed through the door, then came to attention once more out there, his feet slapping on the boards. And his weren't the only feet I heard.

"This is monstrous!" cried Fraulein Graber.

"Do you think so? I find it magnificent. Down the hall, there is a man with no left arm below the elbow. You would discard him. But thanks to Rebirth…"

I felt a knot in my stomach. It wasn't fear, but it was

something in that vicinity. I could see Winter, bare arse and all, unwavering at attention. Meinz whimpered, but then fell back onto his pillow.

I reached for the shotgun.

"No, Herr Kommissar, I don't think so. We are leaving. You would be advised not to try to –"

"Stay where you are!"

That took the smug smile off his face. He hadn't expected Fraulein Graber to pull out her Schwarzlose and aim it at his head. I must admit, she caught me by surprise as well.

I reached down for the shotgun. Von Osterbruck snarled a warning: "One last chance, Kommissar. One last chance to walk away from this. You cannot defy –"

"Put your hands on your head, von Osterbruck. You are under arrest."

"You think so?" His face contorted, and then he screamed: "Company! Kill the intruders!"

My heart skipped a beat; my breath seemed to stick in my throat. Through the doorway, I saw Winter turn around without hesitation and come back into the room. He had nothing in his hands, nothing to attack me *with*, but still he came on, taking quick steps across the bare floor. In my brief time in the Army, and especially at Verdun, I had been confronted by men who wanted to kill me, with bayonet, shovel or club. It takes savagery to come to close quarters intending to kill or be killed. But there was nothing of that in Winter, just brisk, slightly stiff movement. His eyes were as dead as they had been when he was lying in the bed. He lifted his arms as he rushed towards me, his feet slapping on the floor. I couldn't even be sure he was breathing.

"Call him off!" I yelled, but there was no time for van Osterbruck to respond even if he had chosen to. I levelled the shotgun, but that didn't deter Winter – how could it? He more or less ran onto the barrel. His hands clamped around my neck.

I fired.

The Winchester is a brutal weapon, and I have some sympathy with the view it has no place in war, and I say that even though this had been a war of gas, of weeks-long artillery bombardment, flame-throwers and white phosphorous. But a 12-gauge firing nine .33 calibre buckshot pellets does fearful damage to a man. In this case, I virtually cut Winter in half. What was left of him was driven back with considerable force, ejecting his internal organs and spraying blood everywhere.

He had barely stopped twitching when the next pair arrived. They must have been in a similar room to this, just another ten or twelve feet down the hall. The moment they saw me, they came in through the door, almost pushing each other aside in their haste to obey Von Osterbruck's order. One slipped in Winter's blood, but still on he came.

I heard Fraulein Graber cry: "Call them off!". I had no time to see if this had any effect on von Osterbruck. I had no choice but to fire again. The buckshot tore one poor soul to ribbons, and the other was struck in the face and shoulders where he was scrabbling on the ground after slipping.

I worked the action a second time. The Winchester had a five round tube magazine, and I had spare shells in my coat pocket, but I doubted I would ever have time to load them.

"Stop them or I'll kill you!"

Von Osterbruck laughed, dismissing Fraulein Graber's threat. "That won't stop them! Look out, Herr Kommissar, here come the next ones!"

I didn't even let this pair come through the doorway, trying to open the interval so that I might, if I didn't fumble, if I worked the unfamiliar action efficiently, I *might* get one more round into the magazine. The two men collapsed in the hall, but any respite I had gained was lost when I had to club the fellow still crawling towards me across the floor.

"Drop your weapons and I will order them to halt. They will only obey my voice!"

I yelled at the top of my voice, hearing the next pair

approaching. Just before they came into view, another figure appeared, a spindly male in a shabby suit, and also – alarmingly – wearing a gas mask. He was carrying some kind of bulky metal tube under one arm, and two more gas masks in his other hand.

"Put these on!" he yelled, thrusting the masks into my hand and Fraulein Graber's. The voice was muffled and breathy, but I knew it to be Obermeier. As we took the masks, he set the cylinder down with a heavy clunking sound.

Briefly aiming the shotgun one-handed at von Osterbruck, I dragged the mask into place. Instantly, I felt the grip of panic as the leather gripped my face. Everything was distorted through the eyepieces, but I knew what was coming, and as the next pair of von Osterbruck's ghouls appeared, I cut them down.

"Are you prepared?" I heard Obermeier say, and then there was a squeak, like a tap was being turned on, followed by a shrill hiss. A plume of yellow smoke was spilled into the room and towards the door. I was trembling, shaking violently, whispering prayers into the mask, firing again towards the doorway where bodies began to pile high. Rack the shotgun one last time…

Von Osterbruck screamed. His hands rose to cover his mouth. That wouldn't do him the least bit of good.

"What shall it be, Colonel? A bullet to the brain or death by mustard gas? Decide quickly!"

Von Osterbruck hesitated for just a moment. I often wondered if that was what killed him. "Company!" he rasped, but then his throat began to fill with gas and phlegm. We'll never know what the next word he would have spoken might have been.

FRIDAY, 8TH NOVEMBER 1918

I didn't hear Johan come in, but if he had any designs on waking me, I presume he gave up when I didn't come round. Later during the weekend, he told me that he had gone to stay with one of his boyfriends. I asked him what made him realise I could not be roused, and he suggested the empty bottle of cognac on the floor had persuaded him.

I woke up around ten o'clock, having slept the clock around. The later hours of Thursday were a blur. I don't think I contributed anything useful at all, but there were plenty of people drawn to the Armoury as the day went on. Most kept their distance, of course. A few of the more brave, conscientious or foolhardy police and doctors cleaned house. I watched, drained of all emotion. Someone eventually took pity and drove me home, but I went straight to a dismal bar along the street. I drank, I smoked, I stared.

Friday morning, then. I woke up fully-dressed, which wasn't unusual, but in clothes which were not my own, which was. The bedsheets were stuck to my face. I peeled myself out of the bed, fumbled to relieve myself in the chamber pot. That was going to need emptying.

It must have been a mild night because there was no ice on the windows, and the apartment was close to being inhabitable, at least in terms of temperature. I sat in our one chair and smoked my first cigarette of the day. Or, at least I started to, but even nicotine wasn't going to cut through the sour taste in my mouth this morning. I stubbed it out. I'm sure I smoke too many of the damn things anyway.

I located boots, hat and overcoat – none of these being mine either –, and went out in search of a late breakfast. Old Man Mauritz had been open for hours, of course, which meant the place was warm and the ersatz coffee was stewed. It must have rained in the night, because the streets were gleaming wet, but there was a little wan sunlight behind some low clouds as I went down to the café. Old Man Mauritz was in a good mood, and ushered me to a table in the corner where I was far enough away that I wouldn't upset his other patrons. Locked in my personal bubble of introversion, I ate some stew that contained a few bits of rind and some salvaged potatoes. My stomach was somewhat in rebellion after the evening's activities, but it needed filling, so I scraped my bowl clean.

A businessman in a coat last in fashion when the Franco-Prussian War ended left his newspaper behind, so I grabbed it, just so I had something to occupy my mind and keep me aloof from the rest of the clientele. It was the *Berliner Lokal-Anzeiger*, so it wasn't exactly purring with pleasure with the political situation. They had latched onto the idea that perhaps the Emperor could abdicate as *kaiser* but remain King of Prussia, yet just a page or two later they reported on how some of the constituent kingdoms and duchies of the Empire were teetering on the edge of revolution, with soldiers' and workers' councils demanding the removal of hereditary rulers.

I read the local pages twice. There was no mention of the events on Jägerstrasse. Even in its dying days, and despite the anti-censorship laws that had been passed after the socialists took over the *Reichstag*, the state could still function in this one small area.

I heard someone cough and laid the paper down. I wasn't at all surprised to see Obermeier standing there, hat in hand, his face a little more drawn than usual, but still appearing surprisingly alert and good-humoured. He wore a brown suit that appeared to be a size or two too small.

"Don't we get paid today?" Ah, so that was why he'd come to find me. "The widow Moskowizt is being difficult this week. If I hadn't removed my valuables to your dwelling..."

"Yes, you should get paid. Go to the Administration Büro."

"You're not coming?"

"Day off."

He seemed surprised that I wouldn't be rushing in to get my wages. It was his attitude that reminded me that it had been seven days ago that all this had started, just up the street at Friedrichstrasse Bahnhof. My God, I hadn't collected my pay that Friday either. No wonder I had been so broke! As I stared out of the window, a truck went past bearing a squad of uniformed men, with their banners and flags and hand grenades. Reds or freikorps, I couldn't have told you.

"I'll walk in with you," I announced. I paid up, thanked Old Man Mauritz, and we stepped out onto the pavement. It felt like another shower was imminent.

Drawing up my collar, I insisted we walk. Obermeier grumbled a little, but fell into step.

"You missed quite a bit after you left," he said. Drawing that morning's *Vorwarts* from his coat pocket, he added: "Nothing that will ever see print. I should be allowed to claim compensation for lost earnings."

I almost chuckled a this. "So, tell me..."

"Well, we scared the shit out of the Potsdam police, I can tell you!" That much I could remember. The *Leutnant* had stayed true to my instruction to keep clear. "No-one else was that keen to come in until some army lads in masks arrived to check the place out. That's when they took us all outside into that courtyard."

Indeed. Obermeier, Fraulein Graber, myself, and thirty or so of the Rebirth patients, those who had not heard von Osterbruck's commands, and who had not blundered into the mustard gas.

"They burned all our clothes! I couldn't believe that!"

"Mustard gas isn't really a gas; it's an aerosol. The droplets linger on surfaces or in the ground, or on clothing."

"So they said. I wish I'd known that before..."

I thrust my hands more deeply into the pockets of 'my' greatcoat, a recycled army piece of kit that had been patched over whatever wear or bullet holes it had earned. It wasn't half as warm as Fraulein Graber's cousin's coat, and it bore an odour I couldn't identify, but didn't like.

It seemed churlish to hope that more of Fraulein Graber's family could spare an overcoat, but if I had to accept hand-me-downs, I preferred that the donor was still alive.

Once that thought was out of my head, I snapped ai Obermeier. "What were you thinking?"

His face betrayed his helplessness. "What could I do, Herr Kommissar? I didn't have that Luger. I could hear you were in danger!"

"There was an entire magazine of weapons!"

"The gas cylinder was right there, at the foot of the stairs! I heard what was happening, and, well, there wasn't much time, was there?"

"How could you be sure Fraulein Graber and I had secured the masks correctly. We are each supposed to check each other."

He hadn't considered that. We had been lucky in more ways than one.

"What happened that I missed?"

"They took the invalids away. I already checked: they're not in Charité or anywhere else I looked. I suspect the bodies are in a pauper's grave somewhere too." He winced. "What a mess."

"I hope they hand von Osterbruck back to his loved ones in an urn." Even I was surprised by how bitter I sounded. A sudden shower hit the street, and it was stinging cold. We hustled along, but then took shelter in a doorway hoping it would pass.

"What happens now, do you think?"

I lit cigarettes for us both. "What do you think? The only witnesses can't speak. They wanted to draw a line under the whole affair, and now they have. Maercker and anyone else who knew anything will keep their heads low, and who is there to pursue them? The whole government is about to come crashing down."

Obermeier nodded ruefully. "I wonder if there is anything left of Kammerich, in his mind, I mean. He got pretty bad burns from the mustard gas."

"It's probably best if his mind did get wiped clean. I don't think there is any benefit in what he learned in those old books."

"No, I am sure you're right, Gerhard. I wonder what happened to them? When I went to the Praesidium last night, Teske asked me for them, but I couldn't find them." He looked at me from the corners of his eyes.

The rain had subsided. Suddenly, I couldn't face the office. "You go on, Herr Obermeier. I'll pick up my pay tomorrow."

"Oh. Of course. Listen, do you want to join me for dinner tonight, Herr Kommissar? The widow Markowitz always makes a delicious fish stew on a Friday."

"Another time. I have neglected a few things back home. I'll see you Monday."

He tipped his hat. "*Jawohl, Herr Kommissar.*"

A few minutes later, I was back at my apartment, clutching a bottle of schnapps and with my tin topped up with tobacco and papers. I set both down on a side table, and then went to the far wall.

One good thing about living in a tatty old apartment like this is that nothing is structurally sound. By which I mean that there are loose floorboards here and there, and holes in the walls. I moved the chair and knelt to remove a section of skirting board. It felt firmly nailed in place, but the trick was to lift it up a fraction, then out. I hadn't shown this trick even to Johan, but then I was sure he had a hidey-hole I had never discovered either.

I drew out a dirty cloth bag and carried it to the table, emptying out the contents. The three books slid out, landing in a haphazard pile. I picked up the first – the battered drama commentary entitled *The Drama of the Yellow King* I had retrieved from Doktor Luster's office on no more than a whim.I flicked through a few pages, and it made no more sense to me than it had when I had looked at it last. It was surrealist, perhaps, meant to work on some other level than mere words on a page. One comment I hadn't noticed before was in the foreword: the instruction that this play must never be performed, in case it turned the audience mad. Then why write a commentary about it?

I put it back in the bag. To my mind, the author must have watched the play a few too many times, because the book was unhinged. Doktor Luster had struck me as many things in our brief acquaintance, but a fantasist? What was his interest in this patently absurd nonsense?

Instead of pursuing a question I would never answer, I turned to the other two volumes. These were more relevant, it seemed, to everything that had happened. They were also, I felt, far too dangerous to be left lying around the Praesidium when there were people who might turn their thoughts to Rebirth once more.

The first, of course, was that journal of formulations and experimental records I had found in Kammerich's room at Heilig-Giest. This, I knew, was the chemistry for how *Wiedergeburt* was manufactured. From Luster's interest in the healing powers of sleep, through Kammerich's findings on ancient treatments, to obtaining the ingredients and refining *Wiedergeburt*, it was all here. Almost all.

I'm no scientist, so none of the complex formulae meant anything to me. I learned that a key ingredient was a particular grade of kerosene, which prevented *Wiedergeburt* from evaporating, and from solidifying at cold temperatures. This and some other ingredients made the prepared solution flammable.

It was obvious from the experimental notes that refining *Wiedergeburt* had not been easy. Most early compounds just flat out killed test animals, and a few patients. It was intrinsically poisonous. Something else was required, something Kammerich had known was out there, but didn't know what it was. Something ancient and mystical.

Which brought me finally to the book Kammerich had stolen from the Prussian State Library. I wasn't any the wiser with this one either. Professor Von Theriesenwald had shown me that trick with the light through the pages, and I tried to replicate that now, but the light in the apartment wasn't strong enough, and I didn't have the manual dexterity to hold two pages of the book *just so* while holding a lit match behind them. In any case, was I supposed to have become fluent in ancient Sumerian in the last few days?

The pharmaceutical company – the red lozenge people – would have understood all the chemistry. But there was the implication in Kammerich's work that even the best chemist in the world could not have manufactured *Wiedergeburt* without the knowledge in this final book. That secret was now locked away in Kammerich's ruined mind. If anyone else was ever going to unlock it again, they would need this old hide-bound volume.

I set it down along with the others. I sat and smoked for a while, then opened the schnapps so that I could smoke and drink for a while longer.

I hadn't held onto any of these books for any coherent, investigative reason, they just ended up back here at some point in the investigation. All the other evidence was stored away in Amt VIIIb. I had kept them hidden in the apartment solely so that Johan didn't stick his nose in them.

So, what now?

I looked over at the stove. It was almost certainly going to be another cold night.

As I flipped through the pages of the Sumerian book, a single leaf fell from its binding. It was clear the volume couldn't take this kind of rough handling, and now I had no idea from where in the book the page had fallen. I picked it up off the floor, and froze.

If you know the drawing *Vitruvian Man* that Da Vinci

made, it will help you visualise what I was holding. The image was drawn in some kind of dark red ink on rough paper, a material that didn't match the other leaves of the book. Maybe it wasn't part of the volume at all, but had just been placed within. One edge of the sheet was ragged, as if it had been torn from a book or some kind of pad. The paper had a slightly greasy feel to it, as if it was waxed.

The image was of a woman. She was nude, and depicted a little like *Vitruvian Man*, with her feet apart and arms away from her body. Her hair was splayed upwards. Behind her were a number of geometric shapes, including a circle of intricate glyphs, and a rectangle. For a moment, I didn't make the connection. I leaned in a little closer, and I saw there were markings on her ankles and wrists.

I turned the page about, so that she was upside down.

SATURDAY, 9TH NOVEMBER 1918

I slept pretty solidly that night too, once I had that image out of my head, finally. I got up well before dawn or the return of Johan, put on some fresh underwear and a clean shirt to keep a level of insulation between me and those dreadful army fatigues, then went out into the world.

Much like Friday, this was a cold, but relatively still day, washed by showers and even a little sleet. I marched across the city, feeling the pinch of my donated army boots. God knows where I'd start or how I'd pay for it all, but I was going to need a new... everything.

The Police Praesidium is usually an awkward place on a Saturday: busy, but quiet; populated, but empty. Get there early enough, and you will see the drunks being tipped out onto the street before they can think about asking for breakfast. By mid-morning, there might be a small queue of discrete, nervous gentlemen wanting to report the theft of a gold watch or a sizeable sum of money, but being a bit coy about where they were and who they were with when the items went missing. The Robbery Büro can be quite busy on a Saturday, even if the pickpockets and the burglars largely take the day off.

From the moment I walked in, I could tell there was something up. In the main hall, there were quite a few uniformed officers loitering around, looking peculiarly out of place. Some of them were people I recognised: the first one I saw was Kriminal-Sekretär Blume, wearing a uniform that had last fit him properly around the time of the Boer War. I was about to speak to him about it when I heard my name called. Oberkommissar Radel was also in uniform and looked about as uncomfortable. He fidgeted with his tunic collar as he strode over to confront me, his boots shining, and his *shako* wobbling precariously on his head.

"Why aren't you in uniform, Hoehner?"

"Excuse me?"

"Get out of those rags and into proper uniform. Everyone has been called in; all leave cancelled."

"What's going on?"

"Had you been here on time, perhaps you could have learned along with all the others!" Radel was almost being choked by his own collar.

"Oberkommissar Radel, Amt VIIIb has been excused special duties."

Radel spun on his heel at this new intrusion. We were both taken aback by the way Oberkommissar Teske had sneaked up on us.

"I was not informed of this!"

"Perhaps it does not come under the purview of the Chief of Robbery to know such details." Radel bristled. He clearly wanted to come up with a pointed retort of his own, but was over-taken by Teske, who added: "I am going to be overdue for an appointment with Herr Weiss. Please, excuse us."

He took me by the arm and led me away towards the broad stairway leading up to the first floor.

"What *is* going on?" I asked again.

"Matters are progressing quickly, politically. The socialists are planning several marches and rallies against the government. Every policeman in the city will be needed."

"But... the socialists *are* the government."

"Don't be obtuse, Hoehner. Ebert and those others might be the majority in the Reichstag, but they hold no actual power. Prince Max remains Chancellor, though I know he is on the brink of resigning and handing power to Ebert and his cronies in the Council of the People's Representatives. Ebert has been pressing for that. The only obstacle has been the Kaiser, and he cannot hope to stay in power for much longer."

"Not as German Kaiser."

"Not as King of Prussia either; the constitution does not

allow it! Though what good are constitutions at times like this? The country is tearing itself apart. The Spartakists are planning revolution; the Revolutionary Stewards have called for a general strike. Ebert worked against them back in January, but now..."

"All this politics is above my pay grade, Herr Oberkommissar. What's all this about meeting with Herr Weiss?"

"In all honesty, he isn't expecting to see you..." I raised an eyebrow. "Oberkommissar Radel drew an inference I did not intend. But now you are here, it makes sense for you to be present in this meeting. Herr Weiss may wish to question you over this von Osterbruck business. He will want to draw a line under the whole affair. We must ensure he is able to do that."

We were almost at the top of the stairs to the second floor. Oberkommissar Teske took a moment to catch his breath and straighten his necktie.

"Before we go in, let me show you the inside track. If there is a change of government, von Oppen will step down as head of the Berlin police. That means Weiss might be the next Chief. Amt VIIIb is a product of the old regime; there are many who don't know why we exist. You and I know why. Let's not give Weiss any reason to doubt our worth. Are we clear on this, Herr Kommissar?"

I nodded, even though all this talk made me tired. It had never been this difficult in Robbery, but then we hadn't solved that many crimes either.

Weiss' office was next door to the Chief's. It was a little smaller, but only a little less grand. Weiss sat behind his desk, his glasses perches on the end of his nose, working through a stack of papers with a gold-nibbed pen in his hand.

We were invited to sit. Beyond that, Herr Weiss had nothing to say while he annotated whatever he was reading. There was a cigarette lying in a chrome ashtray offering a curl of smoke to the ceiling. I wouldn't have minded being invited to smoke myself.

Weiss concluded reading the document, gathered up the papers and placed them into a folder. He tied a ribbon to fasten it, then added another annotation to the folder. Finally, he pushed his glasses more firmly onto his nose.

"A comprehensive and… final report, Herr Oberkommissar." If there was a question there, I missed it.

"Of course, Herr Weiss."

"Good. I spoke this morning with the Military Governor. He will be relieved to hear that we have plucked out all the rotten apples." Weiss picked up his cigarette. "General von Linsignen has assured me that the Army is available to move against these Bolshevists and trade unionists if the threat to public order becomes too great. There have been discussions about how such efforts can be coordinated throughout the Empire, even should it be that we are an Empire no longer. It is just as well that your operations have been concluded with such dispatch."

Oberkommissar Teske harrumphed a little, at which Herr Weiss looked up with raised brows.

"Great risks were taken, Herr Weiss, because we have such limited manpower."

"You have picked the wrong time to ask for a raise in your department's budget, Herr Oberkommissar. As you know, Amt VIIIb was the creation of *Polizeipräsident* von Oppen, and many questioned the need for it to exist even then. If he resigns in the next few days, as there are strong indications he must, the new Chief may have completely new ideas."

The Oberkommissar chewed this over. I watched him search for the right way to approach Weiss, before he settled on a direct route.

"If things go as you say, can we count on your support?"

Weiss considered this in turn, then reached down and opened the drawer in his desk. He took out a very thin folder, placed it on the desk then closed (and locked) the drawer. He tapped the unlabeled cover with his fingers, then shifted the folder across the desk. "Your previous operation is concluded? Entirely?"

"*Jawohl.*"

"I wondered if this officer was working undercover."

Ouch.

"Kommissar Hoehner's clothes were burned as a precaution at the scene of the incident in Potsdam."

"I see."

"He has been on a Bezirkssekretär's pay since he returned to the Berlin police. That was over a year ago."

Weiss looked at me over the rims of his spectacles. "Perhaps something could be done about that." He then reached for a small metal box at the end of his desk, drew a small key from his waistcoat pocket, and unlocked it. I couldn't see within but when the lid was snapped closed, he had a small pad of requisition forms. He took up his pen, quickly scribbled a few notes, authorised the form with a rubber stamp, tore the sheet off and handed it to me. "Do you know Artur's, the tailors on Mollstrasse?"

"I do."

"Tell him I sent you. It won't be much, but he can ensure that you'll look less like a tramp."

"Thank you."

That was me dealt with. Weiss turned back to Oberkommissar Teske. "Can this matter be dealt with immediately?" He nodded at the folder. "Events may mean that you cannot report back to me here. Here is my home address."

Teske took the business card he had been offered, and rose to his feet, clutching the folder under one arm. "My department will attend to this immediately." And with that we were done.

Rosa Luxembourg

Herr Weiss' 'instructions' amounted to one personal name, Joseph Liebnitz; one business name, Das Metallverarbeitungsunternehmen Liebnitz, and an address south of Landsberger Allee, out east in Lichtenberg, all three typed on a plain sheet of paper with no signature or case number or anything.

"It doesn't say what we are to do there."

"Best you hurry and find out. I will send word to Herr Obermeier and Fraulein Graber to meet you there."

He took the piece of paper back from me once he had assured himself I would remember the details.

"Visit that tailor first," he insisted. "You look more like our revolutionary comrades than police."

I was quite keen to do so. Who knew how long that chit would stay valid for?

My doubts on that score were only increased as I stepped out of the Alex, to find a police cordon around the building, and two armoured cars at one corner. Across Alexanderplatz, there was a throng of a few hundred men and women, largely gathered around a flatbed truck on which a small party of people were haranguing the crowd.

"Red Rosie," commented one of the *schupos* as I walked away from the Alex.

I decided to take advantage of my disheveled state. Thrusting my hands into my pockets and with a nail hanging from my lip, I wandered across Alexanderplatz towards the truck. On the way, I found an abandoned copy of *Vorwarts*, which I thrust into the pocket of the greatcoat to help the disguise. As nonchalantly as possible, I moved to a position on the edge of the throng.

So, this was Rosa Luxembourg. I hadn't encountered her before, seeing as her activities were far more of interest to the security police, but her name was a byword for the Red problem faced by Berlin as the war came to an end.

She was quite an animated figure up there, twisting and turning left and right as she called out to those around her. These were a motley crew of soldiers, sailors, workers and others, men and women, who huddled in their coats against the wind while hard-faced men in red armbands moved among them handing out leaflets and soliciting donations.

As I watched, one of them came up to me, a flat-nosed fellow with a jagged scar on his face that I fancied was obtained from a knife rather than an epee.

"You won't find the truth in there, *kamerade*" he said, with a nod towards the paper hanging from my pocket. He offered to sell me a copy of *Die Rote Fahne*.

"I need what I have left for the soup kitchen," I insisted.

"All the sustenance you need in here." I thought that was a bit rich coming from someone whose leader was demanding Peace and Bread from the back of a truck.

He handed me a crudely printed leaflet which called for a general strike by all workers in all the industries of Berlin. This must have been planned for the 11th, but the date had been over-printed with today's. It didn't entirely line up with Red Rosa's calls for the removal of the Hohenzollerns, an immediate cessation of the war and government by councils of workers and soldiers.

Watching her speak, what I heard was an intelligent woman making arguments that didn't quite speak to the German character. She made some convincing points, but they got lost in talk of 'soviets', socialist republics and Marx. We Berliners had heard all the stories about how the Russians were engaged in a bitter civil war while their people were starving. We were hungry too, but that would end the moment the bastards in the Royal Navy went home.

I pocketed the leaflet and moved around the edge of the crowd. I passed a couple of soldiers in uniforms that looked a lot smarter than mine. They were sneering contemptuously, and reminding everyone nearby that Luxemburg was a Pole and a Jew.

"Do your collar up!" called one of them, a feldwebel as I walked away.

"Go fuck yourself," I replied, which was as clear as I could be on the politics of the matter.

Republik

That was how it ended for me: that first case or two with Amt VIIIb and Oberkommissar Teske. In all honesty, I still didn't understand what we were all about, and I felt as if more people had dodged accountability for what had been done at Heilig-Geist and the Potsdam Armoury than had paid a price for their crimes. Then there was the matter of Fraulein Elisabet Nowak, which hadn't been resolved at all. Waldemar Pabst and I would cross paths again; I would make sure of it.

I thought about all this as I left Alexanderplatz. I was vaguely aware that more people were thronging into the square, coming in from the crowded tenements, attracted by the hum of intrigue and revolution that filled those cold streets. There were marches and protests all over the city, strikes and agitation. In the Reichstag, Friedrich Ebert was brought news at regular, frantic intervals that suggested the Spartakists and their union friends, the Revolutionary Stewards, were moving from strike action to revolution. Still no word came from Spa as to the Kaiser's intentions. By lunchtime, the situation was spiraling out of control.

Sometime in the early afternoon, one of Ebert's SPD colleagues, Philipp Scheidemann, went out onto the balcony of the Reichstag and proclaimed a republic to the crowd down below. "The old and rotten, the monarchy, has collapsed. Long live the new! Long live the German Republic!" Stirring stuff. I'm told Ebert was furious, but what was done was done?

Someone was always going to be first to seize the moment; later in the day, Rosa Luxemburg's co-leader of the Spartakists, Karl Liebknecht, stood up at a second-floor window at Gate Four of the Berlin Palace and pronounced a "free, socialist, German Republic". Perhaps it mattered which order these things occurred in, but by nightfall it was Scheidemann's vision, and not Liebknecht's, which held sway.

It paid to move quickly these days.

There was some constitutionally suspect activity in which Prince Max stood down and gifted the Chancellorship to Ebert. At some point, I forget quite when, we all heard that the Kaiser had jumped onto a train, not back to Berlin, but to exile in the Netherlands.

The old order vanished. Much as Herr Weiss had predicted, I realised later, the revolutionaries, in their various shades of red, took over public buildings, including the Polizei Praesidium. Just as predicted, Heinrich Karl Wilhelm Ehrenfried Hellmuth von Oppen went back to his estates to tell his eight children how he had stood aside for the sake of the German state. His replacement as *Polizeipraesident* was the USPD politician Emil Eichhorn, who had actually stormed the Praesidium, which was surrendered without violence. He set 600 political prisoners free and just made himself chief. Oh, the stories I could tell you about him.

I missed almost everything.

I spent the first part of the revolutionary day of the 9th November being fitted for a second-hand suit by a Jewish tailor who thought the Russians would be in Berlin by Sunday. From that afternoon, the full resources of Amt VIIIb were thrown at the Case of the Liebnitz Metalworking Company, but that's a tale for another day. You'll like the bit where I was almost lynched by both the Reds and the *Freikorps* on the same day…

GLOSSARY

Police Terms

Abteilung: department. Also Büro and Amt.
Kripo, Kriminalpolizei: the detectives of the Berlin police force.
Krmininal-Oberkommissar: a chief inspector.
Kriminal-Kommissar: a detective inspector.
Bezirkssekretär: a detective sargeant.
Schupo, Schutzpolizei: uniformed police.
Polizei-leutnant: an officer in the uniformed police.
Polizei-Wachtmeiester: police sergeant.
Sicherheitspolizei: security police, or political police. The term has more sinister connotations in later history.
Zellengefängnis: the infamous Moabit Prison.

Army Terms

Siegfriendstellung: The Siegfried line, planned defences the German army retreated to in 1918, but couldn't hold.
Paris-Geschütz: long range siege guns deployed to bombard Paris in the spring and summer of 1918.
Hauptkadettenanstalt: the main officer cadet training school in Berlin.
Garde-Kavallerie-Schützendivision: Formerly a cavalry unit, reduced to infantry status in Berlin in 1918, the 'division' will form the basis of a *freikorps* unit in mid-November 1918.
Stielhandgranate: Hand-grenades.
Stahlhelm: the classic late war German army steel helmet.
Giftgas: a generic term for poison gas.

Auswärtiges Amt: the Foreign Office.

Erkennungsmarke, Hundemarken: two different terms for dog tags, or identity tags.

Kriegneurosen or Krieghysterie: shell shock, or PTSD as we might now term it.
Schüttler: shaker or trembler.

Völkisch: a different concept for a glossary entry, but a concept based around race and identity, with a folk tinge to it (back to nature and the soil), but, in Germany, hevaily tinged with nationalism.

Königlich Preußische und Großherzoglich Hessischen Staatseisenbahnen (KPuGHStE): the Royal Prussian and Hessian State Railway.
Stadtbahn: the suburban railway services.
Bahnhof: a station. Hauptbahnhof: the main Berlin railway station. Universitätsmedizin: the university medical centre at Charité.

Berlin Media

Vorwarts: the newspaper published by the Social Democratic Party (SPD).
Die Freiheit: the newspaper of the Independent Social Democratic Party (USPD). Voßische Zeitung: a Centrist newspaper associated with the liberal middle class, the oldest newspaper in Berlin (and one read widely around Germany) and the 'newspaper of record' for Germany at this time.
Nordeutsche Allgemeine Zeitung: a quality newspaper, which is about to change its name to the *Deutsche Allgemeine Zeitung.*

GERHARD HOEHNER WILL RETURN IN 2025